# A Kiss After Dying

## ASHOK BANKER

PENGUIN BOOKS

PENGUIN BOOKS

UK | USA | Canada | Ireland | Australia
India | New Zealand | South Africa

Penguin Books is part of the Penguin Random House group of companies
whose addresses can be found at global.penguinrandomhouse.com

First published by Penguin Michael Joseph 2022
Published in Penguin Books 2022

001

Copyright © Ashok Banker, 2022

The moral right of the author has been asserted

Typeset by Jouve (UK), Milton Keynes
Printed and bound in Great Britain by Clays Ltd, Elcograf S.p.A.

The authorized representative in the EEA is Penguin Random House Ireland,
Morrison Chambers, 32 Nassau Street, Dublin D02 YH68

A CIP catalogue record for this book is available from the British Library

ISBN: 978-1-405-94959-0

www.greenpenguin.co.uk

For Biki, Yoda, Yashka and Leia.
Love, and only love, always.

*The heart asks pleasure first,*
*And then, excuse from pain;*
*And then, those little anodynes*
*That deaden suffering.*

*And then, to go to sleep;*
*And then, if it should be*
*The will of its Inquisitor*
*The liberty to die.*

*— Emily Dickinson*

*The Island, Now*

A woman in a red bikini on a sugar-white beach before a baby-blue ocean.

That's me.

The hunky man in shorts and unbuttoned Hawaiian walking down from the villa to the private beach, weathered, tanned, a little beaten around the edges but all the sexier for it.

That's my husband.

We were married yesterday.

The chopper with his name on the side dropped us off only hours ago. The staff went back with it. Now, we're the only two people on this island and we're pretty much stuck with each other. There's no way off. The undersea reefs make approach by sea too risky. Even if you survived the rocks and could swim the forty-five miles to the mainland, the sharks and undertow would get you. It's not on any flight paths and no joyriding speedboaters or chopper pilots have any reason to pass this way. It is quite literally the kind of desert island they mean when they ask you the What If question. As in, if you were stranded on a desert island, what books, or movies, or people, would you want to bring along?

All we brought is each other.

We're on our honeymoon, after all. We don't need anything or anyone else.

The next three days belong to us, and nobody else is going to steal even a tiny slice of it away. There's no internet, no cell service, no TV, cable, Netflix or landlines. Just a satphone to call the chopper when we're ready to leave. We won't be 'gramming our honeymoon pics for the celeb-obsessed world to drool over, or posting cryptic updates that the gossip websites try to blow up into a scandal.

For the next seventy-two hours, the outside world doesn't exist.

It's just him and me.

He leans over the deckchair and kisses me upside down. I let the book I'm reading drop and kiss him back, tasting vodka and cranberry juice and inhaling his familiar aqua-based cologne. His hand reaches for my breast. I intercept it and use it to pull myself to my feet. I lean in close, breathing on his cheek, and feel the stiffening in his Speedos.

'Last one in's a rubber duck,' I whisper, then break free and run, laughing, down to the water. He laughs and runs after me, overcoming my lead with a power sprint, his muscled thighs pistoning.

The surf explodes as we hit it at almost the same instant. I turn to him, arms raised in a victory gesture. 'I win!'

'You cheat!' he responds, laughing.

The incoming tide is waist-high. The water is warm, just a tad above body temperature. It feels great, the sand deliciously cool between my toes.

He grabs hold of my waist and reels me in, finishing the kiss he started on the beach. This time I let him have his way, and when we break off we're both breathing hot and heavy.

It's a shame I have to kill him.

He's good-looking in a sexy, mature way, fabulously rich and famous, and good company. The sex is pretty good too.

But it's got to be done.

I can't forgive or forget what he did to my family, how he ruined our lives.

That's why I've spent my entire life preparing, training, planning.

And now, after all these years and incredible effort, I'm within reach of my goal.

In a little while, I'll make my move. Catching him unawares, ending his life right here on this private paradise. It's the perfect place and time, after all. I'll never get a better opportunity.

But until then, we may as well have fun.

Enjoy it while it lasts. Indulge our appetites. Relish the luxury of the privacy, the beach, the sea, the bungalow, the superb wine cellar and gourmet repast.

And then, when he's lulled and satiated by sun, wine, sex and indulgence, I'll take him. Quick and deadly. Ending his life and finally delivering what I've worked so hard and long to achieve, what my mother, my family, would have wanted.

Justice.

# ACT I
# Hannah & Ricky

*Zurich, Switzerland*

# I

The first time Ricky sees me, he doesn't think I'm drop-dead gorgeous. If anything, he probably thinks I'm a plain Jane. That's not low self-esteem, it's just a fact. I'm not beautiful and I don't pretend I am. In reality, I don't give a damn what he or any other hetero male thinks of me. I'm good with what I am, and what I have going for me is more than skin deep, as all my past lovers would agree. But Ricky being Ricky, I knew I'd have to play to his outdated binary concept of female beauty, and so I am. From the way his eyes track me, I know I've struck just the right balance between demure and hey-who's-that. Gotcha, male gaze.

I'm walking to the Hans Augusten Building where I attend most of my lectures. It's a cool morning and I'm wearing a blue sweater over a shapeless mid-length skirt with long socks and boots. I'm clutching my sketchpad to my chest and hunch forward a bit to balance the book-heavy backpack. I have bangs this year and they tend to fall over my face, which is angled downwards to avoid making eye contact with the other students. I've not made any friends or struck up conversations with anyone on campus yet, even though I've been here two semesters, and I like it that way.

An autumn gust blows a dried maple leaf off the grass and on to the path and it crunches crisply as I step on it. It puts me in mind of the sound of the chest cavity being cut open with rib shears. More leaves blow underfoot and now the effect is

9

more like a skull breaker hammering in the cranium. It reminds me I have dissection this week and I need to prep for it.

That brief distraction gives me the chance to angle myself in the path of the two girls tossing an American football to each other. One goes long and crashes into me backward, sending me sprawling. I fall sideways into dried autumn leaves and lose the sketchpad, landing hard on my right shoulder, but rolling just in time to avoid hitting the outgrown root. There are leaves everywhere now, under me, in my face, hair, mouth. I lie stunned for a second, spitting bits of dry leaf and grit. The phone I was handling before the collision is nearby, and easily nudged away by my elbow.

An angry male voice yells in American-accented English at the two ball players who reply sulkily in German. I push hair out of my face and see a tall, dark-haired guy jabbing a finger at the wannabe Tom Bradys who both shrug sheepishly and make themselves scarce. It isn't their fault because I deliberately sidestepped to make sure they crashed into me, but they're still asses for not bothering to apologize or see if I'm OK. That's cool. I want them gone.

The dark-haired guy leans over me and offers a hand.

'You OK?' he asks.

I sit up, ignoring his outstretched hand. I brush leaves off my sweater, but they break up and I know I'll feel little pokey fragments scratching at me through the wool for the rest of the day. I swipe at my face, spitting again to get the taste of grit out, and check my shoulder; it's sore but there's no real damage. Even though I haven't been keeping up my Krav Maga, gymming or running since I came to Switzerland, my muscle memory held up well enough to manage the fall. I'll still bruise a bit, but it looks worse than it actually is, which suits me just fine.

'Pretty nasty spill – you should get yourself checked out,' he says to fill the awkward pause.

He thinks he's being cool and classy. He considers himself a master of the game. He's trying hard not to come on too strong while using the accidental encounter to bait this unexpected fish that's just swum into his tidepool.

What he doesn't know is that I've been watching him for seven months and am intimately familiar with every gesture, every movement, every detail, from the way he runs his fingers through his hair, pushing it back on the right – the left side he keeps shaved almost to the skin. The angular shape of his jaw, his heavy eyebrows, the vee-shaped accent of his torso, the bumps and ridges of his eight-pack abdomen, and even the size of his package. There's not much left to the imagination when a guy is in Speedos on both the swim and dive teams.

It's been harder for me to keep from being noticed by him, while watching him, these past seven months. Even with my training, it's taken some doing . . . staying out of his way, making sure he didn't see me until I wanted him to, and if he happened to look my way, making sure he didn't notice me.

All that prep pays off now, as he sees me for the first time – or so he thinks – and comes to the conclusion: no bombshell, but definitely on the doable side.

I haven't said a word yet. I stay silent as I stand. Everything feels fine; no real damage done. I turn in a circle, looking for my sketchbook. He spots it in a jumble of leaves and picks it up. It's fallen open to reveal some of my little doodles of Zurich cafés, buildings and scenery. 'Cool stuff. Art major?'

I take the pad without answering and busy myself brushing off the debris stuck to the front of my sweater. He consciously tries to avoid staring at my breasts, which only makes it obvious that he's noticing them. I start to walk away.

'Heya,' he calls out, surprised. This is a guy who isn't used to women walking away from him without saying a word. I've seen how the women on campus respond to him: flirtatious, coy, sometimes matter-of-fact and direct, but always pleased to have his attention. There's no shortage of rich, privileged students here, but nobody in his league. Billionaire American scions don't usually go all the way to Switzerland to study business economics; the word on campus was that Ricky Manfredi was only here to party. From hacking his transcripts, I know his history of suspensions and expulsions from US schools; this is his parents' idea of a fresh start for him. High hopes!

I keep walking, knowing he won't chase after me. Not his style. A few people rushing to get to class noticed the little accident, but their attention was mostly on Ricky, the big shot on campus. Nobody paid any attention to me after the first glance; I am a non-person to them, just another international exchange student from an Asian country. Ricky calls out to me again. I ignore him. I've worked hard to stay invisible on campus and don't intend to change that by being seen hobnobbing with my quarry now. I've done this often enough before to know how the game is played too: the how and when is everything.

Still, I will be careful not to be too cocky; all the other times were test runs, with other misogynists or abusive men whom I have no personal feelings for or connection to. They were to prepare me for this, the main event. Ricky is not just some stand-up comic with a goatee from Astoria, Queens, who makes college girls laugh in bars and then sexually assaults them when they're drunk on his couch. He's a Yanagiba fillet knife. One mistake, and I'll be the one left bleeding.

As I go up the steps, I see his reflection in the glass doors. The blonde and redhead he had been talking to by the quadrangle when I fell are calling out to him and he turns and walks back to them, shooting me one last over-the-shoulder glance as he goes.

I allow myself a small smile, concealing it behind the sketchpad.

I've hooked my prey.

# 2

I avoid Ricky all of that day. I'm in my last lecture when I hear one of the doors at the rear of the room being opened. The seating is arranged in concentric descending levels, with the professor, whiteboards and screens at the bottom. Ricky enters through the top door and takes the nearest empty seat. His entrance, though discreet, attracts a number of glances and smiles from several of my colleagues, mainly the female ones. Everyone around campus knows Ricky Manfredi and an astonishing number have known him in the Biblical sense as well. He's been busy, busy, busy.

When the lecture ends, I stand up as I gather up my books and see him out of the corner of my eye: he's coming down the steps to my level. I move downward, against the flow of exiting students who are heading upwards. Ricky has to fight the flow – and deal with several admirers, each of whom assumes, incorrectly, that he's here for her. I reach the door and exit quickly. The underground hallway is almost empty at this time, as is the next lecture room. I duck inside, holding the door shut so it doesn't swing to and fro.

The door has small clear glass panes on top. I flatten myself against a wall, able to look out at a slanted angle. I watch Ricky come out of the other lecture room and look around the empty hallway, puzzled. He glances at the door of this room, but from the hallway it looks dark and empty. Still, he starts toward it and I prepare to run up the steps, when his phone pings with a message tone and that distracts him. As he types a message with quick thumbs, he turns away and continues down the hallway.

I go up the steps of the lecture room and exit into a hallway with a fair amount of student traffic, all heading out to start their weekend. I continue upward through the next level to access the skywalk that connects almost all the buildings on campus. During the harshest weeks of the winter, the skywalk is the only practical way to get around, but this being early autumn, and because of the hour, it's deserted.

Halfway across a skywalk between buildings, I spot Ricky down below, coming around the Hans Augusten Building. I clock the crease in his forehead as he slips on his Diors to ward off the slanting late afternoon sun. I grin to myself: he's bugged that he couldn't find me. This is not the way the game is usually played in his world. This is a rich, handsome guy accustomed to having girls chase him, not the other way around.

He gets a call on his cellphone, and from his body language I'm sure it's one of his many girlfriends. He glances around one last time, probably wondering where the mystery girl vanished to, and then shrugs me off and moves toward the parking lot. His jaunty walk suggests a young man with oats to sow en route to an inviting field.

*Go on, Ricky*, I think, still grinning. *Get it while you can. You don't know it yet, but your wild-oats-sowing days are almost done.*

## 3

I share an apartment off campus with a Bulgarian girl named Olga. An over-dramatic blonde who dyes her hair black and has a thing for deafeningly loud death metal, silver piercings and boyfriends with spiked hair and eye make-up. She's like a throwback to the eighties Goth scene with a millennial outlook.

She tried to get friendly at first, but soon understood that I wasn't interested in sharing polka-dotted pajama bottoms and heading out for shots. I get the impression she hasn't personally met or interacted with any people of color before in her young life, and all she knows of India is what she's seen in old black-and-white Hindi films, the kind with Raj Kapoor and Nargis singing in the rain, or Dilip Kumar pushing a plough. What is it about Eastern European countries and old-school black-and-white Hindi films? Did Soviet-era communism only allow the proletariat fare to be shown in cinema halls? Still, she's seen *DDLJ* several times so I'll give her points for that.

Olga has this irritating habit of drunk-livestreaming to her 'followers' – I'm using quotes because most of them are the kind of creeps who use video chat apps just to stalk women like her – and on one or two such occasions, she tried to get me to strip down to my underwear and dance with her to a Nicki Minaj song. I set her straight real quick, and she's kept her distance since then, but she bears watching. I can't be caught on camera, live or otherwise. It's taken me a long time and a lot of effort to stay anonymous and unknown this far, and I can't let that change now, not when I'm so close to my goal.

So, Olga. Friends, we'll never be; but so long as she leaves me alone, we'll get along just fine. If not . . . well, let's just hope it doesn't come to that. I'd like to do this one clean and quick, with minimal collateral damage, especially after the mess on the first test run. Besides, Olga's like edible moss: she's started to grow on me.

She's not home today when I return to the apartment. I can tell from the way the place just sits there in the late afternoon sunlight, the refrigerator making its usual knocking sounds. Empty houses have that feel, like they're waiting for something to happen. I'm relieved not to have to wade through the usual routine of air kisses and pointless pleasantries, and head straight to my room, unlock it and go in, peeling off my sweater.

The mirror on the bathroom cabinet shows me a small, reddish discoloration on my right shoulder and upper back. A small price to pay for having hooked Ricky Manfredi. It'll be purple in a day or two, and feels tender when I poke it, but it'll heal. An ice dunk will hasten the process and quell the inflammation more effectively than ibuprofen. I run the bathtub tap with cold water and head to the kitchen.

The stove top and counter are strewn with the debris of Olga's attempts at breakfast. Like most millennials – I'm one, so I know whereof I speak – she really can't cook but she's pining for home-cooked food and attempts these ill-advised YouTube-inspired cooking experiments. She always asks me to please, please, please taste some Bulgarian specialty or other she's trying and I *always* plead allergies. From the way she and her boyfriend du jour's faces look after tasting the results, I'm pretty sure it's a far cry from Mom's cooking. I admire her courage.

The refrigerator has an ice dispenser. I fill a salad bowl with ice and dump it in the bathtub. Two more bowlfuls and I strip naked and slip in. The water brings out goosebumps all over, but after a minute or two my body adjusts. I scroll through my phone while I let the ice water do its job.

I cloned Ricky's SIM card the first month and use an app which mirrors his phone activity. I keep the cloned SIM in a second phone which lets me read all his messages and track all his calls. If I wanted, I could even call or message his contacts and it would be as if he was calling or messaging them, but that's for the final stage of my plan. Right now, it's enough that I can track his entire life, minute by minute.

My reading of him earlier was dead on. He drove off for a booty call with one of his current regulars: a red-headed Finn named Ursula with a sex drive almost as hyper as Ricky's. Like him, she rotates through a steady stream of regular lovers, bringing new players into the mix to keep things interesting. Ricky tires of his regulars after about six weeks, and he's only midway through the cycle with U. They like to fuck in a hot tub while doing coke, then go clubbing. Sometimes, she invites a friend in to play with them. Ricky's mostly the one-on-one type, and other males are a strict no-no, but he'll occasionally OK an FMF. A selfish me-oriented man; then again, when it comes to singles sex, aren't we all?

I'm scrolling through Ricky's earlier text messages of the day, making mental notes on which asses he's currently tapping, and which ones are 'tapped out' (his phrase, not mine). Ricky tends to go all in on new women for a few weeks, then check out for good. The hotter the liaison gets, the more permanent the break-up. Ursula's one of the rare few with whom he's maintained an on-off linkup; I suspect that's more to do with her own busy sociosexual schedule. He's not had her often enough to get her out of his system.

I'm almost done with his chat history when I hear the front door open and I blink.

Someone's in the apartment.

A minute or two later, the door connecting the bathroom to Olga's bedroom opens and a stranger walks in.

I'm instantly alert, ready to act, but he reacts like any typical coed would if he walked into a bathroom and saw a naked girl in the tub. He stares, caught unawares; his hands, poised to unzip his jeans, rise up, palms out, like a man caught in a police searchlight. He was obviously intending to take a piss and wasn't expecting anyone to be in here.

'Whoa, I'm real sorry,' he says in what sounds like a Texan accent. 'Didn't know someone was in here.'

'My bad,' I say, 'I forgot to lock the other door.'

He tears his eyes off me long enough to register that there are two doors into the bathroom, one from each bedroom. 'Oh, right.'

'Do you mind?' I say.

He looks at me, then looks away again with a sorry-not-sorry look. 'I'll . . .' he starts, then backs away, shutting Olga's door as he goes without finishing the thought.

I lie there thinking, Am I going to have to kill this one?

I've managed to steer clear of Olga's revolving door boyfriends pretty successfully until now. The fewer people who see me and talk to me up close, the better. The campus and classes don't count: nobody really sees you up there unless you're part of their clique or you dress or act in a way that stands out, which I don't.

But it's different in the apartment; guys who are here just

for a night or three to roll in the hay with Olga are happy to note that she has a flatmate. I've avoided that by making sure I stay confined to my room when she has company, which isn't more than two or three nights a week anyway – and she never lets them sleep over, so next morning isn't an issue. But now, this dude has seen me up close and very personal and that might be a problem. Worse: Olga's given him a key, which I'm not too happy about.

I let myself soak another few minutes, then climb out of the tub and examine the bruises in the mirror. The coloring seems less intense and angry now, more muted. My shoulder feels a whole lot better. Ice-baths always work, my Israeli MMA instructor used to say. She was right.

I put aside my accidental flashing of a stranger for the time being; put aside, but I don't forget.

I return to my room, making sure that both the bathroom door as well as the door to the hallway are locked, and change into black jeans, tee shirt and a bomber jacket two sizes too large for me. It gives my torso and chest a shapeless, genderless look. With my hair up on my head and face hidden under a black motorcycle helmet, I could be anybody, any gender. The black motorcycle gloves conceal my hands and light brown coloring, erasing any clue to my race. Now, I'll just be another anonymous motorcyclist like any number of others.

The door to Olga's bedroom is closed, music playing inside. An oldie. The Beach Boys' 'Don't Worry Baby'. So our American gawker is into old-school rock and roll. Interesting. Not that it would keep me from snuffing him out if I think he's trouble, but it makes me like him just a little bit. Hard to hate someone who loves California R&R.

Olga's Golf pulls into the basement garage just as I'm starting my bike. She sees me but doesn't see me. She doesn't know I ride a bike and has never seen me in my hunting garb. I'm unrecognizable, which is the whole point. I watch her get out of the car carrying a heavy brown paper bag as I roll past. She kicks the door shut and click-clacks to the elevator. There's a clink from the bag which suggests booze. Looks like she's going to spend the weekend partying with our mutual American friend. At some point in the evening, she'll probably feel compelled to try out another of her mother's Bulgarian recipes. Thankfully, I won't be around to smell the result.

The Hayabusa purrs up the ramp and on to the street. I erase all thoughts of Olga, the Texan, the bathroom incident, and everything else. I'm done playing the prey for today. Now, it's time to hunt.

# 4

My apartment is located at Kurvenstrasse 24, which is in the 6th District. It's one of the new multi-storey apartment blocks they call 'skyscrapers'. To someone who's lived in New York, a seven-storey building is just a town house to me, but hey, it's their city.

I could have found an apartment in an actual tower – the old Swiss stigma against high-rises is fading slowly as more of them come up – where I could have had the whole place to myself if I wanted, and never had to worry about strange men walking in on me while I was in the bathtub. Two things kept me from renting one: I would have had to provide ID and pass financial and legal checks to get a lease, and that would have meant exposing my identity and getting my name into the system. The second reason is that they're fucking expensive.

It's not that I don't have any money – sharing a 2.5-room apartment in Kurvenstrasse costs too – but I don't have a billionaire daddy like Ricky Manfredi. If you're wondering why I didn't go in for sharing a room or taking one of the cheaper apartments in one of the typical two-storey Swiss town houses I was driving past right now, well, that's because I also wanted the right flatmate.

Why did I need a flatmate at all? Simple: the lease is in Olga's name. I found her through an ad she posted on the university website's bulletin board. I pay her cash each month, it's her name on the lease and she's a foreigner too.

A foreigner; but white. I could have shacked up with any number of black, brown or Asian students; we're a tiny minority here, but there are a few of us. But that would have made me stand out and that's the last thing I needed. I wanted a female flatmate (for the obvious reasons) but she had to be a white foreigner and had to check certain boxes. Olga felt just right to me: financially able to afford her own car, a furnished apartment and a fairly comfortable lifestyle, but not one of the uber-wealthy brats, and not Swiss, German or Dutch. Not perfect – but then again, who is. So her cooking sucks and she drinks and screws around a bit too much, but those are flaws I can live with. If it wasn't for the fact that I was on mission, I'd even have partied with her and her boyfriend *du jour*; that Texas cowboy was cute.

Now, I cruise past the historic main building of my university. In the tour I took a year before applying, they said it's been standing at the center of the city since the mid-nineteenth century. It is pretty impressive, but I'm not here to eyeball the architecture. My apartment is less than a mile from the campus and about the same distance on the other side is chez Ricky.

The street is quiet and deserted except for a tall, elderly lady walking a pair of Pomeranians and talking on a cellphone. She doesn't so much as glance in my direction.

I pull over to the curb at an angle, and turn off the engine. The Hayabusa set me back a fair bit even though I bought it used; I conveniently neglected to file the transfer of ownership with the ch.ch, which is the Swiss government website, and since I'm using a Swedish driver's license I filched from a woman up in the Netherlands, there's no paper trail leading back to me there either. It's a beautiful machine, though, and I will miss it when this mission is done. I rode it on the Great

St Bernard Pass through the Alps down the E27 south toward Italy for a two-day trip in summer, and it's easy to see why every conquering army from the Romans to Napoleon Bonaparte raved about the view. I even stopped at the hospice where the monks first began training the canine breed named after the region back in the seventeenth century.

The elderly woman's Poms stare at me suspiciously from under their fringes. Poms, I have no love for, but St Bernard puppies are the cutest thing in the world. Maybe someday, when this is all over, I'll own one. Or three.

I snap out of thoughts of big, lumbering dogs and snow-capped mountains as I see Ricky's bright red Lamborghini Aventador emerge from the gated drive of his town house. Even in a city filthy with uber-rich overspenders, it stands out. It purrs past me, a sleek, red-furred cat with enough power to do the Great St Bernard Pass in forty-three minutes flat. I timed him last summer, and even though the Hayabusa can technically outrun the Aventador, it gets pretty hairy doing those hairpin turns at 300 kph when the valley is all of 8,000 feet below your wheels, but Ricky arrived looking like he'd just been out for a leisurely cruise. I guess that's what extreme wealth does to you: fucks up your sense of proportion so even the most extraordinary things seem mundane, everyday stuff to your jaded mind.

I give him a respectable lead then follow slowly, keeping my distance so I don't stand out in his rear view. I'm dressed in the ubiquitous all-black gear of your typical motorhead, but the Hayabusa is no typical cycle and Ricky has an eye for stuff like that. It would be a shame if I have to dump this beauty on a routine follow simply because he makes me, but if I have to do it, I won't give it a second thought. The target is all that matters. Now that I've acquired him, I'm another step closer to killing him.

# 5

I follow Ricky up Gloriastrasse, past the uni, then on to Seilergraben, take the bridge over the Limmat river and on to Uraniastrasse 9. I already know where he's headed because I've been tracking his cellphone texts. I switched to audio once I got on the bike, and my phone reads his latest text out loud to me on my earpods as he turns on to Uraniastrasse.

Ricky: *Were u at?*

Irina: *Im heer.*

Atrocious spellings aside, this is Ricky's second assignation of the day. He's already burned the better part of the afternoon in a booty call with Ursula, before heading back to his own place for a shower and a change. Now, he's about to hook up with Irina, a Russian-Norwegian working on her dissertation on 'The roles of redox active metabolite in microbial signaling in gut flora'. It's got something to do with treating stress; my research doesn't dig deeper than required, and my own bachelor's studies are in plain old surgical medicine. Besides, I know Ricky's interest in Irina doesn't extend to discussing microbiology minutiae.

I let the Hayabusa idle outside a Credit Suisse up the street while I watch Ricky make his entrance in the flaming-red supercar, eliciting the expected reactions from the inevitable clutch of pencil-skirted wannabes thronging the entrance of Miko's. He hands the keys off to the delighted valet with no more care than if it were a beat-up compact car. To a guy like Ricky Manfredi, a car that costs a half a million American dollars is just another ride. He has a dozen others just as swish back home in LA.

I know better than to even try to get into Miko's. It's a private sex club with a by-invitation-only clientele. Prostitution is legal in Switzerland and sex clubs are a dime a dozen, but what makes this one special is that it's owned by Danielle Scharrer, the sitting Mayor of Zurich and a power player. She also happens to be queer and a socially progressive Democrat born and raised in Des Moines, Iowa, the grand-daughter of Joshua Silverblatt, a former Republican Whip, hard-right Christian anti-abortionist and Creationist. She was a major force behind the drive for equality in Iowa, and responsible for her neck of the woods having a stellar record for LGBTQIA acceptance and human rights. Quite the contrast to her father, Senator Josh Silverblatt II, who hewed closely to the family tradition. Imagine the dinner table chit-chat in the Silverblatt household. If there's a prize for most unlikely offspring, she deserves a nom.

Maybe because she was tired of the in-family opposition – or just nostalgic for her mother's homeland, where she had spent every summer – about fifteen years ago Scharrer gave up her US citizenship when Switzerland tightened its tax policy and settled permanently in Zurich. She was elected three years ago, only the second female Mayor of the city. Though the title of Mayor (*Stadtpräsident*) in Swiss cities is purely a ceremonial one with no real power, Scharrer is in synch with the current zeitgeist and is something of an icon for the Social Progressive Democratic Party here. All the old money and new money players in the city like to be seen with her, mostly because it plays well to the media and public, but also because she's a hell of a businesswoman. Apart from Miko's, she owns a slew of other businesses and has her financial fingers in more pies than I have fingers and toes. Miko's is also one of the few LGBT-oriented sex clubs, which makes it even more exclusive and chic, and is very high-end even in a city which is already one of the most expensive in the world.

Anyways, the only reason I'm waxing eloquent about her is because she is closely connected with American billionaire Roger Cordry, and hence his son, Ricky.

Since Ricky is an unabashedly cishet, I know that the only reason he's here is because Irina swings both ways. Her constant inventiveness and experimentation is the reason he's continued to swing with her even after discarding several other young women. I guess she pushes his buttons in all the right ways, which isn't easy when a guy's as jaded and seen-it-all, been-everywhere as he. They'll probably party right here in the club for a few hours, then Ricky will head back to his place to grab a few hours' shut-eye before hitting the reset button on a new day.

Then something interesting happens. Ursula texts Ricky after she sees a post on one of his socials, a short loop of him dancing with Irina. Like all Ricky's posts, this one is promotional and it plugs the club as well as a recently launched brand of champagne, both of which are owned by Scharrer. Figures. I eavesdrop on their convo with interest and amusement. Ursula is pissed that Ricky lied to her. Not that he's partying with Irina – she claims she isn't jealous – but that he lied to Ursula about going for a work thing and is actually living it up instead. Ricky's response is that this is the work thing he mentioned. He just made $100,000 for that post. Ursula backs off after that, but I've noted her initial over-reaction.

I do some quick research into her background, using

Professor Luegenbiehl's password to log into the proprietary medical database maintained by the university. It takes some digging but eventually I scrape through the dross to find the gold. Ursula has a well-documented history of mental health issues, going back to her teens. I save the files to my digital locker for future reference. This bears rereading. Useful. Very useful.

It's been a productive evening – and a very productive day. I decide to reward myself with a treat.

# 6

I ride past the National Museum and the bus station to Mattengasse 29, just a couple of kilometers away. I have a hankering for Desi Khana tonight, and while Zurich isn't exactly a haven for Indian food lovers, at least there are plenty of options. I make it a point never to eat more than once or twice at any place, especially a joint where someone might remember me, so even though I liked the Butter Chicken at Tadka, the last place I ate, I have to skip it. Instead, I decide to check out a place called Don't Hurry Eat Curry, partly because I haven't been there before but mostly because I like the name. I smell the asafoetida and saffron from the street and even though I've grown up mostly in the US and kicked around half the world since my childhood in India, it still feels like coming home. Like the NRIs say, you can take the girl out of India but you can never take India out of the girl.

The place is small; tiny, actually. It's really just a delivery-and-takeaway joint with some courtesy on-site seating. They don't get many walk-ins. That's why I picked it over the swankier sit-down restaurants. The fewer people I rub shoulders with the better, especially my fellow South Asians who tend to remember any halfway attractive desi girl. When I parked the bike, I took off the helmet, stripped off my jacket and gloves, locked them in the storage box, pulled on a sweatshirt with a hoodie, then let my hair down. When I walk into Don't Hurry Eat Curry, I'm just another brown girl in jeans, sneakers and an oversized H&M tan-colored hoodie which I got at half-price in a fall sale last year in London. I keep my hands in my pockets, slouch and keep my head down. Nobody would connect me with the disgendered all-black-wearing super-bike rider now, but even if they do, all they'll see is another second-gen diaspora girl with a bhangra pop attitude.

A middle-aged Sikh man carrying a takeaway packet comes out just as I reach for the door. He holds it open, and I slip in without bothering to thank him. The bells tinkle behind me as he exits, his bright orange turban contrasting with the muted stone greys and browns of Zurich architecture. The interior of the restaurant is pleasantly warm and the smells remind me that I haven't eaten anything since this morning.

Two dark-skinned women in Punjabi suits are talking to each other over the sound of a TV tuned to a football match. Tiny, ant-sized players in black-and-red and white outfits are running across a green rectangle. Belgium versus Tunisia. Belgium has the only goal, with less than three minutes to half-time. The feed cuts to middle-aged coaches yelling instructions to their teams, and a packed stadium restless with anticipation and alcohol.

The women are arguing in Tamil; I catch references to both teams and a few English words. The general drift seems to be that Tunisia doesn't stand a chance in hell of beating Belgium or any other team in 'G', which I presume is the Group. I wasn't always a football fan – the kind played in Europe and Asia, not the ball-carrying bull-charging scrimmage Americans mean when they use the term – but it's grown on me, or maybe it's a latent part of every desi. It's like the taste for over-boiled, painfully sweet Indian-style chai: it comes with the DNA.

I pretend to look at a plastic-encased menu while I watch the women out the corner of my eye. They've seen me and called out the usual 'Hello, welcome, welcome, with you in a minute!' before continuing their international debate. The woman in the open kitchen area seems to believe that Tunisia has a shot this year, for reasons that escape me. My Tamil is rudimentary, nowhere near as fluent as my Hindi, Bengali and Punjabi.

The woman in the serving area shakes her head one last time before clapping her hands together in a typically South Asian 'OK, I give up' gesture, and turning to me with a fairly genuine smile on her long, lean face. There's a look to her that I can't quite place. Tamil speakers in Sri Lanka are mostly descendants of South Indian immigrants, who in turn, like all South Asians, are a sub-category of Mediterranean Caucasians. The body structure and features are fairly similar to Middle Easterners, but with much darker skin tones. This lady is dark, but the shape of her face is almost African in its bone structure. Her hair is curly too, which is a contrast to most Tamilian women, who tend to have long, thick black hair. She's tall, at least five nine, maybe an inch more, and has a way of carrying herself that's quite distinctive.

She notices me looking her over and smiles as if she's used to this scrutiny from fellow South Asians. 'Douglas.' She pronounces it not like the male name but like 'Doogle-aas'.

'Excuse me?'

'Afro-Indian. Our ancestors come from India, via the Caribbean Islands, before settling in Kandy.'

'Right,' I say cautiously. That explains the sing-song speech. Race and ancestry can be touchy subjects these days, especially for non-white immigrants in white-dominated western countries. I decide the safest bet is to not comment on it at all. Hannah's Law: when in doubt, say (or do) nothing. If I engage, she may start asking me questions about my origins, parentage, marital status, favorite brand of panty liner, who knows what; my fellow South Asians can't help it, we're naturally born inquisitive.

'So . . .' I continue, glancing down at the menu again, 'what do you recommend?'

She reels off several items, pointing them out on the menu to me, summarizes the ones I inquired about, and after I make my choice, asks me what spice level I want. In most western-owned 'Indian' restaurants, they use the standard terms 'Less spicy, medium spicy, more spicy'.

When I reply I wanted it 'Spicy', she phrases her question in more homely lingo: 'Indian spicy or European spicy?'

I smile inwardly at that. 'Indian spicy. I can take it.'

She leans over the stainless-steel counter to yell the order to the woman in the kitchen area before turning back to me.

'Please, have a seat, I will bring it to you.'

The food is good. Indian spicy as advertised, hot enough to have white patrons steaming out their ears and noses and other assorted orifices. Burns you at both ends, as we say back home; does you on the way in and does you on the way out, as the UK desis put it. Afterward, I use the washroom to scrub as much of the curry off my fingers as possible, although a few faint turmeric stains still linger at the tips, like evidence of an old nicotine habit. I take another moment to pee. When I return to my table and pay the bill – cash is king, as we desis also say, and it doesn't leave an electronic trail – the tall woman brings me my change and a glistening golden-brown ball in a small thermocol cup. It's an Indian sweetmeat called gulab jamun, and seeing it fills me with a sudden, painful pang of nostalgia. I stare down at it.

'I didn't order this,' I say to her retreating back.

She turns and offers, over her shoulder with a toothy smile: 'Compliments.'

I hesitate, then sit at the table again, looking down at the gulab jamun. After a brief inward struggle, I pick it up with a forefinger and thumb and bite off half of it. It's sticky, very sweet, and the soft, milky dough, fried to a deep brown on the outside, all but dissolves in my mouth. On the TV screen above the door, Tunisia scores an unexpected second half goal and the crowd and commentators go berserk. The two Sri Lankan women resume their sporting rivalry, the kitchen side now crowing triumphantly in Tamil while the serving side make good-natured, dismissive remarks about luck and even stopped clocks being right twice a day. The taste of yesterday floods my senses and I'm suddenly flung back in time, into my ten-year-old self sitting in the dining room of the Beck House in upstate New York.

We're all seated around the table, finishing dinner on a warm night, but my attention is on my older brother Brian sitting across from me. The slanting summer sunlight falls through the picture window that looks out on to a picture postcard view of the Adirondacks, washing the large room in soft, buttery hues. It's the fag end of a glorious summer, a summer spent swimming in our heated indoor pool, riding our BMX bikes over dirt trails, tramping through the woods just beyond our backyard, and generally having the time of our lives.

My brother has promised he'll take me along to the pond for skinny-dipping tonight – it's so much more fun swimming under the stars than in a boringly safe indoor pool – and I'm so excited I can barely eat. My mom is watching me and she knows something's up because, as she points out, I've barely touched my food. She's gone to the trouble of making idlis and dosas with sambhar and chutney especially for our dinner guest, my father's partner Rajesh Kadru, whom we're supposed to now call 'Uncle Roger' instead of 'Uncle Rajesh'. I'm always clamoring for her to make dosas and idlis but now that I have a plateful of them before me, I'm not hungry. Later that night, when we sneak back into the house, my hair dripping wet and with leaf crumbs stuck to it, I will be struck with an almighty hunger and Brian will help me raid the fridge for the leftovers which we then devour cold, standing barefoot at the kitchen counter. But right now, I've only taken a bite or two out of my idli and my butter dosa is barely touched.

Brian breaks off a piece of idli with his fingers and makes it hover over the bowl of sambhar, just like we'll be doing when we hang from the tyre slung from the tree branch before letting go and splashing into the pond. He lets go of the piece of idli and as it falls into the sambhar, a few drops splash up into his face. I cover my mouth to hide my giggles. Brian hams it up, waggling his eyebrows, crossing his eyes and sticking out his tongue to try to reach the drops of sambhar on his cheek. I burst out laughing and everyone looks at me. Mom frowns, smiling but suspicious: 'What's up with you tonight? You've been begging for idli-dosa all week and you've barely touched your food!'

I try to control my giggles. 'Sorry, Ma, just not hungry.'

'That's too bad,' Mom says, exaggerating a shrug, 'I guess that means you're too hungry for gulab jamuns too.'

'What?' I squeal. 'You made gulab jamuns too?'

'Yes,' Mom says, 'it's Uncle Rajesh's – I mean Uncle Roger's – favorite sweet, remember?'

'Mine too!'

'Yes, but you're not hungry, you said. So I guess I'll just have to give your gulab jamuns to Reba and Britney instead,' she says, indicating the dogs under the dining table.

'No way,' I yell.

Across the table, Brian makes calming gestures at me, mouthing: *She's joking!*

Everyone laughs at my over-reaction, but Mom stifles her grin and says, 'Well then, you better eat some real food if you want your sweet.'

Brian makes eating gestures to me.

I stick my tongue out at him.

Brian shrugs and says to Mom, 'Sweets aren't good for dogs, Mom. If she doesn't want her gulab jamuns, I'll have them.'

I pick up my idli and fling it across the table at him. The rice cake slaps him squarely on his forehead and sticks fast. Brian crosses his eyes in disbelief, staring at the food stuck to his face, and that sets everyone off again, including me. Even the dogs under the table burst out barking as the dining room fills with our laughter.

In less than three weeks, Brian will be lying dead in the woods, not far from the same pond where we're going skinny-dipping tonight, his chest and abdomen ripped open by savage shotgun blasts at close range; my dad will be found beneath him, cradling Brian's head in his hands, face gummy with tears and the blood from his own terrible wounds. I will lose all desire to eat gulab jamuns again for well over a decade – until one evening, in a curry shop in Zurich, I'm unexpectedly served one.

'Is it good?' she asks, and I look up – at the server, at my mother, at the past and the present blurring together disorientingly, and the too-sweet taste of the could-have-been and never-was fill my mouth and mind like cold water in a drowning lung.

'It's . . .' I start to say, and the tears stream down my face. Regret. Pain. Grief. For what was, what could have been, what was taken from us.

I get up from the table and leave the dining room, the restaurant, New York, the past, the present, the world, my heart.

# 7

Ricky is talking to a pert brunette I don't recognize. She's short, not quite as short as I am, but very pretty. She has a knockout bod, which explains Ricky's interest despite her not being his type, if a screw-everything-in-sight-that-looks-screwable man can be said to have a type. She's really into him, alternating between touching her hair and touching his arm, leaning into him, looking up and laughing at every second thing he says. Ricky's using his height and build to his advantage, looming over her like a NYPD chopper. She's leaning against a red-brick wall, one sneakered foot propped up behind her, her pleated skirt riding up to show off her nice legs, but from a distance all you really see is Ricky leaning against the wall.

I walk toward them with my head down, bangs hanging over my face, sketchbook clutched to my chest as usual, not seeming to pay any attention. I pass them, acting as though he didn't see me, and continue on the pathway. I hear him excusing himself to the brunette – 'Text me' – and then his shadow sweeps across and over my own, preceding his grinning appearance.

'Hi.'

I keep walking like he isn't even there, blowing past.

He catches up again, his smile a little dimmer, but still game.

'We met the other day. You fell. Those assholes playing ball back there.'

I'm still walking. He steps backwards to keep up with me. Two or three steps of mine are equal to one of his strides. The grin stays on: he's not giving up this easy.

'You dropped this when you fell. Someone found it.'

He holds up a cellphone with one hand, thumbing the home button to make the screen light up. It's right in my face, so I have to stop.

The lock screen is a picture of me in my Hannah look, de-aged to make me appear five or six years younger and with a top row of slightly buck teeth wrapped with old-school braces. I Photoshopped it on to the burner precisely for his benefit. In the pic, young adult me is standing in front of the Taj Mahal with a goofy smile on my face, doing the touristy trick-shot thing: holding my palms horizontally above each other, with the Taj sandwiched between them. It's a cliché thing that lets him get a fix on Hannah: small-town desi expat chasing the Great Capitalist Dream but homesick for those bygone salad days.

The screen dies, dispelling the illusion.

'I didn't have the lock code, or I'd have tried to find your deets, shown it around campus.'

Exactly why I didn't use a current pic. Even in my Hannah look, I don't want to leave anything that can be used to visually identify me later.

I reach for the phone and he lets me take it.

'I tried finding you all of yesterday. I would have shown the pic around but it doesn't really look like you.'

'I'm much younger.'

'You look really cute in braces. You know you get the invisible kind now? They're like transparent.'

Yeah, asshole. And they cost five times the shiny metal ones.

'Thanks for returning my phone.'

I slip it into the back pocket of my jeans and start down the path again. He walks alongside me now.

'So what's your plan after class?'

I keep my eyes on the path ahead, not ignoring him but not looking directly at him either. So far, I haven't made actual eye contact, despite his best efforts.

'Nothing really,' I reply, sounding cautious.

'How's about a drink? Or chai. Whatever's your poison.'

I drag him along another few yards, thinking it over. 'I've been wanting to go to Odeon.'

Ricky looks at me skeptically. I can see he's tempted to make a crack but thinks better of it. He's trying really hard to make a good impression. 'Sure. Odeon's cool. Five-ish?'

I'm outside the building now, about to go in, and I stop walking, pretending to think it over. I know he has a booty call with one of his regulars scheduled for three. I decide to test his eagerness. 'Three is better.'

He comes back without so much as a pause. 'I can make that work. Give me your cell.'

I make one last show of hesitation then unlock the phone he just gave me with a four-digit code – 1947, the year India got independence from the British Empire – and hand it over. He thumbs in his own cell number and adds it to my address book under 'Ricky' then hands the phone back.

'Text you,' he says. He grins one last time and walks away with the jaunty stride of a Mercedes salesman who's just topped the leaderboard for the year. I watch his ass move in his Gucci Genius jeans. He does have a nice ass. Along with everything else, I'd bet.

I'll be able to verify that for myself pretty soon.

But maybe not too soon.

The game has to be played as it's meant to be played, after all, and this dance has only just begun.

# 8

He lies naked on his back, a well-maintained young white man in his mid-twenties, with brown hair, brown eyes. Not as buff as Ricky but youthfully trim, without any visible adipose deposits. He used to work out in the gym, although the definition is lost now, muscles smoothened and indistinct beneath the translucent skin. Blue veins stand out in his neck and forearms. He has the advantage of being young and well-preserved, but his body shape is endomorph (Ricky's a mesomorph) and once he hits middle age, he'll start piling on the pounds steadily, no matter how much he works out. Eventually, he'll turn toward pear-shaped inevitability like a weather vane into the wind, the inexorable hand of genetics firmly steering his metabolism. Although, of course, that day will never come: he's been spared that genetic inevitability by the even crueler hand of sudden death, arriving in the form of a massive brain embolism, undetected and unsuspected, of which he dropped dead one morning while playing tennis. A Swiss national and former medical student at this very university, he signed over his body to science in a drive which he himself was a volunteer for only a few months earlier. Which is why he now lies here, under the garish white lights of an autopsy table surrounded by white-coated students peering down at his vulnerable flesh which we are about to dissect with our silvery scalpels.

It's his interiors that I am interested in. The viscous secrets of his organs and viscera, the cranial cavity with its occipital curves and ocular, auricular and thoracic passages, the grey, neuroelectric mysteries of his brain. The body is such a marvel and a miracle. When I learned that Ricky had secured a place at this university, I could have chosen to seek admission in any field ranging from economics to physics to literature; instead, I chose surgical medicine. I always wanted to see the insides of this bag of flesh we call a body; to try to understand the magic of life.

And yes, I thought it might also be useful in other ways: my life is dedicated to killing. Not the emotionless commissioned sanctions of a paid assassin, but the cold-blooded, meticulously planned, justified homicides of one to whom justice has long been denied and who has been compelled to take matters into their own hands. Why not train those hands in the intricacies of saving life as a means of prepping for taking life? The scalpel that saves is after all only a small twist removed from the knife that takes. In the months that I have spent here, I've come to enjoy my studies in their own right. I've learned, somewhat to my surprise, that I could become a good doctor, perhaps even a good surgeon, if I choose to pursue that course.

Professor Luegenbiehl has been speaking in German as we study the cadaver. There are only six of us. It always surprises me that western classes are so small. I studied for a few years in India, where there were fifty or more students to a teacher, and when one teacher was absent, double that number, all packed into a classroom, two to a chair. After those tumultuous, sweat-smelling rooms, the air-conditioned sparseness of a European class seems like a wasteful extravagance. In India, we would have packed thirty students in this same space, some standing on rickety wooden stools or on each other's shoulders, craning their necks to ogle like spectators outside a cricket stadium.

Her brief preparatory lecture finished, she instructs us to put on our masks and take up our scalpels. We do as instructed. One of the young men hesitates before he pulls his mask on, and looks uneasy as he picks up the scalpel, his hand trembling slightly. That's Villeneuve. He's nervous about blood and bodily fluids, among other things; he also has allergies. Red-headed, pale as fat-free milk, with light blue eyes and a barely-there attempt at a moustache, he looks like he might faint at any time. The other students to his right and left whisper to one another, side-eyeing him. I think they might be laying bets on whether he'll faint or not.

I would bet fifty francs at two to one odds that he'll be laid out on the floor after the first cut, but I've successfully managed to avoid hobnobbing with my fellow classmates for the entire semester and can't break cover now. They went through the five stages of social interaction in the first month itself: Curiosity, Interest, Irritation, Anger, Disinterest. They're now at the point where they hardly appear to notice me. I've hacked all their phones and use spyware to track any mentions of me, just to be safe. They stopped even mentioning me on their group and individual chats months ago, after deciding that I was either a snob, a reverse-racist, or just another ABBA, to use their invented term. That stands for Angry Black/Brown Activist, not the Swedish pop group, and I'll admit there are a fair number of ABBAs in the education system; I guess it's even a fair assessment of me, except that it's not the reason why I'm ignoring them – but none of that matters now. One of them happens to be Ursula, Ricky's angsty Finn. Interesting. She's probably curating Luegenbiehl's class, maybe contemplating a switch. I didn't anticipate encountering her at such close quarters, but I don't mind having the chance to size her up.

She's a bit aloof from the rest, either because she's snobbish or just plain unfriendly. I don't think she even knows I exist, let alone that I'm in the class. I'd like to keep it that way.

'Now we are ready to commence,' Professor Luegenbiehl says in German. 'Hannah has requested to go first. Hannah, are you ready?' She sounds skeptical. I have missed previous anatomy sessions, and I am now appearing for my exam directly. She's more concerned about losing a good specimen than failing me. She expects me to fail. Everyone does. They don't know I've done this before, several times. Bodies are cheaper to buy in India, especially when they're low-caste indigents and paupers. Practice makes perfect.

All eyes rise to appraise me. I nod, raising my scalpel and reply in heavily accented, deliberately clumsy German. 'I am prepared, Professor. Shall I initiate?'

Two of the girls giggle softly behind their masks: Scherzinger and Winzenreid, rich, spoiled, third-generation surgical aspirants, from wealthy families in Zurich and Vienna. There will be chatter about my poor German on their Slack group tonight. Good. Wouldn't want them to know that I speak German fluently enough to pass for Swiss-born. The others, Ursula included, don't really care much either way. They're more interested in getting their turn.

Professor Luegenbiehl is a large blonde with a quietly precise manner and a soft, gentle way of speaking that comes across as unexpected in such a big woman. Her blue-eyed gaze appraises me briefly. She's judging whether I'm likely to faint – or botch this up badly – and I wonder how much my skin color and race influence her judgment. She seems to think I'm a good risk, and she nods once, then points to the cadaver. 'The first incision will be made here.' She marks the line precisely with a marker before capping it and putting it back in the pocket of her coat.

I place the scalpel at the start of the marked line, my hand steady as a rock. I can hear the soft hum of the central air-conditioning vents above us, lightly brushing the nape of my neck like the cold breath of someone standing behind me. I hear the breathing of the students, especially Zopfi who's a JUUL smoker. Scherzinger makes a one-word whispered comment to Winzenried, Villeneuve clears his throat once, nervously, then the room is quiet except for the steady beating of my heart. Fifty beats per minute, calm as an astronaut. I've trained for moments like this one; this is truly what I am.

I make the cut, moving the scalpel through the epidermis precisely along the marked line, accurate as a vector drawn by a computer program. The layers part as easily as the petals of an awakening orchid.

'*Ach so!*' Luegenbiehl says approvingly. I hear a barely concealed tone of surprised relief; so, my skin color did influence her judgment in the negative. 'Steady hand, decisive cut. Severing all layers of the epidermis in a single stroke.'

I look up at her, calmly acknowledging the praise without smiling or showing any other response. Scherzinger's dark eyes are small and glittering above her mask; she's jealous. Ursula is watching the path of the scalpel with the keen focus of a future surgeon; makes sense, given her family background. Zopfi looks like he's desperately trying not to cough. Villeneuve is staring down at the long cut in the abdomen of the corpse with a dull fascination. I'm guessing his blood pressure is dropping by the second, though it's hard to be sure with his face already so pale beneath his rubicund shock.

I continue cutting, following Luegenbiehl's instructions

then gradually outpacing them, performing expert, perfectly executed incisions, parting the layers, peeling back the adipose tissues, trimming away the fascia. Now, the abdominal cavity is exposed.

Faintly, I'm aware of the sound of Villeneuve fainting, dropping out of sight in my peripheral vision. There's a soft thud as his head touches the floor. The others virtually ignore him. All attention is focused intently on the body and my hands.

Luegenbiehl cautions me not to cut into the stomach or liver – too late, as I'm already past them and moving two steps ahead of her by this point. This is now an exercise in demonstration: I am cutting and she is explaining what I have just done immediately after I do it. Our roles have been reversed: I am now the Sachin Tendulkar hitting a record innings, and she is Sunil Gavaskar offering expert commentary from the box.

I could do this all day. I'm really enjoying myself. This is amazing. A part of me cautions restraint. I don't want to show off; the whole point of Hannah's low-key persona is to avoid getting noticed. But I can't help it. I really do love this. From the avid gleam in Ursula's eyes, I see that she shares my enjoyment.

As I pull on the tendons – 'Shall we pull on the tendons now?' the Professor says in a futile attempt to try to anticipate my next demonstration – the toes of the corpse wriggle at the foot of the table. Scherzinger startles involuntarily, so absorbed in hating me that she forgets this quite basic tendinous response. The small scream that she utters is instantly suppressed, her hand clapping her mouth, but it's too late. The laughter that erupts from the other four raises a flush of humiliated embarrassment to her white cheeks, visible even in the little areas that show above the surgical mask. Even Luegienbiehl smiles drily: 'No need to panic. He is quite dead, *fräulein*. It is mere puppetry. Like a marionette, yes? And now, shall we cut into the digestive system? Starting with . . . quite so, the esophagus, all the way down to . . . yes, yes, the rectum.'

Now, everyone gags, reacting to the odious exudation that rises from the cadaver as I expose the shit-canal, to use a non-technical term. Zopfi gags.

'No regurgitation on subject!' Luegenbiehl admonishes sternly.

Zopfi stumbles over to a waste basket, grabs it and pukes into it noisily. The stench adds to the delightful atmosphere. The distraction erases everyone's minds of Scherzinger's embarrassing reaction: everyone except Scherzinger, that is. She's staring down at the floor, very obviously avoiding eye contact with me, and I suspect she's wishing it were me on the table and she doing the cutting right now.

'Hannah has a good hand. Yes, well done, well done.' Luegenbiehl's compliments come fast and frequently now as she relaxes, clearly impressed by my work. It's quite obvious now that she was expecting some nervously competent cuts at first then utter cluelessness and confusion at some point. The very fact that I've taken this all the way without so much as a minor misstep or hesitation is outside her scale of expectation.

I pause and look up at her now. 'Shall I extract the heart?' I don't bother with the honorific; I've proved myself competent, and she knows it.

She nods, pursing her eyebrows in a very Swiss-German way that tells me she is genuinely impressed. 'If you wish. Proceed.'

46

When I have the dead man's most essential organ in my hand, surprisingly heavy as the heart always is, she nods again approvingly. 'So advanced already. I see you have prepared thoroughly. Good. You do well today.' She raises her gloved hands. 'A round of applause for Hannah? Good. Yes. Good.'

A smattering of applause from everyone, including Scherzinger who has recovered and doesn't want to look like an envious asshole; I sense I've made an enemy for life, but I won't be sticking around Zurich long enough for it to become a problem. Villeneuve recovered toward the end of my procedure and is on his feet again, looking even whiter and sicklier than before, if such a thing is possible. Zopfi has found a stainless-steel stool and is sitting on it, staring dully at the now-exposed cadaver's insides as he claps slowly, looking like an addict who's just sworn he'll never touch the shit again in his life. I give him maybe six hours before he's JUULing again, and maybe a couple of years before he's stretched out on a hospital table himself, being treated for lung problems. He's not going to hack it as a doctor, though you never know. White male privilege goes a long way.

I drop the stained scalpel with a pleasing clink into a tray and peel off my gloves and mask. No smile on my face or visible sign of pleasure; but on the inside I'm glowing like a hot coal. I know I've shown off more than I should have, especially in front of Ursula, but it was worth it to see their reactions. Besides, it was fun. I love cutting.

# 9

He looks around Odeon's like it causes him actual pain to be seen in such a touristy place. Good. That's exactly why I picked it, knowing he would find it uncool to be spotted here and wouldn't bother posting about it. He's Ricky fucking Manfredi. Places where he's been seen get written up and talked about. Who's been seen at and seen with are stop-the-press news in these social influencer-obsessed times. Sometimes, he'll even deign to post a pic of himself and his party partners at a lesser-known joint, and his followers will like it a couple of hundred thousand times and leave a mess of comments. Once, Beyoncé commented on a place he posted about, recommending the shrimp. Ricky replied with a pic of himself about to bite into one. That particular bistro was booked up solid for the next six months. Celebrity, bitches.

He inclines his artfully tousled head at my just-arrived drink. 'You do know that Cüpli is just house champagne sold by the glass, right?'

I stare down at my stem glass, letting my bangs conceal my eyes. I say nothing, letting him read into my silence what he will.

He's silent for a moment, knowing he's made a faux pas, perhaps even a fatal one. 'Heya,' he says in a softer tone, 'I didn't mean to be judgy. My bad.'

Then, in a brighter tone, trying to undo the damage: 'This is on me anyway. Why don't you try the Bordeaux 'fifty-nine? Or a good Pinot Grigio? They must have some halfway decent stuff.'

If this was a real date, I would glare at him and walk out

48

for judging me and trashing my taste – not to mention flaunting his wealth and critiquing my poverty – but this isn't me. This is Hannah; I'm just playing a part.

I reach for my bag, still avoiding eye contact. 'This was a mistake.'

To his credit, he doesn't grab my wrist or block my way. Instead, he says, 'I'm sorry. I was out of line. I had no right to question your choices.'

I pause, still holding my bag but not getting up. 'It's not you, it's me. I . . . I can't really afford this place. It's just . . . I just always wanted to come here. I mean, it's Odeon. There's so much history. So many famous people came here. Einstein even had a favorite table.'

He nods vigorously, eager to pacify and please. 'Lenin.'

I give him a sudden, surprised glance: our first eye contact. 'Joyce.'

'General Ulrich Wille. He was like, the commander of the Swiss armed forces during World War One.'

'Alberto Giacometti. Sculptor and artist, he lived in the same building.'

We smile tentatively at each other over the polished tabletop. The corners of his eyes crinkle handsomely as he raises his double Scotch on the rocks. The overhead lights refract through the cut glass, scattering diamantine highlights. His movie-star straightened-and-whitened teeth gleam like bleached bone. 'To Lenin!'

'To Joyce!' I clink my willowy stem cautiously against his blocky shard.

We drink in sudden camaraderie, the ice broken.

In his eyes, I read the artfully disguised glee: *Am I the smooth operator or what?*

Dance on, motherfucker, dance on into my darkness.

In the Netflix series *You*, which dropped a few years back, the creeper-protagonist Joe stalks a bookstore patron with a relentless obsession that leads down a dark, spiraling stairway to the basement of his basest desires. I read the Caroline Kepnes novel on which the show was based before I watched the series, and found myself thoroughly creeped out and completely aroused. The show, a fine adaptation, was a huge hit, an ironic counterpoint to the #MeToo and #TimesUp movements raging around the same time. If Caroline Kepnes had been a white, cishet, privileged male, would the book and show have been accepted and absorbed into the cultural zeitgeist so readily? The book, and especially Joe's character, had a particular resonance for me: not because I identified with him – nobody in our present judgy age would dare admit aloud that they relate to a stalker-serial-killer protagonist – but because I *got* him. He was real. He was human. He lived and breathed.

Former President Obama once commented on online activism, saying 'This idea of purity and you're never compromised and you're always politically "woke" and all that stuff. You should get over that quickly. The world is messy; there are ambiguities. People who do really good stuff have flaws.'

Word.

Obviously, Joe Goldberg isn't a good guy; but he is real. There's more Joe Goldberg in you and me than we would like to acknowledge. This one time, I was in a group therapy session for abused women, and one of the things I picked up was how many are obsessively addicted to true crime stories about sexual assault and male abuse. *You* is only one of any number of shows, movies, books and true crime stories catering to the same market, I guess. Is it because fiction is a safe space where we can revisit our past trauma while knowing we're never going to come to actual harm? Your guess is as good as mine.

I'm no master con artist. I'm not even a career criminal, in my view at least. I'm just a girl standing in front of a boy asking him to drop dead, asshole, because your father fucked up my family and destroyed my childhood, and not only did he profit enormously from it all, he got away with it scot-free and blame-free, leaving me with no legal or official recourse other than taking the law into my own hands and bringing down just punishment on him and all those he engendered, because if an eye for an eye makes the whole world blind, well, he already erased my entire family, so I intend to do the same to his.

It's brutal. Extreme. Psychotic even.

I'm sane enough to admit how insane this whole thing is.

But I'm also human; real; sentient; moral; woke; feeling, caring, emotional.

I feel. I hurt. I care.

And I am capable of love.

Even the most broken person on this planet possesses that capacity, that *need*.

Not to be loved, because that can be tricky, a trapdoor to hidden pitfalls, but simply to love. To give.

Make no mistake about it. What I'm about to do to Ricky, to his family, and most of all his father, that OG responsible for setting off this vendetta, will be brutal and shocking. You may even see the acts themselves as pathological. They are certainly criminal. I'm not going to even try to justify them. I am what I am and so will I be. But I am more than the sum of my crimes; I am the engine of vengeance, but I am no avenging angel. If anything, I believe that revenge is the worst crime of all; it perpetuates the cycle of human violence. If we could only eliminate the drive for revenge – justified or otherwise – we would avoid so much of the history of human suffering.

Which is why I'm surprised when he texts me one night while I'm lying in bed, following his digital trail as usual. I'm actually reading his convo with an Indian-American friend where he refers to 'fresh flesh' which I presume (shudder) means me, when his text pops up in my inbox.

*heya that was fun*

Interesting. Either he's totally changed his idea of what 'fun' means or he's really eager to hook up with me.

*Yes,* I text back, *it was, wasn't it?*

He gets a call just then but ignores it. It's from Ursula. I track her on a separate app without even thinking about it. That one bears watching.

*ya want to hang out?* he asks me.

I pause a few seconds, letting him watch the blinking dots as he waits, then type *That depends.*

*lol i dont mean like crazy shit*

*Well, from what I've heard, your life is pretty wild.*

*girl you bin checking up on me?*

*What's to check, Ricky, your life is a public show 'n tell!*

*hyuk hyuk touche*

*So what did you have in mind?*

We go back and forth a few more times, he tries to fix up

for tomorrow, I say I have an important test I need to cram for – I do – and we finally settle on a day and date later in the week. I want to play hard to get but not so hard that he loses patience. I have to admit, I'm kind of smug in my own complacency at this point. I've hooked him and I know he wants more. I expect him to play out his usual smooth operator script, the same as he's done a thousand times before.

Instead, he pulls a David Copperfield on me – Vegas, not Dickens – and pulls a rabbit out of his top hat.

I turn up at his apartment, half-dreading a packed house party with wall-to-wall action, some big-name DJ curating the beats, and an endless supply of recreational stimuli. That would be a disaster, and I'm prepared to turn around immediately: I need to stay off the radar of his friends. Instead, I find a pair of little clay lamps outside his front door, the kind we call 'diyas' back in India, and a beautiful mandala pattern on the porch, drawn using colored powders – we call it 'rangoli'. I groan inwardly and roll my eyes, expecting some crass cultural exploitation passed off as a 'theme party'.

But there are no guests, no DJ, no drugs. Only Ricky, and his entire apartment decorated with Indian motifs, wall hangings, paintings, spotlit statues, and a dining table laid out with a lavish spread of what smells and looks like authentic desi cuisine. There's soft music playing: it's the bittersweet drone of shehnais, the wind instrument which backdrops Indian weddings. The lighting is low, and a prince in traditional Indian garb greets me with a namaste and a bow.

This is Ricky? For real?

It's Ricky.

'Namaste,' he says.

I can't help it. I burst out laughing. I'm so loud, it drowns out the mournful wailing of the shehnais.

When I finally stop, Ricky is watching me with a disarming grin on his face. 'Too much?' he asks.

I hold up my forefinger and thumb an inch apart. 'Just a tad.'

He bursts out laughing too. That sets me off again.

'Sorry. You mentioned that you're missing home, so I thought I'd do something special. If it's too overwhelming, I can have it all taken away, or we could –'

I stop him by placing my finger on his lips. His eagerness and nervous energy are so charming, I could kiss him right now. Instead, I say, 'It's actually kind of sweet and I'm pretty hungry. Could we eat?'

His expression is somewhere north of thrilled, south of trying to be cool about it. 'Sure. I mean, that's what the food's for!'

The meal is delicious. Catered and prepared specially, of course. The perks of extreme wealth. The conversation is awkward, but unaffected. Whatever I was expecting, this is not it. This is the opposite of it. This is . . . personalized. Intimate. Like a handwritten note just for me. Not a copy-pasted text. From my digital stalking, I know Ricky's never dated an Indian before. He's slept with a bunch, but that's not the same thing. So this is a first. He's actually put thought, time, effort, energy into it. It's not the work of some assistant on his team – I know this because over dinner, I ask him judicious questions and he tells me how he put this whole night together. He basically stalked my social media – or rather, Hannah's social media, in keeping with the persona and background I've created for this role, and made notes on Hannah's favorite foods, music, movies, the works. Luckily for him, I knew the best way to build a character is to stay as close to your own self as possible, so these are pretty close to my own tastes.

After dinner he has an Indian movie lined up for me to watch. Not a streaming Bollywood blockbuster: those I can't stand. This is the first new movie by a reclusive genius in twelve years, an artistic exercise as well as a philosophical inquiry into existentialism. In a multitude of Indian languages as well as English. It's eccentric, zany, but thoughtful, aesthetically amazing, and there are some incredible moments. I love it. And it's screened for me in a special preview theater that Ricky and I have all to ourselves for the night, with popcorn flavored with masala powders, the kind you only get in Indian movie theaters.

To put this simply, it's the best goddamn date I've ever been on. I hate to admit that with a swinging dick like Ricky who is clearly doing all this just to seduce me, but damnit, this is one time I'm actually enjoying being seduced, against my better judgment.

Ricky Manfredi. I came to kill you. And already, I think, just maybe, I might be falling for you. You fucking bastard.

We are in his bedroom, my breasts pressed against his chest, his hardness pressing against my belly.

To say we're ready to have sex is an understatement.

After that second date, the electricity between us could have lit up Zurich. I have managed to keep him at bay for just over three weeks in all – a record for Ricky. This is the first time we're going to have sex; he's priapic but impressively restrained.

I've enjoyed the waiting almost as much as I now savor the yielding.

I'm just as horny as he is; he knows it; it's why he's held out this long. I've never once rebuffed his advances these past fifteen days, and he has known it's only a matter of time.

Time's up now.

A brief parting. Exhalations. Hot breath on my forehead, my ears.

Then we resume the pas de deux.

I'm stretching this one out as long as I can. It's the last hold-out before the long-awaited surrender.

Ricky believes he has all the power in this relationship. He's played the game beautifully: wooed me and cooed at me, wined me and dined me, clubbing and dancing, jello shots and spicy tapas, long, high-speed drives on winding Swiss mountain roads. After his misstep at Odeon, he's even dressed down for me to avoid causing me embarrassment at my modest wardrobe (carefully chosen to convey the middle-class-desi-girl-trying-too-hard-to-look-fashionable-abroad look), taken me to obscure eateries and bars he'd never have let himself be seen dead in otherwise, and valiantly resisted clicking selfies or 'gramming and 'tokking pics and vids of us together. He's made adjustments that would severely damage his rep as most desirable slutboy if his usual homies ever saw him in this mode.

My insistence on discretion has worked in his favor too: by staying off the celebrity grid, patronizing the more mundane, un-glitzy joints and avoiding sharing our exploits on social media, he's able to – I won't say 'be himself', because that would be going too far – ease up on the gas. Like any other poor little post-millennial rich boy, Ricky wears his privilege uncomfortably. A victim of his own status, he has to watch every spoken word, every item purchased or displayed, check every relationship for how it plays publicly, double-check everything to be sure it's the right 'look' for that moment in the zeitgeist. That basically means having to run everything he intends to do, or even thinks he might, perhaps, be interested in doing, by a team of expensive image and PR consultants, and having $1,000-an-hour New York lawyers double-check every last line of fine print of his endorsement contracts to be sure he's not violating any sub-sub-clause.

This habit of second- and third-guessing and triple-quadruple-thinking everything is so much a part of him, like a pair of vermilion-tinted contact lenses laser-stitched on to his corneas, that it's never occurred to him before that he could simply shrug it all off and live outside the petri dish. (To us millennials that's like postulating an existence without a smartphone, internet and social media; basically, dystopia.) Not permanently, because sooner or later even reclusion becomes viral news. But just for a short while, a couple of weeks, someone like him can sometimes slip back into the shadows without the gossip websites making a big issue out of it.

I claim responsibility for putting the idea into his head, while making him think he came up with it all on his ownsome.

His cover story, fed to the helicopter team of consultants that hovers over him digitally, is that he is trying to get his grades back on track (also my idea) so that he doesn't flunk his Business Economics course at the uni. (There's some credence to that story, as I'll explain later.) The team isn't happy about the publicity brown-out, there are some concerns about security – but ultimately, the celebrity machine is designed to run itself. Experts tweet, 'gram, post and otherwise manage Ricky's platforms, as they mostly do anyway, and since he doesn't spend every waking hour with me (by my choice, not his), there are plenty of opportunities for him to give them the requisite posed pics and product endorsements that pull in the seven-figure sponsorships that enrich an already super-rich young man.

Ricky even understands my insistence on keeping our relationship private; it's part of the package deal for any digital-footprint celeb who's not sure if their current partner is just another fling or a long-term thing. Think Priyanka and Nick or any one of a hundred other pairings that weren't news until they were. In my case, it's not because I'm managing my feed but because I'm playing Hannah, a girl from an educated, reasonably well-off, upper-middle-class Indian family whose clan would be devastated if my involvement with the wildest billionaire playboy of (partly) South Asian origin were to be splashed across the net.

It works for Ricky too: he wouldn't want his wild playboy image compromised by the knowledge that he's wooing, in the old-fashioned sense, a young fellow desi who is the hardest sexual conquest he's attempted since he can remember. Try, hardest ever.

I admire Ricky's self-restraint.

He's almost a different person from the arrogant, self-centered star boy who first helped me to my feet after that leafy fall. This Ricky isn't afraid to talk about his feelings, to let slip his real views on stuff ranging from TV to music to feminism; to show a glimpse of the real Ricky.

He's even talked to me – only a half-hour ago, when we were still at a nondescript café on the outskirts of Zurich – about how yogis channel their physical desires and needs inwardly, subverting the usual outlets of hunger, thirst, sex, love, comfort, into spiritual energy that builds and grows until it becomes a force unto itself. I already know he picked up this bastardized version of tantra philosophy from an Israeli girl with Sanskrit tattoos who spent two years at an ashram in Haridwar in the foothills of the Himalayas, and that despite this line of bullshit he's been banging his usual booty callers all the while he's been trying to get into my pants. Ain't no tantra, it's just a mantra.

But there is something sincere at the core of his bullshit, some kernel of real, like the soft white meat at the center of a coconut. My white, Anglo grandmother, who grew up in Goa, used to say that's when the coconut is perfect for use in cooking.

He strokes the back of his hand against the side of my throat, a seemingly non-sensual move that shouldn't be arousing but is; he knows better than to actually take hold of my throat, no matter how gently.

Things escalate; I let it happen.

He moves his head back a bit so he can see my face. He looks at me. I give him a compliant, eager look, my mouth slightly open, tongue-tip snaking out briefly to press down my lower lip. Then I nod to underline my approval. Green lights across the board.

For the first time since this encounter began, he lays his hands fully upon me. He takes hold of me by my hips. The apartment is quiet, still, the world at bay. The Bordeaux in my blood heightens my sensations while dulling my inhibitions; I allowed him to select the wine today, a major concession. We stay in this moment, savoring the anticipation of what is to come.

He commences: running his hands up and down my torso now, like a police officer conducting a hostile Terry stop. He'll not find my concealed weapons; they are in my cranium, not in my underwear.

Up, down, raising prickles of static from my woolen sweater and causing the hairs on the nape of my neck to rise horizontally; the static arouses the cilia in my inner ear, and they pass on the message to the tectorial membrane, which passes it on in turn to my brain.

If this had been just a sexual liaison, I would have taken him by force by now, shoved him back on to the bed, mounted him. It's what I do; I take charge, I rule. Men have always liked – or disliked, in a few instances – that about me sexually; color me utterly disinterested in what men like – or dislike.

I'm a lit fuse now, and he knows it. He owns me and he believes I want him to own me, because that is what I want him to feel. What he doesn't know is that even in submission, I am the one in control.

Still in control, I allow myself to take pleasure from his selfish, masculine, muscular manipulation.

His hands are under my sweater and skirt, moving more aggressively now, stroking, sliding, grasping. The clasp of my skirt open-sesames; through my almost-shut eyelids, I glimpse his teeth flash; the grin is in response to his sense of control, of power. Pleasure bursts my brain.

He is mine. I own him now. Sex with Ricky was not a goal; it's a means to an end. The goal is to find out how much he knows about his father's crimes. I'm one giant step closer to that goal now.

## 13

I am lying in the pose of Matisse's *A Nude with her Heel on her Knee*. Buttery sunbeams paint my tan skin, the slate-grey bedsheets, the walnut wooden floor, the giclée-print of Renoir's *Odalisque* on a pastel wall the color of white smoke. A flight of geese are visible through the window, calling distantly, charcoal silhouettes against a cerulean sky; a dog barks, another responds; a genially accelerating car fades, letting in a faint echo of music too soft to make out the song. For no logical reason, my mind produces the memory of Mantovani's orchestra performing 'Vaya Con Dios': I have the vaguest childhood memory of an elderly gentleman removing a shiny black vinyl album from its sleeve, placing it on a Grundig record player, setting down the diamond-tip needle; as the dark whirlpool swirls, he says in a voice from a forgotten era: *Now* this *is music*. Who he is, where I am (a faint sense of large, overarching ceilings, Corinthian pillars, a luxurious mansion, a graveled driveway, a gleaming, two-toned Austin Healey which the old man affectionately calls 'Big Boy') and when this happened are minor details; this is a post-coital wine-flushed daydream, part fantasy, part memory of my one visit to my mother's father's home in Surrey. It was his wealth that my mother inherited and later invested into my dad's business, which paid for the Beck House in New York; it was this wealth that was wiped out when Roger Cordry killed him and my brother and stole the company out from under our noses. But today, I will not let myself be overcome by the anguish of those crimes. Today, I am living in the moment, luxuriating in my femininity.

A toilet flushes.

A naked man emerges, sniffing and swiping his nose.

'Heya.'

I say nothing, still basking.

He looks at me with that I-thought-I-was-done-but-there's-always-room-for-one-more-go-around look guys get. His gaze takes in my body with the efficacy of an airport full-body scanner. His eyes shine with something other than just lust and I know he's done a line or two in the bathroom.

Drug habits, private proclivities, sexual preferences, those are the first things I research about a target. Our secret addictions reveal more about us than our online profiles; despite what you may think about your favorite celeb's squeaky-clean image, they all have something. I once went after this online activist, a poster girl for equality, liberal progressiveness, you name it; she was into some seriously weird shit; like, believe me, you don't even want to know.

'Gotta go,' I say, hauling my ass out the far side of the bed. The little stranger twitches in response to the inevitable jiggling.

'Sunday.'

I pull on my sweater. 'Laundry, cleaning, cooking, groceries, chores.'

He stares at me with a boyishly baffled look. 'Maids.'

I laugh as I step into my jeans. 'Maids!'

He runs a hand through his tousled hair, trying to process polysyllabic thoughts. 'You know, I can always help you with that.'

I drop the smile and raise my eyebrows, zipping up.

His eyes cut sideways. 'I mean . . . It's no biggie. I help out friends all the time.'

By friends, he means his booty call brigade of ever-available ladies. The majority of them are well off themselves, some even qualify as rich, and at least one in the past year was even wealthier than his dad, but there are a couple of poor middle-class Sheilas in there.

I offer the equivalent of a goodbye: 'Text you.'

He trails me to the front door. He isn't ready to give up yet. It's taken him an unusually long time to get me into his bed; he wants more. Men always want more. That's why I don't do break-ups, just ins-and-outs. The sexual equivalent of a mugging. Ricky wants me on the list of on-calls. Uh-huh, not happening. Bad enough that I'm starting to *like* this rich asshole; don't complicate this, Medusa, keep your snakes in line.

'Come with?' he offers as I am pulling on my boots. 'Brunch?'

Brunch sounds amazing actually. I could eat a horse and a stable. But I have to show him who's El Jefe here. I'm the Captain now.

I smile up at him fetchingly as I slap his nether friend. He jerks back, wincing.

'I FaceTime with my parents and my grandma on Sunday mornings. I'm sure they'd love to chat with you.'

Chatting with the conservative South Indian parents and grandmother of a girl he only views as a part-time FWB isn't his idea of a sunny Sunday pastime.

'Text me after. Let's do something.'

I leave one final smile hanging in the air as I bounce.

## 14

Olga is standing in the kitchen-cum-dining-area, eating a bowl of cereal. She has droopy, Sunday morning eyes as she holds a spoon dribbling milk up to her open mouth. She shovels in a mouthful of something crunchy and chocolate and takes in my late/early appearance with youthful interest. From the open door of her room, Bulgarian metal angst screams what sounds to my uninformed ears like a rip-off of 'Sunday Bloody Sunday'.

I avoid eye contact – the bangs help conceal my eyes anyway – and shuffle down the hallway, giving off what I hope are powerful do-not-approach vibes. I feel her watching me as I open my door and go in; I know she's bursting with curiosity to ask me where I spent Saturday night – and if it was a guy, who is he, what's he like, how is he hung, all the usual roomie patter. She knows better than to risk getting shot down again and I hear the spoon and the bowl conversing tinnily as she continues scooping up cereal; she's jonesing for sugar after all those shots with her new Texan BF last night. I track her cell messages too, of course. Big Sis, always watching.

I've roomed with all types; while my vendetta is private and requires isolation, I also have to blend in with 'normal' society to avoid being noticed. Single young women living alone stand out. Besides, shacking up is the best way to study people.

I've learned more about morning-after make-up from a

$5,000-a-night trans woman escort in San Fran than you could pick up from a Mac makeover in a mall; more about deal-making from a hostage negotiator than a hotshot Hollywood lawyer; and more about finding flaws in store merchandise from a secret shopper than a quality control expert. While I can't say I've learned anything new from Olga, overall she's pretty OK. Except for the thrash metal blasting from her room, which isn't doing my slight headache any favors.

I glimpse a blue denim jacket, boots, jeans, scattered around her room. The Texan stayed over – again. I'm not happy about this new BF. He's stuck around longer than her usual fuck-of-the-week; it makes me edgy.

I need a shower.

I strip down to my birthday suit, grab a towel and head for the bathroom. The instant I open the door, the steam hits me like a hot towel in the face. The loud music must have drowned out the sound of the shower running. Still, I should have noticed it right away: if Texan BF wasn't in her room or in the living-dining-cooking area, obviously he had to have been in here. The shower is running, plastic curtains drawn, and the bathroom is a steam room. Either he forgot to lock the door on my side or deliberately left it unlocked. Either way, I disapprove. Little things like that bug the shit out of me.

Luckily, with the curtain drawn, the steamed up room and the Bulgarian death metal breaking down the walls, he has neither heard nor seen me enter. I back out, shut and lock the door and sit on the edge of my immaculately made-up bed. (I did a gig in housekeeping once at the New York Sofitel; when I make my bed, it's seven-star deluxe hotel perfect. I like things perfect.)

I drink a whole liter of water while I wait. Hydration is key: Rule #1 of the Good Assassins Guide.

After another seemingly endless track which sounds almost identical to the earlier one, I hear the shower shut off, followed by the faint sound of the door on her side being shut. The coast is clear. The music and low blood sugar have aggravated the headache. My skull throbs in counterpoint to the mucus, excuse me, music. The laidback, easy feeling I had earlier that morning at Ricky's place has waned; I need a hot shower and a hot meal. Mercifully, the Bulgarian metal monsters die abruptly, followed by blessed churchly silence.

I walk into the still steamy bathroom and am hit by the sight of the tall Texan standing naked in Olga's room. He's six four, six five easy, with long, lean muscles that speak of good genetics and hard endurance training, not just the usual pumped-up gym bod. Olga sits cross-legged on her bed before him, doing about what you'd expect. Her robe has fallen open; she has nothing underneath. The door I heard being shut was her room door, not the bathroom door, which is almost halfway open. I curse myself silently. That's two errors in a few minutes: unacceptable, grasshopper.

Olga is turned away from me, aware of nothing but her own pleasure, but cowboy has a direct view of the bathroom.

His eyes flick up.

My towel is wrapped around me and tucked in carefully, so he sees even less than he saw the time I was in the tub, but he's caught me checking him out and I can't help looking up. He smiles at me, tips an invisible Stetson and lips *Howdy, ma'am* as Velvet Underground's 'Sunday Morning' kicks in on the Bluetooth speaker.

I respond by arching an eyebrow, walking over coolly and shutting the connecting door to the bathroom. I lock it, then stand there for a moment, thinking it through. To kill or not to kill; that is the question. Am I over-reacting or do I need to eliminate him to make sure he doesn't remember me afterward, in the event the cops question him? On the other hand, they'll find out I was staying with Olga anyway, and all he'll be able to tell them is that I have a great bod. It's not like he's seen me with Ricky or anything incriminating.

Fuck it. This kind of thing is totally routine in the coed life; it's not the first time I've seen and been seen naked by other naked persons. No point making a big deal of it. Continue the usual watch-and-wait policy. Besides, I'm not in the mood for bloodshed today. Not until I get a breakfast pastry, at least.

I turn the water on and step into the shower.

After a minute or two of scalding hot water pounding on the top of my scalp, my headache begins to recede. The sweet, low music from next door helps. I dream as water drums.

'Sunday Morning' gives way to Marvin Gaye's 'Sexual Healing'. Cowboy really does have a thing for old-school make-out music. Hmm.

By the time I'm back in my room and getting dressed, Kalai's 'On My Mind' is underscoring Olga's loud, encouraging demands to her new paramour. I tip my own invisible hat to Cowboy as I pass my roomie's room, on my way out the front door. I really hope I won't have to kill these two when I'm done in Zurich; I'm actually starting to like them a little.

# 15

I am lying naked on my belly, diagonally draped across the lower half of the bed, hair hanging off the side, like a Bond belle sans the gold paint. Sounds familiar? What can I say, I'm a woman enjoying my hedonistic pleasures while I can. My tips almost brush the floor. This is the longest I've let it grow out and I like it. I might even keep it after I do Ricky. That's what I always say; more likely, I'll lop it off and revert to my standard military crew, so much easier to maintain and convenient to cover with wigs to alter my appearance.

For the moment, though, it feels nice to be Hannah, to let go of the obsessive high-protein-low-carbs diet and intense workouts. That person I've been my entire young adult life, while Hannah is closer to what twelve-year-old me thought I would turn out to be. You might even say she's me if things hadn't turned out the way they did, the young woman my mother would have expected me to become, but without the vendetta. The most successful performance is one that builds on some aspects of your real personality, then adds fictional layers.

Ricky is sitting on the edge of the bed, texting.

He texts other fuckbunnies while he's with me, the bastard; I track his feed each night. There's an exchange or two with his financial people, some with friends and other celebs in India and the US, where Ricky lives mostly. The only actual voice calls Ricky gets and makes are usually with his brother.

As special as that date had made me feel, I'm unsurprised to see that he's had more than one other rendezvous since we began fucking, and during a two-day period when I went incommunicado on him, he spent a wild day and night at a gabber, or at least what rich kids in Zurich call a gabber but is really just a tame imitation of the real thing. He fucked a bunch of girls there, he claimed later in a chat with one of his sex club regulars, and I took that to indicate overcompensation for the guilt he felt in being with the same girl for this long.

That girl being me, of course.

I turn my head to peer through my bangs at the bedside table. I reach out and tug open the drawer. This is a calculated move: I already know what I'll find in here. I scoured Ricky's apartment most recently that night he was at the gabber, using the spare key I copied weeks ago. I pretend to rummage inside and fish out a photograph placed facedown. It's the only picture he keeps in hard copy, in an uncharacteristically simple wooden frame.

It's a selfie of Ricky and his brother in matching swimsuits on a beach, arms flung over each other's shoulders, laughing almost identical goofy laughs. Ricky looks younger, happier, his hair is different.

'You have a brother? Cool!'

I feel the bed shift, then Ricky jumps up and comes around the bed to snatch the frame from my hand.

'Hey,' he says in a sharper tone than he's ever used with me, 'that's private.'

I raise myself on my elbows and hold out my palm in a warding gesture. 'I didn't mean to pry. I was just looking for some candy.'

He put the frame back into the drawer and shut it with a firm finality.

'That is your brother, though, isn't it?'

He's still standing there by the table, looking at nothing, his eyes unfocused.

'Yeah,' he says finally.

'Are you close? Do you see him a lot? Have I met him?'

He says nothing, just stands there, breathing.

'Is he here in Zurich too?'

'No.'

'Is he in Italy, with your mom?'

Ricky's mom is a fashionista and a minor celeb in her own right: her current BF – Ricky's stepfather – is only a year older than Ricky himself, and their pics feature frequently on the celeb gossip feeds, usually with Ricky's pic and his dad's pic tossed into the mix. She and Ricky's dad split up years ago and haven't spoken or texted each other since. Gabriella Manfredi (she's always used her maiden name) lives in Milan, where she made her name as a supermodel before she caught the eye of Roger Cordry twenty-four years ago.

'No.' Ricky turns and walks away, then stops, his back to me. He's struggling with something and isn't sure how to express it. I'm the first of his lay-ladies (his term, not mine, from some old song that goes 'Lay, Lady, Lay' whatever that means) to get this personal, and he's extremely uncomfortable but doesn't know how to get me to back off without being obnoxious. News flash, dude: as a super-rich, massively over-privileged male slut, you're literally the picture that shows up online when anyone types in 'obnoxious'. All the rest of your facade is just a brilliant disguise. 'I don't keep any sugar. I'm trying to kick it. That stuff's toxic, you know. It's a drug, like any other. Worse than opioids.'

'It's cool. I'll just grab some waffles. Have to get going

anyway.' I am standing too now, looking around for my clothes. Ever since getting with Ricky, I've been leaving my stuff all over the floor; it drives my OCD brain crazy but that's part of being Hannah.

'Hey, do you want to try something? Better than sugar, and way less addictive.'

He returns to the bedside table and opens the lower drawer, the one in which he stores his stash. He takes out a plastic baggie still half-full of fine white powder, along with a copy of a glossy magazine with his visibly pregnant mother posed in naked profile on the cover in a pastiche of the famous Demi Moore cover. There are visible traces of cocaine on Gabriella Manfredi's swelling belly and I wonder, not for the first time, if his choice of this particular issue hints at an Oedipal streak.

He taps out two lines of coke with practiced ease, rolls up and tightens a 500-euro note, and snorts a line. He offers the note to me.

I shake my head. 'Thanks. I'll pass.'

'Everyone does it.'

'I don't do drugs.'

'Sugar's a drug, alcohol, even carbs are a kind of drug. Coke's just a picker-upper. They used to sell it in drug stores in the US a hundred years ago. How do you think the opioid epidemic started in the nineties? Big Pharma looking to get back a piece of the action, legally. Coke's not addictive.'

I've finished dressing. 'I'll text you.'

But I don't just leave like I usually do. I linger a moment longer. 'I didn't mean to get into your stuff.'

He blinks. 'It's cool.'

He holds out the euro-straw again.

I start to shake my head, then stop. I come over to the bed

and kneel down beside him, glancing at the line of coke on his mother's naked thigh. 'I've never done anything before.'

'Shit's awesome. Better than sugar. Picks you right up. Even keeps you –' He cuts himself off.

'Keeps me?'

'Just try it.'

I chew my lower lip, a Hannah thing. 'I don't know . . .'

I'm playing tempted but scared. He's been here, seen this before, like a dozen times: Ricky Manfredi, every shy girl's gateway to the mind-altering realm of controlled substances. Wisely, he doesn't push me, touch me or try to use any kind of physical pressure. Instead, he offers me Positive Reinforcement.

'I'll go down on you while you inhale. You'll come like crazy.'

I pretend to be thinking about it: he's right, cunnilingus and cocaine go together like red rum and Coke. It's been a while, too.

'Let's go away.'

He blinks, surprised by the segue. 'Away . . . ?'

'Like for a weekend. We have that long weekend coming up this week.'

He frowns. 'You mean like Ibiza or the Maldives? Sure. I have a jet. We can bounce anyplace.'

'Airports and private jets are where every celeb and star gets pic'ed. If my family gets to know about us, they'll pull me back home to Chennai so fast . . .'

'Hey, hey,' he says, 'not going to happen, OK.' He looks off to the right, left eye squinting slightly: he's thinking hard. 'OK, OK. I know the perfect place. No paparazzi, nobody from the uni, nobody we know would see us.'

He tells me a few more appealing details. The fact that he's hard-selling this trip tells me all I need.

'OK,' I say abruptly. 'That sounds perfect.'

He nods, smiling. 'Awesome.'

I know he's imagining us reveling in hedonistic splendor in a snowbound Swiss chalet. So be it. I'll go along for the ride because I can sense that I'm close to getting to the inner Ricky, the guy I'm really after. Whatever it takes. That's the only reason he's still alive.

# 16

Oberholz-Farner is an Alpine ski resort in the Canton of St Gallen. I already knew about it from Ricky's chat histories. When he's with the more upmarket women, he goes to the swankier, trendier resorts; this one is where he brings the fillies he's trying to break in. (Again, his terms and phrasing.) He looks at shy, emotionally withholding young women like Hannah as challenges to be overcome, obstacle courses to be slalomed. Oberholz-Farner is perfect because, unlike the other slopes, it only has beginner slopes, with just a bit of intermediate level skiing. Boring to the Eurobabes who practically learned to ski before they learned to walk, but just right for Hannah, who's never even seen snow in her life. (ICYMI: It doesn't snow in Chennai or anywhere else in the Indian state of Tamil Nadu.)

We arrive at the resort early Saturday afternoon in Ricky's bright yellow Urus. The Alps nod their sage white heads in our direction. There's probably only slightly less powder in the newly replenished baggie Ricky has stashed in his luggage than there is on those peaks. He has some wicked fun in mind for the weekend and believes Hannah is finally ready to graduate to beginning level. *About time, bro,* his friend Dev in NYC texted, *was starting to think you lost the magic touch.*

I won't bore you with the details of the entire weekend. We skied, we ate, we drank, we did some lines, we fucked. Well, technically, he tried to teach me to ski, I fell a lot, we both laughed a lot, threw snowballs at each other, laughed

76

some more, got freezing cold, went back and spent hours in the en-suite hot tub, drinking champagne, doing coke, getting up to all the expected shenanigans. Bacchanalia. Ricky got his wish: he broke in another jeune fille, corrupted the innocent and got his perverse kicks every which way. ·

And I got what I was seeking. Not entirely, but partially.

I guess you could say we both got what we wanted.

Somewhere in the wee watches of that Sunday night, after too much wine, coke and sex, Ricky let me have a little peek into his private space.

'We did everything together,' he says, sipping cognac from a snifter at a window with a midnight view of the Alps. The mountains are blue ghouls looming around us, a circle of true believers gathered to witness the sacrifice to the adversary. 'We shared everything.' He stares out at the night, his bare chest moving lightly beneath the unsashed robe. 'We were so competitive, we raced for everything, climbed, took the craziest dares. Nothing was too extreme. Nothing.'

I drink some water to compensate for the copious quantities of alcohol consumed this weekend. I want to guzzle down liters, but don't want to distract Ricky from his reverie. He's almost talking to himself, only peripherally aware of my presence. I have a suspicion that if startled right now, he might be momentarily confused about which young woman he's with. After a while, he said in one Snapchat convo, they start to blur together. It's the reason he's trained himself never to use a partner's name during sex; that way, there's never any risk of getting it wrong. Bastard.

'That summer was so good. We had a really awesome time. We were at our dad's Malibu shack, the waves were bitchin' and we were working on our aerials and three-sixties.'

The 'shack' in question is a twenty-four-room mansion on

a clifftop with an unencumbered view of the Pacific, and he's referring to his and his brother's surfing obsession that year, which he'd already talked about in a brief prelude, unwittingly taking a cue from my strategically planted query about whether snowboarding was similar to surfing.

'That pic you found in my drawer by my bedside, the one of Monty and me on the beach, I took it right before it happened. We were fooling around while waiting for the waves to pick up again. I tossed the phone to some flunkey. I remember her fumbling and dropping it on the sand, just as I did a backflip into the shallows. She was still brushing the wet sand off the screen when Monty did a backflip too and I remember I was laughing and yelling at her to fuck the phone, I didn't like it anyway, just save the pic to the cloud.'

He takes a long, deep draw, draining the glass. The dregs slosh as he drops the snifter to the carpeted floor. It lands silently in the deep pile, the cognac soaking into the snow-pale rug. It'll leave a stain, but the over-generous tip Ricky will leave the hotel will probably pay for a half-dozen new rugs.

'Next thing I knew, the flunkey was screaming her head off. I turned and saw Monty lying in the shallows, his head at a right angle to his body. Turns out he'd hit a sand ledge only a few inches from the spot where I'd landed. He fell on his neck, broke his spine in four places. Caused permanent loss of the use of his limbs. Freak accident. One in a million odds.'

He sounds like he's quoting the doctors' description of the injuries after the panicked 911 call, the ride to Cedars Sinai and the flurry of tests and scans and consults with specialists across the world. I picture Ricky, listening to them with a dull, stunned expression on his handsome face, his father and mother on separate video screens, she tearful in

Rome with her then-lover, an older Italian movie idol, and he listening grimly on a runway in Shanghai, about to board a private jet. That eighteen-year-old Ricky looks out from this twenty-four-year-old Ricky's light grey eyes, scared to death, still in deep shock and denial, completely unprepared to deal with this, the biggest personal crisis of his young, over-sheltered, over-privileged existence.

I reach out and take hold of his hand. It's cold, despite it having cradled the snifter of warm cognac only moments ago. I squeeze it tightly, drawing it to my naked breast, warming it with my own body heat. The gesture isn't meant to be arousing but reassuring, offering a troubled, confused, still traumatized young man the gift of understanding, emotional support, the deep, soul-satiating absolution that a man can receive only from a woman. Words are irrelevant. Snow descends on the mountain, blanketing us in a cocoon of memories and silence.

# 17

He sleeps badly that night, thrashing and moaning, hot sweat limning his hairless chest. I don't need a Psych degree to tell me he's reliving the guilt and shock of that traumatic moment, telling himself for the thirteen-thousandth time: *If I hadn't done the backflip, Monty wouldn't have done it.*

The irony of their having done a hundred worse extreme, unspeakably dangerous, spine-threatening stunts far more complicated than a mere backflip on sand without major injuries – a minor carpal fracture, a hairline crack on the talus, barely worth remembering – but it had to be the most innocuous maneuver, something they'd been doing since they were still in single digit years, a simple backflip, that had caused the life-shattering disaster. The inevitable intimations of mortality that come with seeing a sibling come that close to death, to realize that but for a few inches and a shelf of hard sand that could be you, are a bonus cherry on top of the cake of remorse.

That kind of thing fucks you up forever. Monty is in a wheelchair for life. Ricky is healthy and virile as a horse – but on the inside, he's crippled too; emotionally handicapped. What I want to know is whether that's the only thing that's made him the way he is now – emotionally withholding, sexually over-generous – or if there's also trauma from stuff he knows about his father's past actions. That's what I'm really after.

At one point in the early hours, he breaks down and sobs

into my breasts, awash in a sea of guilt, remorse, regret, self-recrimination, anger, and God alone knows what else. It's a breakthrough moment, the kind that would please a therapist; it pleases me. It's not what I was aiming for but it's a start. I feel more confident now that I will, in due course, get him to open up and talk about the main matter, the reason I'm waiting this long before killing him. I'm hopeful that will come in time now. I've waited my entire life for revenge; I can wait a few weeks more, or as long as it takes.

He needs a drink after that, and as always with Ricky, there's no stopping at one. I drink too, in solidarity with his grief but also because his confessions have awakened the memory of my own pain. At a distance, it's easy to picture those we hate in clear blacks and whites; up close, people are drawn with a richer palette. Now, for the first time, I'm seeing my target as a real, vulnerable human being. It reminds me of my own vulnerability.

At some point, I start talking about my own past trauma. It comes up when Ricky comments self-critically that his 'fucked-up family' takes the prize. I correct him gently, pointing out that if there's a prize for fucked-up families, mine would be at the top of the podium. He looks at me with the over-intense curiosity of the very high. Outside the window, snow blankets the storybook landscape. Something soft and nostalgic is playing on the Bluetooth. The lateness of the hour, Ricky's cathartic confession, the sheer quantities of alcohol and drugs, the shared feeling of utter emotional exhaustion, all invite further confessions. A long-buried memory rises up inside me like a dislodged body from the bottom of a lake, floating up my gullet.

'I had a brother,' I hear myself say. 'Four years older. My role model. Our dad and his partner, they were into hunting that year. It was a new obsession. We'd moved to this huge house in upstate New York and my dad's partner said that we had one of the best hunting grounds right in our backyard and we were letting it all go to waste. My dad wasn't too keen; he'd been raised a vegetarian and an animal lover and hadn't touched a gun in his life. But his partner kept at it, talked him into trying it out, buying a gun, shooting on a range. I think my dad gave in because he was so eager to fit in to American society – all the people they were in business with were gun owners and hunters. One time we spent a weekend at one of their clients' estates – it was like an NRA convention. When we came back, my dad had changed his mind. My mother was dead against it. She was a non-vegetarian and had killed her share of live chickens, even pigs and ducks back home in India, but she didn't want guns in her house when they had kids around. I remember they had a major blow-up over it, but of course that only made my dad more determined about going through with it. So he bought a gun locker, installed it in our basement, kept it under lock and key, put the fear of God into us kids about guns and accidental discharges and all the statistics.'

Ricky is listening. Actually listening. This is the first time he's ever heard me talk about my family, apart from the occasional monosyllabic mention. Maybe it's the lateness of the hour, his own vulnerability, or just the booze and coke, but he seems to actually be interested.

'But somehow, Brian – that's my older brother – figured out the six-digit combination to the locker. He was smart with computers, codes, patterns, that kind of stuff, and always said he was going to be a hacker or a CIA analyst when he grew up. I was there when he opened up the locker.

I remember standing there in the basement, looking up at all those guns. The sleek black hunting rifles, the pistols, the revolvers. There were maybe a dozen in all. I don't know why our dad needed so many just to hunt. Brian said that Uncle – that's what we called our dad's partner – had talked him into keeping guns for home protection because we were rich and rich people were always targets for criminals. So we're standing there in the basement in the middle of the afternoon, my parents are out for the day and our housekeeper probably still thinks we're somewhere in the backyard playing Cops and Robbers or some kiddy game, and I reach out and take one of the handguns. I can't help myself. It's like a snake, drawing me in with that little black eye, hypnotizing me. Suddenly, this heavy black automatic is in my hands and I'm pointing it and I pull the trigger.'

Ricky is about to take another hit of coke. He stops, the rolled-up hundred-dollar bill clutched between his thumb and forefinger, the lines of coke on the glass coffee table laid out next to the platinum credit card, and gapes at me. He was probably expecting some feel-good memory of the time I played peekaboo with my brother or something sugary like that. Not ten-year-olds firing off guns.

'So?' he asks when I don't say anything for a minute. His heavy Latin brows beetle, making a vertical crease appear between them. He looks slightly myopic when he does that, though he has 20-20 vision, and I think it makes him look cute in an intense kind of way.

I shrug and take a drag of my vape device, another bad habit I've picked up around Ricky. 'Nothing much. The safety was on.'

He grins out one side of his face. 'Cool.'

He bends over the table and does a line.

He's doing the second one when I add, casually:

'So then I flicked the safety off and fired it again.'

He chokes on the line and white powder flies everywhere, coating his face, those bushy eyebrows, going all over.

I double over laughing, pointing my device at him.

He looks ridiculous. Is this what they mean by coked up to the eyebrows? I can't stop laughing. He joins me.

When we finally stop, he quietens down and asks me, also quietly, 'So what happened then?'

I shrug. 'I shot my dad's old microscope. It was lying in a box in the corner and the bullet shattered it. No biggie. He only kept it around because he had sentimental memories attached to it. It was the microscope with which he'd discovered his first new microbacillus back in Chennai. It was obsolete and he never even looked at it anymore. Brian moved some boxes around and buried it under some other stuff. Dad probably wouldn't even notice it for years, if ever.'

He never did. My dad – and Brian – were dead within the month.

We come close to something resembling a real relationship that night. Ricky's response to my own story of family history and the tears he cried earlier on me, lull me into thinking I'm inside now, I've got under the sonofabitch's skin like a deer tick.

It makes no difference to me that Ricky Manfredi is innocent of his father's crimes.

Brian was innocent too.

I am almost ready. It will not be long now. I have to do this before I get in too deep; perhaps, after tonight, I'm already in too deep. I never thought I'd get this emotionally entangled;

84

it's dangerous. But I need just a little more time for this to play out according to plan. To line up a few more things so my exit is clear and I get away scot-free. Just a little more time.

But then, like a flash of heat lightning out of a clear sky, everything changes and my plan goes for a toss.

# 18

Out of the blue, our relationship takes a nose-dive after the Oberholz-Farner weekend. When we return to Zurich, Ricky drops me off at a tram stop, for once not making the usual privileged comments about my use of public transport. We part, promising to text each other, and even as the canary-yellow luxury SUV zips away like Reverse-Flash in the CW television series, I know that, this time, he'll be the one who goes incommunicado for a day or two.

What I'm not expecting is the complete blackout that follows.

Total silence.

I always knew that once Ricky thought he'd gotten under my skin – initiated me into enjoying, even embracing his binge-drinking, coke-snorting, anal-fucking excesses – after he'd taken me as far as he knew I would go, or as far as he cared to go with this particular pick-of-the-moment – he'd drop me like a hot tamale.

I just assumed we had one or two more pair-offs left in us; three, at most, but at the least, one.

I wasn't expecting the sudden, total shutdown that happens instead.

After a whole week during which Ricky ignores all my texts and blocks my calls, I slowly, angrily accept the inevitable. It's over. He's burned out on me. Sweet, innocent Hannah is all used up and played out. He's done as much as he wanted to get done with her, and for one reason or another, he's bored, or exhausted, or just plain no longer interested in her ass. Maybe it's my fault for not seeing this coming a mile off. Maybe I'm the idiot here for forgetting that he's done this before: this is who he is. Why would he treat Hannah any differently?

Hannah isn't me, not by a long shot; but she isn't far off from the me that would have been, which is to say, she's one version of me in some alternate timeline that never happened.

Maybe that's why this feels personal.

I scan his texts and chats, monitor his calls, try to find a clue, some hint for the sudden blackout.

There's nothing.

It's as if Hannah doesn't exist for him, as if she never existed.

He doesn't so much as use her name. For that matter, I see, using a customized Boolean search to scan my stored archive of Ricky's communications, he's never really used her name. It was one of the things I had been surveilling him for; even though Hannah was a fictional identity, a person who never existed and would cease to exist the instant this particular mission was over, I still needed to know if her name was out there. Details like that could matter later.

But he doesn't even consider her important enough to refer to her by name. Even when chatting with Dev, his wing-man in NYC, he only mentions her as 'that sweet new piece of ass I'm tapping'. After Oberholz-Farner, when Dev asks how the 'Initiation' went – their misogynistic phrase for the act of turning a conservative, shy girl toward their hedonistic lifestyle – Ricky replies succinctly: *Howdi think it went, bro?* Dev's tear-spouting, laughing brown-face emojis are suffi-cient response.

By Friday, I'm seething mad.

Why am I so upset?

I knew this was coming.

OK, so the suddenness is a shock. I haven't anticipated that. It feels like a personal blow.

But Hannah is just a fictional invention, a manufactured profile and bio for a bot, an act, a performance, fake news.

This is not personal to me; Ricky Manfredi doesn't even know the real me. He hasn't met this woman yet.

Yet it *feels* personal.

Intensely.

Painfully.

Bitterly.

All that work, all that time, wasted. It makes me mad enough to want to kill someone, anyone!

I slam the front door of my apartment hard enough that Cowboy – his name is Stu, we've even been introduced by Olga, but I prefer to think of him as just Cowboy now – looks up, surprised. He's standing over the gas range, a wooden ladle in one hand, wearing an apron decorated with something in Cyrillic script. The heart symbol and the little embroidered kiss symbols make me guess it goes something like 'Love the Chef'.

'Everything OK, hoss?' he asks with genuine concern.

'Yes.' That comes out sounding more acidic than I intended. I dial it back. 'Just having a bad day.'

He nods. The apartment smells of something vaguely spicy and beefy. From the detritus of the preparations on the chopping board, I suspect he's brewing chili, Texan style. I love chili, especially when it's Indian-spicy, the way my mother used to make it. My stomach rumbles to remind me that I've barely eaten today. Apparently, I'm so deep into this Hannah persona that Ricky's blackout has even nullified my appetite.

'Sounds more like you've been having a bad week,' he drawls casually, head bent over the big pot which he's stirring slow.

I hesitate. Cowboy's been around the house so much of late, I wonder if he's shacking up with Olga. Well, so what if he is. It's none of my beeswax. But his noticing things about me is my beeswax. It's a yellow flag, if not an orange or red one. Walk away, I tell myself. Ignore his comment and walk away.

I should make a beeline to my room, lock myself in and get back to work on my laptop, tracking Ricky's whereabouts and thinking of a strategy to turn this around, maybe even turn it to my advantage. At the very least, dress up in my assassin blacks and stalk him on my Hayabusa. If nothing else, riding the cycle helps keep my inner dragons at bay. Holding it inside, doing nothing physical, there's always the risk of them busting out and wreaking havoc. Even Khaleesi knows her dragons need to be unleashed from time to time.

But the truth is, I'm tired.

Tired of being Hannah, of playing this doe-eyed Chennai innocent 'from a decent family' with all the cultural and psychological baggage that entails.

'That smells good,' I say now. Middle ground: don't acknowledge his 'bad week' comment – too personal, potentially intrusive – but stay polite and friendly.

The moment I say it, I realize it's a bit too friendly. There's only one response a cook can give you when you say his cooking smells good.

If he's surprised that I've actually offered an unsolicited word, he doesn't show it. He keeps his eyes on the simmering stewpot, moving the ladle in slow, uneven circles. 'Almost done. Here, try a lick.'

He brings out the ladle, blows on it a few times, then holds it out.

I can still back off now, palms raised, give him a nervous smile and disappear. It's what I should do; must do. Don't compromise the mission. Hannah lives by strict, unbendable rules, not unlike the unwritten, unspoken rules that any well brought up young woman from a conservative Indian family abides by in an essentially patriarchal society maintained by a complicit matriarchy. My life, my purpose, my family depends on my abiding by the rules. No exceptions.

I shock myself by walking over to him, bending over the ladle he's holding out and slurping a tiny bit of the chili. The slurping is audible enough to raise a well-shaped eyebrow.

'Oops.' I dab at my lips with the back of my hand. 'It's good, really good.'

He looks down at me from the vantage of his superior height and his handsome jaw cracks in an aw shucks smile. 'There's enough for three. Six, actually. My mama's recipe was for the whole family, Dad and her and us four kids, so I know better than to mess with the proportions. You'd be doing me a favor by joining us for dinner.'

I nod. 'Thanks. Maybe I will.'

He smiles at me and I can't help but feel an instant of chemistry spark between us. Not for the first time. He sees and feels it too: I can read it in his eyes. My hands betray me by fiddling with my hair, a sure giveaway. The hell are you up to, fool? Back away. Back away before you blow everything up.

I force myself to turn and walk away.

I feel his eyes on me all the way to my room, even after I go in, shut and lock the door behind me.

After a long hot shower, I sit in my bathrobe and check on

Ricky. For him it's life as usual. It's like nothing ever happened between us. Was it me feeling a spark of real intimacy, or was it just my own eagerness to get in close? Sometimes, I can take stuff for granted, and when a plan doesn't come off exactly as visualized, I have difficulty dealing. Even though I've trained myself to adapt to any eventuality, there's a point after which you know that a mission is either a no-go or a go. With Ricky, everything had been green lights across the board, until he just dumped me.

Because that's what happened.

No point beating around the bush, I might as well come out and say it plain.

Ricky dumped Hannah.

He didn't even bother with the courtesy of a break-up text, call, or anything even remotely resembling one.

He just snipped the cord.

And I'm finding it hard to take.

I retrace everything I've done, read through every text, but there was nothing there. I've been careful to avoid leaving digital fingerprints that could be traced back to me. Sure, there'll be proof that he went out with a girl named Hannah for a few weeks, but she's only one of almost a hundred girls he's been with since coming to Zurich, one of a couple of dozen he's currently seeing on a rotating basis. Besides, this is his lifestyle: trying to pin anything that happens to him later on any one girl is going to need way more than just dating texts.

So it isn't anything I've texted, either before or after he dumped me.

Nothing I've said was responsible. I know because I checked. Did I mention that I record everything, every call, every conversation, even our sexual encounters, then run it through an app I bought on the dark web which is a rip-off of one that a US national security agency uses to scan phone cons and social media for certain key words and phrases? I tweaked it to flag anything that might be a potential trigger for Ricky. My history with Ricky is spotless and blameless. I've prepped and trained too well, performed like a pro, and done everything right.

Still, he's dumped me.

And now, it's going to be impossible for me to get back in. Unless and until he gets an itch to see me again and gets back in touch someday. Which is not going to happen, based on his past history as well as common sense. Ricky makes it a point to at least occasionally text and keep in touch with the women he intends to see again someday. He's a master at the game and knows better than to simply ignore me for a week and then expect to come crawling back to me. No, his radio silence makes his intentions perfectly clear: he's one and done. Our field trip wasn't the beginning of a new phase in our relationship as I thought; it was the parting gift. Hannah's out on her ass on the street and he couldn't care less what she says or does or doesn't next. I'm The GF That Never Was. One of a long, long list of exes. Welcome to the Ex Fucks Club.

There aren't any options left now.

I can't go up to him on campus. That would risk a scene: even Ricky ignoring me and walking away will attract attention; too many bimbos will take wicked joy in watching me get shot down. Within hours, I'll have a rep as a Klingon – an unlikely Star Trek reference – an ex who won't let go. There's probably even a support group somewhere online for Ricky's exes that I'll be directed to join. The last thing I need to compound my failure is to become almost famous.

Maybe if I abduct him, stash him in some remote place,

torture the truth out of him? Nah. Too risky. This is a guy whose every move is trolled online. If he's offline for even a few hours, someone is going to get alarmed. Murder is tough enough; kidnapping is deadly dangerous. It always leaves a trail. No. I can't go off-plan and wing it all of a sudden. The murder plan is carefully laid out and almost in place, best to stick with that. But it still galls me that I didn't find out what I wanted to know. I was so fucking close, damnit!

After a frustrating hour which leaves me no better off, I'm ready to go out and pour some hard liquor down my throat. I don't dare surveil Ricky right now. Training and discipline enable me to keep my emotions in check, but even if I don't explode, I don't see how tailing the asshole is going to get me back in. If anything, it'll be a reminder of how far in the game I've been pushed back. This game doesn't come with extra lives. The only way out is forward.

A knock on the door startles me out of my funk. I open it without even thinking about it, just to have something to do other than stewing about the Ricky disaster.

It's Cowboy, sans apron. I'd forgotten about him.

'Your chili awaits, ma'am.'

'Be right there,' I respond, once again breaking protocol.

Thing is, I need something, anything, to take my mind off Ricky for the moment, and I am hungry. Besides, that tiny taste was good, and I won't deny Cowboy's Southern manners make a refreshing change from the Ricky Manfredis of this era. I could use some company right now.

Olga is clearly surprised to see me, but recovers quickly. She puts down her cell and pushes back her chair, bobbing up to greet me with the obligatory air kisses. 'So nice you join! Stu cook real good. You like much. I tell him, you American too, all American eat chili. Please invite.'

Good save. She probably thought he was pulling her leg when he told her he'd invited me to join them for dinner and I'd said OK. Now, she wants to take credit for it. She's probably already having visions of us roomies painting each other's nails late at night while swigging vodka and watching old Bulgarian movies on her laptop. Am I opening a new can of worms here?

I silence the voices in my head and sit down at the dining table.

Fuck it.

I'm going to drink some beer, eat some chili and just be a young woman tonight. The universe owes me that much as an apology.

# 19

Mascotte on a Saturday night.

Or is it Sunday morning? I haven't looked at a clock since Friday and don't care. I'm a few drinks down and feeling chill.

We're at a private bar table, on a raised level over one of the dance floors, and down there, a couple of hundred of Zurich's finest are raving to 'Taki Taki'. When it comes to Reggaeton, I can take it or leave it, but DJ Blackem Dano – the name is a riff on some ancient TV show, I guess, because he keeps dropping *Five-O* references – promised he'd have some deep house vocal in a few, maybe even some Nu Disco, and if he hits the right beats, he may just get me to my feet.

For now, I'm content to soak in a sugary orange-red concoction that looks like overly oxygenated blood.

Cowboy is enduring Olga's drunken nuzzling; she's inhaled the apps and is snacking on his earlobe now. She must be whispering dirty nothings into his ear because he keeps smiling and leaning in to kiss her. God, they're embarrassingly into each other.

'Get a room!' I yell under the deafcon-level pulsing.

Olga detaches herself to purr cattily at me, extending one long, bare hand and crooking a finger in a provocative gesture. '. . . jealous . . .' is the only word I catch.

I laugh. I'm a little drunk. Maybe more than a little. Who gives a fuck. I've taken the weekend off from work. I deserve it.

After the Texan chili dinner last night, which went

surprisingly well, Cowboy, Olga and I have formed a kind of temp triad. Nothing sinister or subversive; just weekend buds. The sparks I felt between Cowboy and me have smoldered into a smoky tinder. How it proceeds now is really up to me: there's no question that he's interested. Keeping things interesting, Olga and I have established a kind of companionable sisterhood; for now, at least.

Mind you, all this is happening only in looks, gestures, body language, pheromones; vocals not required. What the body speaks, the body hears; translation unnecessary; words diminish.

'Yo, yo, yo, Zurich!' DJ Blackem Dano says, announcing the end of one set as he segues into the next. 'DJ Blackem Dano! *Welt zu rocken!*'

Silk vocals bleed into my pores, elevating my ass. I sashay, batting my lashes and stretching out my arms in mock-seductive invitation. 'Dance with!'

Olga squeals, thrilled, and flings herself at me; our body mashing conveys her delight that roomie-me finally melted. She's having visions of eternal GF-hood. Tonight's not the time to prick her party balloons. I slip an arm around her bare waist and we move our hips in synchronicity, summoning Cowboy. He responds with a range-worthy 'Yee-haw!', tosses off an invisible hat and follows us down to the dance floor.

The next couple of hours are a blur of alcohol, sugar, greasy-cheesy bar snacks, pounding beats and kaleidoscopic lasers. There's much FMF action on the floor, all in good fun and good-spirited, with just the right mix of naughty teasing. I let my guard down for once, and it feels great. We're joking around about taking a vacation together – 'threegether!' Olga cries exuberantly – and I even mention Goa at one point, I'm that far gone and feeling good.

We have a good time.

Sometime in the early hours, maybe even morning – Olga's room has blackout curtains worthy of a vampire's den – we are all on the bed, making out. The energy that exploded on the dance floor, the chemistry that smoldered between Cowboy and me, and the suppressed loneliness of two single girls far from home, have conflagrated into a crackling blaze. We descend into the burning bed, three naked animals entwining on satin sheets. For a while, the heat of my rage is diverted to the pursuit of hedonistic pleasure. I partake and am taken.

## 20

I wake sometime in the watches of the night, lava coursing through my veins in place of blood. Olga is sprawled on her back, limbs spread akimbo, snoring; Stu lies face-down, passed out at last. I slip out of bed carefully and pad silently out, shutting the door softly as I go.

Instead of going back to my room, I go through to the living room and out to the balcony. It's a moonless night, or perhaps our sister satellite has already drowned her hairless skull in brine; I sit in the dark, smoking one of Olga's vile fags.

Sitting there in the cold darkness before dawn, I smolder silently.

The night out and subsequent hook-up have banked some of the heat of my fury at Ricky for ghosting me, but the original fire still glows and pulses deep within. Alcohol, tobacco, post-coital depression, generation rage, the hypnotic rhythm of the pounding bass, all merge into a tidal wave battering my self-erected walls of containment.

The sound of young laughter and a car accelerating remind me that others my age – or even much older than I – are still out there, roving the Zurich night in pursuit of private pleasures. I wonder what it would be like to just be like Olga or Stu, to party and pass out and not care about tomorrow. To simply live in the moment: to be. That pathway was shut off from me years ago, the night my mother threw herself off that bridge in New York. I shut my eyes and the hollow, liquid sound of her head striking that iron strut echoes in my ears. My own scream, part wail of despair, part howl of rage, drowns out the sound of her body hitting the freezing East River a hundred feet below.

I am filled with an impotent rage at Ricky Manfredi.

I need to do something.

I need to kill him.

But I'm not ready.

Things have not gone according to plan. I had expected a slightly more enduring liaison. The original idea was to build up trust, while getting him to open up more about his father. That insight into Roger could be crucial to getting on the inside track with my main target, Cordry himself. That night in Oberholz-Farner was a great start. I expected two or three more revelations of that order, to gain some insight that I knew he must have.

The plan was fairly simple. Several pieces are already in place, thanks to Ricky's own promiscuous lifestyle. But it calls for cold, dispassionate murder, an assassination, nothing less. Right now, I'm not sure I want to do it that way. Maybe I want some hot-blooded revenge instead. Something violent and head-on, more in-your-face than a quiet, private death.

I could do it, indulge my craving for mayhem and madness. While on a reckless drive over the Alps, Ricky Manfredi could lose control of his beloved Lamborghini and go careering into those breathtaking valleys. No coming up for air after that dive, swim champ. An autopsy would show his system had illicit drugs and alcohol levels well over the legal limit. His death would be ruled an accident. No trace of foul play, unless you counted the Fentanyl which I had discreetly administered. Given Ricky's drug, pill and alcohol abuse, it would be written off as yet another unfortunate incident.

99

The halls of Young Adult Heaven are plastered with the names of They Who Drove and Died Under the Influence.

I'm tempted. I'm so fucking tempted.

It takes me most of the rest of the night but cooler logic prevails at last. I've worked too long and too hard to risk the whole gig by acting impulsively. I have a plan. I must stick to it. No room for mistakes, or hot-headedness.

By the time I've smoked almost the entire pack of Olga's foul cancer sticks, dawn is breaking over the treetops.

I'm finally calm enough to get to work.

I go into my digital locker and retrieve the confidential psychiatric files on Ursula's mental health. All it takes is a few taps of my finger and I've done what I need. I then turn my attention to the text message archives on the servers used by U's cellphone as well as Ricky's and a few other mutual connections. A few fake messages slipped into the tens of thousands of genuine ones, stored on the servers themselves with no way to trace them back to me, short of checking every single message – and why would anyone bother to do that in a world where text messages are accepted as hard physical evidence in any court of law? – and the ground is laid.

I sit back and enjoy the sunrise, feeling better for having channeled my rage demons into a very productive morning's work. I'm set for the final stage of my plan for Ricky Manfredi. All I have to do now is wait for the other players to make the right moves, then clean up.

The sunrise over the treetops, birds silhouetted against it, the dregs of the drugs, nicotine, alcohol, and the caffeine I'm consuming as I sit out on the balcony, all merge into a sensory cocktail that lifts me out of myself for a few.

In a moment of perfect void, this skywritten epiphany: a time to cast away, a time to gather; a time to embrace, a time to break off embracing; a time to possess, a time to lose; a time to keep, a time to cast off; a time to rend, a time to sew; a time to be silent, a time to speak out; a time to love, a time to hate; a time of war, a time of peace.

Time to kill.

## 21

I am waiting in the apartment when Ricky returns that Sunday night.

A tall, leggy redhead exercises her right to sweep ceilings with a Medusa headpiece. Ursula the Finn for the win. Ricky wanted to hook up with her at Miko's, but U wanted him all to herself. She keeps insisting she's not jealous of his other lovers but Ricky's texts to his other pals make it obvious he doesn't believe her. I think he likes U's possessiveness; he would, of course, because guys like that crap. I like it too because it suits my plan perfectly. I've been waiting for this precise moment long enough and now that it's finally here, I wonder if I'm ready. Shut up, I tell myself. You're ready. You have to be. It's payback time.

It also helps that U is angry with Ricky for ghosting her — *et tu, U!* All the better. Angry sex is the best sex, they say. It won't be the first time for either of them. And there is that matter of pretending to be copacetic outwardly, even if she's seething with rage inside.

All I had to do was let them hook up at his apartment. Give them an hour or so to party. Monitor their activity through a spyware audio feed that turns Ricky's cellphone mike into a listening device. Wait for them to get down and nasty. Then move in. By the time I slip into the apartment, the expected noises from the bedroom are climbing toward an appropriate decibel level. That's my cue.

Ursula is on top, the Medusa headpiece her only attire. Papier mâché tendrils snake out like the rays of a star gone nova. Her back is to me and the headpiece obscures her peripheral vision. Ricky can see me but his eyes are closed at first, then open. It takes him a minute to process my presence. I'm clad in my roadkiller blacks, only keeping the visor open so he can see my face. He reacts.

Disbelief. Puzzlement. Anger.

'*Mitä vittua!*' snarls the Finn as he wrestles her off him and she crashes on to the bed. Medusa tumbles to the floor on the far side and she scrambles after it, so she is preoccupied and looking the other way when Ricky springs up from the bed, obstructing any view she might have of me in the hallway, but she is more concerned about her fallen gorgon than her disposable lover.

Ricky comes toward me, enraged erection bobbing, both heads red and swollen-faced, all three eyes glittering angrily. There is violence in his manner. The rage of drugs and suppressed guilt, of male arrogance and American privilege.

'The fuck?' Angry fists reach for me.

I step back, then away. Out of the range of the doorway now, out of Ursula's sight lines even if she turns back now. Dancing backward, I lead him up the hallway, past the door to the living area where Israeli trance still pounds from his Bose speakers, into the foyer and the front door. He charges at me with righteous fury.

'How did you –' he starts, but never finishes.

He looks down at his forearm, dripping a thick, eager flow on to the polished floor; the irregular spatters counterpoint the 144 bpm beats: a collaborative mix.

'The fuck did you just do?' I hear him say over the beats.

I have just cut his radial and ulna arteries. He will bleed out in minutes if he doesn't get a tourniquet.

His expression registers the shock his body is feeling at being dealt a mortal wound but his anger overrides it, refusing to accept. 'What the fuck?'

Now he sees the twin scalpels in my gloved fists, my instruments of vengeance. His eyes are rising to meet mine, but I have already snapped down the visor of my helmet. Once again, I am Black Strider, the anonymous Dark Angel.

He starts to speak, to say something else. There is still rage in his eyes; full comprehension hasn't reached his brain yet, rationality compromised by the alcohol and drugs in his system. He still wants to abuse me, to hurl insults, demean and diminish. The Trumpian-Brexitian era's version of a table-pounding, call-out, shout-down; rally the mob from the online bully pulpit. 'I knew you –'

The rest of that sentence is still somewhere between his brain and his epiglottis when I reach out with both scalpels, wrists crisscrossed, and slash his larynx with one and his carotid sheath with the other, severing his voice box, jugular vein, carotid artery and vagus nerve all at once. Sudden death.

Rich, full life pours out of his throat, spattering my helmet and jacket, the walls, the floor, the little Giacometti figurine on which he carelessly hangs his keyring and hats.

The rage washes out of his pale grey eyes as he sinks to the floor in an expensive heap.

'My brother died much like this,' I say softly to him, squatting beside his thrashing body. 'His body a ruin as he bled out in the woods in my father's arms. The man who did that to him was your father.'

Ricky's brilliant eyes stare up at me with something that might be comprehension. He understands now that this isn't about him, it was never about him, it's about his father's misdeeds. One in particular.

From the bedroom, Ursula calls out something incomprehensible in Finnish. Or maybe German. The music is too loud. Her irritation sounds untouched by concern, but she will start worrying soon. Anxiety becomes us. It hardly matters. I don't mind if she comes out this very minute. She's welcome to join us now, celebrate the bacchanalia. There's plenty of red wine on tap. Exquisite, twenty-four-year-old vintage, limited stocks.

The heap of bones and flesh shudders, flails. A faint flicker in dying eyes.

The sound of air bubbling from demolished vocal cords.

He's trying to say something. I hear a query in this last gasp.

'I'm sorry,' I say. Because I feel sorry for him now, at the end. I meant what I just said. Children shouldn't have to pay for their parents' sins. But they do. Because blood pays for blood. It's always been that way and always will be.

'Time's up,' I say quietly.

And then he's gone, one eye staring at the puddled floor, the other obscured by clouds of blood. From the bedroom, Ursula repeats her irate demand. In a moment, she will rise from the bed, emerge into the hallway, approach in puzzlement and irritation, take in the crime scene, then process it belatedly. Her first thought will be of herself and how this will impact her life, her social standing, her reputation.

I open the front door, slip out of the apartment, into the hallway, and walk away slowly. I am calm and at ease. Down the emergency stairs which nobody in this upscale building uses I go, light-footed and fleet; I'm almost two levels down when I hear the distant scream. Ursula is in fine voice tonight.

Her aria carries through the apartment building, following me down.

By the time I reach the street corner where I left the Hayabusa parked, the first sirens are sounding in the night. I smile inside my cocoon of plexiglass and give the beautiful machine more gas. It's a fine night to be riding the streets of Zurich.

*This one was for you, Brian,* I tell my dead brother. *A son for a son.*

One down.

Two to go.

# Entr'acte

## Roger

Roger Cordry stares at the face of his son Ricky on the flatscreen monitor. Ricky looks much younger than when Roger last saw him, almost eight months ago. In repose his face has lapsed into boyish softness, slipping back a whole decade and then some. He is now the Ricky he remembers from childhood, the boy who worshipped the ground beneath his father's feet, and for a moment, Roger feels the screen shimmer and shimmy, like a visual effect marking a transition into a flashback.

He sucks in a breath and gets hold of himself. He is shaken by this more than he wants to acknowledge. From the moment he got the call from Mayor Danielle Scharrer, he felt blindsided. Now, he feels as if the earth could open up and swallow him, the sun fall out of the sky, the ocean rise up and float away into outer space and it will all make sense. It's the sight of Ricky, laid out like a freshly caught cod on that stainless steel slab, that does it.

This is real.

This is happening.

Ricky is dead.

The screen dances and Roger closes his eyes, raising his calloused hand, pressing thumb and forefinger into his eye sockets, blanking out vision. He hears Ricky's fourteen-year-old voice, remembers the boy's gangly, awkward gait and bucktoothed smile (later corrected with cosmetic surgery) and experiences a moment of perfect, exquisite grief. An old

Mohammed Rafi song surfaces, linked by association to memories of old, dimly remembered grief: '*Gham uthane ke liye main to jiye jaaunga*'. The heart-rending delivery of a long dead singer, the plaintive score of a forgotten Hindi film, wash over him like a wave in winter, drenching him in pain. In this most intimate of moments, he is no longer Roger Cordry, billionaire and world figure, but plain old Rajesh Kadru, a young executive with a degree in pharmacy working a dead-end job at a barely sustainable salary. He leans against the glass window that separates him from the flatscreen monitor and faintly registers the sound of Danielle's voice beside him.

Back in the time when Ricky and Monty were in their early double digits, Roger could do no wrong, despite being a barely present parent in his sons' lives. Even his absence was looked upon with affection and admiration, as a matter of pride. Their dad was an important man; he was one of the people who built and ran the engines of the world. To that pubescent Ricky, Roger represented everything a man could be, should be. It stayed more or less that way, in spite of adolescent hormones and teenage angst, give or take a few periods of disillusionment, until Monty's accident.

After that, everything changed; Ricky changed. The past several years, it was Roger who sought him out, almost as much as he sought out Monty. The tragedy had shocked him into realization of his children's mortality – a subject no parent is ever truly able and willing to confront – and he had tried to bring about genuine change through his life choices. It had been too late for Ricky by then; when his dad fell from grace in his eyes, he fell hard, crashed and burned. Ironically, Monty continued to love Roger just as much as ever, perhaps even more so. Not a day ended without them FaceTiming, ending, as always, with the ritual kiss, a practice inherited from Monty's Italian mother. In contrast, Ricky sent all Roger's calls to voicemail, and months went by without them even seeing each other in the flesh.

He was here now, in the flesh, and how cold, blue and vulnerable he looked; his boy, his little Ricardo Francis Cordry Manfredi, his firstborn; his son.

Beside him, Danielle finally pierces the veil of grief. 'So, so sorry, Rog. Terrible that you have to go through this.'

Roger turns his head a quarter and says, 'I want to talk to her.'

Danielle hesitates. 'Maybe that's not such a good idea.'

She still has her Iowa accent, even speaks German with an Iowa accent, and the flattened consonants sound out of place in these surroundings. She considers herself a friend, and perhaps she is, as much a friend as Roger Cordry can afford to have in a world of complex, interwoven political and business, often self-contradictory, alliances. Ironically, it is her grandfather he is closest to; Roger and Josh Silverblatt have several boards in common, as well as some interesting political associations. At his level of ultra-capitalist commerce, Roger can't be dogmatic about any one set of political beliefs, but if he has to accept a label, the one he supposes would come closest to describing his complex affiliations would be middle-of-the-road conservative. This makes no difference to Danielle, just as her own political philosophy and personal lifestyle doesn't affect their friendship. He makes regular donations to her causes as well as Josh's, and keeps a foot in both camps. This straddling of sides is an essential, unavoidable part of doing business in the post-post-modern world.

He presents his full face to her, allowing her to glimpse

the pain, the anguish beneath his meticulously manicured mask, just for an instant. Too long, too much, and she will see it as weakness, a fatal flaw in the game of drones that is international politics and business; too little, and she might remain unconvinced that he really cares. After all, he is Roger Cordry, the Mountain, a ridiculously inept analogy made by a news outlet that Photoshopped his face on to that of a character from that medieval fantasy show. The Mountain cannot be moved by mere mortal emotion. The Mountain abides. All men die; the Mountain is no man. The memes had crossed over into ludicrous within an hour.

She sees what he has permitted her to see: a fleeting glimpse of his true self. It elicits the desired result.

'Let me see what I can do.'

He nods, taking her hand in both his hands. 'Thank you, Danielle. You're a true friend.'

His assistant alerts him to the imminent arrival of his ex-wife. She has disembarked from her car outside, arriving straight from the airport. The media at the entrance is slowing her down but he intends to be out of here before she comes in. He is not ready to face the woman with whom he collaborated to create the person that now lies cold and dead on that screen. There is nothing left for them to say to each other – nothing that can't be better said through representatives who have been legally vetted and screened, that is. It's been hard enough to keep the troll army from getting hold of a picture of Ricky's corpse. A picture of both Roger and Gabriella together for the first time in decades would be to die for.

He gives the flatscreen monitor one final look. The sight of Ricky on that slab still pierces him as sharply, and he takes only a little comfort in knowing that, at last, his son is spared the intrusive eye of the camera that dogged him relentlessly the past several years and, in a sense, all his young life. Still, Roger doesn't put it past some wise wag to doctor a pic and pass it off as Ricky's death portrait. There's probably even a filter that does it automatically. Even in death, we are in the midst of life's circus.

Detective Reitmaier is in his late fifties, lean and trim, with soulful grey eyes that look like they have been weeping, but that's probably only Roger's own grief clouding his judgment. He looks a bit like a younger Christoph Waltz but with another actor's eyes. He is wearing a serviceable suit.

The detective puts down the coffee he has fetched, unsolicited, for Roger, and takes a sip from the one he brought for himself.

'Thank you, detective,' Roger says, to be polite. He usually doesn't bother with basic pleasantries, preferring to get straight to business, but this is not business. At least, he doesn't think so; he has resolved to remain open to all possibilities, however dismaying, until he has all the facts. There is always the possibility that Ricky's murder was somehow related to Roger, either peripherally, or more directly. There are already people scanning everyone who might have a motive; it's a very, very long list.

Reitmaier is the detective in charge of Ricky's murder investigation, and he inspires confidence and respect even at first encounter. Danielle has already informed Roger that the man is a highly decorated investigator with a reputation for thoroughness and results. A methodical, sometimes plodding, but reliable professional. He has the highest success record among his present colleagues in the Canton of Zurich.

Roger has been reassured that only the best will be assigned to this case in every department; although to him, personally, apprehending the perpetrator and bringing him to justice seem less urgent than comprehending the why of it. If he simply wanted justice or even revenge, he would hire an entire team to go after the person or persons and do to them what no court of law anywhere in the world can mete out, in considerably less time.

Revenge is not his goal; it seems pointless to respond with anger and blood-lust to such an event; selfish, even. Ricky is dead. His son is dead. Catching the killer and tearing him apart, piece by painful piece, seems incidental to the shocking impact of that inescapable fact.

That might come later: it almost certainly will. Roger has always been slow to anger but even slower to forgive. When the rage comes, he will be obsessed with wanting to punish the person who did this, to take them apart limb by limb, organ by organ. He will not feel an ounce of remorse or mercy for the person responsible. The greater the suffering of the murderer, the more satisfaction Roger will feel.

But that is later.

Now, all he wants is to try to understand.

*Why?*

*Why my Ricky?*

Roger Cordry's entire existence, his sanity, is based on justifications. Everything else is negotiable; *why* is not. In the past, he has hired professionals to dig as deep and as long as required, until they come up with explanations for otherwise inexplicable things. He cannot fully accept something until he understands it. This is why he is here now; not to demand quicker action, or more bodies assigned to the case, or any of the typical things that a father in a Hollywood movie might demand at such a time, but simply to understand. Help make sense of this seemingly senseless act.

He does not say this to Reitmaier. He has said nothing to the detective except the polite thanks for the coffee. He has made a fortune out of letting the other party speak first, to listen and learn and gauge, and when he does speak, he does so with the intent of closing things out in the fewest words. Roger Cordry is the kind of man who never starts a fight, but always finishes it.

The detective sips his coffee, looking across the conference table at Roger, taking his measure with the infinite patience of a man who takes his time, and knows a thing or two about interpersonal psychology and negotiation tactics as well. But this is not an interrogation, this is a courtesy meeting, and Roger senses no stress or egoistic tension in the man. He is comfortable and quietly confident in his role.

Reitmaier refers to his computer now as he speaks in perfect English with only a slight accent.

'The young woman was found at the scene at the time of the murder by Kantonspolizei Zürich on their arrival. She was seen arriving earlier by at least three persons: a lady from a nearby residence walking her dogs and two persons from the same apartment building who were in the elevator when she came up with your son. One of these two, a Mr Jurgens, recalls seeing her on at least one earlier occasion, and recalling her because of her Finnish accent and physical dimensions. She is a large, tall young woman and very attractive, quite noticeable. Mr Jurgens had earlier complained to the building superintendent about loud music and . . .' a brief pause, '. . . intimate sounds . . . coming from your son's apartment on more than one occasion, and recalled seeing her with Ricky on the verandah, somewhat scantily clad, drinking and laughing and engaged in physical intimacy. And, of course, after she began screaming, two or three neighbors came to see what was the matter. They witnessed her too, completely without clothing, covered with your son's blood, quite hysterical. No other person was seen entering or leaving that evening, and your son himself appeared to have been out most of the weekend, until he returned barely an hour before the event.'

Roger remains silent.

Reitmaier finally dismisses the screen with a mouse swipe and says, 'It seems perfectly clear the young lady did it. We have charged her accordingly and there are no available facts to cast any doubt on the matter.'

'What was her motive?' Roger asks.

Reitmaier sips his coffee. 'The accused denies the charges.' He hesitates a moment, considering something, then puts down the Styrofoam cup. 'Mr Cordry, I have been investigating homicides for Canton of Zurich for over two decades. In my experience, one question that is not always answered satisfactorily is the one you are asking now.'

'A motive for a murder?'

'Motive, yes. There are reasons that drive persons to actions. But in many cases, cases like your son's homicide, there is rarely a complete understanding. That is what you are seeking now, is it not? A logical explanation?'

'Or an emotional one. Any explanation will do. I need to understand.'

'Yes, of course. I empathize. But now that the young lady has sought legal counsel, it is very unlikely she will speak frankly, especially to you. At the time of the incident, she was very emotional as well as intoxicated with drugs and alcohol. Whatever statements she made at that time may well be disregarded at the request of her counsel. There are legal complications and maneuvers the lawyers can employ in her favor.'

'Such as?'

Reitmaier takes another sip. 'It seems likely she will plead self-defense in court.'

'She's saying Ricky assaulted her?'

'Not in the sexual sense. She admits freely that the sex was consensual and that she had been involved with your son on several prior occasions. But she may claim that the use of drugs impaired her judgment. Your son has been heard arguing loudly by neighbors at times. He was a very physical young man, given to vigorous self-assertion. He also has a very full sexual history, even for a person his age, and appears to have been seeing several young women at the same time. It is always likely that some jealousy was involved –'

'You are basing all this on?'

'Witnesses to his behavior. Video footage from the clubs. Text and chat messages.'

'Text messages?'

'Your son and the accused had some exchanges before their rendezvous that evening, and on some prior occasions, that seem to indicate that she was extremely upset with him. There was a matter of some private, confidential documents from her psychiatrist's office that she accused your son of having made public. Witnesses say she was "mad as hell" at him and even threatened him on text message. He argued with her, claiming he was not the one responsible. The exposure of the documents and their falling-out caused a minor scandal at the university. It is quite likely these events played a significant part in what happened that evening.'

'You think she killed Ricky because he posted some files of hers online?'

'She denies killing him at all. But yes, it provides motive, such as it is. We have viewed the files in question and her psychiatrist has confirmed that they were the official patient files. It appears that your son may have hacked or hired someone to hack the doctor's records and then uploaded the files to an online forum frequented by students of the university.'

'Appears? You aren't certain?'

'There is a cyber trail but it is inconclusive. It leads to his IP address and one of his devices but a VPN was used which bounced around several international locations. It may not be possible to prove it conclusively for legal purposes, but that is not our goal here. We merely wish to establish whether Ricky was responsible.'

'And he's not here to confirm or deny it.'

'We acknowledge that fact. In any case, it transpires that the files of Ursula's psychiatric history were downloaded several thousand times before we were able to contact the host of the forum and have them deleted.'

'Why is this incident so important? This kind of thing must happen all the time in a university of their size.'

'This is true. However, there is the matter of Ricky's history.'

'What about it?'

'It appears your son had engaged in similar behavior earlier as well, with another young woman with whom he was involved. In that instance, there was also some video footage of the two of them engaged in sexual acts together, as well as several angry, threatening texts from him, and further abusive texts and posts he sent to other friends in which he said disparaging things about her.'

Roger is aware of the details. It cost him money to get all those things removed from the internet, and even so, he knows that complete sanitization is impossible. Once something is on the internet, it lives forever in one form or another. Still, he feels resentful on Ricky's behalf. Roger and he had a major falling-out at the time over Ricky's behavior and only Monty's intervention helped patch things up. Bringing it up now rakes up those unhappy memories he would much rather edit out from his mental home video of his dead son's life.

He hears the slight pique in his tone when he says, 'That was supposed to be expunged from his juvenile file, and the file sealed. The video itself was taken down and deleted.'

'All this was done, I am sure, Mr Cordry. However, there remain ample screenshots and excerpts of the video, and any number of comments and references to it still online. It came up during an in-depth search of your son.'

'I don't understand why you even had to go digging for dirt. Are you investigating Ricky or his murderer?'

'It is necessary to understand the victim in order to understand the crime.'

'What about the texts sent by this Ursula to Ricky, the threatening ones you mentioned?'

'She denies sending the texts. In her first statement, she said she might have forgotten sending those, but if she did, they were sent in a fit of anger. Now she says she never typed them into her phone at all and has no idea how they could have been sent from her device. She admits to being very upset about the online sharing of her private documents. Later, she learned that Ricky was likely responsible. It stands to reason that she would seek to confront Ricky as well. Since they had an ongoing relationship, it could easily have become inflammatory.'

'My son was a fit young man. Why didn't he defend himself, fight her off?'

'It is difficult to say. She is a large, strong woman and could easily have overpowered your son. There also appears to have been intercourse between them at the time of the murder. Perhaps she took him by surprise. They were both found naked at the scene and subsequent tests and the autopsy show that both had engaged in intercourse.'

'If she had threatened Ricky in her texts, I don't see why he would have agreed to see her, or had sex with her. That doesn't make sense. I knew my son. He had his choice of women. He avoided confrontation at all costs. He would rather break up over a text message or a voicemail than ever see anyone who made him uncomfortable.'

Reitmaier hesitates. 'The wording is ambiguous in the texts. They can be interpreted as threats after the fact, but before the murder, they could merely be read as direct questions and statements. There is room for doubt. It is impossible to read tone and intention from texts alone.'

Roger is well aware of this fact. One of the several Silicon Valley companies he has stakes in specializes in designing emojis that capture a wider range of nuances and specific emotions than are currently available. A survey commissioned by the firm found that the majority of online battles, feuds and flame wars were caused by imperfect interpretation of people's posts or texts. Screencapping and sub-posting were among the ways in which such misinterpretations were perpetuated and then compounded, causing a domino chain that eventually led to reputations destroyed or maligned, misinformation disseminated and even, in one extreme case in North India, riots. This business of wilful misreading of words is at the heart of the fake news phenomenon, which is now a substantial, flourishing business area.

'What about other physical evidence? The file I was sent made no mention of the murder weapon?'

To his credit, Reitmaier doesn't make the usual noises of protest about confidential police files being sent to unauthorized personnel; either he has been in a similar situation before and is politically astute enough to let it pass, or he acknowledges Roger's position and influence and is willing to make an exception in this one case.

'The Coroner says it was almost certainly a scalpel. It is a small object, easy to dispose of; it is possible she threw it out the window after wiping it clean.'

'And you searched the street?'

'Of course. The fact that we did not find it does not mean it did not exist. She was a medical student, she had use of such implements. The cuts were precise. Surgical. That fits the facts as well.'

Roger is silent for a moment. The detective waits patiently.

'May I visit Ricky's apartment?' Roger asks.

He walks through Ricky's apartment. Reitmaier waits considerately in the hallway, neither watching him nor following him around. It is greater consideration than he would expect from an American police detective.

Roger looks at the outline marking the spot where the body was found. There are still blood stains on the floor and walls and tiny dried droplets on the Giacometti figurine as well as on the keyring and hats hung on its outstretched arms and head.

The rest of the apartment is cold, impersonal, with nothing specifically indicating that it was Ricky's residence. It is an expensive shell, containing all the things that his son needed on a day-to-day basis but nothing that bears his mark – a realtor's model luxury apartment, slightly used. Even for a generation that carries its entire life on a device, it seems to lack personalization. The clothes in the wardrobe, the drugs, the electronics, the decor, all resemble similar high-end collections that Ricky owned in any of his other half-dozen apartments. There are no artifacts that reflect his personality.

Could Ricardo Francis Cordry Manfredi even be said to have possessed a personality? What a cruel thought to have about one's own child, and yet there is some truth to it. For the past several years, everything Ricky did, said and owned had been selected or purchased for him by others. His tastes were sponsored, his life curated, his communications filtered. It wasn't just because he hated shopping – ever since Monty's accident, Ricky had submerged his own personality in a tub of ice, squared away anything that might reveal his inner self. One young man had been incapacitated physically on that beach in Malibu that day, but two young men had been crippled for life. Like many social influencers, the public persona that people saw on social media, and even in everyday life, was Ricky Manfredi, the rich bachelor celebrity, not the son that Roger had raised and loved. Still loves.

Only in the bedroom does he find a trace of the real Ricky.

He looks at the framed photograph of his two sons, resplendent in the magnificence of their youth. He was not there on the beach that day, but he knows it would have made no difference if he had been. What happened was not his fault, or Ricky's fault, or even Monty's fault. Shit happens.

But it had somehow been him, Roger, that Ricky had blamed afterward. As if a father was somehow responsible for keeping watch and protecting his offspring through every waking minute of their adult lives.

Perhaps he was being unfair.

Ricky had clearly blamed himself the most; his hedonistic excesses and dramatic personality change afterward needed no psychologist to interpret. Yet it had been Roger he had broken off contact with. They had never shared a single conversation after Monty's accident that came close to emotionally open, or even remotely friendly. On the other hand, he had continued speaking with Gabriella and even her parents, and to the best of Roger's knowledge – based on the reports he received – Ricky's relationships on that front stayed cordial and friendly, if not as open and emotionally honest as before.

If he is seeking some answer to these questions, he finds none in this cold, sterile apartment. Except the evidence of the solitary picture frame.

And of course, Ricky's own blood. Perhaps nothing could be as personal and revealing as those grainy burnt umber stains. Only in death had Ricky opened up and revealed his inner self.

Ursula Andersson is typical of the tall, light-haired, leggy, supermodel-shaped young women that Ricky seems to enjoy. Even in her drab prison attire, she conveys a rampish grace and elegance that is only slightly undercut by the expression of dazed bemusement in her Nordic blue eyes. It is not dissimilar to the look Roger saw in his own mirror in the bathroom of his Gulfstream III minutes before landing at Kloten Airport this morning, although he has not allowed that look to be viewed by anyone other than himself, and then only for a few private seconds.

This is a woman who has not yet fully processed her predicament, he thinks. She is still in a state of shock.

He knows such things can be feigned effectively. For all he knows, she might have lashed out at Ricky in a fit of jealous rage fueled by drugs and alcohol, a spur-of-the-moment crime rather than a premeditated one. That is the working theory of the prosecution. If so, she might actually still be in shock, suffering PTSD.

But his instinct tells him this is more than that. There is something deeper in Ursula's eyes, the way they roam the ceilings and corners of the room, flick to the door, the armed guards. She is a trapped animal, someone who never imagined being in this situation, is still trying to come to terms with the reality. Also, she agreed to see him against the explicit advice of her lawyers, and without their being present. Those are powerfully suggestive, coupled with her manner and appearance.

'Mr Cordry?' she says in a heavy Finnish accent even before she takes a seat. 'I am innocent. I never killed Ricky.'

Roger stares up at her. Reitmaier has not given him the usual cautions, but Roger is not new to this rodeo. He knows the statistics: almost all accused assert their innocence, often for decades, and even until the instant the final syringe is inserted into their arm. Is she in self-denial, following a legal script, or telling the truth? It is impossible to be sure.

'You have to believe me,' she says. 'I was not in love with Ricky. We both knew how we are. The police say they have texts in which I say I love him. I have never been in love! It is an outdated patriarchal construct, anyways. I loved fucking him, but he is only one of many men I am seeing.'

She makes no attempt to correct her errors in tense; either she doesn't realize them or her English is flawed.

'Tell me what happened that evening.'

She gives him almost a verbatim reprise of her first statement to the police, seemingly ignoring the later, legally edited and revised version.

She and Ricky were fucking in the bedroom – her choice

of word – when he suddenly threw her off and stormed out. After several minutes, she followed him out, more out of irritation than concern. She hadn't finished and she didn't tolerate selfish partners. When she found him in the foyer she thought at first it was some kind of publicity stunt, a sick prank created for her benefit, something staged for concealed cameras that was being streamed live on the internet. When she knelt down to berate him, her fingers slipped into the gash on his throat. That was something that was beyond good make-up or prosthetic effects. She is a medical student and knows how the insides of a corpse feel.

That was when she began screaming.

'And you saw no one else? In the bedroom, the apartment or outside the front door?'

She never checked outside. She barely registered that the front door was ajar. Her entire attention was on Ricky.

'Did you hear him speak to someone when he left the bedroom?'

If he did, the music drowned it out.

'Why did he leave the bedroom?'

She doesn't know. She was close to her own orgasm when he shoved her off himself. She couldn't see the door from her position, and Ricky hadn't said anything specific when he got up and left, just abuse.

'Had he ever done that before? Broken off sex and walked away?'

She shakes her head. Not in that particular way. Sure, he had pulled out to change positions, or to move to another partner if they were having group sex, you know, the usual. But the way he had flung her off that evening, it was like he was furious, like he was losing his temper at something.

'Or someone?'

She shrugs.

Her lawyer has insisted that there was at least one other person present that evening, the actual murderer, and that, Reitmaier believes, is the theory the defense is most likely to present in court – that someone else came in and murdered Ricky. But to Roger, she seems to be offering stark honesty, as if she believes that by telling him the truth – or the truth as she sees it – he will understand, intervene and somehow make all this go away with one magical wave of his $98-billion-dollar wand.

Roger can do no such thing, of course, and Ursula is worldly enough and her family wealthy enough to know that even power, wealth and influence have their limits. Jeffrey Epstein could have confirmed that, if he had lived to go to trial.

'There must have been,' she says miserably. 'I . . . did not see them.'

She is clearly agitated, confused and upset; but she does not appear to be in denial.

'Who would want to kill Ricky?' he asks, aiming to come off conciliatory rather than challenging.

She looks perplexed. 'Nobody. Everyone wanted to fuck him.'

The rest of the interview is equally fruitless.

When he finally thanks her and starts to rise, she reaches out in a panic and grabs his forearm. 'Please! Help me! I am innocent!'

The guards intervene, compel her to disengage. Even as they remove her from the interrogation room, she calls out tearfully, 'I am a vegetarian!'

He doesn't try to read too much meaning into this parting

remark. She probably means that she is incapable of violence, could never take a life, even of an animal or bird, leave alone a fellow human being. But he knows this means nothing. Back home in India, any number of stone-cold killers are vegetarian. In the history of human violence, meat-eating has never been a prerequisite for carnal mayhem; one notorious Adolf was allegedly vegetarian, a dog lover and an artist to boot, while on the other hand the Dalai Lama has admitted openly that his favorite repast is mutton.

Reitmaier is already seated at an outside table, a thimble-sized cup of espresso pinched between thumb and forefinger. He sets it down and stands to greet Roger.

'She will be convicted,' he says after a few pleasantries. 'Life imprisonment.'

'What if she didn't do it?' Roger asks.

'Herr Cordry, I have been doing this a long time. They all shout their innocence.'

'And there are no other leads, no other suspects?'

'Far too many. Ricky was known to some seventy-eight young women, as far as we know. And that was only in Zurich. We have interviewed every one, accounted for their whereabouts at the time. We find no reason to suspect any.'

'What about Ursula's subsequent claim that there was another person in the apartment? Did you find any forensic evidence to support it?'

'Far too much evidence. DNA matches to at least seventeen other young women who were in that apartment at one time or another. But there is nothing to support the theory of another killer.'

They go back and forth for another few minutes. Finally, Reitmaier says gently, 'Herr Cordry, accept the fact. It is over. The killer is in prison, she will be penalized. Move on with your life.'

A party of young Swiss couples take seats at the tables around them, excited, chattering in German, ordering, flirting, joking. The two older men occupy a tiny island of somberness in the midst of this vivacity.

Roger knows the detective is right. His own people have told him the same thing: Ricky's life and apartment were revolving doors through which paraded an endless succession of attractive young women. Every single one of them had been thoroughly checked and researched by his team, finding nothing significant to add to the Zurich police investigation. Had there been any other girls who might have had means or opportunity? Quite possibly. Motive? None that would fit any better than the one ascribed to Ursula.

Investigating each and every one of those other young women had led eventually to cul-de-sacs, culminating in the overwhelming conclusion that on that particular evening, only Ursula was with him. As for her own denials and assertions, she had a record of some minor scraps with other young women and at least one young man had been stalking her; she was a physically active and vigorous woman, given to loud, aggressive behavior; the very history that had been leaked was of psychological issues in her mid-teens which included a turbulent affair with a teacher, an older man, whom she had stalked and attacked when he was out with his wife one night, a tentative diagnosis of anxiety disorder and possible tendencies toward bipolar disorder which had not been confirmed; she was a medical student who possessed a scalpel and knowledge of how to deploy one, had been high as a kite on a cocktail of drugs and alcohol at the tail end of a weekend of drugs, alcohol, sex, and very little sleep.

If someone had set her up, a theory which was highly unlikely and with no evidence to support it, then they had chosen extremely well. Ursula Andersson was about as perfectly framed as a suspect could possibly be. She checks all boxes, and the forensic evidence points squarely to her.

A brief period of silence follows, into which Roger finally asks:

'Detective Reitmaier, if you don't mind my asking, do you have children?'

'Two daughters.'

Roger looks down at the glass and open bottle of expensive spring water he hasn't touched. 'I know my son wasn't perfect. Neither am I. But I loved him.'

He looks Reitmaier squarely in the eyes. The detective meets his gaze unflinchingly. 'I need to be sure. Are you satisfied?'

Detective Reitmaier nods once. 'I am.'

Roger exhales, stands, holding out his hand. 'Thank you for everything.'

Reitmaier shakes his hand. 'It is my job, Herr Cordry.'

Still, Roger is unable to simply walk away. This is unlike himself. He knows the importance of closing on a note of finality, of maintaining control. He feels an incompleteness, a sense of something unaccomplished. He cannot pinpoint the cause or the solution. There is only this sense of impotent frustration. This is not something he is familiar with.

'I still don't get it,' he says, more to himself than to the detective. 'I still don't get why she did it, why she would do it. It doesn't make sense.'

Reitmaier's cellphone is buzzing in his jacket pocket — Roger can hear the subvocal humming. The detective ignores it. It stops. He looks away, into the distance, at the snowcapped peaks of the Alps above the valley.

'Who can say for sure, Herr Cordry? The human heart is a strange animal. Today it weeps. Tomorrow it rages. The main thing is, we have the perpetrator behind bars. The evidence is compelling. Justice has been done. Go home, Herr Cordry. You have another son. Go to him. Be with him. Heal. Live. There is nothing else to be done.'

Roger watches Detective Reitmaier walk away. He breathes the Swiss air in deeply, then exhales slowly.

He sits there at the café table, thinking of a cold, wet autumn day many years ago, in another lifetime, a day spent in the woods of the Adirondack mountains in upstate New York, a day that ended with blood and corpses. Of all the violent deaths that day, the one he has never forgotten, can never forget, is a boy of barely fourteen years lying on his back on a mulchy, muddy forest floor, a hybrid carbon-aluminium shaft sprouting from his ruined throat, eyes bulging and feet drumming as he gasps for breath.

That image now merges with the image of Ricky lying face up on the cold metal slab in the morgue.

Roger shuts his eyes.

He opens them again to find a man more than a foot taller than himself sitting across from him in the seat recently vacated by the Swiss detective. Hakam Abdi is a Middle Eastern American of mixed Saudi-Yemeni parentage, a second gen American, and the head of Roger's personal security. At least, that's his official designation. In reality, he's far more than that. He's general dogsbody, fixer, strongarmer, bagman, and anything Roger needs him to be at any given time. He speaks with a crisp

British accent, reflecting his Eton schooling. In his rare playful moments, Roger calls him 'Alfred'.

Roger doesn't say anything; he doesn't need to. There are no wasted words between them. He just nods once to let Hakam know that he's ready to hear whatever he has to say.

'Everything Reitmaier says checks out. They've run down all the leads that were worth running down.'

'And the ones that weren't worth running down?'

'We've done that.' Unlike Swiss law enforcement, Hakam had access to resources and budgets that were virtually unlimited.

'And?'

'And nothing.'

'Nothing?'

'Nothing worth reporting. Ricardo saw a number of women, dumped a fair number. Any one of them could have had a motive, all of them had had access to his apartment at one time or another, but none of them line up as perfectly as the Finnish one.'

'Ursula did it?'

'There's no reason to think otherwise. All the evidence points to her.'

'Except she says she didn't do it.'

'Would you expect her to confess it all, while in police custody, to someone who isn't her lawyer, isn't bound by attorney-client privilege, is in fact the father of the man she murdered?'

Roger doesn't answer that. He looks around.

The Swiss couples at the next table look jollier now, full of that bright-eyed, carefree look that suggests the first flush of youth and relationships in the honeymoon stage. Everything that Roger no longer has and will never have again, which money cannot buy. One of the women is flirting with the other woman's partner and neither of the others seem to mind; it's all in good-natured fun and fairly innocent. They all seem to be having a good time.

He drums his fingers on the tabletop, thinking. The image of Ricky's corpse merged with that of the boy from the woods – Brian, his name was Brian, he knows but doesn't want to remember, not really – comes to mind again. 'Keep digging.' Hakam looks at him, saying nothing. The answer, as always, is yes.

Roger looks down at the table. The white ceramic glazed surface glows in the evening dusk. He takes his hands off the table slowly. Only a faint tremble in the left hand betrays the intense river of emotion roaring through him.

He stands up.

He buttons his blazer.

He walks back to the waiting car and gets in.

He leaves Zurich.

# ACT 2
# Kiara & Monty

*Berkeley, California*

## 22

Monty Cordry is a handsome man.

The sharply carved features that yelled arrogant and egoistic on Ricky now suggest sensitive and intelligent in Monty's face. Ricky carried his Adonis body with a cocky swagger, while the atrophied object folded into the wheelchair underscores the challenges this young man has overcome. Ricky's voice and accent comes from Monty's full, delicately shaped lips, but the flow of words is laced with wit, intelligence, and the sense of a man who has found his place in the world and is proud of it. This is a lovely person, even at first encounter, and all of us walking alongside him are more than a little infatuated.

As for me, don't ask me how I feel just yet. It's complicated. It's been only three years since Ricky's death and I'm still not entirely over it. I know it was necessary but it was still a brutal, cold-blooded murder. I'm not going to diminish the horror of the act itself, or the fact that a young man had to be executed summarily, like an animal being slaughtered for the table. It was terrible, as is the taking of any human life; any life, even, if you're a pacifist at heart, as I like to think of myself in my better moments.

Oh, I'm sorry. Were you expecting me to rationalize and justify Ricky's murder? Gee whiz. Get over it. I'm under no illusions here. I know that killing is wrong and Ricky's murder was a heinous, cold-blooded crime. Two wrongs don't make a right, vengeance perpetuates the cycle of violence, revenge is the worst crime of all – you can trot out any tired thesis to show how and why what happened in Zurich was unconscionable, untenable, unacceptable. Just being a young woman of color from a marginalized minority doesn't excuse bad behavior. Bad is bad, and I bear the stain on my human heart to prove it. But there's more to it than just crime and punishment, and that's what makes my experience with Monty so different from that with Ricky.

With Monty, I sense the possibility of a fresh start, of renewal; not redemption, that is no longer possible, but possibly rejuvenation. There's a sense that the tragedy that was Ricky Manfredi's wasted life and unrealized potential is balanced in some undefinable way by Monty Cordry's resilient, buoyant, gung-ho passion for life. This man died and yet he lives; he is not he who was, but he who is now; a better avatar, more deserving of this mortal coil.

'– began as a DARPA-funded research project to develop a functional prototype of a cortical modem. Basically, a device that lets us read into and write from the brain. Exactly like the input-output activity of an internet modem, except you can't use it to surf porn. Though I'm sure one of you bright lights will figure out a way to do that someday!'

Monty is powering through the UC Berkeley campus with the casual efficiency of his brother driving his Lamborghini on the mountain roads of Switzerland. A group of research interns pursues him, struggling to keep up. He slips through the incessant flow of oncoming students with osmotic ease; the rest of us have to work hard to avoid head-on collisions, limb-and-strap entanglements, while still managing to keep pace with him and follow his every word over the cacophony of the crowded campus. Students and faculty members offer smiles and warm greetings as he zips by them. He continues talking, acknowledging them with a smile here, a nod there and a succession of high-fives exchanged with a trio of big-built ball-player types accompanied by a chorus of '*Go Bears!*'

'I got involved in the project just last year. But as those of you who've listened to my podcast already know, I have issues with anything that contributes, however indirectly, to military applications. The fact of the matter is that Cal U has been ground zero for some of the most significant scientific and technological developments and discoveries since 1868, and my little research project is only the tip of the tip of a very large iceberg of achievements of this venerable institution. Am I pleased that it's recognized by the Academy and getting all the press it has of late? Sure! Into even the most dull and boring scientific research a little glamor must fall. But don't mistake that for *wanting* publicity, or even *liking* it.'

He brakes to a sudden halt, eliciting a squeal from a young Vietnamese intern who almost collides with the back of his chair, then holds up a finger. 'Which, ICYMI, is my circumlocutory way of saying that loose lips sink ships – or in this case, your chances of getting a job when you complete your internship. Not that I'm promising you a job, but I am reminding you that you all signed NDAs and it would be real nice if y'all could honor them. Pretty please!'

A student guide leading a tour of parents and prospective students points him out to the group. A couple of them click pics. Monty waves back. He's a minor celeb on campus, and not just for his family name and fortune; he's brilliant, sensitive and a really nice guy.

Sometime later, back in the research lab, his narration continues unabated:

'– flattered by all the Stephen Hawking references but

FYI, they're inaccurate. Hawking had ALS, also known as Lou Gehrig's Disease, which is a muscular degenerative condition. I, on the other hand, had an accident.'

He swings the chair around to face us all. We're clustered in a ragged semi-circle. Around us, the lab-full of scientists continue their work, accustomed to Monty's entourage. We are only the latest batch of interns; in the gig economy, internships are essential building blocks in a nascent career, and getting this particular gig is a sweet spot for anyone building a future in scientific research. We are lucky to be here; I'm lucky to be here.

'We may as well get this out of the way. So. I was perfectly fit and able till the age of eighteen when my twin brother and I were fooling around on a beach a couple of hundred miles down this same West Coast. We were always outdoing each other, Ricky and I. It's a twin thing. He did a backflip into the sea, landing on his feet. I did the exact same backflip and hit a sand ledge – I landed on my neck. Broke my spine in four places, causing permanent loss of the use of my limbs. End backstory. Cue the violins.'

Silence greets this. We've all read up on Monty's accident, his family, his parents' acrimonious public blame game, have all probably consumed more than a healthy share of online natter about stuff we have no business knowing, but right here right now, confronted with the person himself, in the flesh, it's impossible to say anything without sounding trite or facetious. Thankfully, everyone opts for a respectful silence. Monty is copacetic with our choice.

He raises his right hand and waves it at us.

'Now you're wondering how can a quad move his hand, right? Well, I couldn't until I came up with this idea. This nifty little thing is called an electrode sleeve. It's connected to – this hat isn't just a style statement, by the way, though I do love Bogie.' He lapses effortlessly into a convincing Bogie imitation, 'Play it, Sam. Play "As Time Goes By"', then again in his own voice '– under this elegant porkpie hat are micro electrodes connected directly to my brain's motor cortex. This device is a BCI – Brain Computer Interface – which uses the microcomputer under my sexy ass to translate signals in my brain into electric impulses, causing the muscles in my arm to contract. Hey presto! Give me five, intern! Gently, bro, gently!'

One of the male interns slaps Monty's hand – carefully. It helps that he's seen the football players do it only minutes earlier.

'Awright! So that's the tour, guys. This is my lab where you'll be spending the next several weeks. Congrats again on being selected, and if anyone has any queries, my door's always open. Melinda will take over from here.'

A very pretty fat brunette in her early twenties greets us with a smile. 'Hi. I'm Mel.'

As the rest of the group introduce themselves to Mel, I glance at Monty, who's already wheeling away at a fair clip, heading over to the far side of the lab where three white-coated persons are waiting for him.

When I look back, it's my turn, 'Hi Mel, I'm Kiara. Transfer from CU Boulder.'

'So nice to have you with us, Kiara. Now, if you'll all follow me, I'll show you to your stations.'

And finally, after three years of painstakingly constructing an identity, establishing a new career in scientific research, and biding my time, I'm in like Flynn, sporting a brand-new look and personality, embedded in the world of Monty Cordry, my *número dos* target of assassination.

Ricky's murder was payback for my brother Brian. Monty's will be payback for my dad. An eye for an eye, a life for a life. Ricky was a good start – hell, a great start – but it was only the beginning.

## 23

The air in the empty lab smells of chemicals and perfume, an intriguing cocktail. Somewhere in that mix of gaseous chlorides and Dior is the promise of a sensational new scent: LabGeek. That pretty much describes me in this current avatar, though I much prefer the Lancôme *La Vie Est Belle* that I'm wearing. I hear him before I see him at the far end of the room. I have been coming in early each day for the past two weeks, hoping to catch him alone before he is overrun by the unwashed doctoral masses. Looks like today's my lucky day.

Monty is hooked up to an interface out of a science fiction movie, something inspired by a story by Philip K. Dick perhaps: *We Can Rebuild You Wholesale!* He's reading aloud from a prompt screen. I approach cautiously, careful not to interrupt him, and stop when I am some distance behind him. His reading voice is sonorous and pleasing. There is none of Ricky's sneering bitterness and implicit self-loathing; in their place is a gravitas unusual for someone so young. He'll never replace Morgan Freeman or Amitabh Bachchan as a narrator, but I could listen to him reading aloud anytime. In fact, I do listen to him while running my daily route. This is the same warmly intimate, genially authoritative voice that graces his multi-awarded and hugely popular podcast *Monty's Pythons: Amusing Misadventures on the Fringes of Bio-Science.*

'There is always a tone of admonishment, a disapproval associated with women who appropriate agency, who insist upon acting independently. Linda Williams has demonstrated the manner in which the horror film genre actively and gleefully punishes the woman's explorations of independence. The monster she sees is none other than her own projection, a freakish embodiment of her own sexual power, a god-like admonishment of her perversion of her intrinsic feminine nature. She has strayed too far from the patriarchal fold and punishment is inevitable, even desirable.'

A tone sounds from the computer. Monty finishes off the paragraph, or perhaps a chapter sub-section, and begins the laborious process of detaching himself from the contraption.

'Yo, sis, if you're expecting extra credits for brown-nosing by showing up early, it ain't gonna happen,' he sings out cheerily as he works.

I step forward into his field of vision, smiling guiltily. 'Sorry, I didn't want to interrupt your work. I just came in to catch up with something I couldn't crack yesterday.'

He finishes extricating himself from the tentacles of the beast and glances up at me. 'Calibration. Have to do it at least once each day.'

He notices me glancing at the screen. The text he was reading from is still up there, though it doesn't show the title of the book or the author.

'Ellen Kay Hardwick,' I say. *'Hommes Fatales: Dangerous Women and the Male Gaze*, right?'

'I see you know your feminist texts, grasshopper.'

I shrug. 'She's pretty standard reading. I first read her for a feminist film theory course. I've been reading her essays whenever they appear. I like her other book too – *Undesirable Desires*. But *Hommes Fatales* is brilliant.'

Monty nods, wheeling away. 'Walk with me. What do you think about her new one, *The Permanence of Cinematic Time*?'

'I'm ashamed to admit I haven't gotten around to it yet. I have a book budget and I couldn't justify blowing forty-two dollars on a text that isn't directly about feminism.' I'm walking slightly behind and to his right now, to avoid crowding him as we traverse the length of the lab. He seems to be heading for the exit. 'I mean, I'm sure it's brilliant, but it's really more about cinema and modernism and I have to make choices.'

'I'm heading up to the cafeteria to grab something. Join me.' The invitation isn't phrased as a question: as one of his interns, I'm at his disposal, but Monty usually has his meals with Mel, or one of the other campus stars, never us interns, so it's really a compliment. 'It's about archivability,' he goes on as we exit into the still deserted corridor and motor toward the elevators. 'The permanence of time, its irreversibility, and how we process it. Think about it, when we watch a movie, we're really watching still images projected at the rate of twenty-four frames a minute. It's not actually a moving picture, just the illusion of it, and all we really retain are flashes, fleeting images that we constantly Photoshop and manipulate to fit our own evolving narratives. We're not really remembering what happened, so much as remembering how it made us feel at that point in time – very much like the movies manipulate our emotions using the illusion of motion to simulate life. I love the way she unpacks the essence of the cinematic construct of time and how it's shaped our biological experience of temporal continuity. The "beautiful illusion".'

I frown. 'Buñuel?'

He smiles craftily. 'Alessandro Michele.'

He laughs at my blank expression. 'Designer for Gucci. A friend of my mom's. The full quote is "Fashion is the most beautiful illusion." Someone I follow retweeted it, I liked it, and it stuck. What can I say, I'm eclectic.' He taps the arm of the wheelchair. 'And peripatetic.'

The elevator arrives and he rolls on, followed by me. The only other person on it is a young Asian woman I've seen around a few times. She smiles in polite greeting as Monty swivels the wheelchair.

'You're welcome to borrow my copy of *The Permanence of Cinematic Time* anytime, grasshopper.'

'Thank you, Master Po,' I say, sketching a mock bow.

He laughs. 'This one's a keeper,' he says to no one in particular, and the young woman glances at me with an expression that suggests I've made the grade.

'I'm having lunch with her in a couple of weeks, by the way.'

I frown.

He grins. 'Ellen Kay Hardwick, I mean. You're welcome to join us.'

I'm speechless for a moment. The elevator opens on another floor and a pair of early bird students get on. Monty notices my lack of response.

'Sorry,' I say, 'I'm having a fangirly moment.'

'You haven't even met her? You do know she teaches here, right? She's the Class of 1936 Professor of Film and Mass Communication.'

'I thought she was a fellow at the American Academy in Paris. That's where I heard her speak.'

'You do get around, grasshopper. Well, I guess that must have been just for a year. She's been here at Cal for a while. You should join us for lunch. I'll send you an invite through my calendar app. We had a very lively disagreement the last time about the pervasiveness of the male gaze in the works of

144

female filmmakers.' He squints up at me, taking my measure. 'Yup, I think you two will hit it off like gangbusters.'

'Why do they call it that? Cal, I mean? It's not like it's the only UC school.'

He drops an eyelid in a conspiratorial wink. 'Because they, meaning we, consider this the premier educational institution of California. So we pompously appropriated the generic "Cal", thereby relegating every other school in California to basking in our illustrious shadow.'

He laughs good-naturedly to show he doesn't share in the pomposity. Our fellow travelers laugh too. We're all friends here, part of the same liberal arts adventure, an island of resistance in an expanding ocean of populism.

Breakfast is an enjoyable affair.

Monty is erudite, witty, an autodidact with a voracious appetite for intelligent conversation. We are not really dining together so much as I am given a front seat to a scintillating performance. Within moments of arriving in the cafeteria, he is surrounded by a gaggle of admirers and friends. Their diversity itself is testimony to his universal sitcom-level appeal: Everyone Loves Monty.

He tap-dances through an astonishing variety of topics, his segues as entertaining as his opinions. Incredibly for a white-appearing (but in fact mixed-race), privileged, cishet male in our politically charged times, he somehow connects with this diverse crowd, despite glaring divides of sexual, political and even racial orientation; Monty Cordry is that rarest of rare specimens: 'an honest-to-goodness Renaissance man with a post-millennial, post-deconstructionist, post-MeToo mind'.

(That last is an actual compliment paid him by one of the senior Fellows, an acidic radical antifa with a button displaying a picture of Noam Chomsky shaking a fist with the legend 'I punch Nazis. It feels good!')

But there is a moment, after breakfast, when we are wending our way back to the elevators and a pair of preoccupied students hypnotized by their phones – *'Believe this shit Énard? How is he still allowed to be on Twitter! Why haven't they blocked his account?'*– jostle his wheelchair inadvertently and cut in on him in the line for the elevator without even being aware of it; his handsome face curls momentarily in a moue of pique. It is a truthful glimpse into the daily frustration of being a brilliant, super-rich, privileged male who is harshly reminded at such moments of his inherent disadvantage in an ableist world that judges and treats people by their weakest traits, and takes cruel pleasure in kicking sand in their faces.

It's a fleeting glitch quickly corrected, the unpleasant scowl instantly erased – as if it never existed – and only someone watching him as carefully yet discreetly as I would even note it. But it's there, and I see it, and I know that is the true Monty Cordry, the frustrated cripple who had so much taken away so unfairly; and all the money in the world, and influence, and cutting-edge tech, and personality, and privilege and entitlement, will not make up for that life-altering deprivation. What's gone is gone for good; what's left is the dealing-with and surviving-in-spite-of, and it sucks. It truly, deeply sucks.

This momentary glimpse confirms what I already know, that the persona is a mask, a brilliant disguise, one grown organically and well integrated with his real face, but still a disguise.

That's a glimpse of the real Monty Cordry, the one I'm interested in.

That's a start.

Now begins the arduous, painstaking process of paring away the mask to reveal, scrape by scrape, the skull beneath the skin.

Over breakfast, we also chatted briefly about my research project: the reason why I was one of the lucky few selected out of the hundreds of applicants to intern with Monty Cordry. The project itself is something that I came up with purely to get into Monty's lab and his inner circle, but it had to be convincing in order to impress him. When he asks me to pitch it to him again, as if for the first time – which in a sense it is, since I was selected based on a written essay, not a verbal pitch – I'm tongue-tied at first. It's one thing to come up with an ingenious medical research idea all on one's own-some; it's a whole other thing to pitch it in front of a cafeteria full of brilliant young minds, all either jealous of me for being in Monty's lab, or thinking I must be just another over-privileged rich kid whiling away the summer.

But once I start, I find myself warming to it and hear the enthusiasm in my own voice. Soon, I'm rolling along like a freight train. 'So, to sum up, by using DNA samples from indigenous South Asians of various tribes, we hope to be able to isolate the markers that cause these genetic predispos-itions to chronic and fatal diseases in these populations and develop a vaccine to eliminate them from future generations. A side effect, wholly unintentional, but which also shows up in several of our computer models, is the use of the vaccine on non-indigenous South Asian as well as other diaspora-related populations. That's a pool of a potential billion plus individuals globally!'

'Wow, do I know how to pick 'em!' Monty says aloud, and pumps his fist in the air, Breakfast Club style. He shoots two fingers at me: 'Kiara, you rock!'

I suppress a blush and do a full curtsy instead. That gets me another round of applause, and spontaneous laughter.

Later, reviewing that first week, I find myself daydreaming about what Monty said. Getting funding, greenlit, actually running the project. It's the kind of thing my dad would have been proud of me for doing. For a while, my imagination runs away with me and I find myself picturing a life in which Monty and I are business partners, running our own bio-pharma boutique company, doing work that actually benefits humanity, unlike the soul-sucking, profit-vaccuuming, megalithic corporation Roger Cordry runs.

Then I remind myself: Dad. Think about Dad. Yes, he would have been proud of you for doing something like this.

But he's dead.

He was killed by Monty's father.

That's why you're here.

Not to get funding and support out of Roger fucking Cordry's son.

But to get the truth out of him, by any means necessary.

And then, to kill him.

# 24

The first major impediment turns out to be a fairly predictable one: Mel.

Monty's assistant has been observing me work my way into his inner circle. I've caught her watching me closely more than once in the past several days. Her pretty face doesn't convey any specific emotion; if anything, those two sapphires conceal rather than reveal; their diamantine beauty is a cunning lure, like the baby-blue eyes of a Leucistic ball python, inviting the prey to admire their jeweled beauty while the constrictor slowly tightens her coils around its throat.

Viewed in context, that very absence of visible emotion is itself an indicator. That she hates me is a given; any likeability points I earned in the first weeks were doused out by my growing friendship with Monty. In Mel's tightly ordered corner of the universe, interns aren't supposed to fraternize with 'actual' scientists; trying to get close to Monty himself is unacceptable. Previous interns have been dismissed for lesser transgressions.

Her rancor is ill-justified: after all, it's Monty who's taken a shine to me, not the other way around. He's the one who's been inviting me to join him/them for meals, introducing me to other professors and even visiting celebs, roping me into his social circle and activities; I've never invited myself or asked him for anything.

In fact, I've begged off a few times, just enough to assert my independence and make the point (to her and my insanely jealous fellow interns) that he's the one who seems to have a thing for me. I've consciously issued these polite refusals – 'Monty, I'd love to, but,' or 'I have something that day I can't get out of, I'm so sorry to miss it,' – when there are witnesses around, largely for their benefit but also because after what happened with Ricky, I don't intend to risk Monty's attraction to me burning itself out too soon.

In a sense, I'm just playing a variation of the classic 'hard to get' routine, even though I've been careful not to give him any indication that I have the slightest bit of romantic or sexual interest in him. In this regard, at least, Monty is not dissimilar to his brother. The less attainable object of desire is always more attractive.

Don't get me wrong: Monty is not falling for Kiara in the love-at-first-sight sense. Just as his elder brother wasn't actually in love with Hannah either.

What lies between us at this point is fantastic chemistry, that's it.

But even in the most asexual tug-and-pull between two potential partners, there's always a secret whisper of possibility. Not just the possibility of sexual coupling – that awareness is a basic species-survival instinct – but the deeper, truer human goal: intimate connection.

I'm speaking here of the kind of intimacy E.M. Forster meant when he wrote: 'Only connect.' For an emotionally effusive, empathetic young person like Monty, that connection is more rewarding – and harder to attain – than horny fornication. Deprived of the majority of physical interactions once available to him as a young, hormonal, highly sexed young man (he was no less active than his brother), such sapiosexual matings are all that remain. I researched and studied him for years before molding myself into the ideal prospective partner, and with every passing hour, evening, and day spent together, he finds new facets and aspects of my personality that surprise and stimulate him. The hook is deep, the bait is digested, and the only thing left is the delicious dance of alternately playing-out-and-reeling-in until, unable to delay the arrival of pleasure, both partners yield to fruition.

Monty being Monty makes it easier for me and harder for himself: while he can be appropriately raucous or delightfully vulgar at the right times and in the right company, he never takes his popularity for granted nor mistakes the fangirl entourage for groupies. He's what publicists and image consultants would call an ideal client: a rock star who never once takes undue advantage of his god-like power. You'll never see Monty Cordry's name in a #MeToo context, unless it's to provide an antonym to the Harvey Weinsteins of the world.

This means that he has to constantly deny his own attraction to me, ignore the obvious signs of chemistry writ large on the envious, amused and voyeuristic faces of all around us who read it as clear as tags on a white wall, and suppress his own hormonal indicators that are issuing urgent summonses to his id.

He likes me. A lot. And can see that we have the makings of becoming best buddies for life.

BFF? Why not. What's the harm?

And if my equally attractive physical charms trigger his hormonal responses in a pleasurable way, well, nothing wrong with that either. Even a hetero best friend can recognize their queer pal's attractiveness to others of their gender, right? I'm looking at you, Hollywood cliché. *So desirable that even their gay friend admits to finding them hot!*

(In case I haven't mentioned this yet, Kiara is queer.)

So to Monty, I'm an excellent option. He can desire me, even lust for me secretly, yet continue fraternizing with me openly and intimately, with no fear of censure about the possible sexual harassment implications. He's looking to me as a close friend, and my being gay is just the icing on the cake, shuttering any idle gossip before it even reaches wagging tongues. In a safe space the size of Cal U, anyone critiquing Monty for befriending, in an utterly platonic-intellectual way, a queer, marginalized woman of color would be asking for instant, irrevocable ostracism, if not actual expulsion.

I'm the perfect BFF for him and that's not even the reason he enjoys spending time with me: he actually, genuinely, likes me. And can see that the affection is mutual. In mere weeks, we're as thick as metaphorical thieves.

Mel has been noting all these signs and reading them with growing alarm. I sense her unease ramping up despite her carefully polished veneer of efficient neutrality. She's deeply concerned, and not just for Monty, but for herself. The prospect of my actually getting romantically (or sexually – even quadriplegics have sex lives) involved with Monty is too far beyond the pale for her to consider, but there now looms the very real possibility that her boss may enjoy my presence enough to consider making me a more permanent part of his daily life.

After all, before Mel there was Naomi, and at that time, Naomi seemed as inextricable as a prosthetic limb to Monty, as indispensable as his electrode sleeve. Yet Naomi was dispensed with and disposed of, by none other than Mel, who sashayed into her boss's life in a manner not dissimilar to my own unheralded entry as one grape among a bunch of interns. (There are several differences – Mel was an assistant to another professor at the time, not an intern, to name just one – but you get the point.)

The point is, Mel replaced Naomi.

And that means, Kiara could replace Mel.

She doesn't know, of course, that this is far from my intention.

Being hired to work as all-round dogsbody to a brilliant, lugubrious, insanely rich, massively popular rock-star-scientist is not one of my life goals.

My real intention is far less ambitious and far more insidious.

But Mel doesn't know that.

And what she doesn't know might end up killing her.

The thing is, I can't afford to kill her.

Or disappear her.

Or force her into quitting.

Or any of the alternative ways to push her out of the picture.

Too risky.

With Ricky, there was the advantage of being one of dozens of young women parading in and out of his merry-go-round lifestyle. Monty is friendly with a ton of people, but not close friends with all that many. Like most compulsive extroverts, his garrulous nature is overcompensation for introversion and borderline depression. He isn't medicated any longer, but there was a patch there, following his accident and incapacitation, when he waged a desperately lonely battle against the thirteen reasons why.

Unlike the trite simplifications of the Netflix teen soap, he found his salvation not by succumbing but by directly confronting the specter of Camusian Absurdism and coming to terms with it, a kind of resigned acceptance of the Hardyan

Naturalism of his life event and a careful backing away from the larger Nietzschean void that irised open in its wake. He was taken off suicide watch about seventeen months after the accident, but in mental health terms, he never really stopped considering it a valid option; he simply decided not to act on it.

In a course I audited on The Purpose of Literature at CU Boulder, the lecturer talked about the two principal raisons d'être of all great fiction: Mystery and Manners. She was referring not to the garden-variety 'mystery' of genre detective novels but to the Mystery of Existence: WTF are we all doing here anyway? Are we actually heading someplace or is our rideshare driver's GPS broken? Is there even a driver and a GPS, or is it all just some cosmic roulette spinning eternally in the abyss? Manners, not as in know-your-wine-glass-from-your-water-glass table etiquette but as in the Tragic Reality of Human Relationships, or *La Comédie humaine*, as Balzac called it.

The same incident that caused Ricky Manfredi to shut down his loftier faculties and reduce his existence to a non-stop pleasure-seeking, hedonistic Bacchanalia drove his brother up the next turnpike, to the higher highway of rigorous rationalism and a pursuit of Platonic ideals.

Different strokes for different folks.

The point I'm making is that if there had been a murder or inexplicable disappearance or similarly creepy incident in Ricky's social circle, it wouldn't have made a dent in his titanium-clad mental armor.

In Monty's artfully balanced, meticulously maintained universe, it will topple the whole fucking house of dominoes.

Bad enough that Ricky's murder caused a seismic event at the time, forcing Monty back into intensive counseling – five two-hour sessions a week for thirteen weeks, then three one-hour sessions for the next thirty-one weeks – and brought back the dream-fantasies of himself murdering himself in numerous Grand Guignol surrealistic scenarios (I hacked his psychiatrist's patient records, what else?), but a murder in Roger Cordry's surviving son's immediate proximity would draw public attention, media and law enforcement like trolls to a trending hashtag.

I can't risk everything I've worked for just to get an inconvenient assistant out of the way.

Turns out I don't have to.

Mel's obsessive envy of my growing intimacy with Monty is not simple professional insecurity. It's more complicated than that.

She's got a thing for me.

# 25

She doesn't know it herself at first, but I spot it a mile off.

The signs are written all over her.

The instant I push elimination out the window and start looking at other, sustainable alternatives, I start to see them.

The woman has the hots for me.

I'm not the first, nor will I be the last. It's not like she's in lurv; puhleez.

It's a power thing.

She gets attracted to young women or men who are in junior positions but ambitious enough to be viable rivals.

The more ambitious they are, the more determined to succeed, the more attractive she finds them. As a woman with a certain agency and privilege, she feels a sense of power in that she can choose to aid them in their rise, or cut them off at the knees. In a very real sense, their fate is in her hands. And knowing this is a major turn-on. I see this reflected in the way she looks at me, watches me, checks me out. Men aren't the only hunters in this naked jungle. Melinda Lutz is a power-seeker, and she recognizes others like herself. In me, she sees a kindred hunger.

There's something more. There always is. The rules of attraction aren't based on logic and psychology alone. There's always that indefinable thing we call 'chemistry' and sure, maybe a big part of it is down to pheromones and mutually arousing body odors, yucky as that may sound said out aloud, but the truth is, there's something more to it that science can't put its finger on, the indefinable X factor, the unknown ingredient, the secret sauce. Whatever it is, it lies between Mel and me like an invisible cord slowly constricting.

The inevitable happens — because I let it. I have played into this mutual hate/love attraction, doing unto Mel what I have been so careful not to do to Monty: I play with her, teasing, flirting, provoking, inciting, leading on. And finally, one evening, after an irrelevant disagreement over some forgettable non-error she accuses me of having made, the tinder ignites.

From that argument in the lab late at night to her apartment off campus is a short, breathless ride. We proceed from lab to bedroom and arrive naked in a surprisingly messy boudoir with little awareness of the intervening steps, writhing hot and sweaty in intertwined coils.

There is something about swapping sweat and bodily fluids on a cold night that is so powerfully arousing, and nothing smells sweeter than two female bodies spent and limned with hormone-rich exudations.

I have made myself into a machine with a singular mission, like a programmed cyborg in a sci-fi movie, pursuing this path for so much of my young life that if you ask me at any given time who the real person is behind the Kiara mask or the Hannah mask, I would be hard pressed to answer honestly. But tonight, I feel as if I could stay here in this bed, this apartment, this identity, this life, forever. I could give up my quest, release my quarry into the wild, let Monty go about his own life unmolested, put Roger Cordry out of my mind and heart, and just be this person, whoever she is, that I am right now. Lesbian? Very possibly. In a committed relationship? Why not.

'Penny for yours,' she says.

I sit up, peering up at her through my natural hair, which can get wanton when I don't pamper and primp it with spa treatments and timely trims. She is lying on her side, ambient light breaking and entering through the slitted blinds, the alternating bands of light and shadow playing sweet music on her beautiful naked body.

'I wanted to do this since the first time we met,' I say, with more truth than she knows.

She blinks several times, surprised at my honesty.

We're not an honest generation; we can't afford to be. Too much of our lives is on constant display. The Orwellian nightmare of an authoritarian overseer granted unlimited access to our most private spaces has come true: except *we* are Big Brother, watching each other, knives out, ready to carve and slash and slice and dice at the slightest provocation. Even the most confessional social media accounts are really just carefully curated fakery: give them enough to make it believable, but never at the cost of your own privacy.

My admission surprises her: she isn't sure how to take it. Am I one of those painfully honest types who will turn all clingy and weepy, or worse?

'You're a saucy one, aren't you?' she says, tracing a faint scar on the inside of my right forearm. 'So tell me about your family. Dad, mom, siblings, the usual?'

I shrug. 'Just mom and me. As for family, all you really need to know is that things kinda fell apart after my father disappeared.'

She nods as if she's familiar with the condition, or its like. 'Went out for pack of smokes, never came back?'

'Something like that. I was old enough to know what it meant, too young to deal with it effectively. My mom was a mess too, which didn't help. I guess I was fucked up for a while.' I paused. 'Maybe I still am.'

'Aren't we all?' she asks rhetorically. Then kisses me tenderly on the lips. 'I've lived on that street for a while. Fuck, I own property in that zipcode.'

'Your dad's MIA?'

'I wish. He's Republican.'

'Jeez. You win.'

I'm bullshitting, of course: the scar is from a roughhouse scramble in a congregate care center in rural Illinois. An older girl, a mean butch named Mira Delmore, was shaving her legs with my only razor and when I asked her to give it back, she tried to cut me. She was aiming for my face, or neck, or chest, anyplace would do so long as it bled nicely, but I got my arm up in time – living a childhood in free fall sharpens your reflexes – and took one slash before I put her down. She ended up not interested in shaving her legs for a while after that, and I got tossed back into juvie, but that was how it went: you stood up for yourself or got stomped on. There's an ounce of truth in that, though: I was fucked up after my father and brother's deaths, my mother's too, and it defined my life. Still does. That wasn't directly connected with that scar, but I am Kiara and this is Kiara's backstory I'm feeding Mel.

Once Mel and I start seeing each other, the tension in the lab eases. Not that it was bothering anyone – everyone's too caught up in their own thing to really care, except in a scandalous, gossipy way. *omg kiara and mel are like a couple now.* The person that it affects most positively, and the only one I give a fuck about, is Monty.

He and I are at breakfast in the cafeteria, as we so often are, and it's a testament to how far we've come since that first day he invited me to join him, when he says, 'I'm happy for you and Mel.'

I look at him with a shy, tentative expression that's all Kiara. 'You knew?'

He smiles. 'It's pretty obvious. The two of you are like . . .' For once he can't find the appropriate analogy.

'Thanks,' I say, saving him the effort. 'I was worried you might get upset.'

'Why? It's your personal life.'

'Yeah, yeah, but you know. I mean, like, she's your assistant and I'm just an intern.'

His fork halts en route to his mouth; a chunk of folded pancake with a blueberry speared by one tine bleeds sugary blood on to his plate. '*Just* an intern? Ki, you're way more than that.'

I shrug. 'You're sweet. But it's the truth. I'm only here temporarily, after all. Once my internship's done here, I'll be heading back to Boulder. I promise I won't screw things up for you with Mel. I know how much you count on her.'

*I have much worse things in store for you, so an unhappy assistant is the least of the problems you have to worry about – in fact, pretty soon, you won't have anything to worry about at all,* I don't say.

He puts down the fork, his bushy eyebrows beetling. Ricky used to have his plucked and shaped so expertly, in the preferred gender-neutral style of the day, but I like Monty's naturally bushy brows better. They set off his light eyes so perfectly. 'Whoa. Whoa, there. What are you talking about? Haven't you heard anything I've been saying these past weeks? What's in Boulder that you have to flee to? You have a real future here, Ki. I hope you know that I wasn't just saying that. I really mean it. You're very smart, you have great ideas and you've already been a great asset to me.'

I toy with my muesli and yogurt, pushing cranberries and shaved almonds around my bowl to avoid looking at him. 'So you're offering me a job?'

He spreads his hands in a 'help me out here, guys' plea, shaking his head as vigorously as science and a broken body permits. 'A job? It's not just a job, Ki. It's a breakthrough. All I want is for the world to benefit from your brilliant idea. Is that asking too much?'

I nod nervously – acting nervously, that is. It's not hard because I am not just playing Kiara, just as I didn't really play Hannah. They are both extensions of my own self. I am simply letting that part of me out, allowing that particular package of neuroses and drives free rein. *Go to town, girl. Let loose. Go big or go home.*

'I believe you, Monty. You're awesome. But I have stuff going on that . . .' I break off, pushing dried fruits till the spoon screeches on the ceramic bowl. 'It's just a bad time, that's all. I wish I could explain, but it's complicated.'

'Then simplicate it.' This is a very Monty phrase, his comeback to the ubiquitous 'It's complicated' which everyone tosses around as if, before the invention of this Facebookish cliché, life was perfectly quotidian and infantile, and complexity was only invented in the 1990s. Truth is, Henry James used the phrase in his novel *The Tragic Muse* when it was serialized in *The Atlantic Monthly* in 1889 and it had probably been in common use long before that, not to mention its frequent usage throughout the last century. All this, you guessed it, was info gleaned courtesy of one of Monty's jocular rants. 'Tell me what's going on, and help me help you. Is it personal, family, relationship stuff – are you married to a cultist, do you have a terminal disease, were you a communal wife in a Utah compound? – whatever it is, Ki, you can talk to me, you know that.'

I smile at his attempt to cheer me up. He can see I'm blue; he's learned to tell my moods now, and I let him see them as proof of how close we have become. Far from being offensive, as the words alone might seem on reading, his rambling coverage is amusing, endearing to me. He can say all that shit because he knows my problem has nothing to do with any of the above-mentioned. The truth is, I'm the one reeling him in, not the other way around. I hooked him with the project – him and Mel, both, and Mel's opinion matters a lot to Monty – and now, he's afraid he's going to lose me and the project. That was my plan and it's gratifying to see it shaping up so well. Now, for the hard part: to get close enough to Monty for him to open up to me about more than just DNA and microbacilli.

I flick a look at him, apologetic and contrite. 'You know my situation, M.'

That was the second hook. I've been feeding Monty Kiara's story, one that's consistent with the yarn I spun for Mel. Abandoned as a child, I'm supposed to be flat broke and up to my pretty nose in credit card debt, I got evicted from my last apartment and my credit score is shot so I can't get another rental again.

Now, when I refer back to that predicament, he whirs closer, lowering his voice and waving off an incoming friendly – the casualness of his gesture suggests a student-admirer rather than a fellow professor – to maintain the invisible cocoon of privacy around our table in the bustling cafeteria. The clatter of voices and flatware provides a comforting contrast to our private moment. 'Ki, I've told you this before, but in case I wasn't clear, because, you know, I can sometimes start ranting and rambling, and wander miles off the hiking trail and into bear territory, let me make myself crystal clear. I'm here for you.'

'I appreciate that, Monty. I really do. You've been a good friend these past few weeks. I mean, you didn't have to listen to my crap. It wasn't fair of me to lay all my personal issues on you in the –'

I break off.

He's holding one hand bunched beneath his chin, while he saws at it with the other hand, elbow held perpendicular to his chest. 'This is me playing the world's tiniest quantum violin.'

I manage a shaky grin.

'Ki, Ki, Ki. I'm not trying to be patronizing and patriarchal here. I'm just saying,' he spreads his hands again, this time keeping the elbows tucked in and swiveling from the ball-joints, 'you can always talk to me. You know I'm here for you.'

I frown. 'What exactly does that mean?'

He hesitates. 'Why don't you come over to my place this weekend. We can talk about it at length, without being interrupted every few seconds.' He gestures at the inevitable crowd of hopefuls waiting for a moment of his time.

I accept politely, not making a big thing out of it.

Inside, I'm going *Yee-haw! Monty Cordry just invited me to his home this weekend.* He never invites anyone there. And I mean, *anyone*. Not even Mel. This is a very big deal. It means I've done more than hook him. I've got him in the bucket. Now, all I have to do is fillet him and see what he has inside.

Proceed to Stage 3 of my plan.

## 26

I'm walking a tightrope over an abyss, like Philippe Petit walking on a wire between the Twin Towers in 1974. My goal tonight is to use Monty's interest in the project as a way to sidetrack the business talk into personal confessions about my dad. The intent is to get him to commiserate with me and, if I do this right, talk about his own relationship with his father. After that, hopefully I'll be able to draw him out on the subject of his father's past sins. Once I have him talking and get a sense of something worthwhile, I'll do whatever I have to in order to get the rest out of him. *Whatever* I have to.

But like all best-laid plans of mice and men and, in this case, women, nothing goes according to plan.

It first starts to go off the rails during the business discussion.

We are sitting in the living area of his house on Lyon Street, a large, rectangular glass box that resembles the set used in the movie *Ex Machina* (which, ironically, is actually a hotel in Norway). Sited on top of the highest hill in the area called Billionaire's Row, it looks out on to a spectacular view of the Bay, the Golden Gate Bridge and downtown SF. His neighbors include novelist Danielle Steel and a tech billionaire who gives away ten billion annually to charity without making a dent in his personal fortune. I'm sipping a glass of apple cider and Monty is having a special organic shake which contains ingredients flown in by jet every morning from halfway around the world. There's art on the walls and on pedestals placed around the house that cost about as much as the budget for the next *Avatar* movie. Talk about hanging out on the Tony side of town.

'I don't know, Monty,' I say. 'This isn't just a research project for me.'

'I get it, Ki, this is personal. You've put a lot of yourself into it. That's exactly why I'm proposing going this route. All the hard work and brilliant coding you've done deserves to be followed through to the end. Once we do that, the end-use application could be a vaccine that helps save others in that endangered minority from falling prey to the same genetic diseases. It's important work and it's not just a great research project. I see great ideas all the time. This is way more. It's social justice through genetic coding.'

I wait a few beats, then shake my head slowly. This is *exactly* how I hoped this might play out – fuck, it's even more perfect than I could ever have hoped. The thing is, when I played this out in my head a hundred times beforehand, I never factored in the emotions it would awaken inside me. While the set-up and scene are scripted, the things I'm feeling are not. I hear my voice thicken, the tone change as I say, 'That's not exactly what I mean.'

I'm not looking at his face now, but I can sense him frowning in my peripheral vision. His voice softens, his tone changes. 'Then tell me what you mean. Help me understand.'

I pause a minute or so longer, looking out at the view. I allow myself to think about the project's original seed, the glimmer of an idea that first came to me when trying to think up something that would impress the notoriously hard-to-impress Monty Cordry. It was thinking of something my father had once talked about, one afternoon as we were driving home from his workplace. It was one of those rare occasions that we kids had been granted a glimpse of the hallowed 'lab', the place where all my father's genius ideas came to fruition. I was still too small to sit in the front even though I always yelled 'shotgun' in echo of my brother Brian, who called it out every time we were heading for the car, so I was in the rear passenger side seat. That made it easier for me to see my father's face, or rather his profile and his eyes when he turned to glance over at the back seat when stopped at a red light. I still remember the excitement on his face, the glow of passion, the way his eyes lit up when he talked about the magic of genetic codes. He really and truly believed in what he was doing and that it would benefit people, especially the people who needed it most. I probably didn't understand any of the science he was referring to, I was just a kid then, after all, but I remember that passion, the fever of enthusiasm for something truly worthwhile.

I drew on that same passion, and the same germ of an idea that he had talked around, when I came up with the breakthrough idea that became, over time and after a great deal of painstaking investigation and some laborious scientific calculations, the project that was currently under discussion.

'I was in the car, coming back from the lab with my father,' I say now, letting the real emotions I feel color my words, 'he was talking to my mom. I don't think he even realized we kids were still awake in the back seat. I know I was, though my sister might have been in and out. I don't remember everything he said but a few phrases stuck in my head, and when he was tucking me into bed later, I asked him what one of them meant. He smiled – he had this wonderful smile which started at his eyes and spread lower to the rest of his face – and promised to tell me the next day. Then he kissed me on my forehead and said good night. I remember he smelled of the cologne he always used, something aqua-based with a French name. That was the last time I ever saw him.'

Into the quiet that follows, Monty asks gently, 'He left the next day?'

I'm silent long enough that he knows not to prompt me again. Finally, I say, 'Later that same night, someone broke into his lab. He got a call and left. I vaguely remember stirring and being aware of my mother's and his voices talking in the hallway, then the sound of the car starting up again and driving away. Turned out his own partner had broken into the lab and tried to steal some important samples that were crucial to my father's research. Security caught him and kept him until my father got there. My dad had told them on the phone not to call in the cops just yet. That's what my mother and he argued about before he drove off. He didn't want to have his own partner arrested and he thought they could sort out whatever the misunderstanding was. My dad went to the lab and never came home. The next morning the cops showed up and told my mother he was dead, shot three times in the chest and head, along with the two security guards. My father's partner was gone and so were the samples. He was never caught – we suspected the cops were bribed to cover up the crime – and they pinned it on a burglar afterward. The guy died in prison before he could be sentenced, shivved in a prison brawl, so the case was deemed closed and shut. My mother never recovered, it destroyed her, it destroyed us as a family.'

Monty sucks in a long-held breath. 'Jeez, Ki. I'm so sorry. I can't imagine . . .'

'It's OK,' I say, sounding very much not OK. 'It was a long time ago. The point I wanted to make was that this project, the basic germ of the idea, came from the things I heard my father talk about in the car that night, the night he was killed.'

'Wow,' he says. 'That's . . . very personal. I see what you mean now.'

I go on. 'When people ask me about my family, I always say my father left and never came home. Because to tell them the whole truth hurts too much. It's what I told Mel. I know she must have told you the same thing, that my father just left and never came back. Please don't tell her the whole story.'

'Of course,' he says quickly, 'I get it. You don't have to explain anything to me, Ki. I'm just so, so, so very sorry that you went through that. I can't begin to imagine what it must have been like for you. You're incredibly brave to even talk about it now. I'm honored that you shared it with me.'

'I want you to understand that this is more than just a research gig. It's my father's life work, in a sense. Well, not literally, because he was working on a whole lot more and this was just a side project that he was tossing around as a future possibility. But it came from his brain, so it's like he's in it. His DNA is in this project, as much as it's inside me.'

He wheels forward, places his hand over mine. 'I get it. I didn't before, I guess. But I do now.'

I lower my head, letting my hair, which I've left untied for this reason, fall over my face, concealing it from his view. I hope I'm coming off as a vulnerable young woman still mourning for her lost childhood and family, and not a J-horror ghoul. Either way, I'm a vengeful spirit.

A tremble vibrates through my hand, the one Monty is still holding, and is echoed in my tremulous voice. 'My father was a good man, a wonderful human being, a really hard worker. He worked his ass off to come to the US with his wife and babies and try to build a new life here. He had brilliant ideas, things that could have revolutionized the field he worked in. Instead, he got shafted by his own business partner, killed because he wanted to give the bastard a second chance instead of just turning him over to the cops. He was murdered and his work stolen by a man who got away with it clean and free. That bastard is still out there, untouched by his own crimes, grown fat and rich off the work he stole from my father. God knows how many other people he must have shafted to get as rich and powerful as he is now.'

Monty's voice is very soft. 'You mean the guy's still around? That's really awful, Ki.'

'I've had thoughts, terrible thoughts, sometimes. Buying a gun, going to his house one night, emptying it into his face.'

'I understand your rage, your wanting justice.'

'Fuck justice,' I say bitterly, this time meaning it, letting my own genuine emotions show through, 'I'll take vengeance.'

Monty is silent for a long time.

'Would you like a drink?' he asks at last.

'Very much, thanks.'

He rolls over to the wine cooler, picks out an aged Pinot Noir, flashes the label. 'This OK?'

I nod.

He pours for us both.

He raises his glass. 'This one's for you, Ki.'

We sip quietly for a while. I'm patient. I know I've brought us to a point we've never been before. This is the most personal, intimate, Monty and I have ever been. There's a connection here, no question about that. Maybe even something more. Something . . . romantic? No, that's not the right word. That sounds like a Hallmark card. What's between us is a deeper connection, a sense of shared loss, of pain.

'I always knew my dad wasn't a saint,' he says unexpectedly.

I feel my pulse jump.

'Which billionaire is, right? Who was it who said, if you want to make a buck, try working your ass off for a living. If you want to make a million bucks, start by getting an expensive education and privilege worth at least that much. But if you want to make a billion, figure out a way to take a buck apiece from a billion people. There are no billionaires with clean hands and consciences, at least that's what I think. They've all got skeletons buried someplace, all done things they wouldn't want dragged out into the light of day. But even by that low standard, I always knew my dad was a . . .'

He pauses, contemplating his wine glass, highlights sparkling in the slanting light of sunset. They're reflected in his eyes, glittering darkly. 'Robber baron? Let's settle for that. I knew he had done stuff, to people, some of them close to him. Hurt them. Financially, for sure. Emotionally, psychologically, mentally, definitely. Physically too? Maybe. It wasn't outside the realm of possibility. At least that's what my mother yelled at him during one of their flaming arguments. It got worse during the divorce and just after. Ricky and I heard stuff, saw stuff on court documents and legal documents that maybe we weren't supposed to see. And that was probably the sanitized version.' He pauses for a moment, shaking his head.

'I know my mother hasn't talked to him directly since then. She resents the fact that I'm in touch with him. I mean, it's not like we're close in the usual sense. But, hey, he's my dad. We only get one. So what's a guy to do? I try to look past the stuff in his past, the Roger Cordry people talk and write about, and see him as what he is to me now: my dad. A hard-nosed but fair-minded guy with a brilliant business sense, some very wise insights into people and problems, and yeah, sure, I'll admit it, a shipload of moolah. After all, it's there, and with Ricky gone now, there's nobody else to enjoy it. So sure, I use his name, his privilege, his position, to my advantage. I know it's what gets the funding, the government research contracts, opens all kinds of doors for me. In an ideal world, I'd make it entirely on my own, cut off all ties, build my own little sandcastle on my corner of the beach. But that's bullshit. I was born Roger Cordry's son. That kind of privilege can't be shucked off like an unwanted coat. It's stitched to your skin. It's who I am, whether I like it or not. I might as well do some good with it, try to make reparations of a sort, in my own small way. And I am doing some good work with all my privilege. Wouldn't you say so, Ki?'

I'm surprised at the question. I was listening too intently, excited to have him opening up in this manner, hoping for revelations. 'You don't need my acknowledgement, Monty, you know you're awesome and you do awesome shit.'

'Yeah,' he says, grinning briefly, 'I do, don't I? I do awesome shit.'

More sipping, more pouring, the light slants slower and longer, the shadows grow. Lights come on, low, soft, subtle backlights, unobtrusive. I realize belatedly there's music playing somewhere in the background, that it's been playing all along, like a distantly heard soundtrack in a theater next door.

'There was this one time,' he says now, his voice subtly different. 'Ricky and I were both in the Malibu house with our parents. They were arguing. Ricky had on his music, he did that when they fought, he couldn't take it. Ricky always turned away from the dark, toward the light, wanting to party more, drink more, mess around more. I guess it was his way of dealing. I felt conflicted. I didn't want them to fight. I wanted to go down there, tell them to please stop. But I knew it would only make things worse. I'd become a football in their scrimmage. Why do couples always use their kids as weapons against each other? They're supposed to protect us! Anyway, I stayed upstairs, trying to read a book, but I couldn't help hearing almost every word from downstairs. At one point, it got really ugly. My mom said something. She always started abusing him in Italian when she got really pissed. I don't know why. It's not as though Ricky and I don't speak it as fluently as she does. Didn't speak it. After she hurled abuse that would have made my Sicilian grandfather proud, she said something that stuck in my head and I've never forgotten since. She accused him – I won't try to quote her exact words, because I don't remember them now – but she accused him, I think, of murdering his own partner and stealing his research to get his start. That his whole empire was founded on a crime.'

I'm holding my breath now. The wine waits darkly in my glass, untouched for the duration of this extraordinary monologue. *This is it*, I think. This is where he tells me that he knows Roger Cordry killed my dad and brother. That he knows who I really am, why I'm here, why I killed Ricky. The game's up. I gave away too much, I slipped up, and he's on to me now. The fuck am I going to do now?

## 27

The soft whirring of his wheelchair as he turns around to face me is overbearingly loud. The twilight has carved his features, turned those fine Italian lines into veined marble, leaving dark creases and pools of shadow. Ricky looks out at me through those striking grey eyes. There's accusation in his eyes, and pain. Why, he asks silently, why did you kill me?

I shift uneasily. That was Hannah, my mind replies instinctively, Hannah did that to you. My name is Kiara.

Then Monty speaks and the illusion is dispelled.

At first, I don't hear what he says. I'm so focused on the past, on what he just revealed about what he heard his mother say, that my ears are only expecting to hear more in that vein. Maybe even a direct accusation leveled at me.

He repeats it twice before I finally catch it.

'I'll fund it.'

I stare at him, still not fully caught up.

He mistakes my dull, stunned look for something else, leans forward, taking both my hands in his. 'Ki, you and I, I won't pretend we're the same. We come from different worlds. But at some level, the level we're at in the lab, when we're discussing your project, when we're debating something intellectually and something just *clicks* in mid-air, the coding, the science involved, and what we can do with it, at *that* level, we're on the same floor. I feel it. I know it. There's a meeting of minds here. Maybe even . . .'

My heart feels impossibly loud in my chest. He must feel the thudding through his fingertips.

He leaves the sentence unfinished. 'I guess I wish my father was more like yours. But he isn't. What he has given me, though, is a lot of money and resources. I couldn't have got to where I am today without it. The perks of privilege. So I've dedicated my life to not being like my dad. To trying to be, if you'll excuse my using the example, more like your father. And, right here, we have this amazing opportunity.'

He swallows, and looks me directly in the eye. 'My dad's money, and your dad's wonderful project. Let me use my wealth, influence, privilege. I can't bring back your father himself, or punish that bastard partner who killed him, but I can atone in some small way for my own father's misdeeds. So I ask you, Kiara, let me do this. Let me fund your project.'

I'm silent, still stunned. I grope around for a response. My mind is reeling with the realization that he actually doesn't know who I am. He hasn't figured it out.

And he doesn't know what his father did, not really. He's clueless about the true extent of Roger Cordry's past crimes and sins. That's very clear now. He has no idea of the depths of evil his father has sunk to. Which means that this was an exercise in futility. I've walked the tightrope and survived, but it wasn't between the Twin Towers after all; it was just a pole laid down between two first-floor balconies. There was no real danger here at all, because there was nothing worth finding out.

And, finally, he really does want to fund my project. My dad's project.

That awakens such feelings in me, the thought that I could be making my father's dreams come true, that I'm a bit of a

174

mess on the inside, although I'm trying hard not to show it outwardly.

My mind is in turmoil. But for the moment, I need to play this scene out without arousing Monty's suspicion.

I hear myself say: 'You said entrepreneurs should never fund their own projects.'

'And that's true. However. It's not my project. It's yours. Besides, if I fund it, that will give me, which means us, total control. We wouldn't have to sell out to just anybody for a payday. No pressure from VCs or anyone else. We choose to hold on to the patent until the right buyer comes along, OK, we hold on to it. When you're ready to sell, we sell. Not a day sooner. No compromises. It'll be your project to run as you see fit, all the way down the line.'

I'm silent for another, shorter minute. I am torn between conflicting thoughts, emotions: frustration at knowing that neither of the two sons of Roger Cordry really knew anything worthwhile, that this whole game could have been simplified – or simplicated – into a much cleaner, one-two pop-pop pair of quick assassinations. Instead, I've somehow got entangled, way more than I ever thought was possible. Monty is really invested in this project, intellectually as well as psychologically. Maybe because I was so focused on my mission until now, I didn't realize he was actually dead serious about seeing this through. I see it now, in his earnest tone, in his face, lightly flushed from the wine and from the emotional exertion of this evening. He really wants to put his money where his mouth is – no, where his *heart* is – and his heart is in my project. If I were to, for instance, say yes, right now, then we would be going ahead with my dad's project in a manner of speaking. I would be seeing my father's vision through, continuing his work, perhaps someday achieving the very results he dreamed of. And the irony of it all is that a Cordry would be funding the project. Crazy, crazy world, and all of us caught inside it like bugs in a lightbulb.

Because I still have to play out this convo, I say:

'Monty, you've already contributed so much. I mean, I could never have figured out that glitch in the coding if you hadn't pointed it out. Using simian DNA to patch that gap? That was so awesome. It's as much yours now as mine. What am I even saying? If it wasn't for you, I'd be sitting in my windowless room back in Boulder and searching for a zero-hour gig so I could pay the rent while working on the project, freezing my ass off because I can't afford to run the heat more than a few hours a night. I mean, Monty, you're saving my entire life here and I'm giving you such a hard time about it. I already feel so shitty. I can't possibly take your money!'

He waves off my generous praise magnanimously. 'Like I say, it's not really my money. Secondly, I've been doing this for a while now, and I have fantastic advisors and consultants whose opinion I really trust, especially when it comes to money management, and I wouldn't be making this offer if I didn't think this is a great investment. Let's not lose sight of the ball here, Ki. I'm offering because I smell a big payday. Sure, it's years away, and there's a bunch of risk. There always is. But it's there for the taking, and the fewer investors we bring in on the ground floor the more pie there'll be for me to feast on. Profit, it's my ulterior motive, so don't go thinking I'm a white knight in shining armor. I'm just a late-stage capitalist who hopes to do some little good while lining his bank vault with crisp currency. Lastly, and most important of all, Kiara, I believe in you. I really, really do. You have something . . . special.'

Coming out of that face, and off those lips, that last part almost sounds like a line Ricky would spin when trying to get a young nothing into the sack. Except, I see, looking into Monty's beautiful grey eyes, he really means it. He does believe in Kiara. In her talent. Her science. Her potential.

This, I wasn't expecting. It's not part of my carefully laid plans.

I'm searching desperately for some sign that he doesn't really mean it. But everything I'm seeing only confirms what I've already read in his eyes. He does mean it, every word. He's backing me not for any other reason but the fact that he believes in me and the fact that this project will do some good. He's bought lock, stock and barrel into Kiara's intention to use science to help the indigenous population in India.

Could it be . . . is it possible . . . that Monty Cordry is the genuine article? Not a greed-is-good Gordon Gekko to the max, willing to do anything and then some – kill his partner and his partner's son, ruin the family – to get the money and power he craves? Or is there some angle here that I'm not seeing and is he just stringing me along? No, that last question answers itself: Kiara is a broke intern, a grad student with bad credit and questionable job prospects. Monty Cordry is the son of one of the world's richest men, a multimillionaire in his own right, and in line to inherit all his dad's considerable wealth, ill-gotten though it may be. There's nothing Kiara has that he needs to angle for or scheme to get. Any other person in this situation might simply steal my idea and insist it was work product created during the internship and therefore, under the terms of our work-for-hire contract, his intellectual property. He would even be right, since without his lab, oversight and tech support, my idea would have remained just that. I'm the one who has an angle here, the one who set out to deceive. My little DNA project was dreamed up solely for the purpose of impressing Monty and getting hired as an intern. The very fact that he's willing to back it with millions of his own money with no guarantee of any return – the project is years from even proving itself viable, let alone successful or commercially exploitable – comes down to nothing more than philanthropy.

This is one of the good guys.

An honest-to-goodness modern day saint, or as close to one as you can get in Silicon Valley. The kind that you *don't* get in Silicon Valley because *nobody* in San Jose or the Greater Bay Area funds tech startups, especially med research projects, out of the sheer goodness of their hearts.

*Fuck you*, I think, even as I smile at him through shining eyes; shining because I am feeling genuine emotion for once – OK, I admit, I am capable of it at times, now shut up – fuck you, Monty Cordry. I had this all neatly worked out to the last detail. You were supposed to turn out to be another Ricky, if not in lifestyle and personality, then in character, but still the son of Roger fucking Cordry. The devil's son. Instead, you've turned out to be something else entirely. Oh, fuck you, you bleeding heart asshole. Fuck you for getting in under my armor and pricking my well-shielded heart.

'Fuck,' I hear myself say. 'God, Monty, I don't know what to say. No, wait. I do. Yes. I say yes. I know I'm a fool about business and money and stuff, but I'm not that stupid that I can't see when the best thing that ever happened to me falls into my lap. So yes, Monty. Let's do this. Oh God, oh God, look at me, I'm shaking. I'm crying. I'm such a putz!'

And I am. Shaking and crying. It's not entirely a performance,

I'm also kind of laughing-crying out of frustration, and anger, and confusion.

What am I going to do now? I actually like this rich bastard, this . . . *Cordry!*

How the fuck am I going to kill you now?

## 28

I'm running down a wooded pathway lit by dawn gloam on a cold, wet November morning. My headlamp fills the shadows caused by the overhang; my waterproof jacket keeps the leaf-drip off me; my deep lugs embrace the sandy soil. Sweat pools in the crevices of the jacket, slips between my vest and soaks into my cotton tee. I suck in cool fluid from one of the two hydration straws below my chin, keeping my eyes on the uneven trail. The hydration vest's two liters are almost drained, but I have two bottles, one in each vest front pocket, both freshly filled. I'm locked and loaded for bear: after running twenty-four-hour ultra-marathons several times in the past couple of years, a mere half-dozen miles a day is almost literally a walk in the park. The Lands End trail overlooking the Bay is just 1.5 miles, and I run it anywhere from four to five times every morning most mornings since moving to SF; I know every tree, rock and twist in the trail like the veins on the back of my hand. The air is refreshing, a pleasing low sixty-something, and I feel like I could go for five, six, or even seven circuits today easily. Jeez, but it's great to let out the Hannah in me and let her run free.

To my right, the Pacific Ocean appears and disappears like a moody ghost, shrouded in fog. Somewhere in the distance, faintly visible, the rusty bones of a dead giant poke through holes in the grey shroud. For some reason known only to my inner, inscrutable-even-to-me self, the Golden Gate Bridge is my favorite public monument. I can't explain it and won't try: I just love it. Being able to see it every day is one of the invaluable perks of living in SF, and even if I hadn't taken up ultra-running back in Colorado, I would come out here each morning just to watch the first kiss of sunlight touch her naked limbs. It's the closest to religious ecstasy I come. The gruff god of labor rousing the sweat of thousands of toilers to rack this beast of engineering in order to span the mouth of the Bay, arouses a profound sense of wonder and calm inside me.

When I am on my final circuit of the morning, I always make sure to go down to Lands End Point and sit and commune with the Old Lady in Red. One of the reasons I run at Lands End instead of Golden Gate Park, or the Embarcadero, or any of the other more popular trails, is because fewer people know about it, and even fewer use it; I'm talking about San Franciscans – the tourists don't even know about it, which is a blessed relief. The few people who do hike or run here tend to be hardcore runners like myself and they know well enough to keep to themselves. Running is a serious business; it's the most precious kind of me time in our too-connected world, and there's a code we pros respect. I know that technically I'm not a pro per se, but I consider myself one in spirit, if not in practice. This is a lifestyle that makes sense to me, as against being an e-girl or VSCO girl and typing sksksks while preening for flattering filters.

Talk of the devil.

I'm making my way down the path to Lands End Point when I see them.

They're on the labyrinth, looking around with the skeptical surprise of YouTubers disappointed by reality.

'This is it?' says the tall ghost blonde, splaying her palms as she looks around. 'They call this a labyrinth? Hello! Fake

news! I've had tangles in my hair more artistic than this . . .
pile of pebbles!'

Her outrage is understandable: the word 'labyrinth' conjures up visions of cavernous catacombs winding endlessly through the bowels of the earth. Take our own legendary Bhul Bhulaiya in Lucknow, India, for instance: it's a marvel of engineering and you could spend days in there without ever finding your way out. The Lands End labyrinth is just a collection of rocks placed on the ground in a pattern. You can literally walk out of the maze at any time; it wouldn't even keep Pacman in. It's the way she expresses it, that I'm-offended attitude that takes even this simple naturalistic work of art so personally, that irritates me.

The labyrinth is just that, a work of art created by an artist named Eduardo Aguilera who wanted to pay homage to the classic seven-circuit Chartres labyrinth which was itself an adaptation of the ancient Cretan labyrinth – yes, the one from Greek mythology built by Daedalus for King Minos to hold the Minotaur which was eventually killed by Theseus – and Aguilera chose this beautiful site to place his artwork to serve as a shrine to, in his own words, 'peace, love and enlightenment'. The point of the labyrinth is to walk through the circuits until one reaches the symbolic center, which represents enlightenment. The artist meant it to be anonymous and obscure, since few people ever came down here – the cliff path is steep and treacherous, and even the gentler, longer way down can be daunting – but people keep finding it and destroying it, forcing him to rebuild it every now and then and earning it publicity which he had never intended.

Watching this young woman's reaction, it's evident she'd like to destroy it too – hurl the stones into the ocean perhaps – and is prevented only by her ludicrously inappropriate attire and footwear. The fuck is she wearing anyway?

I have stopped halfway down the path, which is so steep and narrow as to be little more than a goat walk. A patch of grass growing on the face of the fall conceals most of me from the people below, but I can hear them and glimpse their colorful attire through the wind-swayed blades.

The first young woman, the one outraging about the labyrinth, is now posing for pics taken by another young woman. From the constant barrage of instructions and her tone, I gather that the one being photographed is the other one's employer. From this angle, I can't see their faces too well but I've already formed an impression of them as e-girls, or at least I think the outraged one is. Maybe the other one's some kind of intern or flunkey or just a shamelessly exploited BFF. For all I know, Ms Outraged could be a social media celeb, maybe even a famous 'influencer' being paid five figures for each post ranting about tourist spots that don't live up to the hype. She definitely thinks she's some kind of hot shit, trekking all the way down there dressed like that in this weather.

But it isn't her outrage or her questionable fashion sense that's attracted my attention.

It's her voice.

I know that fucking voice.

I've heard it in my nightmares – still hear it some nights, when my pineal gland sparks off another surreal trip to that white-tiled gym bathroom thirteen years ago.

It's Mira Delmore.

## 29

Mira Delmore was the queen bee who came after me in that juvie center bathroom. She'd already tried swiping me with my own razor seven months earlier and learned her lesson. The second time she brought help. Five other juvies, all of them mean as sin and built for pain; but it was Mira Delmore who called the shots. She ran the chain-gang.

She was the oldest, at nineteen, and made sure everyone knew how rich and powerful her family was. All her flunkies had been promised jobs of a kind after they got out of juvie. Fools that they were, they probably believed her jive too: I would have bet that Mira wouldn't remember a single one of them within ten seconds of leaving the center.

Toward the end, when I was barely conscious and sincerely believed I was going to die from the pain, I heard her say, 'That'll teach the bitch.' They all laughed, Mira the loudest. It was the last thing I heard before she swatted me in the head with the Louisville Slugger again, and it all went dark night on me; it was the first thing I remembered when I came out of the coma, gasping and sweating, expecting to feel the hollow sound of that aluminum bat striking my skull again. I carried that voice in my head for the next thirteen years and knew every inflection of every syllable.

It's the voice I hear now, standing on this precarious path overlooking Lands End Point on this wet November morning.

I peer down through the waving fronds, trying to make

out a face without success. Then I start to creep down the slope, more careful than usual. Neither of the women below have heard or seen me yet and there's nobody else around right now. The serious runners are pounding the trail and then they'll run back to their cars to head home to shower and change before starting another workday; the adventurous amateurs aren't likely to venture down here today when there are so many fine spots to look out at the Bay and the Bridge along the city's coastline. Both QB and assistant QB down there must have a commercial reason for making the trek down, otherwise they wouldn't be risking their precious Brandy Melvilles and Vans.

If you have to come across your worst enemy in SF on a foggy morning, this is either the best or the worst place for it to happen, depending on your intentions and preparedness.

The face of the cliff is convex, and by the time I reach the bottom of the goat track, my view of the labyrinth is cut off. Wet sand crunches beneath my shoes as I touch down, and I move forward slowly, careful not to pop suddenly into their field of vision. The bright neon colors of trail wear are meant to make runners easy to spot against the dull beiges, greens and greys of natural landscapes, and on a day as dull and grey as this, I'll stand out like a signal flare on a moonless night. When I glimpse the bright, pretty pinks and mauves of their outfits, I stop and crouch down. There's no cover once I step out into the open now, so it's decision time: Should I reveal myself and see what follows, or turn back and head up the path again? I could be back in my car inside of ten minutes, swap out this cold, sweat-drenched tee for a fresh dry one, turn the heater up full blast, and listen to Fernando and Greg, or maybe the Breeze, on the way home. Kiara is scheduled for an 8 a.m. breakfast with Monty and Ellen Kay

Hardwick, and a full day ahead; I need to be there. I don't have time to go down memory lane; especially not this exceptionally shitty memory lane.

But something makes me stay there, waiting. Maybe it's all the nights waking up with the covers drenched and my hands held up to ward off the memory of metal blows. Or maybe it's just that voice and the outrage she expressed at such an innocent, sweetly intentioned work of art. Whatever it is, something has turned over in the lizard part of my brain and it doesn't want to leave just yet. It wants to hang and chill a little bit longer, waiting for what, I don't know. I'm not really thinking now, just being. Riding the metro to see where the train stops.

Ten, fifteen, twenty minutes pass.

The sun comes up behind me, but it's not really making a big thing about it because the sky is too overcast.

Luminous light saturates the air around me.

Seagulls scream as they fly overhead.

The briny smell of the sea fills my nostrils.

My wet tee dries from the warmth of my body.

I suck some water from the vest bottle straw.

I have to pee soon; the price of staying well hydrated.

The voices of my tormentor and her flunkey critique various aspects of San Francisco's eternal appeal in neat, prepackaged Gen-Z hashtags, and I start to wonder if I'm going to make my breakfast at all, because I don't know what I'm even doing here or how long I'm going to stay.

And then something happens that I wasn't expecting, but maybe I was, but don't ask me how, because I couldn't have anticipated it even if I'd planned this encounter down to the last detail, which I obviously haven't, since I didn't even know Mira Delmore was in SF until this morning.

She has an argument with her flunkey over a backpack with a change of accessories that Mira wants for some pics because they will go so perfectly with a particular set of filters on Instagram, and then the flunkey leaves to trek back to the car to fetch said backpack, and Mira is alone at the point.

The flunkey takes the easy path up – not that easy with the kind of shoes these chicks are sporting, but less likely to send her to an early grave than the goat track I came down by – which is on the other side, so she doesn't have to pass me, thankfully. It takes her several minutes, during which their voices can be heard talking on their cellphones even as she is climbing up the cliff face. Mira is giving her instructions about various things since she's heading up to the car anyway, and the flunkey is sulkily noting them and asking follow-up questions. After what seems like hours, they finally end the call, and then there's silence for a bit.

I peer around the corner.

There's Mira, standing with her shoulder to me, thumbs and eyes on her phone like a good Gen-Z gal.

My heart seems to beat faster, though my Fitbit still shows a reliable 55 bpm. These past two years of ultra-running have paid off. I've also been getting back in touch with my Krav Maga routines and I feel better than I've ever felt before: lean, mean, centered. Except: my heart sounds louder and faster than it really is. Despite the digital readout on my wrist, it echoes the drumming of a fourteen-year-old girl's panicked cardiac pace as she fights a losing battle that she thinks at the time can only end in her lying spattered like a deer struck by a semi on a mountain road.

I really shouldn't do this: I have a plan. I've worked too long and hard on the Cordry family to risk it all with spontaneous combustion. I haven't prepped for this, haven't done the due diligence, there could be a hundred unforeseen complications; this is how criminals slip up and get caught.

The reasons tumble through my mind like clown acrobats, but counterpointing them smugly, arrogantly, is the thought: but what if killing Monty Cordry doesn't happen anyway? That's how things appear to have been shaking out, isn't it? Kiara came here to SF for that sole mission: to kill Monty. And if Kiara isn't going to kill Monty, then she's free to do whatever else she likes, right? Including killing a VSCO YouTube girl if she feels like it. So what's the fucking harm? Besides, everything's a risk. Even chemotherapy. There aren't actuarial tables for serial murderers, or if there are, the reinsurance companies aren't sharing that private memo with Joan Q. Public, so it's all just a toss of the coin. Besides, there might be a way to pin this one on that flunkey.

And then, just like that, I tell all the voices to take a hike.

Without thinking further about it, I step out from my hiding place and into the open, walking toward Mira.

She senses me before she sees me, peeks over her shoulder.

Her first glance shows blank disinterest.

Her eyes flick back to her screen.

Then, a shadow of a memory passes across them.

She looks at me again, closer now, maybe ten yards away and coming in.

She frowns at my face.

The frown clears.

Her face goes blank for an instant.

The phone slips a few millimeters from her hand. She closes her fingers before it actually falls, blinking rapidly, but it's there in her face now.

Recognition.

Disbelief.

Confusion.

There's no concern yet; she's still processing what this means, playing out scenarios, possibilities.

She's Mira Delmore.

An influencer, former VSCO girl, minor social media celebrity, 104k follows on Instagram, a handful of mid-level sponsors that pay her for 'curated posts', nothing major, not like the Emma Chamberlains and real movers and shakers of the online world, but good enough to pay for her sweet lifestyle, bouncing around the country to post filtered pics of herself in various touristy locales, an All American e-blonde with a swole musclehead BF who does much the same thing, pimping organic protein supplements and eco-friendly workout gear. And it's not like she needs all that anyway; her trust fund may be controlled by her disapproving dad now, but sooner or later, that whole pile of moolah will be hers.

I know all this because I looked her up, like I look up everyone in my life, and considered going after her but then shelved it until after I'm done with the Cordry family, except I hadn't expected her to land up here, fall into my lap as it were, here in SF. Sure, I know her, and even if I wasn't planning this brief encounter, it's not a total shock to me. I knew her the instant I heard her voice, and I know her now as I stride toward her over the rocks of the labyrinth.

But she has had no reason or occasion to even think of me, the bug she squashed back in juvie during that awful stint during her teens, a time she's successfully expunged from her social history and her memory, and never talks about to anyone, because if nobody knows about it – and you don't even think about it – then did it even really happen? Like they say on social media, if it really happened, where are the receipts?

And I'm . . . what?

Less than a nobody.

I'm surprised she even recognizes me. People change a lot between their early teens and late twenties. Almost like different people. But I guess there are some things about me that haven't really altered that much: maybe it's the lean, lithe body and the way I move, on the balls of my feet, like a jaguar coming in for the kill. Maybe it's the face, sharper, more intense, but still the same basic shape and features. Handsome, not beautiful, remember? The kind of face you wouldn't notice in a crowd, but when you see it coming at you on a deserted rocky seafront on a San Francisco morning when you thought you were the only one here at this hour can unnerve you and make you think dark thoughts.

'Hannah?' she says, 'What the fuck are –' and brings the phone up again, like a warding wand, a fiberglass shield, an all-purpose weapon. In her other hand is her Hydro Flask, every VSCO girl's compulsory accessory.

She never finishes whatever it is she plans to say. Starts to back away, holding both her hands up now, eyes and mouth dilating to form a triangle of Os.

'Hello, girlfriend,' I say, showing a lot of teeth, '*so* good to see you!'

And then I'm on her like brown on rice.

## 30

'Vegas?'

Monty jabs his fingers in the air and sings a line or two of 'Viva Las Vegas' in an Elvis parody.

I can't help smiling. I've been doing a lot of that lately in his company. 'Really?'

He shrugs and sucks on an organic infusion. One of the new concoctions his personal herbalist invented. His expression suggests it's more sucky than suck-worthy, but of course he's too nice to say that aloud. I've come to know Monty fairly well by now and he's the kind of person who doesn't want to express anything that could possibly, maybe, even remotely, cause hurt to another person. IMHO: he's too nice. The herbalist is a nut; she's even recommended urophagia to him at one point. To us ordinary folks, that's urine therapy: drinking your own urine for medicinal and health benefits. She even tried to push her case by trotting out a list of celebs who did it or are doing it, from MMA fighters and boxers to actors, and, of course, our own late Prime Minister Morarji Desai.

Yuck, ew, omg. There aren't enough emojis to express my feelings when I heard her suggest it the first time. But Monty listened to her with the same attentive expression that he wears when listening to one of his colleagues delivering a talk. He's a better person than I am.

The list is probably off Wikipedia and no scientific study has ever found any evidence to confirm the benefits of swilling your own pee, but that hasn't stopped Radha Pillai. She argues her case with the utter conviction and absolute authority of an upper-caste, upper-class expat. She never makes eye contact with me or converses, even on the occasions we've been alone in the same room or elevator or vehicle, and while I can't say definitively that she's a caste and class bigot, there's really no other way to explain her aloofness. She's a third-gen immigrant and, as I've learned over my own lifetime and from my mother's many experiences, casteism is far more vicious and extant in these United States (and the South Asian diaspora globally) than it is in most parts of urban cosmopolitan India. So I know that the cold shoulder she gives me – while greeting even total strangers in public places, including other persons of color, with unfailing politeness – almost certainly has a caste and class basis. No matter how well an upper-caste and -class Hindu integrates into mainstream American society, their deep-rooted bias against us lower-caste, lower-class South Asians is always somewhere in the mix.

Monty has seen this, of course; he's exceptionally good at sensing biases in people, and I suspect it's the reason why he now lets me see the occasional eye-flutter or fleeting grimace when he tastes or tries one of her 'home remedies' and finds it, well, lacking. He strongly disapproves of her treatment – or lack of treatment – of me too. I have a feeling Ms Pillai isn't going to be employed by Monty Cordry much longer, despite being recommended by someone whose opinion he values highly. And he isn't going to try slurping his own piss; in fact, I think he's had about enough of her pushing it as insistently as she does. Even good folks have their limits.

'Why Vegas?' I ask. 'I mean, why can't we just do it here in the Bay Area? This is where we're setting up shop. I don't get why we have to go all the way to Nevada. Is it a tax thing?'

He nods. We're in a self-driven vehicle specially adapted and outfitted for his use, taking the I-880 from SF to Fremont. The car's a prototype of an all-electric SUV which promises a mileage of 200 miles on a single charge. It was a birthday present from a fellow billionaire pal of his dad's, and I guess I should be at least a little nervous about being in the passenger seat of a self-driven car operated by a quadriplegic. 'Doesn't Roger Cordry care about his son's life?' asked one blogger on the day the news broke. 'He's lost one son already. You'd think he'd be more concerned about the surviving son now.' I can't speak for Roger Cordry, of course, but I'm not concerned. Monty is many things, but he's not reckless. He's looked into the specs of this particular traveling robot as intensely as if it was a lifesaving device for neonatals. If he's willing to trust his life to this glossy hunk of metal, plastic and faux wood paneling, so am I.

I trust Monty. And I think he trusts me. We've formed a bond that is something more than just congenial co-working. Since that night at his residence, we haven't had a chance to talk intimate, personal stuff again; but I'm biding my time. Those aren't the kind of conversations you can have in a crowded cafeteria, or while in the middle of a busy day. I'm itching to know more about what he heard, thought, learned – whether from his mom or dad – about that fateful night that Roger Cordry killed my dad and brother. Every time I'm around Monty and we have a rare moment alone together, I'm tempted, oh, so tempted. But the last thing I'm going to do is endanger our relationship and his trust in me by bringing it up out of the blue. It has to flow out naturally, the way it did before, and that requires the right time, place and circumstances. In short, patience. To be honest, that isn't a tough call with Monty; he's such pleasure to be around. I'm willing to wait until the right time comes again, even if it takes a while.

'Partly, yeah. We're registering the company in Nevada and that's where we'll be doing our manufacturing. We'll run the lab here so you'll have to pay income taxes, sorry about that, but everyone we hire will be based out there. But that's only going to happen down the line, probably next year based on your projected timelines. Right now, the reason we need to head down to Sin City is because I want to announce our startup at VentureCon.'

When I don't say anything for a minute, he turns to look at me. We're doing about sixty-five in the middle lane, and traffic is fairly light at this hour, but I still feel queasy riding shotgun with a driver who isn't looking at the road and doesn't even have a finger on the wheel.

'You're OK with that, right?' he asks. 'You can't hide your light under a bushel forever, Ki. You've done some great work on this. It's time we told the world about it. Not the details, mind you, at least not until we've filed all the patents, but broad strokes. And especially our goals. Helping an already marginalized and endangered minority group to find better medical treatment, live better, healthier and longer lives – that's big. It's about as big as it gets in STEM. We should be shouting this from the rooftops. You should be proud of yourself.'

'I get that,' I say, chewing my lower lip, a Ki habit when she's undecided or nervous, 'I'm just not sure I want to make promises yet. It seems kind of cruel to be promising a cure that we aren't able to deliver immediately.'

'Ki,' he says, 'this is part of the process. It's not an ethical thing. We're not going to be able to develop this in secret. The moment we file the patents . . .'

'Sure, I know that. I'm not saying I don't want to announce it. I was hoping we could maybe wait until we have the first batch ready, or the first trial results, or maybe even the first successful trial.'

He smiled. 'Do you hear yourself? Those could be three, five, seven, even ten years from now. Progress can be painfully slow in this area, you know that. Besides, if we don't announce it, someone else will get hold of it sooner or later and spin it. I know you think I'm the big dude on campus at Cal, but that's just home field advantage. Out there in the big dirty world, I have my share of detractors. Hell, I even have a fair share of them in my own backyard. You wouldn't want the wrong persons twisting our work into something other than what it really is, would you? Well, you'd be surprised at how deviously even the best things can be spun by the right choice of words and pictures. I mean, let's face it, that's what alternative facts is all about. It's all about the pitch and the lede. And once that spin is spun, we'll be spinning our wheels just trying to deal with the damage control.'

'You have a point,' I admit.

I'm silent a few more minutes.

He reads my silence this time as a contemplative one and lets the quiet sit comfortably between us, like a contented dog. The lush green hills of the Bay Area travel past us as the AI-driven car carries us smoothly southward.

I can't tell him what's really bothering me: I never intended things to go this far. I expected to be done with the Monty section of my autobiography a couple of weeks before now, around the end of my internship. Becoming his partner on an actual tech startup was definitely not something I meant to do: announcing it at a major world platform like VentureCon, with over 200,000 techies from around the globe, and some of the world's biggest tech company heads and all the media present, is way more public than I ever intended to go. It's still not practical, not really. But for the moment, I just can't bring myself to end this. I want to stick around for this ride with Monty, not just to Fremont, but to wherever we're headed together, to see how it plays out for a while longer. I really want to know what he knows before I . . . well, before I do what has to be done. And if I sound ambivalent about that, it's because I am. Something changed that night. The voice inside my head keeps reminding me – let's call it my Hannah-voice – the Hannah voice keeps saying, *Girl, you know you have to continue with the plan, kill Monty and then move on to Roger. And I will, I will*, I keep reassuring my inner Hannah, *I just need some time.*

Except, time has its risks. The longer I hang around in my Kiara persona, the greater the risk of my blowing my cover and jeopardizing the whole operation. As this conversation has just proved. I can't afford to have Kiara go to Vegas and come face-to-face with Roger fucking Cordry! As it is, Kiara is becoming too visible, too much a part of Monty's life – and Mel's. It's only a matter of time before their social media followers get hold of a pic of me, or worse, and this whole thing unravels. The reason they were never able to catch Ricky's killer was because they thought they already had her: Ursula was the perfect patsy and that whole mission worked out so well. If Hannah had been as high-profile in Ricky's life as Kiara is now becoming in Monty's life, it might have gone differently. There's a reason why assassins stay in the shadows. Light exposes the truth.

I'll cut loose before Vegas, I reassure myself; it's over a month away. I'll bail before that. I'm full of doubts because that's what I told myself a week ago, and a week before that too. But now is not the time or place to prevaricate with Monty. I have to keep playing Kiara for the time being.

So aloud, I say, sounding cheerful and convinced: 'OK, M. Let's do this!'

'Yee-haw!' he yells, holding up both his hands for a double high five.

I oblige. His palms feel warm and soft against my own hard, rough, fighter's hands.

'You climb?' he asks after a minute, referring to the conditioning of my palms.

'Sometimes. But mostly abseiling with ropes, not free soloing.'

'That sounds cool.'

'It's awesome. I get such a rush out of the descent.'

'Ever tried spelunking?'

'Just once. I want to try Moaning Caverns sometime. I had a friend in Colorado and she said it was rad.'

'You should totally do it.'

We chat about different types of climbing, gear, the best gloves to avoid rope-burn, moisturizers. The hour breezes by and before I know it, we're pulling up outside a nice suburban house in the Fremont hills.

'About this guy we're going to meet,' he says, 'I should warn you. He can be a tad inflammatory.'

'I'm chill,' I assure him. I am. I've looked up Énard and to be honest, I don't really care about the dude either way. Sure, I have views. I believe Black Lives Matter and that assholes like Énard are harmful to many people, while feeding the ugliest part of our messed-up society, but Kiara doesn't really share my opinions. Besides, I'm not going to alter my smooth dynamic with Monty over that turdhead. Monty asked me if I wanted to take a drive down to Fremont in his new electric buggy, and I said sure. It was nice getting out of the lab for a couple of hours and seeing what a self-driving Tesla could do. The actual meeting is Monty's business, I'm just along for the ride.

'That's good,' he says, sounding relieved. He pauses while we wait for the rear ramp to lower itself. 'Because there are a lot of people in Cal who really take issue with his views.'

Something in his tone makes me glance at him. 'Are you expecting trouble?'

He nods as if to say, *hell yeah, I am*.

I grin at that. It's so Monty.

'Not that I agree with him,' he hastens to add. 'Au contraire. But it's the principle of the thing. Free speech and all that jazz.'

'I hear you. Isn't that what Cal's famous for? An open forum?'

He sighs. 'Used to be that way. Now, maybe not so much.' He sings the chorus line from Dylan's 'The Times They Are A-changin''.

Outside the SUV, wheeling up the walkway to the front door: 'At times, I wonder if cancel culture might not eventually cancel itself out.'

I'm surprised. Coming from someone as universally likeable as Monty, that's an unexpected insight. He's a guru of the SJWs, a folk hero of sorts, despite his billionaire scion stigma; or maybe because of it.

It sounds like he's actually concerned.

As it turns out, he has reason to be.

There are almost two dozen of them, packed into Mel's apartment, sitting on the bed, couch, squatting cross-legged on the rug, leaning against the furniture. They're a fairly typical cross-section of Cal folk: I know a couple of them by first name, a few more by sight, but several I've never seen before. They're all colors, all mixes, even a half-dozen white kids. I don't need a pamphlet to tell me what their common cause is: antifascism. *I punch Nazis, and I like it!* A bunch of them even have the half-masks with the skull-face dangling around their necks, like they might need to be ready to mask up and wade into action right here in Mel's living room in case Nazis start popping up out of the cracks.

Mel makes a sound like a person shooing away gnats and comes over to me, her face twisting irritably. 'You should have texted.'

'I was just cruising by,' I lie. I deliberately dropped in uninvited to see if my suspicions were founded.

I've been noticing Mel acting weird the past week or two. Ever since Monty announced that he was hosting Ansel Énard for a special session of the DClub Talks. The Democracy Club Talks are an institution unto themselves, a regular feature of Cal U dating back, oh, like a hundred years or so. It's a famous forum for controversial speakers on a variety of topics. A tenured prof can invite one speaker each year. Monty chose Énard. The minute Monty announced his speaker, Mel's face turned bright red; several of the lab peeps, even the new batch of interns, wore varying expressions of outrage, shock, betrayal, disappointment, disbelief. One surfer-dude-type from Malibu even laughed, thinking Monty was joking. When he realized he wasn't, he stared blankly at the ceiling for a good ten minutes, like he was scanning for a reason that helped him make sense of it.

But it's Mel whose reaction troubled me the most. Which is why I'm making this unannounced visit tonight, despite her clearly telling me this afternoon at the lab that she had 'this thing she can't get out of' with her brother and suggesting we hook up tomorrow.

'You should have called,' she hisses to me, grabbing my arm and trying to lead me back the way I came. 'It's not a good time.'

'Which one's your brother?' I ask, still playing the part. 'Is it some kind of family thing?'

'I'll explain later,' she says soothingly, making a shooing gesture, 'right now, you need to go, OK?'

'Oh God, I didn't mean to interrupt,' I say. Aloud to the roomful of intense, suspicious faces: 'Sorry to barge in, guys! I was just passing by and thought I'd stop and see my girl here.'

Nobody responds. A few are either looking at the floor, the wall, their phones, or anywhere but at me. One tall, red-haired dude, the man who was speaking when I walked in, tracks me with hot-coal eyes burning into me from the instant I walk into the room till the time I exit to the hallway.

'Y'all have a good meeting!' I call out from the hallway as Mel bustles me out the front door. 'Is it some kind of AA thing? So sorry I interrupted. Text you later!'

Mel's florid face lingers in the doorway. 'Next few days are stacked,' she says, 'and with my brother here in town . . .'

I raise my hands. 'I get it. Say no more. I've got stuff to take care of too. The project.'

The door shuts and almost immediately I hear the rumble of querulous voices inside, followed by Mel's high-pitched tones. I don't have to hear the words to know that she's apologizing and explaining that I don't know anything and will not be a problem. Yeah, right, girl. We'll just see about that.

Mel's place is a loft in a post-war town house just off International Boulevard, which she, aligning herself with other Oaktowners, still calls East 14th Street. She's no more an Oaktowner than I'm a San Franciscan, or a Coloradan, or *eine Zürcherin*, but that's the whole point. Mel hails from a New England clan of German–Irish descent, staunch Republicans and hardcore right-wingers. She's the lone hard-left Democrat in the family and sees herself as a radical anarchist revolutionary speaking out for the marginalized and disenfranchised of the world. The holidays are a tempestuous time in the Lutz house in Boston, especially after a certain Mr Trump took office and Mel took offense with her family's public support, including the wearing of pink hats on Thanksgiving. Like so many other white women hailing from generations of wealth, stature and privilege, Mel turned woke in college at Dartmouth when a black girl was sexually assaulted at a frat house. She sincerely feels she has a responsibility to utilize her privilege and social power to fight for social justice.

I've known all this even before I came to Cal U, and I suspect it plays more than a small part in predisposing her toward having an affair with me, but there was no indication it would pose a problem.

Until now.

I wait down the block from her place, parked in a

nondescript rental I picked up this evening. I don't own a car in SF. Property crime rates, especially car break-ins, are the highest in the country. One intern at the lab naively drove her BMW M4 all the way up from Scottsdale, Arizona, and was rewarded by having it broken into fourteen times in just under three months before it was finally jacked two days before her internship ended; she left crying and swearing she would never come back to SF, boo hoo poor baby. Besides, parking's torture and traffic's a bitch. I keep the heater in the rental on to combat the unseasonal cold wave; it's snowing in Southern California this weekend, even LA County, and I haven't got much sleep the past few nights. I rub my palms briskly in the warm blast while I wait.

An hour and seventeen minutes after my unannounced visit to Mel's, the door of the house opens and what looks like the majority of her party troop out, breath condensing from the temperature contrast. They shuffle their feet for a few minutes, then go their separate ways. I let them go: I'm after bigger fish.

The last one to leave is my *poisson du jour*.

Jordan Rappaport, aka hot-coal eyes.

Six feet four, built like a basketball pro, he stands on the sidewalk barely a minute, eyes scanning the area with the efficiency of the perennially paranoid.

He has good reason to be: Rappaport is an extreme-left activist known to promote and engage in violence. He's on a number of lists. There are three separate alphabet-named law enforcement agencies who would love to get him in a black site detention center and ask him some hard questions. He has ties to at least one underground group on OFAC's SDN list, and is himself a Specially Designated National and Blocked Person. In plain English, that means that US citizens are prohibited from dealing with him – and his assets, the ones known to the Treasury Department anyway, are blocked.

He pulls up his hoodie, stuffing both hands into the pockets, and a minute later, a jacked-up Impala coasts up the street, two men in the back and one driving. He gets into the shotgun seat and they take off.

I follow at a cautious distance. My hoodie's up too, a different one from the one I use in the lab, and I'm packing heat. I know the brothers are carrying, and this is their turf.

I'm treading dangerous ground here. These guys are pros at spotting tails and should they get hold of me, even my Krav Maga skills won't get me out in one piece. But I have to get a fix on what they plan to do. That was no group hug they were engaged in up in her loft; it was a full-on antifa strategy meet. They're planning something for the day of the DClub talk and I need to know what it is before it happens.

My concern isn't for Mel. She's a sweet person, most of the time anyway, and I've enjoyed the time we've spent together; in an alternate timeline on the quantum singularity, we might have made a fine couple. It was a nice dream but this is the real shit. For reasons I can't explain easily, I can't, won't, don't want to let anything bad happen to Monty. If harm is going to be done to him, I'm the one who's going to be meting it out.

I follow them through some of the seediest parts of Oakland. I get a few glares and sharp looks from brothers and sisters on the street, but my low-rent ride and brown skin get me through. I wouldn't want to park for long on some of these corners though; my being a WoC isn't going to get me a pass on a car-jacking. As it is, I have a couple of close shaves: once when a guy steps out in the middle of the street and tries to wave me down, a piece tucked into the waistband of his tracks – I respond by gunning the accelerator and forcing him to dance out of the way, cursing; another time, a trio of cholos in a jacked-up convertible tail me for a few blocks, clearly more interested in me than the rental. But I manage to pick up Rappaport again, and finally, about forty minutes after leaving Mel's place, I hit the jackpot.

I come around the corner and pull up slowly next to a chain-link fence. The Impala is in a vacant lot with a defaced sign that bravely tried to warn off trespassers once. Rappaport and his homies are standing around another vehicle, already parked there, examining it while a black dude wearing more bling than Snoop Dogg talks to Rappaport softly. Rappaport is listening, while his bros check out the ride.

It's a white panel van with faded lettering on the sides that I can't read from this angle. A moment later, Snoop Dogg leans in to the van's driver's seat and does something. A ramp starts to winch down out the rear of the van, like the ones at the front doorway of the BART buses. The kind that people in wheelchairs use to roll on and off the vehicle.

The instant I see that, I'm done. I don't need to see anymore. It's clear what they have in mind.

## 32

Cal U is a war zone tonight.

It's the day of Ansel Énard's DClub talk, and the streets are sibilant with the promise of violence.

Anywhere from a thousand to twice that number of protestors and supporters on both sides are out in the neighborhood of Echelon House, the redbrick building where the talk is scheduled to be held. There's some police presence outside the building and cops in riot gear along the route that Énard will take to get there, but as usual, it won't be anywhere near enough if the protests turn nasty. The odds of that happening are two to one. I don't mean figuratively; those are the actual betting odds posted on the WhatsApp group students use. My intern has twenty dollars on WhiteRight being the catalyst – yes, I have an intern of my own now – while other protest blocs like Oath Bringer, Alt Rite, AntiFa4u, and Whatever It Takes, among others, are also attracting strong odds.

Monty has refused bodyguards.

Hakam Abdi made a trip down to Monty's place yesterday, bringing three impressive-looking associates for Monty's protection. There was some arguing, a FaceTime con with Roger Cordry, and then, at Monty's insistence, Hakam and his party left peacefully. I suspect they're still around here somewhere, standing by, but Monty was adamant that he would not tolerate any 'personal presence'. He only just stopped short of filing a restraining order – against his own bodyguards. That's Monty for you.

Hakam's arrival was precipitated by my anonymous text message tip (via a burner) to the Alameda County Sheriff's office about there being an 'imminent threat to Cordry' tonight from an individual named Jordan Rappaport. I had to sound the alert without drawing attention to myself. I had expected Monty to put up a fuss at first but assumed he would reconcile himself to the idea; after all, Cal U has seen its share of student protestor clashes in the past decade, and talks by similarly controversial speakers have had to be canceled at the last minute due to violent protests. Calling them 'protests' is just a pretty name for riots, which is what they were. Even if I hadn't seen Rappaport and his crew with the van that evening last week, Monty still has good cause to be careful about his own safety. His stubborn refusal frustrates me.

I've tried talking to him. Ironically, so has Mel. She's not shown up for work the past two days, calling in sick, but the day before she seemed to be sincerely trying to convince Monty to get police protection. Was she suddenly afflicted with a last-minute case of the willies or did she just grow a conscience? Whatever the reason, she's chosen to stay out of the fray. I'm tempted to give her the benefit of the doubt but I'm not going to let her off that easy.

Rappaport might well have done whatever he's planning to do even if he hadn't met her, but her complicity is a betrayal of Monty's trust. That's the only reason I didn't try tattling on her: Monty would just laugh it off and trot out the old Evelyn Beatrice Hall saw: 'I disapprove of what you say, but I will defend to the death your right to say it.' I very much doubt the protestors gathering in the streets tonight have that same sentiment at heart, but Monty is an old-school die-hard idealist and won't hear a word against Mel. To be honest, I can't be sure that she knows about Rappaport's sideshow with the van, although her last-minute change of heart does suggest she knows more than she told Monty.

Monty and I are in Echelon House, awaiting Énard's arrival. The French-Canadian national is staying at a friend's place in Fremont, the house we visited last week, and is driving directly to the venue. We're all on tenterhooks, interns as well as the faculty members and volunteers who are here. Monty and I are waiting in the lobby, a walnut-paneled space with brass-framed portraits of old white dudes and a Sheriff's deputy standing off to one side, talking on his cellphone. The police presence is light but visible.

There's a big climate change rally marching down Market Street in San Francisco. They're expecting a substantial counter-protest there too, and every spare law enforcement body is on it, with our little campus speech getting the leftovers. I've spotted at least one dude in a suit outside, touching his ear and watching the street, and I'm pretty sure he's one of Hakam's team. They're all ex-Secret Service guys, and despite the low-key presence, there's no mistaking that hyper-alert yet deceptively relaxed look, like coiled springs ready to launch at the slightest touch. I'm glad of their presence, even if Monty isn't acknowledging it, because there's no doubt that there will be violence tonight; the only question is, will any of it be directed at Monty. I don't give a fuck about Ansel Énard; I've not read any of his books except for a skim-through of the one that won the Prix Goncourt, but he's a provocateur who knows exactly what he's getting into here. My only concern is Monty's wellbeing.

'Is he running late?' someone asks anxiously. Another

person shushes them and whispers something reassuring. The atmosphere here at the venue is tense too: the trustees, two of whom are present – they're the ones whispering – aren't happy about the crowds gathering outside. Someone reads off a text message saying that more activists are converging on the east side of MLK. That's the park a few blocks from here. There's already a substantial presence at the park organized by the left radical group Whatever It Takes where some prominent alumni speakers are supposed to be talking – a live video feed I checked a minute ago showed feminist author Laurel Boone speaking. She's pretty intense. My Twitter feed says that the new arrivals are hard rightists. That's a combustive combination.

Monty is making a call. His normally smiling face is trying hard to appear cheerful and relaxed, but it's not very convincing.

He feels the pressure: nothing that may or may not happen here today is his fault, but in an era ruled by social media gangs it's no longer about truth, it's all about the 'look'. Inviting Énard is 'a bad look' for him, according to the online pundits. Already, there's a lot of hate being spewed against him by SJWs online, with some deeply unpleasant false accusations and unfair hashtags being slung around. An equally vicious onslaught of counter-attacks is spewing from the alt-right, neo-Nazis, and #alllivesmatter gangs; not the kind of support a progressive liberal like Monty wants.

In the real world, things haven't been much better. There have been placards around the campus, graffiti, and even tags sprayed on cars. On one of Monty's rounds of campus, there were mixed responses in place of the usual universal smiles. Several people pointedly snubbed him, a few clicked pics and hate-tweeted, glaring at him over their phones as their thumbs pounded out angry hashtags. A famous black YA author tweeted how she was 'disappointed' in his choice of speaker. That served as a rallying call for tens of thousands of other online activists and their followers. Another influencer rage-tweeted that it was 'time for Queendom to kick this disabled ass'.

It's a full-on dumpster fire now.

On the plus side, if you can call it that, Énard is trending. The talk has aroused more media and public interest than any other in recent times, except maybe for the notorious Milo Yiannopoulos one a few years back. For what it's worth, I think Énard at least has literary talent, which is more than could be said about Milo, the rabble-rouser, and there is a democratic spirit to Monty's choice. It's a shame that his bipartisan gesture is being reviled and dumped on so mercilessly.

'I just want you to know,' I tell him now, 'I think you're doing a very brave and commendable thing.'

Monty looks up at me with a wry smile. 'Thanks. That means a lot to me, Ki.'

I bend down and kiss him on the cheek. It takes him by surprise. Being a disabled person means most people are wary of physical contact with Monty. It's like they're afraid they might break him. The fact is, he likes to be touched – affectionately, not aggressively – just as much as any human being. In fact, he's always calling for hugs and offering to shake hands and mostly gets just an air-hug and air-kiss. An actual smooch on the cheek surprises him, in a good way.

This time his smile is broader. 'Hey,' he says, 'nice.'

I sketch a salute. '*You're* nice, skipper!'

His expression changes. He looks up at me with a distant thought in his eyes. I know Monty well enough by now to recognize one of his 'checking out' moods. 'Everything OK, Monty?'

'Huh?' He comes back with a blink. 'Yeah, sure. Just wool-gathering for a minute. Thinking about that night on my porch.'

My heart skips a beat. 'Yeah. We'd both had a few!'

He grins. 'We did. It was nice. We should do that again sometime.'

'Yeah?' I'm surprised – and thrilled. This is the closest we've come to even referencing that night. I was starting to worry that maybe he had blocked it out as a drunk-talking mistake.

'There aren't many people I can do that with, you know,' he says, and he looks up at me in a way that reminds me so much of Ricky during his most vulnerable moments in bed. 'It's a rare privilege. There's stuff I'm still trying to deal with about my past. My dad, really. My dad's past, I guess. Thanks for listening. I never got round to thanking you for listening that night. I must have bored the hell out of you.'

'No way,' I say, reaching for his hand instinctively. 'Any-time you want to talk, I'm there. Like you said, it's a rare privilege. Makes two of us.'

He smiles up at me. 'You're awesome, Ki. I'm so glad you came into my life.'

I'm about to say something to that when a flutter of move-ment behind him catches my eye. I straighten up, wary.

It's Hakam. His suit and walk give him away as he approaches Monty, noticing our connected hands, briefly making eye contact with me, sensing the moment between us, then looking at his employer's only surviving son.

'We need to get you out of here,' he says crisply. 'Now.'

Monty's face, caught in the smile meant for me, shuts down as he turns to Hakam. 'Get the fuck out of here.'

His tone startles the trustees, the student volunteers, campus security, all of us gathered in the lobby. It startles me. That hardness is so unlike Monty. It's so Ricky.

Hakam is undaunted. 'Your speaker's not coming. Let's go.'

'Wait, what?' Monty is frowning at his phone.

One of the volunteers makes a sound. She holds up her phone. 'It's on the news. They've surrounded his house.'

The live feed shows a crowd of rage-chanting protestors thronging the street outside the Fremont house. Other volunteers, and one trustee, exclaim as they find other news stories breaking.

'Oh, thank God!' one volunteer cries out, running his hands through his shock of red hair in relief. 'We don't have to go through with it now!'

'Yeah, man, I really didn't want to have to sit through that fucker's crap,' says another volunteer.

'So much for supporting free speech,' says a young white woman, looking disgusted at her fellow students.

Redhead rolls his eyes at her.

'Dear God. They're rioting at MLK,' says a trustee, his white goatee quivering. 'What is happening? We used to be such a peaceable community.'

'This is not democracy,' says the other trustee, an elderly black lady, 'this is hooliganism.'

'Now,' Hakam repeats to Monty who is staring, dazed by the flurry of events. 'We have to go, Monty.'

Two of Hakam's people have appeared, seemingly from nowhere, an Asian man and a young white woman. They cover our flanks while Hakam takes point, leading the way down the ramp and out the side exit which was our contingency plan. Monty stops short halfway down the ramp.

'I'm not going to be carried,' he says firmly. 'I want my own car.'

Hakam scowls at the black SUV, one of three parked in the accessway. 'We don't have time, Monty. We have a credible threat against you.'

'You're being ridiculous,' Monty says, not budging. 'They were only agitating against Énard. Now that he's not coming—'

Hakam makes a sound. 'You don't get it. You're the target now. There's a lot of angry fanatics out there who want blood. They're after you.'

Monty's face drains. He stares at Hakam, eyes screwed up in an inscrutable expression. It's hard to tell if he's furious or on the verge of crying. 'Me? The fuck you talking about? It was Énard!'

'It *was*. Now it's you. That's how it works. You know the drill. This is a photo-op, a media magnet. They need their pound of fame. Whatever it takes. You'll do.'

Monty isn't ready to deal with this; he's still processing the fact that Énard isn't coming. The idealist in him really believed that the talk would happen as planned, confirming his conviction in the enduring power of American democracy. News flash, bro: American democracy is what the richest, most powerful, meanest guy in the room says it is at any given point in time; right now, that dude is named Intolerance.

'I need my car,' he says instead, rolling down the rest of the rampway and turning toward the front of the building.

Hakam blocks his way, bends down and says gently, with genuine kindness, 'There's no time. We really have to get you home right now, Monty. We'll have it picked up later.'

'No!' he says. 'I need my own car. I can't get the wheelchair into your ride!'

'It's OK. I'll carry you myself. It's the only way right now. I'm sorry.'

Monty's lower lip quivers. I know what that means, even though I've never actually seen Monty cry before. I know it from Ricky, from the moment after I cut him and before he died. It stabs at my insides.

'I'll get it,' I interject, breaking up their face-off which has nowhere left to go but down. I don't want to see Monty cry; I can't see Monty cry. 'I'll bring it round the back and meet you guys there.'

Hakam is saying something even as I'm sprinting up around Echelon House to the front parking lot where the Tesla is parked. I pay no heed: he's smart enough to know that ordering Monty out to get him to safety is one thing, but picking him up and bundling him into a van to be carried all the way home like a child is the worst thing he could possibly do to a disabled person. It's the kind of humiliation Monty will never forgive. Hakam is efficient and loyal enough to not care right now: his only priority is Monty's safety. But I think he'll give me the few minutes more it will take to bring the vehicle around. At least I hope he will. Even in duress, dignity matters. In fact, the worse the situation, the more it matters. When the chips are down, what else do we really have except our dignity?

The gates to the compound are wide open and unattended. About half an hour ago, when I last checked, there were at least two OPD black and whites cross-parked outside, blocking the way. They're gone now and from the sound of sirens, shouts and general disturbance further down the street, I'm guessing they got the word that the speech wasn't happening and took off to join their buddies at MLK. As if on cue, a red Fire Department ambulance flashes past, lights and sirens going. A few seconds later, a Sheriff's vehicle blazes past too. The overlapping sirens, combined with the other commotion out in the dark evening, adds a sense of spiraling chaos.

Monty's SUV has only one front passenger seat, the rest of the space left open to allow him free access. I can't stand crouched and drive, and if I sit on the floor I won't be able to see over the wheel.

There's a cardboard box on the passenger seat. Monty requested me to bring it when we rode up from his place; hardcover copies of Énard's books, the ones that are translated into English. When we arrived, I had to get out to speak to the officers manning the gates, so Monty told me to leave the box and get it later. I pull it off the seat and on to the floor. It's just high enough to serve as a temporary seat. The edges of the box squish down under my haunches, but the books hold my weight.

I push the ignition button and use the hand controls to drive out the gates then turn right. Instantly, I see the fire down the block, and the flames of tiki torches and the Christmas lights of the 911 vehicles. There are a mess of fireworks going off too, and the night sky blazes with color and sparkles as they go up, while crackers and what sound like cherry bombs go off at several places at once. The uproar swells and what might be gunshots or maybe just M-80s ring out. Shit is going down. My phone has been pinging constantly with notifications and updates, but I can't waste time checking on the latest: it's obvious the clashes at MLK have erupted into violence.

As I start to turn the corner to drive around the boundary

wall of Echelon House, several dark-clad figures come sprinting up the street, waving menacing objects.

They're dressed in the anonymous uniforms of black bloc activists: black clothing, ski masks, scarves, stoles, sunglasses, hoodies, bike helmets, even a Guy Fawkes mask. In case you're not up to scratch on social activists these days, that's the ubiquitous 'uniform' they use to anonymize themselves, make individual details harder, if not impossible, to detect, and escape criminal investigation. It's hard to tell if they're all part of the same group or rivals, but right now, they're all running away from something. The cops, most likely. Nobody is hot on their heels so far as I can see, which is only to be expected with a couple of thousand protestors loose and maybe a hundred cops at most to deal with them.

The runaways see me and slow briefly, then when they realize I'm not law enforcement, speed up, coming straight at me. These dudes are lusting to do as much damage as possible tonight and I'm available. They're waving baseball bats, metal pipes, a couple of two by fours, and a few have knives. But it's the one with the revolver that I'm watching. He stops running and takes aim at me, not just the vehicle but at me personally, in the driver's seat. Fucker doesn't give a shit who he shoots: mayhem is the point.

I gun the accelerator as the revolver flashes and the bullet whickers off the windshield. The Tesla is bulletproof, of course. Son of a billionaire's car. If I can get Monty into it, we'll be safe. I want him to live through this night and come out safe and sound, for my own selfish reasons – tonight might even be the night we end up talking further about his memories of his father's past misdeeds, if our earlier convo was any indication – but also because it simply isn't right that a beautiful human being like Monty Cordry should be the target of such random, misplaced violence. Don't you have real human monsters out there who deserve your attention, asshole? Suddenly, I want to take this bastard down. I aim the two-ton vehicle straight at the shooter. The bastard shot to kill, I don't intend to show him any mercy. But he's an agile fucker, leaps out of the way like a Parkour pro. I hear something thump against the undercarriage but it doesn't feel big enough to be a person; maybe the gun, or a baseball bat. The others scatter. Yeah, run, you asswipes: go target another Capitalist. This one's already taken.

Hakam's people are at the back gate, scanning up and down the street as well as checking the houses just in case. Hakam is hanging back, with Monty.

He gestures to Monty, who rolls out on to the curb as I open the door and push the box of books behind the passenger seat. The wheelchair ramp is already winding its way down.

Shouts, sirens and fireworks – or gunshots, it's hard to tell for sure with all the competing noises out there – vie with screeching vehicles, and a metal-and-glass-voiced boom that sounds like a vehicular collision.

A roar goes up from a street or two over: sounds like the mob is enjoying its run-in with the authorities.

I'm betting this shitshow has the climate change march beat for action, but who knows these days; it's not really the issue at hand, it's the rage in their hearts that drives this kind of violence. Those kids out there are wreaking havoc even though the talk got called off, or maybe *because* it got called off.

Monty rolls up the ramp and Hakam starts to get in, then sees the lack of seating.

'I'll ride home with Monty,' I tell him.

He holds eye contact for a second, comes to a decision, exits.

'I'll drive,' Monty says. His voice brooks no argument. I wouldn't want it otherwise: the driver's side and shotgun seat have the only two seatbelts and airbags.

I strap in as he starts down the street. Hakam's SUV is in the lead, with the second SUV bringing up the rear.

'Avoid Hampshire,' I suggest.

He doesn't reply but turns left on Oak, skipping Hampshire. I'm still hyper-alert. That asshole taking a potshot at me has me worried. Despite Hakam's team, the police presence and the wail of yet more approaching sirens, I have no illusions. If Rappaport and his peeps really want to hurt Monty, they can always find a way.

'Thank you,' Monty says quietly as we wait at the Merck Clinic crossroad while a half-dozen FD and PD vehicles fly past, lights and sirens burning the night. As Hakam starts across the intersection, Monty follows. 'For everything.'

'Cool,' I say. 'I'm sorry the talk didn't —'

I never see the truck that comes out of Elm and smashes into us, never hear the boom of impact or feel the bulletproof window bouncing off my head when I'm slammed sideways, never see the bulletproof glass starring but not shattering. It's only the seatbelt that saves me, that and the fact that the truck struck the driver's side of the vehicle at a precise angle, just the right angle to punch the driver's side door into Monty, deflecting the energy diagonally and forward.

Turns out it wasn't bullets or knives we had to worry about.

Later, I will learn it was a Dodge Ram doing at least 120, lights off, and even though Hakam and his crew are on it less than twenty seconds after the collision, the driver gives them the slip while a bunch of possibly unrelated activists exchange fire with Hakam and his team, mistaking them for right-wing opponents, whooping mob crows at the wreckage. Hakam is naturally more concerned with checking on Monty, and although his crew chases the bastard/s for several blocks, there are too many other dark-clad peeps scurrying around for them to tell one apart from the others. They will be hung up four blocks away by Sheriff's deputies who see them running with guns drawn and draw on them, forcing them to end pursuit while the driver and accomplices get away. The Ram itself has been stolen just that afternoon and there's no DNA or prints found inside that will supply any useful leads.

I will survive with a concussion – not my first – and a few bruises and pulled muscles.

Monty's body is protected by the heavily armored side-plates that buckle but don't fully yield even after being, well, rammed by the Ram.

But the side-on impact throws his head sideways then back against the driver's side window, where it connects with an impact hard enough to give him a contracoup brain injury, which in turn causes an acute subdural hematoma and a dural rupture. EMTs are on the scene within three minutes and try to stabilize him on-site, but they're too late.

Monty Cordry is declared dead on arrival.

When I'm questioned – by Abdi, by the cops, the feds, and I don't know who else – I say the same thing over and over again. 'All I saw was a big black shape coming at us, then it hit and we went over, and I lost consciousness for a minute. By the time I came to, all I could see was Monty. Then Hakam was by my window. I never saw the driver, or even the car, really. It all happened so fast.'

But in truth, I do see something.

There are a few seconds between the instant I regain consciousness and Hakam gets to me and Monty.

In that small sliver of time, a face appears at my window, looking in.

The face has a black mask on, only the eyes and mouth are visible.

Brown eyes.

Brown girl.

'Ki,' she says, anxiously. 'You OK?'

I glare back at her.

I'm mad.

Even at that moment, half-dazed, not sure if I'm alive or dead, broken or whole, I'm mad.

The kind of anger that can only spark up between sisters.

'What the fuck, Hannah?' I say hoarsely.

Then she says, 'Huh.'

Just that one word.

And she grins.

And disappears, like the Cheshire Cat.

Because she knows that if I'm able to croak angrily at her and think clearly enough to be mad at her, then that means I'm alive and going to be all right.

She's right about that.

But she has no idea how mad I am with her at this moment.

She's my sister, goddamn it.

She isn't supposed to be here.

This is my mission, my call to make.

I *chose* to call it off, to *not* kill Monty Cordry.

But she decides to step in and kill him anyway.

Damn it, Hannah.

What? You thought Hannah and Kiara were the same

person? Whatever made you think that? If you've been paying close enough attention, you'd have seen that we're two separate women with separate voices and personalities. She's older than me by two years. She's my sister.

And she has no idea how mad I am with her at this moment.

# Entr'acte

# Roger

Roger presses the heel of his palm against the cold plate-glass window in Monty's bedroom and looks out at the three snow-capped peaks on the far horizon: Mission Peak, Mount Allison and Monument Peak have already received more than their due of snowfall this season, as has the rest of California. They look spectacular. This view was largely the reason why Monty chose this house. The thought that he will never look out at it again is unbearable. It makes Roger want to erase the scene from existence, to obliterate it by a nuclear strike, burn it down to the ground. If Monty no longer exists in this world, neither should those peaks.

He turns away, heading to the refrigerator and picking out a bottle of water which he sips.

He feels like he's losing his mind.

To lose one son was a blow.

To lose a second feels like Armageddon.

He chose not to remarry after his union with Gabriella was dissolved. The experience taught him that he was not a marriageable man; or even a companionable one. He elected to keep himself company thereafter, and has found no reason to question the decision.

He has lady friends, a far smaller number than people impudently assume, and those assignations are comfortable and comforting, but he has never cultivated or maintained close friendship with anyone for too long. It was always the knowledge of his own sons, his flesh and blood, out there in the world – living, breathing, going about their lives, be they as they may, engaging, interacting, influencing and being influenced, their existence on this physical plane – that brought him the greatest satisfaction. The paternal pride of fatherhood; the knowledge that his seed, his DNA, has proliferated and will outlive him. Of knowing he had contributed something to the world which is beyond the daily fluctuations of the stock market or the vagaries of big business. Something real. Something human.

It's also the warmth of sharing blood, life, filial links with his own, with pack, with family. Of being able to pick up a phone, or fly out in a private jet for a lunch or a dinner, and share space and time with his own blood-children. To see the two handsome young men who will continue his legacy after he is gone and hopefully, someday, extend that legacy through their own offspring.

And now that is gone.

Erased.

Obliterated.

The best parts of himself are gone from this world and all he has left now are possessions and things.

In the balance sheet of karma, his accomplishments have yielded a zero sum return.

What does he have to show for these nearly five decades on the planet now?

First Ricky.

Then Monty.

Why?

That is what maddens him. The unanswered questions. The enigma of departure.

Why Ricky, and now, why Monty?

Why *his* sons? Why his *sons*? Why *both* his sons?

He feels the rage flaring again, and this time, can't bring himself to repeat the breathing exercise. He needs to experience this rage. To feel something other than hopeless, paralysing grief. Anger is a gift.

When Ricky was murdered, he did everything he could – within the confines of the law – that was humanly possible, yet was left with no answers. Even now, the investigation continues, driven by his limitless resources and Hakam Abdi's relentless, checkbook-fueled persistence. Over time, slowly, very painfully, Roger somehow overcame the helplessness, the despair at being unable to make sense of that horrific tragedy. Yet it still rankles. The frustration that all his power, wealth, influence, connections could not secure a lucid answer.

Monty's enduring support played a major role in his overcoming the shock and grief, expensive consultants helped with the anger management, and even then, more than a few business rivals and people who made the mistake of crossing him at that most sensitive of times paid the price for Roger's lack of closure. For a time there, he almost lapsed back into the old Roger. The man he had worked so hard to leave behind in the fog bank of the past. There was a moment, an empowering yet terrifying moment, when he thought, *why the fuck not? Who am I pretending to be Mr Good Guy for anyway?* The world had fucked him over, he wanted . . . *needed* to fuck it over in return. That old Roger, his dark passenger, had never truly left him, had always ridden in the back seat, smugly biding his time in the darkness back there; the shock of Ricky's death had propelled him into the shotgun seat, had flashed him the green light, and it would have been easy to yield control then, to let that guy take the wheel and drive all the way to the hellmouth, because a part of Roger knew, had always known, that was the final destination keyed into his life's GPS, and he had always been destined to end up there anyway.

Monty was the reason he had resisted and fought the desire for self-destruction. Grappled the dark passenger and forced him back into the back seat, way, way back.

Monty, his sweet, beautiful, bleeding-heart liberal genius of a son, who was everything Roger (and Ricky) and Gabriella were not, yet so brilliant and successful in his own hippy-dippy way. Monty had given Roger a reason to stay the course, to keep it positive, to resist giving in to his dark side. Every time he was about to lose control in those dark days after Ricky's murder, Roger had only to think of Monty or to call him for a quick chat and it had left him feeling better, that there was still something – some*one* – worth living for. *Think of Monty* had become a life mantra.

He had become a better man because of his sons.

He was a sane man because of Monty.

He didn't know how he would have survived Ricky's death if Monty hadn't been there. Simple answer: he wouldn't have. Not as Roger fucking Cordry, that was for sure. The dark passenger would have taken over, have owned him, just as he had once, a long time ago, a dark, dangerous time. And while that might have been something he could get away with back then, when he was a nobody, it would be impossible to do so now. No. He couldn't afford to give in to that side of himself, the worst side; it would be his ruin. Monty had helped him keep that monster at bay.

Now, Monty is gone too. Lost in another mindless, meaningless tragedy. And who will Roger turn to for help now?

Roger feels ... *knows* ... that this time, he can't lull his confusion, rage and grief by consoling himself with karmic explanations and meme-gif platitudes. Even a hundred Deepak Chopras billing him a hundred thousand dollars a session can't talk him out of this one. And the only person he could speak to about Monty's death, the one person in the world who might have anchored him long enough to find his bearings again, was Monty himself. In losing Monty, Roger has lost more than a son. He's lost the best friend he ever had. The only friend.

Like all super-rich, super-famous individuals, there came a point in his life when he could no longer trust anyone, not a wife, girlfriend, business partner, former college-buddy, therapist, doctor . . . *nobody*. Everybody wanted something from him. If not an actual ask, then their own agenda. He was always a doorway to something they sought, a gateway to the impossible, an opportunity to be exploited. 'If I could just have five minutes with Roger Cordry . . .' was like a mantra to Gen Z. Everyone had an angle. It was only a matter of time before it came out, no matter how obliquely. The fix was always in.

And in these days of instant sharing, it only took one recorded convo or secretly clicked pic to monetize their secret fantasy, or kickstart it.

Roger had been burned too often to ever trust again.

Oh, he had burned them back, for sure; he had to send a clear message to other potential gold diggers. Mess with the bull, you get the horns. If someone touched a magic wand to the statues of the defiant girl and the bull on Wall Street and they came alive, what did you think would happen? That little girl wouldn't be the one left standing, that was for sure. It was a dog-eat-dog world, and Roger was a very, very big dog indeed. Dire wolf to all the stray mutts who thought maybe they could be the exception to the rule and get past his guard to get just one teensy weensy favor out of him. He had to slap them down hard so the next one would think twice.

So, OK, maybe he slapped them a little too hard at times. So much so that they could never get up again.

Like the nurse in the post-op private room at Cedars Sinai who had somehow found a way to leak out private info about his stay there and monetize it so she could get 'just a little help' for her disabled son-in-law. What she had gotten instead was fired. He hadn't taken any pleasure in having her sacked and deprived of health insurance when she needed the money and the coverage so desperately, but it was necessary to drive home the message.

The same went for the movie star he had dated for a while. When that sex tape 'leaked', and she had begun trending on the socials, he had made it his personal mission to make sure she never worked in that town again: her 'go' projects were canceled, studios stopped calling, directors skipped meetings with her and sent their interns instead, audition tapes got erased, and a major movie already in pre-release suddenly got yanked from the schedule – it was still lying in the cans, unreleased. She was now eking out a living on a reality show on a free-to-view YouTube channel, the kind where everyone has to live naked on a desert island and survive insects, animals, and all kinds of creepy crawlies. From Oscar nominated to breakfasting on bugs: the Julie Seymour Story.

Yessir, you mess with Roger Cordry, you get the horns. Both prongs, right in your guts. Hook and rip, no mercy.

It was the way the world worked and how it had worked for him, and it damn well worked the same way for everyone.

Monty had had some harsh words to share about Roger's treatment of those unfortunates. What was that phrase he'd used? He told Roger to 'check your privilege'.

Privilege: that word everyone loved to toss about these days. Sure, Roger knew he was privileged. But he was no to-the-manor-born aristo. He was a brown immigrant in the white, white West. A Chennai pharmacist's son who had built one of the largest financial empires in the world. One of the Ten Richest Men in the World, boo fucking ya. He had damn well earned his privilege. And the only way you were going to take any of it away from him was by prying it out of his cold, dead hands. It belonged in there with the sacred Second Amendment: the right to bear arms and be powerful, a God-given privilege of every American citizen. And if you didn't like powerful, rich men, like Roger and his Tea Party buddies, then you could go back to whatever mortar-shelled hellhole you had crawled over from. And take your bleeding heart with you, if you please.

But to Monty he had said only, OK, son. I'll try to do better.

Because it was Monty.

And if the dark passenger riding in the shadows back there was a monster who had to be leashed at all times, then Monty was the sunshine angel who lit up the world with hope and optimism that Roger hadn't thought possible outside of a Disney movie.

And now that Monty is gone, that sunshine has gone out of Roger's life.

All that's left is a heart-sized hole in the center of his being.

And the dark passenger.

He calls his PA Sharon while he's walking out to the car. 'The Fremont house. The one Monty lived in. I want it gone.'

Her response is sympathetic. 'I understand. I'll have it listed.'

'No. I don't want it sold. I want it burned down to the ground.'

A moment of silence. She's accustomed to his odd instruc-tions but is trying hard to strike a balance between sounding sympathetic and telling him he can't get what he wants this time. 'That may be difficult. The Fire Department probably wouldn't allow it. The house probably contains materials that could produce toxic fumes, things like that.'

He gets into the car. It starts moving at once. He looks through his tinted window at the retreating property. 'Then I want it taken down, brick by brick, plank by plank. Then have everything carted somewhere where they don't have as strict a fire code and have it all burned down to ashes. I want there to be nothing left but a bare patch of ground. The property isn't to be listed, leased, sold or used for any pur-pose, official or personal. I want it left like that, empty and bare. Am I understood?'

He disconnects the call.

Hakam is about to sit in the chair opposite to Roger.

'You can stand,' Roger says, his voice as hard as he knows his face must appear. He's not in a friendly mood today, and Hakam is no friend. It's time the man remembered that he's little more than an overpaid fixer and is replaceable. Everyone and everything is replaceable when you can afford unlimited replacements.

Hakam remains standing without comment. His inscrut-able face reveals no trace of his feelings. He has seen every shade of Crayola in Roger's mood-coloring box, and then some.

He brings Roger up to date on Monty's homicide. That's what SFPD is calling it officially, although Roger already knew that. Most of what Abdi recites is familiar chapter and verse but Roger listens anyway. Repetition is necessary to solving a problem. Most solutions come by trying out minute variations on the same process. It's something Roger learned in chemistry, applied to pharmaceuticals, and it applies to investigative science as well. Go over the facts. Everything you need is almost always right there, looking you in the face. You have to learn to spot it and weed it out of all the other stuff.

As the media has already reported, Monty was killed by what appears to be an anarchist activist protesting Énard's talk, or protesting the protest against the talk; in the tangled web of left-to-the-right-of-the-center mess that is political activism these days, either motive is equally plausible, the methods equally likely to be violent. In any case, the unknown assailant was driving a stolen Dodge Ram doing at least 120 mph at the time of impact, had kept all lights off, and even though Hakam and his crew were on it less than a minute after the collision, the driver had already abandoned the vehicle. He then gave them the slip and disappeared into the night. Hakam's team glimpsed more than one black-clad masked figure sprinting away a few blocks from the collision, but it was impossible to be sure if any or all of them were the persons involved.

Over 4,700 persons were apprehended that day in the violence that erupted on both sides of the Bay. There was literally insufficient space to hold that many. The authorities were certain that Monty's hit-and-run driver had to be one of that number, but if they were, then they were never identified and charged. Once again, through a bizarre mix of circumstance and timing, there are too many possible suspects. The person about whom Alameda PD received an anonymous text message tip, Jordan Rappaport, was apprehended almost an hour before Monty's death. There was nothing to implicate him in the incident.

Kiara, who was in the van with Monty that night, survived with a concussion, a few bruises and pulled muscles, and, after being kept overnight for observation, was discharged from hospital. She's still under observation – by Hakam's people – but she was obviously not the one driving the Dodge Ram.

Monty's assistant, Melinda, proved another dead end. She was questioned in connection with her association with Rappaport and other extremists as well as for her ominous warnings to Monty in the days prior, but that had led nowhere. Melinda turned out to be just another privileged young white woman from a rich family who had felt compelled to try to make up for the wrongs of her ancestors; her involvement was purely symbolic. Apart from taking part in a few protests, chanting slogans, donating to Black Lives Matter, holding up placards and the like, she had done nothing violent, certainly nothing that came close to willfully killing a disabled young man in a vicious hit-and-run.

At the funeral, she had been one of the most distraught, and Hakam informed him that she had returned home to her family in Baton Rouge and was under psychiatric treatment for her mental trauma at the loss. She blamed herself for being part of the protest movement that demonized Monty and appeared to be genuinely contrite. Roger didn't give a fuck about her contrition or her general mental wellbeing, quite honestly, but he had been polite, if cool, at the funeral when she broke down and had even asked one of his people to make sure she got home safely. She too, like Jordan Rappaport, was still under observation but there was no real connection there to Monty's murder as far as anyone could see. Later, when she's no longer in the public eye, he will have Hakam Abdi go after her, punish her somehow for even conspiring with the activists, one of whom might have been Monty's killer. Whether that punishment is public humiliation and ignominy, lawsuits that tie her up for the rest of her life and drain all her family's finances, or actual physical retaliation, he will decide later – or perhaps he will leave it up to Hakam, who has done this before for Roger and will find a punishment that befits the misdeed.

There is nothing else to go on. Surveillance cameras of houses on the street, at the Merck Clinic, on the route the driver had supposedly taken after the hit-and-run, have been more conflicting than helpful: even with high-resolution enhancements and facial recognition software, it's hard to be sure which of the dozens of black-clad figures running about on those streets was in fact the driver. Either the killers had planned the murder very deviously, or it had been, as one working theory went, a for-real accident.

This theory proposed that the driver might simply have boosted the SUV as a means of escape from the cops chasing them and their associates through the streets, and it was only bad timing that had led them to burst out of that alley just when Monty was passing on an otherwise deserted street.

Roger hates that theory.

It's like karma sticking up a thumb at him and cackling: these things happen, dude.

But theories and suppositions are all he has left.

At least Kiara survived.

Roger hasn't met her after the accident, or visited her in hospital, but his people have instructions to make sure that all her expenses and treatment are covered, whatever it takes. Like most young millennials she has no health insurance and could ill afford the bill, based on Hakam's check of her finances.

As Hakam approaches the end of his daily recitation, Roger finds himself circling back to the same conclusion.

He blames himself personally for Monty's death.

He should have done more.

For one thing, he should have dissuaded Monty from going ahead with the talk. Sure, Roger had tried. In fact, on that last FaceTime, it was the closest he had come to losing his temper with his son. It had been impossible to shake Monty's resolve. As stubborn as his mother, although Gabriella would say the exact opposite: 'as bull-headed as his father'. Roger should have lost his temper. He should have paid off Énard. He should have called in a favor from the Mayor and asked him to shut down the talk. Or the Dean of the university. Or SFPD. He should have called whomever and done whatever it took. But as Monty had pointed out to him on the last video call: he wasn't going to live his life with presidential-level security and loss of privacy, so back off, Dad.

It doesn't really matter anymore.

The time for doing, for saving, for talking, is past.

Monty is dead. Whatever Roger does or says now, nothing will change that.

'If it even was an assassin,' Hakam continues. 'SFPD and the FBI's joint task force are of the opinion that it was a black-mask protestor. They expected Énard to be in the passenger seat of that vehicle, with Monty driving. They believe he, not Monty, was the target of the driver.'

'And yet it was Monty who got hit. Not Énard. Not Kiara. Not you, Hakam, or any one of your agents. Only Monty who died. Everyone else walked away unscathed. I have problems with that.'

They go over the timeline in greater detail, slicing each

minute down to the seconds, then the microseconds. Roger has asked for a 3D animatic to be made recreating the crash and they watch it together. It's been designed by an Oscar-winning art director and executed by the same firm that pre-visualizes the visual effects sequences in $250 million dollar movies produced by a studio Roger owns a controlling interest in. He pauses it and asks more questions. They are at it for hours, taking only bathroom breaks and replenishment breaks. At some point, Hakam seats himself without asking permission and Roger grudgingly refrains from ordering him to remain standing. He has made his point; no point being churlish. Besides, Hakam is his best shot at finding his sons' murderers.

At the end of the grueling day-long process, Roger is no wiser than when he began. It all seems to come down to either a brilliantly planned and executed assassination by an unknown assailant or assailants who then vanished without a trace, or the work of some cosmic force that aligned several things at once perfectly. He doesn't believe in cosmic forces.

'This can't be the work of just a student protestor,' he says at last, staring out at nothing, seeing only Monty's face, laughing, talking, whirling around on his wheelchair. 'It's too precisely timed, too perfectly executed. Whoever drove that Ram knew exactly when Monty was leaving, which vehicle he would be traveling in, where he was seated, which street he would take . . . There are too many elements here for it to be just some activist striking it lucky. Besides, there still haven't been any groups claiming responsibility for the event, have there?'

Hakam sounds ambivalent. 'Several anarchist – ultra-left as well as ultra-right – groups have "celebrated" the incident for their own variety of reasons.' He uses air quotes. 'It could be they don't want to take credit directly because it would bring down too much heat. The core leadership in such groups tends to be a pretty small, tight group, often just a handful of individuals. Once a group claims the hit, it wouldn't be hard to track each of the ringleaders and pin them down.'

Roger feels even more frustrated than before. 'So it could be anybody. But it isn't. This is personal. It has to be. First, Ricky, now Monty. This has to do with me. I feel it.'

Hakam says cautiously, 'I'm not disagreeing. That's the strongest theory we've been working on since Day One, but it's also the one theory for which we've found absolutely zero evidence. Besides, they're both such different methodologies. If this is some kind of serial killer with a family fetish —'

Roger slams his palm down hard on the conference table. Mugs, plates, glasses, paperclips and laptops jump and rattle. 'This isn't some serial killer, Hakam. It's an assassination. Assassins use whatever method works in each scenario. It's no different from political targets, except that I'm the common link here, not an ideology.' He thinks about that a moment. 'Unless it's some ultra-left group backed by one of my rivals. In that case, there could be a political angle too. My Tea Party affiliations are public knowledge. So are my campaign donations.'

'We've got a separate team in DC looking into that angle. Everything we get is being fed into the common database, which my analysts go over in real time as new data comes in. But if it's political, then why target your sons? Why not you directly? You would be a prime target. Political assassinations are about sending a message, making a loud bang in the media. These were quiet, off-the-grid murders, few or no outside witnesses, no "audience" to play to. Our analysts . . .'

Roger cuts him off brusquely. He doesn't give a shit about the analysts. He knows they're capable of deducing completely contradictory conclusions given the same set of facts; it's what causes the uncompromising dualistic dichotomy that plagues all contemporary news analysis these days. CNN or Fox News, no middle ground. 'Maybe because I'm too hard to get to? Or because they want me to suffer first and then come after me? Who the fuck knows. I just feel it in my bones, this is personal. Keep digging. Pursue anything, however unrelated and irrelevant it seems.'

Hakam rises with Roger. 'We already have a sizable task force working on it, coordinating with authorities in the US as well as Switzerland and other countries where we're following up on leads. The budget is . . .' He names a figure.

Roger buttons his jacket. 'Double it. Triple it. Same goes for the task force. I don't care. Put all the bodies and funding you need behind it. I don't want to be bothered with logistics and invoices. These are my sons, my family we're talking about, for fuck's sake. I want results. Get me something. Get me anything.'

As they walk out, Hakam asks, 'Sir, if you are right, and these people are targeting your family, then shouldn't we at least warn your ex-wife? She was Ricky and Monty's mother. They might go after her next. She should increase her personal protection measures to be on the safe side. I could arrange a team.'

Roger thinks about that for all of half a second before saying: 'Fuck her.'

Hakam seems confused for once. 'Should we at least warn her that there could be a potential threat to her life? Perhaps even her family?'

He means Gabriella's new husband, and new kids, one a

step-daughter from a previous marriage, the other a young daughter from the new husband.

Roger shakes his head once, decisively. 'Don't bother. I don't give a shit what happens to them. But have them surveilled, just in case. If the assassins take them out, we could get more evidence to work with. Don't interfere if there's an assassination attempt, just observe. Consider them bait. Expendable bait.'

Hakam offers no further comment.

The ride down in the elevator is a silent one.

# ACT 3
# Kiara & Hannah & Roger & Reitmaier

# 33

## KIARA

I love coming home. The smell of the sea, the palm trees, the red soil of Goa, it all smells like paradise to me. The familiar colors and sounds and sights of Vagator are manna to my senses. Each time I emerge from Dabolim Airport into the coastal air of my mother's home town feeling like everything I did while away in the wicked wide world was worth it; it was so I could come home to my family, knowing I've earned my time with them.

This time it's different.

Even the sea smells sour. A nauseating stench wafts into the auto-rickshaw from somewhere, making me crinkle my nose in disgust; I cover my mouth with my blouse sleeve. Seeing my reaction in the rearview and mistaking me for an off-season tourist, the driver explains that the stench is coming from medical waste dumped by private hospitals into the river. Typical. The fucking unauthorized dumping has started up again, because the bastards know it's the off-season and this is their chance to cut corners and costs. A municipal employee or ten have been paid off again.

I listen to the driver, a native Goan Catholic from Saligao, droning on and nod in all the right places. Right now, I don't have the bandwidth to outrage over the corruption. Or the growing inequality caused by the rich European and diaspora Indians who continue to swarm into Goa and gentrify the beautiful, old-world Portuguese charm of the state. Or even the growing saffron tide that is washing through our once inclusive, tolerant, diverse communities. Or any of the hundred other problems that are now infused in our beautiful lady's bloodstream like the drugs that flow through like a perennial torrent.

My head is too full of rage at Hannah.

(That isn't her real name, of course, just as Kiara isn't mine. They're mission identities we both built carefully over years, leaving a curated internet and credit trail. And call me paranoid, but I'm not about to break the habit by telling you our real names here.)

I haven't seen my sister again since that night in San Francisco when she fell out of the Dodge Ram and stumbled away down the alleyway into the darkness.

The night Monty died.

Correction.

The night she killed Monty.

Murdered him by smashing a two-ton pick-up truck into our vehicle at 120 miles per hour. And almost killing me, incidentally.

I have a bone to pick with her.

Despite my anger at my sister, the sight of the villa soothes me somewhat. *Susegad*, it says to me, the Konkani word which is roughly the equivalent of 'Don't worry, be happy.' Its cheerful parakeet hues shout out gaily from its private grove of tall, gently swaying coconut palms. Birdsong and the distant shouts of children kicking a football barefoot from a nearby field are the only sounds. From time to time, the diesel grunts of the occasional passing truck, the impatient honk of a rickshaw or the drone of a motorbike on the nearest paved road about a kilometer away punctuate the calm, but for the most part, it's a quiet place. The dogs make up for that by rushing out to leap around the rickshaw as it pulls up, barking joyfully, leaping up to aim licks at my face even before I get down.

Ronaldo covers my right eye in slobber and I laugh in protest, bending over to grab and rub his wriggling body. That excites the others even more and I surrender, planting my ass down on the flagstones to let them have their way. They swarm over me and it feels so good to be missed. For a moment, I almost forget my anger at Hannah and what she did. Almost.

I have raised all of these lovelies myself; the older ones, Shania Twain and Lana Del Rey, were nurtured during the Ricky years when Hannah was away in Zurich. Shania and Lana are siblings and dams of this little doggie army, and look on proudly as their children and grandchildren dance and woof and expend their love on me. I don't forget to give them their due; they accept my petting and stroking and affectionate words and kisses with pleasure.

The house is furnished much as you might expect any old Goa home to be: low wooden armchairs with nylon woven backs and bottoms, a grandfather clock, colored-glass lamps, floral curtains, windows and doors painted bright primary colors, ancient ceiling fans hanging from the high beamed ceilings, stone floors and painted walls. Even a picture of the Sacred Heart of Jesus with a colored wall lamp highlighting the white Jesus's beatific, upturned face. Hannah likes it this way, she says it gives her a sense of tradition and community.

I have been trying to persuade her to sell, and move to a modern apartment in one of the many new developments that have overrun Goa, a place with modern appliances and amenities and a security system. She won't hear of it. I used to think I would wear her down over time, but of late I've begun to wonder if *I'm* the albatross chipping away at the rock of ages. Hannah can be obdurate; it's one of the many lovely qualities we share in common.

The pungent odor of pork sorpotel leads me to the kitchen, dogs following.

'No coming in the kitchen!' Hannah admonishes the dogs, holding up a red-stained wooden spatula.

Lana and Shania growl and nip at their puppies' tails to warn them to obey their mistress. The dogs retreat, leaving us alone in the old-fashioned Goan kitchen, painted wooden shelves laden with spices, balchão, pickle, and our grandmother's old cookbooks, large annual diaries in which she put down her recipes, amending and revising as the years wore on, and a few marginal notes on stray observations and thoughts – *Herbert dislikes vinegar!! What does he expect me to use instead? 'Sherry,' says the man. Pshaw!* – most written in the nascent months of her marriage, duly arranged to a suitable brahmin Portuguese Catholic from a respectable family.

When Hannah and I were growing up, we used to pore over the diaries and laugh over those comments. I'm not sure why that memory comes back to me right now; perhaps to remind me of how different we are these days, how far we've come from those precious few days of girlhood innocence. Our lives are compartmentalized into two distinct sections: Before Ma's death. After Ma's death. Like two acts in a Shakespearean tragedy. Except, of course, there are usually five acts in those melodramas: we are currently living through them.

Hannah opens her arms to greet me. 'Bring it in,' she invites.

I fold my arms over my chest and stare at her. I hope my

eyes are burning holes into her conscience and the heat from her own guilt is scorching her.

She raises her eyebrows heavenwards and lifts her shoulders, not saying anything.

'That's it?' I say, hearing the anger in my tone.

I try to dial it down. I don't want this to turn into a scene before the girls the very day of my return home after months. They don't deserve that.

But it's hard.

The anger is so palpable, I am almost shaking with rage. I would love to grab her by the hair and shoulders, shake her up and wrestle her down in the red Goa clay of our courtyard like we used to do when we brawled over a decision in a football match as girls.

She picks up her spatula and stirs something simmering on the stove. It smells of cinnamon and coconut.

'I had to do it,' she says, 'because it was obvious you weren't going to.'

'You stop to think that maybe I had a good reason?'

She cuts her eyes sideways. 'Your mission was to kill him. There was no reason not to do it.'

'Sure. And I was all set to do it. When the time was right.'

'When was the time going to be right? You were at it long enough.'

'Does that really matter? When you were partying with Ricky, did you keep a calendar? When I asked you about it, you were the one who told me that when you're in the field, on mission, you have to call it as you see it. Monty was my mission, I had a plan. You had no right to interfere.'

She cocks a brow as she slips on oven gloves. 'I had no right? Really, Ki?'

'I would have handled it!'

'I saw how you were handling it. You were falling for him! You two were like Ben Affleck and his girlfriend du jour. The only thing left was for him to give you a ring and set a date.'

'It wasn't like that and you know it. I liked him, yes. He was a great guy.'

'A great guy? Honestly?'

'I don't expect you to understand. You told me all about Ricky. He was an A-grade asshole. He used women. Objectified them. He deserved to get what he did. When you killed him, I didn't say a thing. I congratulated you on a great job when you came home from Zurich.'

'It *was* a great job. And so was San Francisco. That's two down in our book, sis. We got the fuckers. Let's celebrate.'

'You're not listening to me. Monty was not Ricky. He was different. He knew his dad isn't a good person, that he did some terrible things back in the day, that he hurt some people. He didn't know all the details but he heard his mom Gabriella and Roger fighting when he and Ricky were kids, and he overheard her saying some stuff. Back then, he thought it was the kind of thing that spouses say to each other when going through an ugly divorce, because that's what Roger told him when he asked, but once he was older he realized that, in Roger's case, it was all true. He knew his father was a bad man. And he was trying to make up for it.' I could still remember every word of our conversation that night. 'Monty was blazing his own trail. It took me a while to see that clearly. To get close enough to him so he opened up and showed me his heart. Until then, I was on mission one hundred percent. And then he opened up and told me all this. That's when I realized that Monty Cordry was not Roger Cordry. He was his own man. He rejected the things that his father stood for, and worked hard to distance himself from them and build his own name, make his own karma. He was a good person, Hannah, probably a better human being than a fuckhead like Roger Cordry deserved. He didn't deserve to die for his father's sins.'

'It was an act! Monty Cordry was the spawn of Roger fucking Cordry. He was every bit as guilty as his bastard father. Don't tell me you really fell for his "Look at me, I'm just a poor little rich paraplegic with an awful, awful dad! Feel sorry for me! Boo hoo! Come suck my dick" act, Ki. I thought you were smarter than that!'

I haul off and slap Hannah a good, tight one. She's untying her apron and is looking down, so it catches her unawares. She is rocked sideways, unbalanced by the impact, and grabs hold of the countertop for support just in time to keep from falling on to the steaming hot food.

'Goddamnit, Ki!' she yells. 'What the fuck?'

I jab a finger in the air, pointing at her. 'You have no right to mock me. I was the one on the mission. I was the one inside. I was there. I knew Monty. You didn't. So fuck you for making fun of my empathy, little Miss Terminator!'

She touches a finger to the edge of her mouth and holds it up. It comes away bloody. A thin line of crimson trickles out from the corner of her lips. She takes several deep breaths, exhaling slowly. 'OK,' she says. 'Maybe I deserved that. I was out of line . . .'

'Fucking right! You were out of line!'

'. . . I had no right to mock your feelings, but I was right to kill Monty Cordry. It needed to be done, and everything you've said just now only confirms what I already said, that you didn't have the stomach to go through with it.'

I walk away several steps, resisting the urge to smash something, throw things, break stuff. That's not me. That's

Hannah. She's the angrier, less patient one. She's the one who can stay calm enough to dissect a corpse without flinching or kill a naked lover with a scalpel without turning a hair, but loses her shit when it comes to personal confrontations. I'm usually the calmer, more centered one of us two around the house. Everyone knows that: our cousin Manuel, his wife Philomena, our other cousins, the aunties and uncles, the football coach, the teachers and the girls.

But right now, we're channeling each other, it seems. Body swap.

I walk around the living room, through the hallway and back to the kitchen. I haven't cooled off any by the time I complete the circuit, but it gives me something physical to do with my body instead of getting into an all-out dust-up with my sister.

If it comes right down to it, and I do fly at her, I will lose.

Even after two kids, and being off-mission for a few years, Hannah can still whup my ass, make no mistake about that. She's not just my big sister, she's physically bigger. And tougher. And meaner. And willing to do things I might balk at in the moment. That's why she took on Ricky, the tougher physical mission of the two, and gave me Monty. I could cause her some pain but in the end she would take my ass down.

But that isn't the reason I hold back. Right this moment, I'm mad enough to actually go at her. It wouldn't be the first time either. We've been in our share of fights, with each other, and together against others, and we have both been through too much shit to not have a bunch of unresolved anger issues. Still, I restrain myself because this is our home, the place where our girls live, where we live as a family. Our safe space. Our quiet place. Our haven. We don't allow violence in here. When we walk through that door, we leave it all behind. Right now, I'm finding that a hard thing to do, but somehow I manage. All the pictures of the girls on the wall, their bikes and stuff lying around, their shoes and dirty socks by the door, the smell of Hannah's cooking, help me regain control. This is not a mission; this is our home.

While I'm taking my time out anyway, I decide to go shower. I need to wash the salt of the journey off me.

The water pressure in the upstairs bathroom is lousy as usual, and with Goa's hard water, it takes forever to get the shampoo and conditioner out of my hair. Still, sitting on the cushioned stool in front of the old rosewood dresser – the same one our mother and grandmother brushed their hair before each night and morning – I feel better. The air is cool, cooler than it was when I left in October, and I'm glad to be home. Though it be ever so humble.

When I think I'm calm enough to talk again without getting physical, I go back to Hannah. She's sitting on the back porch, smoking a cigarette. Without asking her, I snatch it out of her mouth and suck on it like a junkie straight out of rehab, which I'm not. She doesn't object or ask me for it back, just lights up another one and smokes it casually. I avoid looking directly at her but can see her every expression and gesture in my peripheral vision, the way we both learned to do while training.

'You could have killed me too.'

My voice surprises me. I sound calm now. Almost sad, regretful, like a mourner at a Goan funeral, the way they apologize like they're personally responsible for your loss and hope you'll forgive them. Ah, Catholic guilt. They get you before your first Holy Communion and you're never truly free of it.

Hannah's head droops. Her voice is a hollow whisper. 'I know.'

Then, even softer: 'I'm sorry.'

Then, she says, still softly: 'I was worried about you, Ki. I was afraid you were taking too long, getting second thoughts. The mails you were leaving at our mail drop . . . they made me worry about you.'

'You had nothing to worry about, Han.'

'I wanted to act, to do something, before . . . well, before I reach a point where I can't do anything.'

I frown at her, trying to figure where she's heading with this. 'What are you talking about? We still have the main mission. Roger fucking Cordry. That's the big one. You could have waited till I finished with Monty and then put all your fury into taking down Roger Cordry. We even talked about maybe both of us going after him together, remember? We had that backup plan?'

She looks at me strangely. Are those tears in her eyes? Hannah, crying?

'What's wrong?' I ask her, unable to make sense of this sudden shift in her.

'There are no more backup plans for me, sis,' she says, 'no more missions. I'm done. That's why I wanted to do Monty, while I still could.'

'The fuck are you talking about, Hannah?'

She sucks in a deep breath and lets it out slowly. She's wearing a sleeveless tank top. She raises one arm and shows me her armpit, pointing to a little bump that to my clueless eye looks like nothing more than good muscle tone. 'The big C. I have lymphatic cancer. Hodgkin's.'

# 34

## *HANNAH*

The girls return like a summer storm ravaging the house. The dogs start barking the instant Manuel's motorbike turns down the dirt lane that leads to the villa. By the time Kiara steps off the last stair, they're in the front door and come barreling at her, two sun-browned dolls in football shorts and tees and cleats all caked with red mud, screaming at the tops of their voices. The dogs compete with them by barking raucously and dancing all around us. I barely catch Manu's wave and shout as the Norton roars away.

I swat at them ineffectually with my apron. 'Lucy! Megan! Auntie Ki's just had a bath! You're getting her all dirty again!'

Kiara grins to show she doesn't mind. A little honest dirt never hurt anyone; besides, she knows I yell at them enough for the both of us. Over the years, I've fallen into the role of the 'bad guy' parent while she's always the good one. But I'm happy to indulge them tonight. It feels so good to see them hugging and kissing and laughing together while the dogs bring the roof down with their yoodling and yowling.

'Kiara's home! Kiara's home!' they chant in perfect harmony, their voices indistinguishable. Lana picks up their pitch and sings, a perfect high-pitched yodeling yowl that makes the short hairs on my forearms stand up in pleasure. Shania joins her, her slightly gruffer tone complementing her sister's fine voice. The puppies and their parents form an enthusiastic chorus. There's nothing like a band of singing bassets to make one feel warm and gooey inside.

Ki grins up at me. Her eyes reflect the pain of my cancer revelation, but as agreed, she's trying hard not to let the girls see it. That was what I made her promise before they returned. Now, I shake my head in mock disapproval but can't help smiling back too. For what it's worth, the smiles are genuine. She waves me in. I join them in a group hug. Over the heads of my babies, I see the withheld tears glistening in Ki's eyes. I close my own eyes, saying a brief prayer for this, our little family.

Oh, blessed Mary. There's no place like home and no one like family. Thank you for all we have.

Dinner is a series of football stories which segue by dessert into eager questions about Kiara's time away. She tells them about the project she was working on with Monty Cordry, glancing at me from time to time as if challenging me to shut her down. I let her talk. I know she's in shock over my revelation and is talking too much to cover it up. The project was genuine, after all, and maybe Monty Cordry was the real deal too, if she's right. Obviously, she doesn't say anything about our assassin shenanigans: the girls don't know about that side of us. Hopefully, if we pull off the last part of our plan, they never will.

Either way, it's moot now, since he's dead and done.

Both girls listen with solemn attention. They have no clue about my adventures abroad, or the shit I got up to in Europe and Zurich for the Ricky Manfredi mission. They know about my and Kiara's birth and girlhood in the US, with occasional trips home to India, but like all children, they can't truly imagine their mother as ever being a little girl like them, so it's more mythic than real to them.

Auntie Ki, on the other hand, with her foreign trips and the gifts she always brings back to them, is the glamorous one, especially after this most recent San Fran excursion. She's avoiding looking at me by this time, because I know it makes her want to burst into tears. I keep my head averted too, listening, enjoying the domestic bliss of this situation, trying hard not to think about what it will be like for me to waste away and die in a hospital bed with my girls watching. At least, I tell myself, at least they'll have Kiara. For all our differences, now more than ever, we share a common love for these two little angels. That's what carries us through this difficult evening.

Then I feel the pain, like hot lava coursing through my veins, and I must have winced or something, because her face clouds over and she looks anxious. I give her a warning glance then look pointedly at the girls: I respect honesty and all that, but right now, I don't see any point in scaring them out of their wits. They're happy and innocent and I'd like them to stay that way as long as possible.

If push comes to shove and the chemo fails, and D'Souza tells me it's no good, I'm a goner, then yes, I will tell them. That could be three months, six months, a year down the road, maybe never, there's no way to be sure. After that first lecture, D'Souza chilled out and told me that there had been cases like mine which had seen a full recovery. There were new treatments coming up all the time. She even mentioned one by Cordry BioPharma which made me laugh out loud. D'Souza looked puzzled and irritated, but I thought it was funny in an ironic way. If and when I'm facing the wall, I'm going to tell the girls, but not one fucking day sooner.

I frown a time or two when Ki starts talking about the protests, which leads into a side-discourse about protests in general. She uses the Black Lives Matter movement against police brutality and the changes it wrought in the US as an illustration of a legit protest and I find myself frowning disapprovingly when she gets into a tad more graphic detail than I like. But I tolerate it because I know as well as she does that it's a violent, bloody world out there – and no matter how much we may want to protect our bunnies from its excesses, it's better if we guide them through those labyrinths than leaving them unprepared for the true extent of the cruelty. It's not a safe world for women, and to us women of color, it's filled with way more teeth and claws. These are teachable moments for our girls.

Both Ki and I learned those lessons in the hardest way imaginable. Innocence is not an option anymore. If there was ever an age when people actually lived in innocent bliss, which I doubt, it ended for us when Roger fucking Cordry destroyed our family. We don't want Lucy and Megan to have to grow up as we did. The money we've got stashed away for them won't help cushion the blows of actual heart-loss; it's only there to ensure they never have to do some of the things we had to do to survive. Dealing with the dirty games life plays is a barehanded task and they need to understand it before they can prepare to fight it themselves.

'Please tell us a story, Auntie Ki!' they plead when Kiara tucks them into bed. I'm perfectly happy to hang back and watch tonight. There's only so many times a mother can read *Goodnight Moon* and *I Am Brown* over and over before she burns out. I passed that point several hundred rereads ago.

The girls are both avid readers, as the bookshelves stacked with books attest, but they still love either Ki or me reading aloud or telling them stories. Best of all, they love it when we both tell one together, taking over the narration unexpectedly from each other or adding background effects and character voices as required. Tonight, I leave Ki to it, exiting the room to go downstairs. I've spent the last few months as the only Homer in the house. It's her turn to pick up the slack.

By the time she comes down, I'm stretched out on my favorite chair on the back porch, a glass of cashew feni and soda in my hand. She gives my drink and then me a look that I know all too well. I take a defiant sip. I know I'm not supposed to be mixing alcohol with my other meds, some of which she doesn't even know about, but hey, you try cooking and cleaning and running a household full of dogs and two madcap high-energy ballbusters all by your lonesome for a few months and then you earn the right to lecture me on taking a drink or two to unwind at the end of the very long day.

She's holding a beer and sips it while we sit together, staring out across the empty fields. Distant headlights pierce the darkness as the occasional bike or car drones by.

The insect zapper by the door crackles and fizzles constantly, working away busily. The younger dogs are all inside where it's warmer but Shania and Lana lie by our feet, their greying muzzles whistling with exhaled breaths. From time to time one of them attempts a snarl in her sleep, reliving some canine adventure fantasy. I rub the sole of my bare foot gently against Shania's haunch; the luxuriant fur makes my nerve endings tingle. Crickets keep time with the faltering heartbeat of some sleeping god. Fireflies sketch abstract outlines on a dark canvas. The alien beacons of a passenger plane headed for Dabolim pulse a warning.

Is there anything more comforting than a warm dog asleep at your feet, warm liquor in your belly, children asleep in their beds upstairs and the simple comforts of home? The knowledge that all your loved ones are under one roof, sleeping securely, and there are no wolves at the door tonight is the closest we get to bliss. For this fleeting moment in an otherwise uncertain life, all's right with the world. I rest my head against the lumpy cushion and let the exhaustion, alcohol and meds take me. I am almost dozing off when Kiara speaks at last.

'Why didn't you tell me sooner?' she asks.

I sigh inwardly. I wish we didn't have to go through this. I already know how it plays out. It's so predictable to me. But that's why a cliché is a cliché, because human behavior is pretty damn predictable.

'You were on mission,' I say.

'You could have told me in one of our emails.'

We use an anonymous, ultra-secure email drop to send coded messages to one another when traveling or on mission. Most of mine in the past year or so have consisted of updates about the girls, without using their real names or any real details, of course.

'Like I said, you were on mission.'

She turns to look at me, eyes boring into my temple. 'Come on, Han. This is big. You knew I'd want to know.'

I shrug and take another sip.

'You didn't want to tell me because you were already planning to come to SF and do Monty. That's what I think.'

'Maybe you think too much, sis. There's a time for thinking and a time to act. When on mission, you have to do things, not sit around thinking. Or worrying about sisters with cancer.'

'Maybe women with cancer shouldn't fly halfway around the world and kill people without telling their sisters.'

I'm tempted to take that bait, to launch into another fight.

Instead, I bite back my first retort, think for a minute, and opt for jocularity instead. 'Would you say that's a major statistic? Women with cancer who jet-set around the globe assassinating people? Is it like a thing that women do these days? There's a streaming show in there: Women With Cancer Who Slay.'

She's silent for a moment. Then she takes a long pull of her beer, and says, clearly, 'Fuck you, sis.'

Before Monty, we would have laughed at that exchange. Now, we both sit sullenly, stewing in our separate angst.

Then she tosses me a curveball.

'He wants me back in San Francisco.'

For a moment, I struggle to make sense of her words. Is she talking about Monty Cordry? Then it clicks. Roger fucking Cordry.

'Fuck him,' I growl drowsily, knuckling my eyes. When you eat spicy Goan food with your hands, even washing doesn't seem to get rid of the sting. You never, ever touch your fingertips to your eyes. Even Lucy and Megan learned to use their knuckles by the time they were eighteen months old.

'It's the project. He says he intends to go ahead with it. Because it was what Monty would have wanted. I think he means it, Han.'

I bite my lip. I was about to retort: Fuck Monty too. That won't go down well with Ki's present mood. In time, I expect her to grow out of the funk over my killing Monty Cordry, but right now, it's the bonfire between us and I don't want to light it up again. The girls (and the dogs) are sleeping peacefully, for one thing. I'm half-asleep too, and in no shape to fight anymore.

'You just got back, Ki.' I appeal to her sense of domesticity. Before San Francisco, before Monty Cordry, Ki was the more domestically inclined, the happily homebound one, the contented surrogate mom. (She doesn't cook as well as I do, but that's no biggie. There's a bunch of stuff I do better than her, always have, and she knows it. It's the price of being the big sister: I've been at it longer.)

'And you just found out you had Hodgkin's lymphoma, but it didn't stop you jetting across the world and committing murder,' she shoots back, straight from the hip.

I wait a moment before replying, letting the heat dissipate. 'I was there barely a week or so. In and out. You've been away ages. You can't go back now.'

'Why not? That's the last target. He's the one calling me. All I have to do is get on a plane and I'm there. Besides, it's not as if you're in any shape to build a new persona, take the time to get close to him, and take him out. So it has to be me anyway. Why not now?'

'Because I need you here. With the girls. While I'm doing chemo.'

'Manu and Philomena are there. The girls love them. Besides, you said it was early stage. You'll probably just be gone a couple of hours three or four times a week for a few weeks. You'll probably be in remission before I'm even back.'

I bite back the urge to tell her it's far, far worse than that. That D'Souza is recommending going straight for stem cell transplants. Time is short, and she's afraid that if we try chemo and radiation and they don't work, it may be too late for even the transplants. She knows I have the money for it, but I told her I'd think about it. I have to give her my answer tomorrow because it's not something she can just set up overnight and I'm running out of time.

Kiara blindsided me with the news about Roger and the project. I thought that research thing died with Monty. I mean, it was a great idea and all, but it wasn't the reason she went to SF.

'I don't like the set-up,' I say, shifting the focus away from myself to the mission, or the absence of one. 'We haven't prepped for this, it's not what we talked about or planned for. Going into the lion's lair, he controls all the variables.'

'Yeah, but he doesn't know that I'm a lioness and he's the prey I'm hunting. Surprise, the biggest tactical advantage, remember?'

She's throwing my own words back at me. I ignore my irritation and try to dull my pain with more booze, which I know is a bad idea. 'I don't want you to do it. You're not going. That's it.'

She laughs softly, a mocking chuckle. 'You're laying down the law now? That's rich, after the stunt you pulled in SF.'

'For fuck's sake, let it go, Ki.' There's a long silence.

'Anyways,' she says at last. 'I want to go back. I'm going. That's my decision, and I've made it.'

I sit up. It takes me a few seconds; the chair is low and I've slunk down into the cushions, and I'm already miles from the shape I was in when I drove that Dodge Ram into Monty Cordry. I'll never admit it to Kiara, but the time I spent in SF cost me. By the time I got back, the jet lag alone wiped me out for twenty-four hours. 'What the fuck, Ki?'

She stares straight ahead, avoiding eye contact. 'The project means a lot to me. It's a real thing, Han. We never expected it to work as brilliantly as it did, but it did. Roger's hooked, and I didn't even have to do anything. He really thinks it's something big and he wants me to be there because he knows it's my baby.'

'The baby you had with your dead boyfriend?'

Her eyes light up, jaw hardens. 'Don't push it.'

'*You* don't push it. You need to back off for a bit. We have a plan. Do Monty. Take a gap of a couple of years – at least. Then, when the time is right, we accidentally happen to run into Roger fucking Cordry someplace. We pick up the pieces there, work him like we worked his asshole sons, and when the time is right, make our move. By then, I'll be over my chemo, be back in shape, the girls will be a little older –'

'There's no *we* in this anymore. You killed the team when you pulled your solo. Now I'm the one in the hot seat and I'm making the call. I'm going.'

'You listen to me, Ki,' I say, my blood as hot as the fire in my lymph nodes. 'This is not up for discussion. You go off plan like this and Roger fucking Cordry and his people will eat you alive. Hakam Abdi is no muscleman in a suit, he's the real deal. He'll see through you in a New York minute and put you down before you get within a yard of his boss.'

'I have a plan for that too,' she says. 'There's this island Monty told me about. It's remote and not on the commercial routes, and Roger only goes there to be totally alone. As in, no flunkeys, security, nothing. Even Hakam Abdi won't be around. It'll be just Roger and me, all on our ownsome. Even if he comes at me, I can take him down. I have moves.'

Of course she does. I showed her those moves, drilled them into her stubborn head. And a part of me perks up at the sound of this island. It sounds . . . it sounds . . .

'Too good to be true,' I say aloud. 'It could be a trap, Ki.'

She snorts. 'A trap for what? They don't know I'm coming. Or that anyone's coming. It's real, Han. He goes to this place once a year. Always alone. No exceptions.'

I frown. Something's wrong with this picture, but I can't put my finger on it. I'm not feeling great, and the booze and the argument and the long, exhausting day are presenting their bills now and I'm all out. 'If he . . .' I take a deep breath and start over. 'If he always goes there alone, why would he take you?'

She smiles at me, and it reminds me so much of our mom, and Brian. All three of them had the exact same smile, an impish look, twinkle-eyed and dimpled cheek. 'Because we'll be on our honeymoon.'

# 35

## *ROGER*

Zurich feels bohemian, relaxing, after the summit in Davos. A florid-faced musician in traditional Swiss garb is playing a cheerful ditty on an accordion nearby, singing along in German. Tourists are stopping to click selfies with him in the background; other patrons at tables nearby are tapping their feet. One little girl is even singing along sweetly. Her eyes meet Roger's by chance, she smiles at him. He looks away. He's not in the mood for indulging children. Especially someone else's children. He's more comfortable leaning into his rage and angst these days. The happiness has been knocked out of his heart like a bung out of a wooden barrel, and all the good stuff has gone down the gutter. He returns his attention to his phone. He is reviewing the deal notes from Davos that his lawyers have sent him. The music washes over him like water over a macintosh.

Roger enjoys his work, in a manner of speaking. More accurately stated: he enjoys the dog-fuck-dog art of negotiating major deals, the give-and-take between powerful people who control much of the wealth of the world and influence the lives of millions. He also likes sticking it to those who've stuck it to him before, now more than ever.

In parting, Van Hoffman, the silver-haired grand master of the art of the billion-dollar deal, shook his hand grimly after sealing a complicated, multi-national, multi-political arrangement that would make enormous sums and resources flow to those who had signed on – while cutting off the same to those who hadn't made the cut – and patted Roger's hand in that patriarchal way only he could get away with. 'They said you had lost your edge because of your family tragedies. But I see that your horns have sharpened with time. Pleasure doing business with you, Cordry.'

That was what passed for condolences and compliments among the uber-rich. It was the most flattering thing he had ever said to Roger.

Roger raises his eyes to see Reitmaier of the Zurich Police approach. The detective looks a little more beaten about the eyes than the last time Roger saw him, which was several months after Ricky's murder, while Roger was in Switzerland on a business trip. There seems to be more grey dusting his temples, and less hair on the top than Roger remembers. Time is not treating the older man kindly.

'May I sit?' the detective asks, seating himself even as he asks.

Reitmaier orders a Chasselas. Roger asked for the meeting at this café after Reitmaier's shift, without specifying a reason. Reitmaier's reluctance was evident on the phone but he had agreed to come.

After he takes his first sip, Reitmaier says, 'I am not certain why you wished to speak with me, Mr Cordry. As you are well aware, your son Ricky's murderer is in prison, serving out a long sentence for her crime. The case is closed. We have done our job.'

'I'm not so sure.'

Reitmaier sets the glass down carefully on the paper coaster with a picture of the Swiss Alps. 'I have complied with every one of your requests, the ones made officially as well as the unofficial ones from your man.' He indicates

Hakam Abdi standing not far off, watching the crowd attracted by the musician. 'Your people have all the information we have. I have been completely transparent with you. You can see how thorough we were. There is simply no doubt. Ursula Andersson killed your son Ricky Manfredi. She is paying the price for her crime. Justice has been served.'

Roger leans slightly forward. 'We have something new.'

Reitmaier looks skeptical and cautious, which is pretty much his default mode, as Roger has learned by now. He has extensive profiles of this man, knows his life inside and out. Reitmaier himself has been surveilled, a forensic examination of his life, his family, his finances, all conducted with the thoroughness and resources of any CIA or NSA surveillance. Roger had to be sure the man wasn't compromised in any way that could affect his investigation. Apart from some interesting but unimportant hobbies – Reitmaier collects Edo-era Japanese *shunga*, or erotic art, in the form of woodblock prints and sex toys, and has occasional liaisons with young men – he is a boringly typical middle-aged European bachelor with no skeletons in his closet.

'A piece of evidence?' he asks.

Roger taps and swipes his phone screen, calling up the image he wants. He holds the phone up for the detective to see. 'My people found this on a Japanese national's 4chan a few weeks ago. The person who took it was a tourist whose phone was stolen, and he only just restored his photo library from the cloud and uploaded some of the pics he took while on vacation in Zurich years earlier.'

Reitmaier raises his eyebrows, still looking at Roger and not the phone as he sips his wine. '4chan?'

4chan is an unregulated bulletin board site notorious for its controversial content and internet pranking. Roger shrugs, acknowledging that the skepticism is justified. 'It's genuine. My people analysed the raw image data and said it was the real deal. Please, look at the picture.'

Reitmaier looks at the phone screen. He stares at it for a moment, then blinks and sets down his wine glass carefully on the placemat.

He glances around at their surroundings then back at the phone. 'This was taken in this same location?'

'Yes. The person was right here.' Roger points at the plate-glass window of Odeon through which the interior of the café was visible. 'He took a selfie of himself and when he checked it, he saw who was in the background. Then he pointed the camera at that table there.' Roger points at a table only a few meters away, inside the café but separated from them only by clear glass. The table is currently occupied by two very chic black fashionistas. 'And he shot a video.'

Roger swipes the picture of the Japanese tourist aside. Goodbye, Mr Hiromoto. The next file is a video. He taps the screen to play it and holds it up so Reitmaier can watch it. A few seconds in, the detective reaches up to take the phone from Roger, who gladly yields it. He waits as Reitmaier watches the entire thirteen-second clip through.

Reitmaier watches it two more times. The third time, he taps the screen to pause it, then uses his thumb and fore-finger to expand the image. He turns the phone back to show Roger.

'You confirm that this is your son Ricky?'

Roger nods. 'Quite definitely. Mr Hiromoto, who also happens to follow Ricky's Instagram feed and has frequently liked several of his posts, tagged the video with Ricky's IG handle when he posted it yesterday. That was how it popped up on our radar.'

Reitmaier frowns. 'Your son's social media accounts are still active?'

Roger shrugs. 'We all live forever on the internet.'

Reitmaier seems about to comment on that, then thinks better of it. He taps at the screen again and then shows Roger another blowup. This time of the young woman sitting opposite Ricky at the table inside Odeon.

'This young lady . . . who is she and what is her connection to Ricky?'

Roger looks at Reitmaier. 'That's what I want you to look into. The date stamp embedded on the raw data confirms that the date mentioned by Hiromoto in his IG post was the same date the picture was taken.'

'So this was several weeks before Ricky's murder.'

'Yes, and as you can see from the video, they appear quite friendly, even flirty. My people tell me that your list of women whom Ricky dated doesn't include her.'

'This is the first time I'm seeing this lady,' Reitmaier confirms.

'So you missed her somehow. If she was seeing Ricky at the time, she should have been a suspect.'

'Not necessarily. They could simply be having a drink together. Men and women do socialize without going to bed, Mr Cordry.'

'Not Ricky. If he was going out with her, he was fucking her. Count on it.'

Reitmaier thinks for a moment. 'Let's say they were involved. That still may not mean anything. Ricky had a lot of lady friends. You have been sent all the files and interview transcripts.'

And had each of those women thoroughly surveilled and investigated, Roger thinks but doesn't say. Reitmaier probably assumes as much, since Hakam was feeding the detective links and leads while the case was still active. 'I would still like you to look into it.'

Reitmaier considers him. 'The case is closed officially.'

'Then do it unofficially.'

Reitmaier sighs softly. 'I am uncomfortable doing this. While the investigation was active, I was happy to cooperate with you, Mr Cordry. After all, you were an interested party. But now, it would not be right. I have active cases right now that require my attention. I cannot devote my time and energy to a closed case. I am afraid you wasted your time.'

Reitmaier drains the last of his wine and stands up, reaching for his hat.

'Sit down,' Roger says softly.

The detective puts his hat on.

'Unless you want to piss away your entire career and your life savings, sit the fuck down.' The words are delivered quietly and politely, but the threat is clear.

Reitmaier looks at him with barely suppressed anger. He doesn't like being told what to do, or being threatened. But he sits down slowly, keeping his hat on.

'Your investigation put Ursula Andersson behind bars for the murder of my son. She's serving out a life sentence, her life and reputation destroyed. How would you look, how would Zurich Police look, how would Switzerland look, if it turns out that you imprisoned the wrong woman – an innocent woman – while the actual murderer went scot-free?'

Reitmaier looks sourly at Roger. 'That would not be good, obviously.'

'And that doesn't take into account the civil lawsuits you'll be charged with, by my lawyers and by Ursula Andersson's lawyers. You will be disgraced, your career and reputation tarnished. Your life savings depleted by legal fees fighting cases that will bankrupt you when judgments are awarded, which they will be, both against you as well as the department. My lawyers will look into your past history and dig up anything they can to show you were an incompetent and careless investigator. It could lead to all your cases being re-opened and re-examined, even overturned in court. It would be a disaster.'

Reitmaier is silent for several moments. The server returns with the bottle of Chasselas and refills the detective's glass. Reitmaier takes his hat off and places it on his knee. He sips more wine. 'What do you want, Mr Cordry?'

'I want you to do your job.' Before the detective can object, Roger raises his hand: 'Unofficially. Look into this mystery girl. Find out who she is, where she is now, what her relationship to Ricky was. Correlate it with the other evidence you have, figure out if she could have been the real culprit. Show her video around to all Ricky's other girlfriends, his male friends . . . If she was involved with him, someone must have seen her. Follow the lead. I don't need to tell you how to do your job.'

Reitmaier considers. 'And if I find she was just a casual acquaintance?'

Roger shrugs. 'Then you go about your life, and you never see me again.' He leans forward. 'But if she's connected to the murder . . . If there's *any* evidence that it might have been she, not Ursula, who murdered Ricky, then I want to be the first to know. Correction: I want to be the *only* person to know. From your lips to my ears, directly.'

Reitmaier gulps wine unhappily. 'What happens then?'

Roger spreads his hands. 'Let's cross that bridge when we get to it. I know you believe in following investigation procedure scrupulously. Do your thing. Follow the lead wherever it takes you. Let's worry about the destination when you get there.'

Reitmaier thinks some more. 'It would not be proper for me to do this during my official duty hours. I have vacation time due. I can take a leave of absence.'

Roger smiles graciously. He's shown the man the stick. Time to hold out a carrot. 'I'll pay your expenses, whatever they may be, no questions asked, no receipts required. Consider yourself a security consultant. You will be paid a retainer and a fee for your efforts. Off the books, of course. In an offshore bank account, if you prefer, or a Swiss account of your choice, to be drawn on at your free will. You have carte blanche.'

Reitmaier looks at him for a long moment without replying. He picks his hat off his knee, plucks an invisible speck of dirt off the felt and flicks it aside with a moue of distaste. He sets the hat on his head again firmly. 'Thank you for the pictures.'

'Are you sure we need him?'

Roger's eyes are still tracking Reitmaier as the detective walks into Café Odeon and speaks to one of the staff.

The woman nods and smiles, indicating another, younger lady standing by the bar, evidently the manager. Reitmaier walks over and has a conversation with the manager. At one point, he shows her his cellphone with the picture and video which Roger has forwarded to him.

'Our people could have handled the investigation,' Hakam adds.

'Sure you could,' Roger says, still watching Reitmaier at work. 'And you might even find her. But this is his turf. He's great at his job. He knows the case inside out, he's lived with it for years now. He knows the city, the people. He won't just find her, he'll investigate the shit out of her. If she's guilty of Ricky's murder, he'll prove it beyond the shadow of a doubt. I know what you'll say next, that we can hire the best in the city too, follow the same procedures, but it's not the same thing. Reitmaier has skin in the game. This is personal to him now. If he was wrong about Ursula Andersson, then that means the real killer put one over him. He was played. He doesn't like that idea. He'll make it his life mission to hunt the killer down.'

'But if he does, he'll risk ruining his career. You just spelled that out for him.'

Roger smiles. 'That's the difference between you and me, Hakam. That's why I'm Roger fucking Cordry and you're just a grunt in a suit. Men like Reitmaier aren't bothered about public relations and image. He's the old-fashioned kind of detective. The kind who cares about the truth. He wants to know. Sure, he'll try to prove that this mystery girl was nobody and Ursula was the killer after all. But if the evidence points another way, he'll follow it. He won't do it for the money, or because I threatened him. He's a bachelor, he doesn't have any immediate family or siblings, he's not responsible for anyone except himself. All he has is the job. He can't live with himself wondering if he put the wrong suspect away while the real killer is walking around out there. He has to know the truth, even if it kills him. What I do want you to do is keep a tight watch on him. If he leads us back to the real murderer, I want to know at once. I don't trust him to call me, or even to take my money. I only trust him to do his job.'

# 36

## HANNAH

The river is lovely and cool. I'm swimming against the current, which is pleasantly strong at this time. In a little while, it'll be high tide and the current will become fierce; fierce enough to carry me out to sea. Well, not me, not even in my current weakened state, but every now and then some foolish tourist does get washed away and has to be rescued – or not, depending on how strong the current is and when the authorities are informed, and how much weed or other substances the idiot has consumed. I'm careful to avoid taking in any of the water. It looks and feels clean but I wouldn't consider any Indian river safe for either swimming or fishing – or even for the fish, poor souls, who have to live in them. At least it's not like the legendary 'pure' holy River Ganga – 'Ganges' to non-Indians – which is so filthy with offal, trash and countless human remains dumped in it that the Indian government has to release giant flesh-eating turtles in it to consume the corpses, and later, sharks to clean up the turtles who invariably get sick from the pollution. The sharks manage to thrive, though, as do the crocodiles and gharials that prowl the sacred river. Our Mandovi is nowhere near as great, sacred or polluted, and if you want a kilometers-long swim, it's the only game in town. Splashing around in a five-star hotel's infinity pool isn't exactly my idea of exercise, unless eyeballing thongy celebs is your idea of cardio.

I feel the boat coming up behind me before I hear it. It draws alongside and keeps pace with me. The nut-brown individual in the banana-yellow shirt and pink slacks leaning over the side calls out a few endearing insults in Konkani, before switching to English.

'You have a death wish, cousin?'

I flash a grin as I twist my head to come up for air, then show him a quick middle finger before cutting through the tide. The current is tugging me out insistently, demanding enough to require my total concentration. After a few more attempts at banter and earnest requests to let him pull me aboard, Savio gives up and chugs alongside, keeping me company. Finally, as I see the mouth of the river up ahead, opening wide to wash out beside one of the most crowded tourist beaches in Goa, I call it quits and wave to him. He sits cross-legged a moment or two longer, glaring down at me through his Ray-Bans, before leaping to his feet and tossing me a line.

I pull myself on to the deck, trying not to gasp aloud. My chest is heaving and I feel like I've been swimming the English Channel, not just a mere five-mile stretch of the Mandovi. When I've regained my breath, Savio takes off his sunglasses and admonishes me with the in-your-face enthusiasm of a fellow Goan Anglo-Indian.

'You out of your coconut, woman? You could have been taken out two miles and nobody would have known. Lucky for you, we were just coming downriver after a tourist swim and Ramesh saw you.'

I wave at Savio's partner, in both the business and personal sense. Ramesh waves back, still at the wheel. Among other things, they run a tourist swimming class at low tide every day, picking up their boatload of mostly foreigners and a few adventurous Indians, near Reis Magos Fort in Quegde-velim, Verem.

'I needed the exercise. I need to get back into shape,' I say, finally trusting myself to speak without wheezing. This fucking cancer is really messing with my stamina.

Savio gives me an exaggerated up-down once-over. 'Girl, you in great shape. Unless you planning to try out for the Olympics, you better quit this foolishness. This's no place to get your cardio.'

I grin. 'Where else do I get to meet the likes of you, brother?'

He invites me back to our cousin Manu's beach shack res-taurant for breakfast, but I decline. Instead, I accept his offer to drop me off at a point close enough for me to get to Mani-pal Hospital.

Did I mention yet that today's my first day of chemo? Well, it is. I knew that once I start the regime it's going to kick my ass, so I thought I'd put in some quality workout time be-forehand. If Kiara was here, she would have held me back and chained me, but Kiara isn't here, so I'll fucking go for a swim if I feel like it.

Dr D'Souza looks relieved when she sees me. 'Ah, good,' she says, before taking in my still-damp hair with a frown. 'Just showered?'

I shrug. If I tell her I swam five miles at high tide, she'll chew my ears off. I don't need a surrogate sister to take Kiara's place.

Sitting in the chair, watching the drip ooze its poison into my veins, I take out my phone and check the email drop for messages. It's too soon, of course. Kiara barely left here. She'll take a couple of days, meet up with RC in Chi-Town, then, when she has something worth sharing, leave me a message. Or she won't. The way we left things, it's possible she won't want to talk to me for a while.

To my surprise, there's a message in the Inbox.

I frown at it for a moment. Ki can't have already gotten into something, could she? I mean, she isn't even scheduled to meet Roger until – when? Later tonight? Tomorrow morning? My head starts to swim a little, trying to calculate the US–India time zone difference and factor Daylight Savings Time and Central Time into it. Or maybe it's the chemo. From the feel of it, I'm guessing my electrolytes are off. I haven't touched a drop for the past couple of days but I did hit the feni bottle a bit too hard while Ki was here; it's the only way I could deal with the constant catfights. Maybe the swim this morning wasn't such a hot idea – on an empty stomach too. On the other hand, if I do hurl as all chemo-takers are expected to, then I'd rather not bring up Goan blood sausages and spicy chutney.

'You OK, sona?' says the middle-aged lady in the next chemo chair. She's half my height and twice my weight and looks like she could roll sideways rather than walk if she wanted. She has a nice voice and a grandmotherly air. 'Your first time?'

I nod, my thumb still hovering over the unread email. 'You too, auntie?'

She smiles wearily. 'First time doctor says, Do it for your family, Agnes. Your grandchildren need you. Second time she say, Do it for yourself, you still have many good years left. This time, she not say anything. I ask her, this time who am I doing it for? She give no answer. So I say, OK, I do it for Jesus. He needs more time before I go to heaven and start telling him how to run the world.'

She cackles loudly at her own joke. I laugh too, but cut off almost at once because of the way it makes my insides churn and head swim. I shut my eyes tight and squeeze, trying to regain focus. The phone trembles in my hands. Yeah, maybe swimming five miles against a strong current isn't the best thing to do before your first chemo session.

D'Souza comes back to check on us. I nod when she asks me if I'm doing OK. She pats my shoulder maternally, then spends a few minutes with Agnes auntie talking about sorpotel and the state of the country.

Finally, I bite the bullet and tap the unread message. It takes effort to convert the code to normal English and sweat is popping out on my forehead. Am I too hot or isn't the damn air conditioning working in here?

*Best if we take a little time off. I think we could both use it. You've got enough on your hands with the treatment and the girls. You take care of yourself. I'll be in touch once I've taken care of business here. See you when I see you.*

What the actual fuck?

Is she . . . is she ghosting me? What the hell, Ki? The whole point of this drop is so we can stay in touch if we need to. Sure, we don't need to right now, and during the last two missions – me with Ricky and you with Monty – we didn't really need to send out an SOS, but that doesn't mean something can't go wrong this time. What if you need my help? I mean, you sure as hell weren't 'taking care of business' with Monty, were you?

The phone slides from my slippery palm and clatters to the tiled floor. I try to lean over and grab it, but suddenly I feel like the ceiling is on the wall and the wall . . . the wall . . .

Next thing I know I'm on a hospital bed and D'Souza is checking my blood pressure while a nurse draws blood. The pinprick wakes me up. Kiara had intended to off Monty with a syringe, pump him full of just enough of his own medication to OD, which would look like he'd forgotten and double-dosed. That was before I slammed him with the Dodge Ram, but would she even have gone through with it? She says she would've, but I doubt it. She doesn't have the killer instinct that I do. I'm worried about her out there in wild, wild . . . um, Illinois, in the lair of Papa Tiger himself. I should be there, FFS. I need to be there. She needs backup on this mission. She needs me.

'You need to calm down,' Dr D'Souza says grimly, and I realize I've been rambling aloud. 'Your electrolytes are terrible. What have you been doing, Hannah? I thought we talked about this. When are you going to act more responsibly?'

She goes on for a bit but I tune out and eventually she goes off to do some other doctorly thing. I gather that I'm being interned here overnight for observation. OK, whatever. I just need to call Manu and let him know to take the girls home for the night. They love their Uncle Manu and Aunt Philo and they love sleeping over, so it's no biggie, and I know they're in safe hands at least.

At some point, I ask for my phones, a bit more testily than I should, and a nurse looks at me sharply, and points with her eyes. 'Nobody touching your fancy mobile, poree,' she says, using the Konkani word usually used for daughters or immature girls.

They're right beside me, on the nightstand. I feel foolish and embarrassed. I think I might have puked up bile and been given something to help balance my electrolytes, because I'm feeling a little better. Maybe ten percent better, which isn't saying much. I don't think I'll be swimming any rivers for a while. I don't feel like I could take a shower on my own right now or in the near future. Fuck chemo. Fuck cancer. Fuck Kiara. What do you think you're doing, girl? Ghosting your own big sis? Damnit, we talked about this. Whatever happens, we stay connected, remember?

Then I see it. The notification blinking on the screen of my secure phone. I fumble with it, my fingers feeling like fat sausages, thinking it's another message from Ki, apologizing for the last one, and saying, of course I'll be in touch, and all is well.

It's not a message from Ki.

It's an alert on the email account of Danielle Scharrer, Mayor of Zurich and Roger Cordry's buddy. She's writing to tell him she's stepped in discreetly to grant Detective Adalbert Reitmaier a leave of absence on health grounds. She hopes the detective proves to be of use to Roger.

What the hell is this?

Why does Roger Cordry need Reitmaier now? The Ricky Manfredi case is history. Ursula was convicted and is already serving her time. Reitmaier isn't a player in the game any longer.

I feel stupid and clumsy, struggling against whatever sedative they've given me and my own messed-up condition as I work my phone furiously, trying to figure out what's going on in Zurich. Finally, I find it. A pic from a 4chan account, leaked by an account I trace back to a security agency managed by Hakam Abdi. The online rumor is that the girl in the pic is the one who actually offed Ricky Manfredi and that Ursula is innocent and was set up.

The nurse comes back in and makes a noise about my blood pressure and heart rate. I ignore her as I tap on the pic. It expands to show me a not-very-good but still passable shot of Ricky and a young woman sitting in Café Odeon.

Fuck, fuck, fuck.

I put it all together as the nurse threatens to call Dr D'Souza at home. Night has suddenly fallen, and somehow an entire day has passed since I checked in here for chemo. Roger Cordry – Reitmaier – Hannah with Ricky. It doesn't take a brain surgeon to see what he's up to.

Roger Cordry knows I was the one who killed Ricky.

That in itself doesn't worry me. The Hannah that Ricky met in Zurich is not really me. I laid down a fake trail a mile wide that will lead any investigator up multiple garden paths and ultimately nowhere. There's no way in hell Reitmaier or anyone else is going to track me down here. Nothing in Zurich will lead him to Goa.

The worry is that it means Roger knows way more than we thought.

And that means he could know Kiara is not who she claims to be.

Maybe that's why he wanted her to come back to the US.

Not for some damn project.

But because he wants to lure her into the tiger's lair.

And that's exactly where she is now.

## 37

## REITMAIER

Detective Adalbert Reitmaier exits the elevator and walks down the hallway. There are only eight apartments on each floor. The door to 304 stands ajar. He pauses for a moment as the smell of some pungent culinary preparation assaults his nostrils. He fights back the urge to press his handkerchief – scented with cologne as usual – to his nose; in an increasingly multicultural Zurich, one can hardly expect everyone to eat Swiss cuisine, and he does not wish to appear rude. For that matter, Reitmaier himself prefers Mediterranean food and enjoys trying out new cuisine, but this concoction smells off. Too much paprika perhaps? And there's a burnt odor as well. It is irritating his throat.

A heavily accented voice in English calls out, 'I am Olga.'

The possessor of this accent emerges from the open doorway. She's a young woman with black dyed hair streaked with veins of white, green and red, the colors of the Bulgarian flag. She has an attractive, heart-shaped face marred (in his personal opinion) by nose, tongue, lip and ear metal piercings. She wears black boots, black leather short shorts, and a fashionably ripped black tee shirt displaying horrific imagery with the name GUTSLIT in dripping crimson letters. Her ghoulishly pale complexion matches the skeleton on the tee shirt.

Reitmaier shows her his ID and hands her his card. She turns to lead the way into the apartment, talking non-stop.

'I worry when she go. No explanation. Suddenly one day here, next is gone.'

He lets her prattle on as he surveys the apartment. It's about what he would expect from a somewhat well-off university student living on her own, away from her country and unaccustomed to housework. In short: it's a mess. A lifelong bachelor (except for one live-in partner for a very uncomfortable seven-month period), Reitmaier takes pride in keeping his own apartment scrupulously neat and clean.

The room the visiting foreign student named Hannah was occupying is the only space relatively untouched by the hurricane that devastated the rest of the apartment: probably because, as Olga explains in the course of her running commentary, it is currently unoccupied. She even asks him if he happens to be 'looking for apartment'. She then launches into a lengthy explanation of how she is still here because she decided to take a 'break year' to explore her identity. She looks at him meaningfully, as if wanting him to ask about her quest, but he is wise enough not to take the bait.

They end up in the kitchen, for some reason, where he is assaulted full-on by the malodorous cooking. The source of the air pollution is a pot that is smoking lightly. Olga curses liberally in Bulgarian, uses oven mitts to take the offensive concoction off the gas range and places it, not in the sink as Reitmaier would have assumed, but directly on the dining table. His sinuses plead for mercy. When she invites him to join her for lunch, he declines and beats a hasty retreat from the apartment, pulling out his kerchief the instant he's out of sight of the garrulous Miss Olga. In the vestibule of the building, he finally pauses for a clear breath, thinking he must visit the sauna this afternoon to clear his lungs. He suspects his clothes will have to be laundered to be rid of that memorable stench.

His cellphone rings as he is standing in the street, making some last-minute notes on the interview in his Moleskine notebook.

Reitmaier sighs and answers. 'Good day, Mr Cordry. What can I do for you?'

'You can start by updating me on your progress.'

Reitmaier is tempted to remind Cordry that he is neither his supervisor nor his employer. Instead, he explains how the video taken at Café Odeon helped him identify the young woman seen with Ricky. A professor at the university recognized her as one of her former med students named Hannah. She did not recall the girl's surname but knew it was a foreign name. She looked up her records, but was surprised to find no record of her at all. She was certain the girl had been a student, so the only thing that made sense was that the student's file had somehow been deleted from the system. Luckily, the professor in question, Professor Luegenbiehl, didn't require records to remember that the girl had shown exceptional talent and that she had recommended she pursue a career in surgery. Hannah stopped attending class around the same time that another girl had been arrested for murder.

'That would be Ursula,' Cordry says.

'That is correct,' Reitmaier replies. He has walked down the street to his car and is now entering the vehicle. He shuts the door and shifts the phone to his left hand.

'They were classmates,' Cordry points out.

Reitmaier explains that apart from that obvious connection, Hannah is a cipher. Except for attending classes with fair regularity, she may as well have not existed. No one else, apart from Luegenbiehl, seems to have seen her or interacted with her. Even Ursula has only a vague memory of 'the brown girl' in her med class but doesn't recall ever seeing her with Ricky. There is no trace of her in the university records.

'I suspect that someone hacked into the system and deleted her file,' Reitmaier informs Roger Cordry as he takes a sip of water to clear his throat of the after-effects of inhaling Olga's cooking. 'However, after a thorough canvassing of the students, I found a young man, an American student, who recalled a fellow American student from Texas who, he said, had been seeing a Bulgarian girl named either Helga or Belga, he thought. This Bulgarian girl had a roommate. Subsequently, I contacted all the Bulgarian female students at the university and was able to locate one Olga. I have just visited Olga's apartment in the Sixth District, Kurvenstrasse 24, and she identified the girl seen with your late son as being Hannah, an Indian student. She did not recall any last name. This girl, Olga, and Hannah had spent some time together with Olga's boyfriend, an American from Texas named Stuart. She lived with Hannah for a year and a half, then one day, she was gone. No note, no forwarding address. Her phone was switched off, texts received no replies. She simply disappeared.'

There is a long silence at Roger Cordry's end. Reitmaier, ensconced in the cocooned silence of his Mercedes, thinks he hears the faint hum of a jet engine in the background and the tinkling of ice in a heavy glass.

'You need to find this Hannah,' Cordry says at last.

Reitmaier once again resists the urge to tell this troublesome man that he is belaboring the obvious. But decades of dealing with inconsolable parents and relatives of victims has left him sensitized to their repetitive patterns. Like a tongue returning time and again to a painful cavity, the bereaved are compelled to harp on about the same things over and over. The difference is that, this time, he's dealing with a man who possesses the power, influence and wealth to take his obsession to dangerous levels. Which, Reitmaier reminds himself, would include Roger Cordry ruining the detective's career out of sheer pique.

'I am exploring all avenues,' he says, as he starts the engine.

'What about a forensic sweep of the apartment?'

'That would be pointless, Mr Cordry. Some years have elapsed since Hannah left the apartment. Several other young men and women have lived in the same apartment, some as co-tenants with Olga, others as live-in partners, not to mention an unknown number of visitors and friends who had access to the entire apartment. It would be a herculean task to track down all of them, secure permission for their DNA samples, then compare them to any DNA we might find on the premises. If you recall, we found no DNA evidence at Ricky's apartment that helped in our investigation at the time. Or rather, we found too much DNA evidence. Literally hundreds of people passed through that apartment. In any case, any potential DNA evidence we might find now would be degraded and rendered inadmissible as evidence in a court trial.'

'I don't give a fuck about evidence or court trials. This girl murdered my son. I want her found and punished.'

'I understand your eagerness. If she is in fact Ricky's murderer, it is quite certain that Hannah is not her real name. Even if we isolate her DNA after eliminating the other previous and current residents, we would still have no way to use it to locate her personally. What purpose would the DNA serve?'

'I'm not just talking about DNA, detective. Fingerprints, a personal item, a hair . . . anything we find could help locate Hannah.'

Reitmaier has mastered the art of sighing inaudibly. But he feels the weight of the decades pressing down at such times.

'Mr Cordry, you could have sent someone else to give me the video, or had my own chief, or even the Mayor contact me. You could have emailed it to me. Instead, you took the time and effort – your very valuable time and effort, I'm sure – to come all the way to Zurich to show me the video personally and make your request. That tells me you respect my skill as an investigator. Trust your own judgment now. Allow me to proceed with the investigation as I deem fit. Whatever the outcome, you will be the first person I contact once I have something of value.'

Another silence. This time, Reitmaier catches the distinct sound of a jet engine and ice cubes tinkling.

Without another word, Roger Cordry ends the call.

Reitmaier looks at his screen to confirm that the call has in fact been disconnected. He shakes his head, smiling faintly at the ego of the man. Still, he knows he trod close to the fire when he told Cordry off. This is not a man known for his patience or his compassion. Respect apart, he expects results and he wants them now. If Reitmaier doesn't deliver the goods soon enough for Roger Cordry's liking, there will be a price to pay.

Adalbert Reitmaier is accustomed to pressure. At his age, at this stage of his career, only a step away from retirement, he has little to lose. Despite Cordry's threats against his family, which could be viewed as a thinly veiled form of blackmail, he intends to pursue this investigation as diligently as possible. He will leave no stone unturned.

Part of his calm assurance comes from knowing more than what he told Cordry on the phone.

## 38

## KIARA

I use my real ID to fly to Chennai, which is where my made-up 'Kiara' persona is supposed to be from. From there I use the Kiara ID and passport to buy a ticket to Chicago which is the seat of Roger's corporate headquarters. After two full days, little sleep and a diet of airline food, I find myself in the slow-shuffling immigration line for tourists at O'Hare. Ironic, since I'm a US-born citizen and could breeze through using my US passport in minutes, but I have to assume that Roger has his people tracking me electronically and I have to be uber-cautious, now more than ever.

This is the real deal, the main event, the one Hannah and I prepped for and trained for all those years.

When I looked out of my window and saw Chicago below, my pulse was racing at the realization that I was finally doing it, stepping up to take the shot. Soon, I will avenge our mother, father and brother and end Roger Cordry's ill-gotten fortunes. I feel the anticipation grow inside me, like a powerful buildup of static electricity. I'm almost afraid to touch anyone near me, for fear I'll shock them into instant cardiac arrest. I'm coming for you, Cordry; you're mine now, you bastard.

Almost as if he senses my murderous rage, his name pops up on my screen while I'm still in line for immigration. I stare at the text message. The auntie behind me, wearing a woolen longcoat over a saree, peeks over my shoulder with the eternal inquisitiveness of the Indian middle class. When I lift my head and stare her in the eye, she doesn't flinch, turn away or apologize. Instead, she nods knowingly, as if reading my murderous thoughts.

'*Aap boyfriend ko text bhejiye, mein nahin padungee,*' she says generously. Go ahead and text your boyfriend, I won't read.

'Thank you,' I reply in Hindi. I almost tell her that not only is he not my boyfriend, he's more than twice my age, but I stop myself; partly because we've trained ourselves not to attract attention in public, but also because it would be a lie. The fact is, I fully intend for Roger Cordry to be my boyfriend, my lover, and if my plan works out, my husband. If only for a few days.

*Welcome to Chi-Town, Kiara,* Roger texted me. *Dani will take care of everything for you. She's waiting outside. Anything you need, just ask.*

I wonder if he actually typed those words himself, or if one of his numerous PAs did. Unlike some front-facing billionaires like Elon Musk and Bill Gates, Roger Cordry doesn't have a social media presence and famously keeps a low profile. After Monty's death, it's like he's disappeared off the media radar completely. I've combed through all the pieces on him since the funeral and there's a whole lot of speculation and blatantly phony sympathy but no real meat. No mention of the Monty project. That's made me wonder if this invitation could be some kind of a trap. What if Roger's people have found a connection between me or Hannah (which amounts to the same thing) and Ricky or Monty's murders? This whole invitation to come lead the project could be just a shrewd way to lure me into an ambush. I'm going to have to keep my eyes open and stay on full alert from now on.

Not that I was dozing off during the Monty mission, but this is different. With Monty, there was never any danger that he might actually suspect me of being an assassin. Roger is a whole other ball game. This, ladies and gentlepersons, is the major leagues. We're playing hardball here, and nobody gets to take their bat and go home crying to momma.

Or to big sister.

I feel the lack of Hannah on this trip. Like I'm about to walk on hot sand without sandals. The water seems a long way off, and the beach is scalding.

Even during the year or so when we were put into separate foster homes, I never felt this alone. Then, I was lucky enough to get probably a couple of the few really decent foster parents in the system and they were really nice to me. But now I'm not a kid anymore, and there are no surrogate families to comfort me. It's just me on my own, up against the biggest, baddest wolf of all.

Coming out of immigration, I take a deep breath, exhale and send up a silent prayer to our patron deity, St Mary. When we first embarked on the Roger Cordry vendetta, Hannah said that technically we should be praying to St Michael, the patron saint of warriors, but right now, St Mary and her namesake, the mother of Jesus and our own mother's patron deity – Ma was clutching a rosary with a locket picture of Mary and Baby Jesus when she jumped off that bridge into the East River – seems more comforting, and appropriate. I don't know how much I really believe in organized religion anymore, but if there was ever a time when I could use some patronage and blessings, it's now.

I step out into the cold slanting light of a Chicago autumn afternoon.

*

'Kiara, you look stunning,' he says as I walk up to him. He's dressed in a midnight-blue suit with a light blue silk shirt inside, no tie, and he looks disgustingly suave and handsome for a man who I know is capable of some of the worst acts a person can commit on God's earth.

I smile back radiantly – the floor-to-ceiling mirror on the wall of the restaurant shows me a reflection that looks radiant, at least – as I take my seat and let the maître d'hôtel slide in my chair. I'm wearing a black D&G cocktail dress with a satin bustier I bought on my new company charge card, one of the perks of being a newly minted CEO of Monty Cordry BioPharma LLC. My shoes are Jimmy Choo, a darling pair of strappy stilettos with a satin finish. To mix it up, I've gone in for just a suggestion of seventies retro-chic make-up and hairdo, with a Kristen Stewartish waif-cut, a light dusting of pink mascara, and kohl-lined eyes, because kohl brings out my melted-chocolate-brown eyes. I've turned a few heads while walking through the lobby and restaurant, and don't need Roger to confirm that I look like a million bucks, but it doesn't hurt to hear it said aloud.

Roger beams at me across the table. 'I am so pleased you accepted my invitation.'

The one to rejoin the project or the one to join him for dinner? I sip from a glass of water and smile politely. The best response is always silence. If he really wants me, let the bastard work for it.

'So,' he says after we've placed our orders and the maître d' has left us. 'Are you enjoying Chicago?'

'Thank you for the car and the hotel. And everything.'

I'm referring to the weekend I spent luxuriating in a suite the size of our Aunt Edna's coconut grove back home, then shopping on the Magnificent Mile, or 'Mag Mile' as Dani said it's called, charging to the courtesy credit cards she gave me a shocking quantity of clothing, footwear, cosmetics and some daily-wear jewelry. The hotel also had a spa the size of Anjuna Beach, a beauty parlor that our cousin Manuel would die for, and room service meals that cost as much as all our relatives back in Goa might spend on a year's groceries.

Roger makes a small hand-waving gesture to acknowledge and dismiss my gratitude. I'm sure the bill for my weekend would probably be less than the meal we're about to eat tonight, and to him, even that mid-five-figure check would be like you or me dropping a dollar into a homeless person's hat. Even the water he's ordered costs $300 (plus tax) a bottle.

I have to hand it to the bastard. He's good. He's really, really good.

Even with my guard up and all my flags flying, he still manages to slip in under my barriers somehow and disarm me. I want to order a Negroni but somehow he overrides me without seeming overbearing.

Try your hardest, bastard. You're not going to get me this easily. Who do you take me for? One of your rent-a-bimbo wannabe starlets? Go ply your Harvey Weinstein act somewhere else.

On the outside, I smile and laugh, and toss my hair back and act exactly as he expects me to act: like I'm falling for his BS.

We're barely through the first drinks, a reverse martini for me, and a peated single malt, single rock, for Roger, and he's probably thinking he has me. Yeah, sure, go ahead and think you've got me – because that's exactly what I *want* you to think!

It's pretty evident that everyone in this (very expensive) room knows him, including the movie star with her very pregnant pop star wife, to both of whom Roger introduces me. They're surprisingly warm and friendly and so ... normal. I enjoy that part of it, at least. It also helps me keep from throwing something at Roger. At one point, I wonder if the pop star sees through me, but then I wonder if maybe she knows what sort of man Roger really is and is being protective. Either way, I enjoy her attention and our conversation. The truth is, she's one of my idols and it's pretty amazing to be spending time with her.

I'm also relishing the food and beverages. Despite my decision to stop at only one drink and eat like a bird, the succession of breathtaking hors d'oeuvres he orders has me helplessly tasting every single thing, and feeling like I've died and gone to culinary heaven. Before I know it, I'm on my third reverse martini and ready to nominate the inventor of this delish drink to the Cocktail Hall of Fame.

This flamboyance continues throughout the meal but I get the point pretty quickly. He's trying to impress me. Since he doesn't need to do it for business reasons – I'm already here, aren't I? – it must be personal. I can't help feeling a grudging respect for his persistence. The bastard is good at this game. This isn't Ricky, this is the Master of the Game.

Somewhere between the hors d'oeuvres and the entrée, I excuse myself to visit the ladies' room.

I wait until a pair of similarly aged young women finish touching up their make-up and leave, after glancing over at me and whispering to each other. The instant they're gone, I turn the latch on the door, glad there isn't a bathroom attendant. I need a moment alone.

I rest my hands on the cold marble platform around the bathtub-sized sink and stare at myself in the mirror.

I want to yell and scream and smash the glass. That's really not my style at all. Call it a Hannah moment. Maybe I am channeling her. After all, she's the one I watched and learned from; everything I know about this deadly game, I learned from her. I've spent hours and days and nights talking to her about Ricky and Zurich, getting her to tell me every last detail. I'm in awe of her. But I'm not Hannah. My anger and frustration at this moment comes from the sense of humiliation I'm feeling at being treated like a pliable plaything by Roger fucking Cordry. It's humiliating to even have to pretend that I'm available to him, accessible to his seductions. Well, who says I have to be the kind of girl he expects? In fact, fuck Roger fucking Cordry and what he wants. I'm Kiara. I don't swoon and blush when a male predator, even a rich, good-looking, sexy, mature male predator, invites me to dance under the moonlight.

I'll bring the knives out and turn it into a *real* dance.

Yeah. That's what I'll do then. If he wants me, he's going to have to do more than wine and dine and woo. He's going to have to learn to take some rejection, to be led rather than just lead. It's the third decade of the twenty-first century; a girl isn't just a girl standing in front of a guy, asking him to love her. She's living her life. She decides where you might fit into that life, and lets you know when you're needed. Don't call me, I'll call you.

When I slip my hand inside my clutch to replace my lipstick, it touches the curved corner of my phone. I'm tempted to check my Inbox, to see if Hannah's read my message yet — or left one for me. Nah. She didn't think I could go through with this gig. Just like she didn't think I would have actually killed Monty. I could see it in her eyes. She doesn't think I have the . . . what did she call it? The killer instinct. Well, fuck you, Hannah. I'm doing this, and I'm doing it my way, and

292

I'm going to get this bastard, and I don't need you breathing down my neck and undermining my confidence.

I got this covered.

I hit the restroom door with the heel of my hand, walking out and back to the table, turning heads as I go – there goes the girl who's with Roger Cordry. Roger sees me coming and maybe he senses something different in me, maybe just the set of my jaw, or the more confident line of my shoulders. He smiles, getting ready to turn on the charm again, while I smile coolly and lean back, ready for battle.

## 39

## HANNAH

The chemo knocks me on my ass. Cousin Manuel, Philomena and Aunt Edna are angels as always, taking care of the girls and even bringing food in so I don't have to cook. Not that I'm able to keep anything down. God, how I hate cancer. You'd think with all the trillions of dollars that big pharma mints from us, they'd have a cure for it by now, and I mean something that doesn't kick your butt worse than the disease itself. Did I mention that chemo sucks? Cancer sucks ass but chemo sucks cancer's ass. Fuck them both and no, don't excuse my Sanskrit. Sometimes, you just have to say it like you feel it, and chemo really fucks you up.

I'm alone at home. Even the dogs are with my cousin and my aunt at their place, along with the girls, having one big sleepover. I love my kiddos and doggos but, right now, it's all I can do just to breathe and stay alive. By the second day on my own, I'm starting to feel like I might survive another day or two. I try to sit up in bed and do some breathing exercises. They make me feel better but also bring back the pukeyness. Everything brings back the pukeyness. They should just call it pukeymo, not chemo; that's the girls' term for it, which I promptly appropriated, like any self-respecting parent would.

I'm lying back in bed, praying for the pukeyness to go away and trying hard not to think of trigger things – food is especially triggering – when I hear the doorbell ring. It's very loud in the empty house, feeling like it's bouncing off the inside of my skull. It sounds weird because I'm so used to the place bursting with noise at all times. Girls screaming and yelling, dogs barking, whining, me and Ki yelling at them and then yelling at each other not to yell at them, which always makes the girls yell even louder ('but you and Aunt Kiara were yelling just now!') and the dogs bark even louder, going into their doggie a capella act. If they ever make yet another *Pitch Perfect* sequel, they've got a ready-made group right here, ready to cast: Vagator Vagabonds!

'Go away,' I murmur, only half in my senses.

The doorbell rings again.

I ignore it.

The nausea has finally passed. The breathing exercises are paying dividends. I'm starting to feel lighter, my chest clearer, and I can feel myself starting to feel nice and relaxed. Maybe I can grab an hour or two of sleep. Ah, wouldn't that be bliss. I start to reminisce about the days when I could get through an entire day without puking even once. True story.

Doorbell, again.

I make a mental note in my drowsy brain to find a screwdriver or a crowbar and rip the damn thing out of the wall. Who had the bright idea to make the damn thing so loud? That would be me, of course, because when our house is at peak noise level, even Big Ben could sound the noonday twelve and not be heard.

Finally, a spell of blessed silence.

Good. Whoever that is, they've gone away. Smart person.

I've just slipped under that sweet, velveteen level of unconsciousness where all life's troubles, the body's aches and pains, and the everyday anxieties of a mother, homemaker and older sister seem to recede to a pinpoint on the distant horizon: still there, but if you raise a thumb, you can block it all out and catch a few winks.

A half-heard, half-imagined male voice penetrates the sweet umbra like a laser.

I snap awake.

'. . . ah . . .'

Did he just say 'Hannah'?

No way.

That's not my real name, as I've mentioned before. Just as Kiara isn't really Ki's real name either. Nobody here in Goa who knows us, the real us, knows those names. Only we two, and the people we interacted with in Zurich and San Francisco respectively while assuming those aliases and the fake identities that went with them.

I must have misheard.

He must have said something else entirely. 'Anna' maybe? Or 'manna'?

My chemo-addled, sleep-deprived, cancer-whipped brain doesn't stop to wonder why someone would be saying 'manna' outside my front door. It doesn't matter. Anything but 'Hannah' will do.

Then he says it again.

'Hannah?'

In that instant, I'm fully awake. One hundred percent.

I sit up too quickly, the nausea making my head spin. My blood pressure must be on the floor. I can't even remember the last time I ate and actually kept any solid food in my system. I'm shaking like a leaf as I make my way over to the window, which, mercifully, is already open. I don't think I'd have the strength right this minute to open it if it was shut, because it tends to stick.

Even with my disorientation and pukeyness, I'm still

careful enough to peer down at an angle, making sure I'm not visible from the front porch if he should look up at exactly this moment.

I hear myself gasp, my hand clapped over my mouth to stifle the sound. It echoes in my head, reverberating.

I know that man.

An elderly, distinguished-looking white dude.

He's the detective looking into Ricky's murder.

Reich . . . no, Reit . . . Reitmaier. That's it. Detective Reitmaier of the Zurich Police.

The fuck is he doing here? Asking for Hannah?

I stumble across the room, check the window on the other side. It looks out to the side of the house, into the coconut grove.

Then I blunder out into the hallway, to the girls' room, and check that window too. Then the windows in Kiara's room. I even stand on the bathtub, almost losing my footing, and manage to crane my neck and peer down through the high, narrow, slitted window to check the fourth and final side.

No men with guns and bulletproof vests.

No uniforms and flashing lights.

No masked men creeping in from all sides to surround and seal the house.

I slip down to the bathroom floor, my back against the cold, hard lip of the bathtub, breathing heavily, my head throbbing from my exertions, trying to will my brain to work.

Why is Reitmaier here?

No.

Wrong question.

Not why.

How.

How did he find me?

What did I overlook?

It's been years. I know I got away clean because Roger fucking Cordry spent a fortune beating every bush, double-checking every single lead, real and imagined, to make sure that Zurich PD hadn't missed anything. Even after all that, they found nothing. That's why they tried, convicted and sentenced Ursula, who is still rotting in a Swiss prison.

So what's happened now, after all this time?

How did he track me down out of the blue, with no warning, without triggering any of my electronic alarm bells? I've got programs in the cloud tracking everything. If Reitmaier found something, I would have known about it the instant he did. The same goes for Roger fucking Cordry and his war-dog Hakam Abdi. They haven't sent Reitmaier so much as an email about the case in over a year.

Then why now? Why here? And how, how, how the actual fuck?

Outside the house, I hear the sound of an auto-rickshaw engine cranking up, then sputtering to life.

I stagger back to my room, which overlooks the front of the house, and look out the window just in time to see a yellow and black rickshaw pulling away down the dirt road. I glimpse a white elbow and forearm sticking out of a colorful Hawaian-style bush shirt and catch a flash of khaki-colored Bermuda shorts in the back of the rickshaw. In another second, it's out of sight and the sound fades as the cab joins the traffic on the main road.

I sink down on the floor again, gulping in air.

He's gone for now.

But he'll be back.

If he's tracked me here, then he knows.

Somehow, he knows that I'm Hannah.

And that must mean he knows I'm the one who actually killed Ricky Manfredi.

And if he knows, then that means Roger fucking Cordry knows as well.

Which basically means I'm fucked.

We're all fucked.

I clench my fists hard enough that my unmanicured fingernails draw blood from my palms and I scream with a fury and strength I wouldn't have believed I could muster fifteen minutes ago. I scream until a murder of crows in the coconut grove responds with raucous caws, mocking my anguish. In my confusion, fear, paranoia and rage, they almost sound like they're calling out to me.

*You did this! You fucked it all up! You're the reason why you're all going to end up dead now!*

The venting should drain me of whatever little energy I have left. Instead, it revitalizes me. Maybe revitalizes isn't the right word. It's not that I've stopped feeling the nausea and weakness that comes with chemotherapy, and the general sense of debilitation. It's more like Reitmaier's visit has lit a fire under my ass, forcing me to forget all those things and shove my own infirmities in the freezer. My only concern right now is for the girls. If Reitmaier has tracked me here to our home, then it's only a matter of time before the girls are in Roger fucking Cordry's crosshairs.

It's times like this that make me think I should have kept a gun in the house. Guns, plural. I would, except Kiara wouldn't have it. When she found the SIG Sauer on the top shelf of our bedroom closet, she went ballistic. It erupted into one of our biggest fights. I finally gave in because she also showed me a doll's shoe that one of the girls had left on the same shelf, right next to the shoebox in which I'd hidden the pistol. That meant either Lucy or Megan – I'm betting Lucy, she's the bandleader on these expeditions – had managed to push a chair over, then place something else on the chair, and then climbed up to reach the top of the closet. Even then, they would only be able to reach up and feel around. That would be when they'd left the doll shoe. It was enough to convince me.

But this is an exceptional event.

I go downstairs, holding on to the bannister some of the way when the nausea threatens, and make it to the front hallway. I reach for the front door handle and am about to open it so I can go into the coconut grove and dig up the plastic sack I've buried there, when my foot touches something.

I look down.

The white square of paper shines brightly against the brown wooden floor.

I pick it up, take a breath, then unfold it.

It has only two sentences, written in neat, Palmer method script, and a phone number.

*I know why you killed them. I know what he did to your family.*

## 40

## REITMAIER

Adalbert Reitmaier is playing with fire and he knows it.

He puts down the phone and takes a sip from a tall glass with a little red umbrella. He is sitting on a comfortable chair in the air-cooled dimness of a restaurant designed to resemble a large shack. The restaurant is on a cliff, overlooking one of the more popular tourist beaches in Goa. He can see people of all nationalities, races and skin hues cavorting in swimsuits on the beautiful white sand beach below. There are para-surfers, water scooters, speedboats circling around pods of dolphins, white women lying face-down on their beach towels, naked backs shiny with suntan lotion, children screaming and splashing in the surf, vendors selling snacks and beer. Wooden stairs lead up here to the cliff where there are restaurants like the one he's sitting in, and dozens of shops selling souvenirs, cashews, feni, and all the other paraphernalia of modern con-sumer culture. The mood is very cheerful and festive. It's his first visit to Goa and he likes it quite a bit.

He has been here less than a fortnight and most of that time was spent working, but for him, it is a perfect vacation. Adalbert Reitmaier has never been a person who can simply lie in a hammock all day and drink rum. He has always found a way to take pleasure in the everyday pursuits of life. A good meal in a pleasant spot. A scenic view. A warm cli-mate. Colorful locals, foreign languages, exotic cuisines, sites of historic interest that one might not find on the list of Top Ten Things to See In ... but are nevertheless fascinating glimpses into a region's history and culture. A conversation with a street vendor, an auto-rickshaw driver, a server in a café. A visit to a perfectly ordinary house and family. To him, life is in the minutiae.

'Can I get you anything else?'

Reitmaier looks up to see his very nice-looking Goan server with his even nicer body. He smiles back. 'No, thank you. How much do I owe you ... ?'

'Manuel,' says the young man.

'Here you go, Manuel. Please keep the change.'

Reitmaier gives him a currency note with a picture of Gandhi on it and a smile.

He gets an even nicer smile and a cheerful 'See you again soon!' in return. Reitmaier waves back. He likes Goan people very much. Especially the young men. Maybe once he's done with this Cordry case, he can linger a week or two and simply enjoy himself?

The walk back to his hotel is a pleasant one, although the street vendors do get quite clingy now that they recognize him. He smiles but shakes his head at the boy from whom he's bought far too many packets of raw cashew nuts already. Even charity has its limits.

His pretty hotel receptionist greets him warmly. She also works room service sometimes and Reitmaier has been a good tipper. He collects his key and heads to his room. The poolside is packed with a large mixed family playing a friendly game of water polo. He smiles to himself as a father picks up his infant daughter who dunks the ball into the basket, accompanied by a chorus of cheers and yells of complaint. The pool sounds fade as he reaches his suite at the far end of the property. Even from here, he can smell the sea. He unlocks the door of the villa – really just a cottage – and goes in.

The place is exactly as he left it. A prettily appointed villa, quaintly furnished in a style resembling Portuguese fazendas in Europe. If he wasn't here for work, he would happily spend a month, three months, and enjoy the warm climate and even warmer culture and people. Hot food too! Too hot for his Swiss digestion, but very delicious. He must try those prawns with that spicy dip again.

He sits in a chair and looks over his files as he waits. It will not be long now. Hannah will get his note and will respond. He will occupy the time reviewing what he is about to propose to her. And then, if she is willing, perhaps the two of them can combine forces to help bring down the monstrosity that is Roger Cordry, together.

He never liked the man to begin with, since the first time he met him after his son Ricky's murder. Perhaps he has seen too many rich, privileged individuals like Cordry over the years; somehow, even when they are at the receiving end of a criminal act, deserving of immediate sympathy for their plight, Reitmaier has found it hard to empathize with them completely. What is that saying, *Into every life a little rain must fall.* Someone like Roger Cordry has had far more than his fair share of the world's resources, most if not all of it gained, no doubt, through exploiting, manipulating or even outright deceiving his fellow men; surely he was overdue for a little rain. It is the genuinely needy whose cases tug at Reitmaier's heart. Immigrants fleeing a despotic regime intent on erasing their very existence from the face of the earth, forced to flee their humble lives with little more than the clothes on their backs, arriving in Europe in the hope of asylum and, perhaps someday, through hard work and struggle, a chance at a better life. Or at least a *life*. More often than not, they end up face-down in an alley somewhere, knived, assaulted, bludgeoned to death by white supremacists, just plain criminals, or even, in some cases, their own fellow refugees. Children torn from their parents, families ripped apart, decent, educated people forced into prostitution, extreme poverty, crime. Those are people who have received more than their fair share of rain. After seeing a hundred cases like that, it's hard to find genuine sympathy with someone like Roger Cordry.

As for the man himself, the more Reitmaier has interacted with him, learned about him, the less he has liked him – or rather, it would be more accurate to say, the more intensely he has come to dislike him. Especially the things he has learned since Cordry returned to Zurich and gave Reitmaier that little demonstration of the tyranny of extreme capitalism. Did he really think threatening Reitmaier was the best way to secure his services? Well, Reitmaier had guessed, correctly as it turned out, that any motive for Ricky's murder had to lead back to the father, and his subsequent investigations had proved him right. Roger Cordry had secured Reitmaier's services, but at a price: the price was Reitmaier learning some unpleasant truths about Cordry himself. Especially the one truth that Reitmaier was now certain had led to the death of first Ricky and now Monty. The sins of the father visited upon the sons.

During the conversation with the Bulgarian flatmate of Hannah, Reitmaier had asked if Olga recalled any mention of places in India. At first, the young woman had nothing to offer but later, when talking about Hannah's activities during her last few days, she mentioned a night out at the club. Hannah, Olga and Olga's then-boyfriend Stu, an American exchange student from Texas, had gone clubbing and in the course of the night, had consumed a fair amount of alcohol.

Reading between the lines, Reitmaier thought perhaps there had been more than alcohol consumed, but he had no interest in that aspect. At some point, they had been daydreaming about taking a vacation together and had discussed the best destinations for a holiday. Hannah had mentioned Goa, in particular a little village and beach resort named Vagator. Olga remembered that because, clearly inebriated, Hannah had lapsed into a brief moment of nostalgic reflection, wishing she was 'back home' right now. She had quickly stopped herself, clearly embarrassed with having revealed what was apparently a private thought, and had deftly changed the topic, but Olga had been intrigued by that solitary glimpse of real emotion beneath Hannah's armor-like facade.

That little clue was the key. Reitmaier had known right away that he was on to something there.

It had led him to two golden pathways: One was the Texan boyfriend Stu, who had a few more insights to offer, which in turn led Reitmaier back to Cordry himself, and his past life. The second was Vagator, Goa.

Reitmaier had made the difficult, perhaps even dangerous, decision to keep these two reveals from Cordry. He investigated both avenues further on his own.

And that is what has brought him to Goa now. Sitting here in this lovely beach resort on a sunny day in Vagator.

Into every life a little rain must fall . . .

Perhaps it is time for Roger Cordry to get his fair share at last.

His cellphone rings, interrupting his reverie.

'Adalbert Reitmaier,' he says automatically.

'You came to my house,' she says, her voice clearly fraught with rage and something else, fear perhaps.

'Hello, Hannah,' Reitmaier says.

# 41

## HANNAH

'You came to my house,' I say when he answers the phone. What I really want to say is: *You know where I live! Where my babies sleep at night! I should kill you just for that, you son of a bitch!*

I have to make an effort to remain calm. As it is, it took a considerable amount of effort just to make this call.

*I know why you killed them. I know what he did to your family.* That was what his note said. What does that mean, really? How much does he know? Is Roger fucking Cordry listening in? What's this guy's real agenda?

As I reminded myself after an agonizing hour of procrastination: there's only one way to find out. That's why I'm calling him. I need to know how much this bastard knows. Will Roger Cordry's goons come bursting into my house one night while my babies are asleep? What's going on here?

'Hello, Hannah,' he says.

The Samsung feels ice-cold against my feverish ear.

I say nothing, trying to get him to keep talking. He doesn't say anything. I try to wait him out but he's more patient than I am. The seconds, then the minutes tick by.

Finally, I decide I'm the only one who stands to lose in this game of chicken.

'What do you want?' I say, trying not to sound irritated, anxious, pissed-off, take your pick.

'We need to talk. I have learned some very interesting things.'

My fist clenches the phone hard enough that all my phalanges and metacarpals are clearly defined.

I lower the phone because my hand is trembling. I don't know if it's the adrenalin, the chemo, the shock, or all of the above. I'm sitting on the stairs when I make the call. Below me is the shoe rack and on the walls on either side are pictures of Lucy, Megan, Ki, me, Manuel, Edna, Philomena, and all the assorted aunts, cousins and their broods, taken at various times over the years. The one that catches my eye is a pic of me with Megan and Lucy the night they were born. I look exhausted after my fifteen-hour ordeal delivering two seven-pound brown buns, but it's the best kind of exhaustion. I've never felt happier in my life. The joy captured in that image helps me center my emotions.

I can hear the detective's voice from the speaker. 'Hello?'

I raise the phone to my ear again, ignoring the faint tremors that make me knock it against the side of my head. 'Where and when?'

He names a resort hotel only a few minutes' walk from Manu and Philo's beachside café, and a time.

I shut my eyes and try to think. Leave me alone, I tell the universe. For fuck's sake, I'm no longer Hannah the assassin! I'm just a mom raising her kids while undergoing chemo, trying to survive one day at a time!

But the universe doesn't give a fuck. It never has. I'm on my own. Even Ki isn't here to help me out. I could leave her a message at the drop but what good would that do? She's on the other side of the planet. Whatever shit is about to go down, it's going down right here right now. Even if she starts back now, this will all be over before her plane reaches the Atlantic, maybe even before she takes off.

Reitmaier has forced this engine into motion, and it ain't stopping until it rolls into the terminus now. I have only one choice: get on board or accept whatever happens when I don't.

With my babies' future at stake, that's no choice at all.

'I'll be there,' I say into the phone, then hang up without waiting to hear what he says back.

I pass a hand across my face. I would give anything for three weeks to recover from the chemo, regain some weight, work out, train, get my head and body in the game again.

I don't have that luxury.

I pull myself up by the bannister struts and rise back on my feet. The first thing I need to do is get my guns.

# 42

## KIARA

'No,' I say. 'That's not the way we're going to do this.'

The room falls silent.

Roger frowns. I ignore him.

There are twenty people present around the large table, all the heads of department and senior scientists of the Monty Cordry BioPharma project, a few bean counters and lawyers from Roger's corporate headquarters who flew in from Chicago for this meeting, and the CEO of MCBP, yours truly. As Chairperson and Main Trustee of the Monty Cordry Foundation, Roger controls the purse strings of the company, while I run the project. In the past several weeks since I joined, I've been on a whirlwind tour of activity and decision-making. Just before we came into this meeting, Roger admitted that he's impressed by the progress I've achieved in this short time. Yeah, well, I'm not doing it to impress you.

Earlier, we sat through the presentations from the HoDs followed by my own presentation, Roger watching me with his deceptively please-carry-on-don't-mind-me air. I know he and some of the others here were a little surprised at how confidently I took charge of the meeting and the room. Perhaps some of them have been judging me by appearances and gender/age expectations. They thought I'd be a little ditzy, scatterbrained, self-doubting and disorganized. Instead, I've been crisp, professional and meticulously organized. Years of prepping and training – including taking speech and acting classes and workshops – have proved useful. I got a few chuckles from time to time and at the end, even Roger's main bean counter, Freddy, who is also CFO of MCBP, raised his eyebrows at Roger. The girl has something, that's for sure, he was commenting without saying it aloud. Damn right I do. I've proved myself a project leader, and also a damn good research scientist. I've handled the most difficult part of this startup, the actual startup phase, about as successfully and smoothly as could be done – much smoother than is usually the case with biopharma startups, one of the more supportive HoDs, a greying woman named Kesha, told me confidentially. 'You're kicking ass, young lady. Keep on doing what you're doing.' What started out as a charity research project Roger decided to keep afloat for Monty's sake now looks like it may actually turn into a viable proposition. That's nothing to sniff at.

Roger has funded enough startups that he's probably lost count of how many dozens couldn't get past the usual teething issues and find their feet, some of them floated by reputable Silicon Valley guys with track records. Startups are always a gamble and when it comes to biopharma research-based projects, the odds are stacked even higher against any kind of real success. Yet, somehow, on my first time out of the gate, I've managed to buck those odds and am firmly in control of the wagon team. It's early days yet but I think I might actually pull this damn thing off after all.

During this time, I've only seen Roger on weekends and on the occasional night when he flew in or I flew out to wherever he happened to be, for maybe a handful of dinner dates in the past month. I used that to my advantage: better to have him wanting to see more of me than too much too soon. I also made sure I never talked too much about work when we were out together, just enough to whet his appetite, while making him focus on the woman in front of him. That's working for me now as he is genuinely, pleasantly surprised at how much I've achieved, and how clearly in charge of this whole operation I am.

I also know I'm the best date he's had in a while. OK, so I don't know that with absolute certainty. Roger Cordry is not the kind of man to text his buddies about his new girl or share gooey posts online. But I'm pretty sure I've rocked his world. While making him think all the while that he's rocking mine. Yeah, in your dreams, uncle.

At one point, when we were joined, at his invitation, by a big-time yesteryears movie star turned producer and his Oscar-winning director wife for drinks at a gala, I know I impressed him by how comfortably I interacted with these starry celebs and entertained their table all evening. 'This one's a keeper. You could do worse. Hell, you did do a lot worse! Hold on to her,' said the old-time star to Roger, who smiled over his wine at me. I smiled back and winked. Enjoy it while you can; nothing lasts forever.

And now, I'm rocking his business world too.

After my team and I finished our presentations and the applause died down, one of Roger's people, a white-haired douche named Lerouche, former CEO of Merck and a board member of several biopharma companies and other businesses, suggested that it might be time for human trials in a few months, maybe even before the end of the year.

I gave Lerouche a withering look and said, clearly and unequivocally, 'No, that's not how we're going to do this.'

Now, everyone in the room is dead silent. No one's actually looking at Roger but I can feel their eyes on him anyway.

They're all expecting him to say something, to smack me down for acting too big for my boots. I know Freddy is, for sure. The lawyers are all but smirking in anticipation of the smackdown; they've probably seen their share, including the times when Roger has fired people on the spot for lesser cause. Everyone who works for Roger Cordry knows the Golden Rule: when Roger's in the room, he calls the shots. There is no compromise, no middle path on that. It's his way or the highway, always. The phrase he most often uses at such times is something of a mantra: *This isn't a democracy.*

Lerouche isn't happy, that's for sure. I can tell the man is one breath short of tongue-lashing me right here and now. He's furious at my put-down, coming in front of the entire room. If Roger's a whip cracker, then Lerouche is a boot-heeler. He doesn't like being contradicted at a meeting like this by 'a mere wisp of a girl' – a phrase he used in an email to Roger when he first asked him to serve on the board of this company. He expects Roger to knock me down a few notches.

So be it.

If he does that, I won't take it. I'll stand up to him and re-mind him of what he told me – *promised* me – when I agreed to lead the project. I'm the one running it, not him. He may be Roger Cordry to the whole wide world; but in this room, I'm boss. And he's the one who made me boss, so either he stands up for me, or I stand up and walk. But Lerouche doesn't know that. He thinks I'm just a pretty protégée Roger is giving a twirl here.

And then Roger surprises them all, including me.

'I think Kiara has a point,' he says. 'The FDA has ramped up its actionable guidelines about testing after that last disaster. I think legal has done a cost-benefit-risk analysis on the upside and downside of testing too soon versus testing on a more comfortable timeline and there's a substantial liability cost that could accrue. We don't want to rush into this and have it come back to bite us in the ass later. Isn't that the case, Freddy?'

Freddy raises one eyebrow but nods, acknowledging the fiscal wisdom in Roger's words. 'The last company that was found at fault got slapped with a class action suit of just over $1.7 billion, and that's not counting the sanctions and fines imposed by the FDA, or the PR fallout.'

'It was a disaster, in short,' Roger concludes. 'We wouldn't want that, would we?'

His lawyers and PR consultant all nod in effusive agreement. They would probably have shown just as much enthusiasm if he'd said the exact opposite, but that's beside the point.

The HoDs and team members are blinking and stealing glances at Roger, then looking at me. They murmur their agreement with my call. *The pack falls in line,* I think to myself, resisting the urge to pump my fist, *Breakfast Club* style.

Only Lerouche still looks nettled. He seems about to say something and I'm pretty sure that whatever he says, it won't make things better. At the same time, I can see Roger watching him closely. He also doesn't want to antagonize Lerouche: the man has formidable connections and we will need him once we're past the trials and moving toward the production and distribution stages. Even I know that.

'But Martin makes an excellent point and we should keep in mind that there's also a downside to losing momentum,' Roger says and sees Lerouche blink, disarmed by the sudden change of direction. 'Let's agree to review this at our next progress meeting. Does that work for you, Kiara?'

I give him a look, a narrowing of my eyes combined with

a small smile that tells him I've seen what he's just done and I acknowledge it, but if he's expecting a hallelujah in appreciation then he'll be waiting a long time. I see how he's walked the line between ticking Lerouche off and cutting me down publicly, and have to admit, it's not bad. Not bad at all. But it'll be a cold day in hell before I show admiration for Roger fucking Cordry.

'I think Martin's suggestion is something worth thinking about,' I say, playing it as cool as I can. I then surprise Lerouche with a bright girlish smile, as if to say, I'm still just a kid so don't be too hard on me, big daddy, OK? Out the corner of my eye, I see Roger's eyebrows twitch. He gets what I'm doing – the present-day equivalent of batting my eyelashes and speaking in a Marilyn Monroe lisp – but keeps silent. Lerouche, fortunately, is too gauche to see through my parody.

Lerouche is pacified. The man has granddaughters Kiara's age and he probably thinks this is me backing down. He clears his throat and says gracefully, 'That's all I'm asking.'

Like hell it is, I think. Lerouche is taking his cue from Roger. He doesn't want to come off as the bad guy in this scenario and, I know now, he's more than a little charmed by me, despite our differences of opinion on management styles. Besides, if this thing does pan out, as I'm starting to think it might, there's going to be money to be made. Lerouche has been around long enough to have fought his battles and vanquished his foes; the only true measure he has of achievement now is to add to his considerable wealth and legacy. It isn't worth foregoing all that potential just for the pleasure of slapping down an upstart young woman. And that, friends, is the way to a rich man's heart – not through his stomach, but through his wallet and ego.

'You handled that nicely,' Roger says to me over lunch later that afternoon.

I give him a cool smile but say nothing. I don't need his patronizing praise.

He notes my silence and nods, getting it. At least I think he gets it. It's not always easy to tell with Roger. Like, for instance, I'm sure he doesn't have a clue about how I'm playing him here. Not with the project, but with his whole life. If he knew who I really was, what we've done to his family, he wouldn't be sitting here having lunch with me and talking business, while hoping to get me into his bed sometime soon. I can afford to smile and play it cool. I'm the one holding all the cards here. I'm coming for you, Roger Cordry, you just don't know it yet.

One of the endless stream of celebs who always seem to find him on our dates appears by our table, greets me politely, then chats with Roger for a moment. The guy's a senator from Georgia, a QAnon conspiracy theorist who has ties to white supremacy groups. Not my kind of folk, thank you. Roger probably knows enough of my politics – Hannah and I decided early on that the best way to stay in character is to keep certain everyday things the same as our real personalities, political attitude being one of them – and steps off to one side to chat with him briefly.

I reach for my glass of water and happen to notice Roger's phone light up just then with a message notification. My hand freezes in mid-air.

**Abdi:** *Goa Team in position. Hannah ETA 30.*
Hannah.

That must mean *my* Hannah. Who else?

Hakam Abdi is in Goa? He's meeting Hannah in thirty minutes, and he has a 'team in position'? Where?

I track his GPS back to the source, down to . . . Vagator, Goa.

Fuck, fuck, fuck.

That can only mean what I think it means: Hakam is on to Hannah and is about to close the net on her, using a team of armed and lethal operatives.

I have to get a message to her *now*. Warn her. Tell her to get the hell out of there, take the girls, go to Plan X, our Armageddon option.

Roger is still occupied with the senator. He glances at his watch, looking less than interested in what the blowhard has to say, then looks over at me and gives me a *Can you believe this guy? I'm so sorry* look. I smile back reassuringly. I want to run from here, get on a call to Hannah right away, but I don't know how much Roger knows yet. Do he and Hakam know about me too? That Hannah and I are sisters? Do they know about San Francisco? Or is this only about Ricky? Did Hakam somehow find something linking her to Ricky's murder? Damn, damn, damn. This is totally unexpected; Hannah and I never anticipated it. Well, we anticipated a lot of possibilities, just not this exact situation. Now, I'm wishing we had talked, kept in touch. But that's on me. I'm the one who decided to cut her off and sent her that message.

The drop.

My fingers racing over my screen, the phone angled so Roger can't catch even a glance at it, I check the secure email drop.

There's an unread message there, from Hannah.

My heart pounding, I tap it.

316

I have a brain fart trying to break down the coded message. Our system requires us to do it mentally, never once writing it down or using a decoding app to make it easier. This way, only we know what the messages really say. I fumble it twice and have to start over. Using Vedic Mathematics as a code sounds like a radically cool idea but when you're under extreme pressure, it can be frustrating.

Finally, I have it.

*They have a pic of me with Ricky in Odeon. Reitmaier back on the case. I'm activating Plan X. We're all safe here. Take care of yourself. I don't know if they know about you yet. Watch your back. Eyes on RC.*

That's it.

The message was sent weeks ago.

So does she know about the trap?

Damn my stubbornness.

Why didn't I check this sooner? If I had, I could have watched Hakam and Roger more closely, learned about their Goa plans, the trap they've probably laid for Hannah, warned her in time. Now, it might already be too late. I try calling her, not caring anymore about Roger. We're in a public place; I hardly think he's going to pull out a gun – he doesn't carry one anyway – and shoot me right here and now. Besides, he won't even know who I'm calling. Unless he's already on to me. In which case, it hardly matters, does it?

Hannah's Goa cellphone is switched off. I'm about to call Manu or Philomena, then I stop myself. Hannah said she's activated Plan X. That means the girls are safe and secure, and Hakam can't get to them.

Presumably.

The plan has never been tested before.

But it's all I have, so I hold on to that hope for now.

Hannah's my main concern.

I have to find a way to warn her, tell her she's walking into a trap.

Think, Ki, think.

I'm still staring at Hakam's GPS location in Vagator. It's triangulated by three cell towers in a neighborhood that's very familiar. In a moment, it clicks: I know exactly where that location is. I know where Hakam Abdi is right now.

There is one thing I can try. It's a long shot, but maybe, if I'm lucky – if we're lucky – it just might work.

But Roger's right here. If he hears me, my cover will be blown, and then we'll both be up the creek.

As if on cue, Roger returns to the table. 'Drain the swamp! Once the 'gators get a-hold of you, they never let go.'

I laugh, rising as he sits down. 'I need to visit the ladies' room. Back in a tinkle.'

I let my fingertips touch his shoulder as I pass by, my hip graze his bicep. I sense him turning his head to watch me walk away. Keep watching my ass, motherfucker, just so long as you don't watch my lips.

The instant I'm out of sight, I dial the number of our cousin Manu. It rings out several times. *Pick up, Manu, pick up, please.*

The phone is answered by a female voice. 'Manu's phone. Who dis?'

Not Manu, but it's the next best thing, his wife Philomena. I grin through clenched teeth. 'Philo! Kiara. Listen, I need the number of your cousin who works at Vagator Resorts.'

When I return to the table, Roger manages a smile but he's already preoccupied. 'Hey, everything OK?'

'Yes,' I say brightly, 'Lady stuff!'

He nods politely, looking at his device. 'Listen, Ki, I have to jump on this con call.'

'Sure, go right ahead,' I say, glad I won't have to suffer through small talk and flirtation.

'See you back at the lab?' he asks. Then corrects himself, 'No, the office, tomorrow morning, right? Ciao, bella!'

'Ciao!' I say too brightly and I have to fight to keep my face from twisting with rage as I watch his tight little ass walk away.

The 'con call' he's going to jump on to is the op headed by Hakam, designed to take down my sister. I can only pray Hannah has got my message. Otherwise, the clock's run out.

# 43

## ROGER

Ki has changed.

He smiles inwardly.

He thinks of her as 'Ki' now, not 'Kiara', although he's always careful to address her by the latter in public. Perhaps he will allow himself to call her 'Ki' publicly as well from now on. After all, though it hasn't been very long, it *feels* long enough for it to be real. Not a fan of letting emotion drive his actions, Roger acknowledges that there are exceptions. This isn't business anymore. It began as that, but he can see that what he wants from Ki isn't black ink on the balance sheets, or just her brown hair on the bedsheets. It's more than that now. He wants all of her.

At first, he thought of her as a smart, possibly brilliant researcher who had come up with this one breakthrough idea but had the usual set of emotional and mental health issues that all young people seemed to suffer from these days – or allowed themselves to suffer from. Yet she had surprised him in these past few weeks, not only by turning out to be a formidable leader and handler of people and processes, but also as a person with a strong vision and the moxie to do what was needed to realize that vision. She's a far more practical, get-your-hands-dirty-but-get-it-done kinda gal than he'd thought at first glance, and she's impressed him. That in itself turns him on in a woman, but add to that the fact that she's *not* his type, physically or otherwise, and the fact that he is able to relate to something in her that is beyond the physical, a sharing of something that passes between them only in looks and shared moments, and is the stronger for it. She has an endoskeleton of titanium, speaking metaphorically, of course. Something within her that belies the soft, smiley, millennial youthful exuberance she wears as an alias; a person within the person, the skull beneath the skin. And it's that Ki that attracts him powerfully. That Ki is a perfect match for Roger, himself a chameleon. Their titanium-infused endoskeletons joining together in a perfect storm of mating.

Perhaps even mating for life.

Is he thinking seriously about proposing to her? Does he really intend to marry this young woman?

Well . . . why the fuck not?

It's been long enough since Gabriella, and he isn't naive and stupid enough to believe in shit like eternal love. That's what prenups and lawyers are for. It's not as if he's a spring chicken anymore either. What would be so wrong with spending a few years – or decades – with someone young enough and hard-boned enough to take all his cruel crap and maybe make him feel good about himself, if only for a few minutes, or hours, or days? He's always been a taker. Why shouldn't he take her? If she gets used up, he can always distance himself and take his pleasures elsewhere. And if she turns catty and mean as Gaby did, he can always dump her, hard. Either way, it's worth consideration.

He's still mulling on this when his phone awakens.

'Alive, Hakam,' is the first thing he says when he hears Abdi's voice. 'I want her alive.'

'I've instructed the team to shoot to wound only.'

'Good. Call me again when you have her.'

There's a moment of silence on Hakam's end. Roger knows that silence well. He doesn't like it. 'What?'

'Reitmaier gave my team the slip for a couple of hours. Went AWOL. We think he's using a burner because there was no chatter on his registered cellphone.'

Roger resists the urge to yell at Hakam. Instead, he opts for silence. It's as clear as a threat to his security chief.

Hakam continues: 'We've got him under surveillance now. He's in his room in the hotel. It's possible he's meeting Hannah here, but if so, he hasn't texted or called her.'

'So you don't know for certain that he's meeting Hannah. He could be just another European tourist, enjoying the sights. Jesus Christ, Hakam, why did you just text me that Hannah's expected in thirty? Because it sounds to me like you don't know if she's coming, or even if she's in Goa!'

'She's here. She's coming. Reitmaier left a message earlier with the hotel receptionist that he was expecting a young lady to visit. He just called them again to say she's on her way and to send her straight in.'

'How do you know he didn't just call for someone to help keep him entertained tonight? Slipped a bellboy a few bucks to send in someone young and nubile?'

'Because he's queer,' Hakam said flatly. 'He only likes men, preferably in their thirties.'

Roger realizes he walked straight into that one. 'OK,' he says sharply, 'so let's say it's her. You have the room bugged, of course.'

'Yes.'

'So give them a few. Let them talk.'

'We should go in right away, go in hard and fast, before they have time to settle down.'

'Did I ask you for tactical advice? I want to hear what they have to say, Hakam. Let them talk. Send me the live feed. I want to hear what the Swiss has to say to her.'

Hakam hesitates again.

'What?' Roger snaps, out of patience now.

'It could get bloody. She could be armed and dangerous. We don't know what kind of skills she has. There could be collateral damage. Civilians. It's a beach resort. Families, kids.'

'I don't give a fuck, Hakam. If anyone gets in the way, if seven pregnant woman with their arms full of babies get in the way, cut them down. I want that bitch. No excuses. Comprende?'

Hakam says curtly, 'Yes, sir.'

Roger disconnects.

This will work. It has to work. They will get this young woman, this Hannah. And when he has her in his custody, he will make her tell him about Ricky, about the how and why. Mostly the why. That's all he really wants to understand. Why the fuck did she kill his son?

Once he's gotten the information out of her, he will make her wish she had never even looked at a Cordry in her life.

He will make sure of that.

# 44

## *HANNAH*

I'm finishing my third circuit of the hotel. It's still daylight and this is full season, so there are tourists everywhere. I'm trying to be as low-key as possible, dressed in a tracksuit with an oversized coat that's out of place in Goa's warm 'winter' season. Can't be helped. The ball cap helps cover my hair and face and adds to the androgynous look. A stray dog follows me around, wagging his tail hopefully. He probably smells Britney on me; she's in heat because the girls refused to let their 'puppy have an operation'.

The hotel is surrounded by a high stone wall but there's no wire on top, only lights mounted at regular intervals. Burglary isn't a worry in this part of Goa; there's plenty of money to be made trafficking in drugs, blood diamonds and human beings. India is the biggest redistribution center for all the three illegal trades and the beating heart of the world's three biggest criminal industries; Goa is the nerve center of that unholy trinity.

It also means that there are always plenty of mercenaries around, guns for hire for almost anything under the sun who've worn out their welcome in most of the western world but can fly under the radar here.

The goons I spot around Reitmaier's villa all fall into that category. Israelis, I'm thinking. They have the look and the equipment.

Besides, I recognize Oshri.

That means this is his team. At least now I know who I'm dealing with. I know how they operate, their training methodology, their individual strengths and weaknesses.

That's the good news.

Oshri is fucking good at what he does. His team is just as good. They're a tight crew. If they're working for Roger Cordry, this must be the biggest payday of their young, post-Sayeret lives. Not one of them is over twenty-three and they're all in prime condition. They do everything as a team, bonded unto death. It's a formidable opponent to go up against in the best of times. I've partied with them back in the day. They kill as well as they fuck, and vice versa.

I'll be lucky if I survive the first few seconds of any armed encounter against any one of them when on my best game. In my present condition, against the entire team at once? No chance. Game over before it's even begun.

But then, I already knew I was screwed even before I showed up, right? So boo fucking hoo to me.

Like I said, that's the good news. At least I know Oshri and his team, how they think, how they operate, what their tactics are likely to be – correction, might be.

Here's the bad news.

They're not the ones running this show.

The man who hired them is on site and he's the one heading this operation.

Hakam Abdi, in the flesh.

That's Mr Bad News himself, in person.

Oshri and his team were a mission impossible for me in this condition anyway.

With Hakam leading them, I'm as good as dead ten times over.

But like I said, I already knew the odds going in, right?

So what do I have to lose now that I didn't already have to lose?

It's a minute to showtime now. I could be late by a few minutes. Or even a few hours. Or even not show up at all. But I'm here now, and I have a plan – of sorts. If I run, I'll be looking over my shoulder for the bullet chasing me all my life. And with two little girls who depend on me, that's not an option. No way. I have to confront this head on right here and now. Take the bull by the horns and either bring it down or let it gore me to death. It's kill or be killed time.

If only I didn't have this fucking chemo messing up my system.

If only I didn't have cancer.

If only I had a week, a month, a year to train and prep.

Suck it up and get it on, girl. Time to go to work.

I find a suitable spot and work my way up the wall, using the imperfections in the stone blocks as hand and foot grips. I slip twice, landing once on my ass and the second time on my back, which sets my bones rattling. The stray licks the side of my face supportively and I pat him on the head. 'Whatever you do, don't get cancer,' I tell him. 'And if you do get it, don't get chemo. They both fucking suck.'

He licks my face again before turning his attention to my crotch. I brush him aside gently and try a third time.

I almost lose my grip at the top because my palm is slippery with sweat, but I snake my other hand over just in time and dangle for a moment. Stray dog barks once from below, begging me not to fall.

'You and me both,' I mutter and pull myself on top.

I lie on the wall for a moment, catching my breath.

If climbing one eight-foot wall does me in, how the fuck do I hope to survive an encounter with Oshri's crew?

Simple answer: I don't.

Just one small comfort: Philo's cousin in Room Service, I forget his name now, got Kiara's message to me in the nick of time. The real importance of Kiara's message reaching me is simply that my sister is looking out for me. It feels good to know that our falling-out hasn't damaged our relationship permanently. I mean, I know she loves me and we're sisters for life, but she was really pissed with me after I took out Monty Cordry, and there was a moment there when I thought she might never forgive me. This reassures me in a way that's hugely relieving. If I have to call it quits today, at least I'll go down knowing Ki and I mended our differences.

God alone knows what price Ki is now paying for having taken that risk, sending me that help just in the nick of time. If she's even still alive . . .

I close my eyes against the darkening twilight and focus on the positive. I have to believe in Ki. It's the only way I can get through this. I have to believe she's OK, and she's still in play, and that she'll finish this game.

If anything happens to me, I know she'll take care of my girls. Raise them like they're her own.

Reitmaier wouldn't be looking for her – he has no reason to, right? He's tracked me down somehow – how? – so why would he bother to keep looking? I killed both Ricky and Monty. I'm the one he wants.

My heart rate eases as I think past the panic.

There's absolutely no reason for Roger fucking Cordry or any of his goons to suspect her.

Whether it's true or not, I force myself to believe it.

I cling to that thought.

I take three deep, slow breaths, forcing the air out of my lungs each time, like the opposite of hyperventilating, before drawing it back in slow and easy. I will myself to calm down, centering myself.

The sky is almost dark overhead. The trees are packed with birds of all varieties making a godawful racket. The sounds of tourists and music and traffic all mingle together to produce one loud, mangled mash-up. Another Goan night in full season.

I open my eyes and slip down off the wall, into the bushes that skirt the perimeter of the hotel compound.

Time to face the music.

# 45

## *HANNAH*

The detective is looking at his watch as he rises and walks toward the bathroom.

I raise the gun, allowing the gleam of the fading light from the window to catch the barrel, drawing his attention instantly. A lifetime of criminal investigation has made spotting a weapon second nature to him. He stops.

I come forward from the bedroom, knowing my all-black outfit blends in with the dark room behind me, making me barely visible in the gloam.

'I suggest you seat yourself again, detective,' I say softly. 'We have some things to talk about.'

Reitmaier stares at the gun then at me.

'Hannah?' he says uncertainly. 'You look . . . different.'

'Cancer, chemo,' I say shortly. 'Fuck them both.' I feel out of breath. I gesture with the gun. 'Actually, if you don't mind, I would rather that you get down on the bed.'

'On the bed?' he repeats.

'Yes, please. Lie down flat on your chest, arms wedged under your thighs. Do it now.'

I keep my voice quiet but knife-edged. The gun underlines my commands.

He does as I say.

The room darkens abruptly. He turns his head and glimpses me pulling the drapes shut by standing off to the side of the window, careful not to pass across it. The drapes drawn, I toss the roll of packing tape to the bed beside him.

'Tape your hands behind your back.'

Reitmaier starts to ask, 'How do I –?'

'Figure it out, detective,' I snap. I don't have time for any banter.

Reitmaier feels around with his right hand, finds the roll of packing tape, and uses his fingernails to probe until he finds the loose end. He unpeels it with a ripping sound, wrapping it around one wrist, then passing it around the other as best he can, and repeats the action several times. It looks clumsily done, too tight on some turns, too loose on others, but I'm pretty sure it will be nearly impossible to break free of. He knows better than to ask for a blade to cut the end off, and tries to shift the roll until it's no longer beneath his weight. Good. Now he is effectively disabled. Short of leaping off the bed like a ninja and trying to head-butt me, he is defenseless. And I don't think Detective Reitmaier has had any ninja training.

My hip strikes something in the dark – the sideboard on which the flatscreen TV is mounted – and I hitch in my breath. I know the room is bugged and I don't want Hakam Abdi and his team knowing what I'm up to.

My knees pop as I squat down. My breathing sounds loud in the dark room. Why is it that sounds are always louder in darkness? As I work, I glimpse Reitmaier turning out the corner of my eye. He is trying to look over but his own large feet in the bright yellow flip-flops block his view. He tries to turn the other way to look around but, from the looks of it, he can't do that without risking losing his balance and rolling off the bed. I know he can hear the sound of things being moved around the room and is probably wondering what I'm doing.

'Is everything all right?' he asks, sounding genuinely concerned. 'Are you –?'

'Shut up,' I say hoarsely from somewhere near the floor. I cringe at how loud I sound and lower my voice. 'Shut up.'

He shuts up.

He lies still and waits.

A moment or three later, I straighten up again – I'm feeling the effort and stress now – and work at keeping my voice level, hoping he as well as all those listening can't hear the strain in it.

'Start talking,' I say. 'But listen very carefully to my questions and answer only what I ask. Not one word more or less. Do you understand, detective?'

I'm sure he doesn't understand at all but he says, 'Yes.'

'What do you know about Roger Cordry? Keep it short and to the point, like you're testifying in court and there's a judge and a jury in audience.'

He clears his throat and speaks carefully, choosing his words. He's a good detective, and a smart guy. I think he's figured out that we're bugged and others are listening in.

'Roger Cordry and your father were both from the same city in India. Chennai. Around the same age. Both were eager to seek their fortune in America, where they felt their initiative and acumen would be better appreciated. Your father, Jogesh, changed his name to Joe, and Rajesh became Roger. Roger was a chemist. Joe was a microbiologist. He had been conducting independent research and had developed a process that he felt could save many lives. He wanted to focus on the science and use his ideas to change the world, to help his fellow South Asian people and other underprivileged people of color get access to cheaper medicines and vaccines for endemic diseases. Roger was enterprising and a smooth talker. He succeeded in raising some venture capital funding to get them started. They became partners in the venture, but Joe owned and held the patent for the process.'

I break in. 'Why are you wasting my time telling me my own father's life story? Do you think I don't know all this already?'

He hesitates, then says gently, 'I'm a detective. I need to tell you everything I learned and put together, so it all makes sense to me, as much as to you. I'm sure you know your father's history, but I think, Hannah, that perhaps you do not know everything about his murder. Particularly the details and the specific motivations.'

'What makes you think that?'

'Because you would only have had access to the official police file and the news reports, which are woefully inadequate. Also, if you had known all this, you would not have taken so much time before killing Ricky and Monty; you would have done away with them quickly and efficiently, which was the more logical way. I think you took so much time getting close to them because you wanted to know what they knew.'

I'm silent for a minute, digesting this. He is a damn good detective; maybe too good. On the other hand, he's face-down on a bed with his hands taped behind his back and I have a gun. I came to the party, I may as well let him have a dance or two.

'Go on,' I say.

'Joe and Roger did very well initially, but the money soon ran out, probably because of Roger's predatory nature with women, and because he acquired a bad reputation. They had some disagreements over Roger's habits and lifestyle. Around this time, Joe's wife inherited a considerable sum from her mother, your grandmother, who passed away in Goa. Unlike Joe and Roger, who were South Indian Hindus, your mother's family were Anglo-Indian Christians from Goa. With her money, Joe was able to buy a fine house in Upstate New York and fund the company and his research for several more years, long enough for him to complete the research and perfect the process and vaccine. He kept Roger as a partner because of their friendship and original commitment, even though all the money and scientific talent was Joe's. Without his knowledge, Roger siphoned funds from the cash-rich company and used it to play the stock market, gaining some, but losing a great deal more. Joe found out about the money and told Roger he would forgive him and not press charges if he returned the money and left the partnership. Roger came back to Joe with an offer he had brokered with a bio-pharma giant who wanted to buy out Joe's process and patents. The biopharma company wanted to sell the same vaccine at several times the price Joe wanted it made available, catering to the rich instead of the poor and underprivileged. Joe refused. Roger was desperate. He had no way to pay back the money he had lost, but if the deal went through, they would both be very rich and all his troubles would be over. Joe was adamant. He liked money, up to a point, but he refused to sell out his life's work just so the corporation could make billions in profits.

'Roger resolved the situation by killing Joe and making it look like a hunting accident. Joe's eldest child, your brother Brian, happened to follow the men into the woods that day, and Roger killed him too. He paid off the authorities to pass the incident off as a hunting accident and a bear attack. Evidence was made to disappear, and files misplaced. As the surviving managing partner, Roger forged Joe's signature on a power of attorney, claiming he had been given control of the company, and sold it to the biopharma corporation for $260 million. Through clever legal and financial wrangling, he managed to cut Joe's widow out of the deal entirely. Your mother lost the house in New York and was left with only a small sum of money. She used the last of her inheritance to continue fighting the legal battle against Roger Cordry, refusing to go back to India with you. She was convinced that Roger had killed her husband and son, and stolen the company, and she wanted justice. When she finally lost the last appeal, several years later, it broke her heart. She killed herself by jumping off a bridge in New York City. You were orphaned. Roger Cordry used that deal and his newfound fortune to start a new company called Cordry BioPharma, using Joe's remaining patents. It formed the cornerstone of his billion-dollar empire.'

There is another period of silence. I can hear him breathing but my own breathing sounds louder.

This is a lot to process. While I knew – or guessed – the broad strokes, these details that Reitmaier has just unfolded are news to me. I know what a thorough procedural detective he is. If he's telling me all these details, it's because he has verified them. But I ask anyway.

'You have evidence of all this?' I say softly.

'The narrative is my . . . how would you say it? Recreation? Assumption? But yes, I have evidence too. The evidence that Roger Cordry paid to conceal at the time.'

My mind races. *Evidence.* Can it possibly be true? A reputable Swiss detective has actual hard evidence incriminating Roger fucking Cordry in major crimes? I don't know about the forgery and fraud, but there's no statute of limitations on murder – two murders, in this case. Is this really happening?

Could there actually be a chance that the bastard could finally be brought to justice after all?

But then I think of Ricky. And Monty.

Even if what he says is true, I can't exactly walk into a courtroom and expect to be interviewed by the media after Roger is found guilty and sentenced. My crimes are still my crimes. And in a twisted world, murder for vengeance is still murder. Besides, no jury would exonerate me for killing his sons. Roger, maybe, but not his sons. So nothing has really changed for me, legally and publicly.

And yet, everything has changed.

This information, this confirmation of Roger's evil acts, his premeditated crimes, is huge. It's more than we ever hoped to get from either Ricky or Monty, or even Roger himself, once Kiara gets her claws into him.

Kiara.

She won't have killed Roger yet. I know, because that was the plan, so I'm confident she'll get him to the point where he proposes to her fairly soon, but it'll be a while before she does away with him. As of now, her hands are still clean. She can still walk into that courtroom and be interviewed afterwards by the media, still come out of this vindicated and victorious.

That's what gives my heart a jolt of happy juice more powerful than adrenalin. This will change Ki's life forever. She can live out her entire existence without actually having bloodied her hands. Between the chemo and Hakam's team waiting to get me tonight, I'm as good as done anyway. But Ki can go on, and she can find the closure we both sought.

All these thoughts and emotions swirl through me as I say hoarsely, 'Tell me about this evidence.'

'There is a hunting license, a receipt for the gun that was

used to kill your brother and father, bought months earlier. The testimony of the instructor and the range where Roger learned and practiced the use of the weapon. There was no evidence of any other hunter in the woods on that particular day, as it was the day after the end of bear season and hunting for that particular animal would have been illegal. There is proof from handwriting experts that can show conclusively that Roger Cordry forged Joe's signature on the power of attorney and other documents. There is a paper trail with a New York Stock Exchange broker showing that Roger, not Joe, used the company funds to invest in the stock market. It is not very much, but it is enough to justify reopening the investigation into the murder of your father and brother. As you know, there is no statute of limitations for the crime of murder in New York State. As for the financial crimes he committed, I am not knowledgeable enough about American civil law, but I am sure with the right legal and possibly forensic accounting and document experts, a case can be made on some basis or other.'

This is awesome. This is superb. It's almost too good to be true. Even in the worst monsoon-riddled life, a little sunshine must fall. Maybe it's our time in the sun at long last.

'How did you get all these things?' I ask.

'Only by sheer luck. The files were all destroyed by the county sheriff's department after Roger bought them off. He paid them more money than they earned in five years, and got them promoted through his connections.'

'Then how?'

Reitmaier shifts uncomfortably on the bed. 'FBI reports. The ones Cordry paid to buy too. One of the agents was not comfortable with the corruption and cover-up. He took the money but he made copies of the FBI case file. The federal authorities were investigating Roger Cordry to try and build a RICO case against him for his dealings with an Italian crime syndicate in a New Jersey construction deal. There was a murder there too. Cordry did not commit that one personally but he was complicit, which is the same thing in US law. His crossing state lines to commit another crime in New York State gave them jurisdiction. Cordry made a deal with the FBI to testify against his Italian friends. The federal authorities gave him immunity on that crime and agreed to let the deaths of your father and brother go unresolved. To them the Italian gangsters were a much more important target. But this one agent kept copies of the evidence as insurance, and they remained in safekeeping with him all these years.'

'Where is this agent now?' I ask.

'Dead,' Reitmaier replies.

'How convenient. And he just happened to drop by your house and leave this file with you before he checked into the morgue?'

'No, of course not. I happened to contact him because I found his name on one of the case files. I tracked him down to his residence in Louisiana. He said he was happy to hear from me. That he knew that someday someone like me would call, wanting justice against Roger Cordry. He was dying of a terminal condition, he would not say what, and he would be happy to share the files with me. He sent me scans and couriered the actual documents to me care of my sister's residence in Zurich, where they will have arrived by now.'

I consider this. I have to move the gun to my other hand so I can wipe the cold sweat off my palm.

'And what do you propose to do with that evidence and all this information?' I ask finally.

'I was thinking perhaps you and I might collaborate.'

'Collaborate,' I repeat doubtfully.

'Team up. Roger Cordry killed your brother and father, stole your family's wealth and made you destitute, destroyed your mother's life and mental health. You want revenge against him.'

I want to jump on the bed and hug him, haul him to his feet and dance the polka around the room with him. But I have to be careful. There are other ears listening to us. I need to be sure Reitmaier isn't working for Cordry and this isn't some elaborate attempt to lull me into a false sense of security before they drop the hammer. 'I got my revenge. I killed his son, Ricky. That is why you are here after all, isn't it? Your job was to bring Ricky's killer to Roger Cordry. That is why he sent you here, isn't it?'

'It is true. Roger Cordry asked me to reopen the case. He gave me the picture that eventually led me here to you. It is also true that I am an officer of the Zurich police force and it is my duty to bring you to justice for your crime. But I believe that you have a defense, and that if you present this new evidence I have unearthed, it will lead to Roger Cordry being prosecuted as well.'

And with that response, my fears are allayed to some extent. He's just announced his rebellion against Roger Cordry. That makes him their enemy as well. And as the old wise war experts said in China and India: *My enemy's enemy is my friend.*

Still, I press him, just to be doubly sure: 'And that is what you want? To take me back to Zurich to stand trial, and to use these files to then point the finger at Roger Cordry? That is quite a long shot, isn't it, detective? What makes you think that Swiss courts and authorities will be able to deliver justice against Roger Cordry? Besides, wouldn't his crimes against my family be US jurisdiction, not Swiss?'

'Yes, but –' Reitmaier cuts off as he hears the same sounds I do.

Footfalls outside. Soft, almost silent, but audible because of the dry autumn leaves underfoot which crunch as large men with heavy weaponry move quickly across the yard.

The time for talk is over.

# 46

## *HANNAH*

Reitmaier is dead in the first few seconds. He has to be. I tried to keep him out of harm's way, but there was no way to protect him from a stray bullet. And there are a lot of bullets flying around.

Oshri and his team came in hard and heavy, laying down flashbangs and suppressing fire the instant they burst in. They're trained to scan and shoot in micro-seconds. What they weren't expecting was for me to plunge the entire hotel complex into full darkness minutes before their attack. The assistant manager of the resort happens to be Philomena's brother, and thanks to Ki's message, all it took was a couple of phone calls for him to provide the support I need to survive this evening.

Correction: *try* to survive. There's no guarantee I'll make it out of here alive, but if I die here, it won't be because I walked into a trap and got blindsided. I'm going to give these bastards a fight and I'm going to use everything I can against them.

Which is to say: not much.

While Reitmaier was talking, uncomfortably, on the bed, I was moving furniture around. Oshri and his team will have memorized the layout of the villa's interior. They aren't expecting a dresser to be in the middle of the hallway, turned at an angle, or a coffee table to be in the middle of the room, or for the floor to be slippery wet, thanks to an emptied out bottle of liquid soap, or for the piles of laundry bags – thanks, Josie, head of housekeeping, who left the laundry cart by the door of the villa and let me in through the adjoining villa, which shares an interconnected door. The piles of laundry, put up on chairs which are arranged at unpredictable intervals around the suite, pass for human-shaped figures in the darkness. Even if Oshri's team use night-vision scopes, which they wouldn't have had time to slip on, and might not have even carried, they would still fire at the shadowy lumps just to be sure.

Hakam Abdi follows them into the room, not firing, but scanning the whole space intently. His large, bulking form is the one I've been watching for. Oshri and his team are all lean, young and mostly on the shorter side, with only one person, Izzie, being over six feet. Hakam stands out even as a silhouette.

I notice him out the corner of my eye.

He comes in barely a second after the team breaches.

They're still shooting at the laundry bags, tripping over furniture, slipping. Already, their gunfire is going wild, and one of them is hit by friendly fire, as I'd hoped.

That's when I open up.

Still lying on the floor by the bed, invisible from anywhere in the room, I pick them off one by one. My eyes were well adjusted to the dark. I could have brought night-vision goggles but I chose not to. In an enclosed space like this hotel suite, the muzzle flares and flashbangs would have blinded me, costing me vital seconds. I chose to stay au naturel.

It pays off now.

I take down Oshri's team like targets at a shooting gallery. They're all upright and moving around, lit by the muzzle flares of their own weapons. I only take head shots, seeing the dark spurts flare around their heads as they go down one by one. There are only five of them in all, including Oshri. That's plenty when it's five against one in a brightly lit, neatly furnished hotel suite, when they have the element of surprise, as they'd assumed they would. But it's not that much when they're blundering about in the dark, shooting at each other or at laundry and pillows hung over lamp stands, slipping on wet floors and tripping over glass coffee tables.

Hakam dodges back agilely as he sees what's happening. He has the advantage of being just behind the team, observing rather than assaulting, and he's also much better at this kind of thing.

Now, the room is suddenly quiet, as quiet as a – no, I'm not going to say 'grave' – as a church between services. My own breathing sounds very loud in the silence, and I struggle and fail to muffle it. I'm pretty sure Hakam can hear it, maybe even hear my heartbeat, doing way more than the 50 bpm I could once muster. That Hannah, the one who took down Ricky Manfredi, isn't here tonight. I'm all that was available. I'll have to make do.

Where the fuck is Hakam?

Then, his voice, quiet yet clear in the silence of the death room.

'You won't get out alive,' he says softly. 'Turn yourself over. I'm not here to kill you. I'm here to take you in alive.'

Like hell you are. If you weren't trying to kill me, why the fuck were they shooting up the place like they're in a John Wick movie?

After waiting several seconds and getting no response, he says: 'Reitmaier is dead. I saw him on the bed in the muzzle flares. He's been shot more than once, his eyes are open. The evidence he was expecting to receive at his sister's place in Zurich has been intercepted. We have it. There's nothing else left. Nobody else is coming to save you. You're on your own, Hannah. You were smart here. Oshri underestimated you, maybe because you never let him see just how good you were when you hung out with him. But I knew better. I respect you a great deal. You're quite an assassin to have taken down Ricky Manfredi so smoothly and framed Ursula. But it's all over now. I'm here and you're not walking out of here alive except in my custody.'

I remain silent. I've crawled under the bed and over to the other side while he's been talking, moving slowly and being very careful not to make any sound. As I emerge on the far side, my elbows slip on a patch of hot, gooey wetness. Reitmaier's blood, dripping down the side of the bed. Damnit. I try to back away from it and go around; my elbows and chin are already covered with it. Hot blood is sticky and slippery and it stinks like a rusty nail. There are other stinks in the room too, but they're not the ones bothering me.

From where I am now, it's only twelve or fourteen feet to the front door of the villa. Or better yet, the window. The flashbangs shattered the glass panes and I could jump through and roll into the bushes. But that will mean standing up or at least crouching and running across that many feet of distance, with the open window and the ambient light from outside backlighting me for that second or two. That's all the time and opportunity Hakam needs to put a bullet in my back. Or my head.

He probably has orders from Roger Cordry to take me alive, so the big man can torture me and make me suffer for what I did to his sons. But I know Hakam. If he has to choose between letting me go and killing me, he won't hesitate.

'I know you're somewhere by the bed. It's where I would be in this situation. Stand up slowly, hands raised, and let your gun drop to the floor. Then walk slowly toward the hallway. No sudden moves. No tricks.'

So he still thinks I'm over there. Good. Maybe I have a chance after all.

I have to take it.

Going up against Hakam one-on-one isn't an option.

Even at my prime, I couldn't have done more than give him a good fight. Maybe, with some luck, I could have hurt him or maimed him, but he would have done the same to me. One of us would be dead for sure, maybe both of us.

Now, the way I am, there's no chance at all.

He'll eat me alive.

As for letting him take me to Roger Cordry, ha ha ha.

Hell will freeze over before I even consider that.

Time for the final option.

I grope around under the bed, in the corner nearest to Reitmaier's head. The texture of the nylon backpack is a comfort to my bruised fingertips. Working open the zip slowly, I slide out the device I prepped before coming in. It's a simple enough one. By now, Philomena's cousin will have made sure this section of the resort has been evacuated and everyone, guests and staff, kept back at a safe distance.

They had better. This package was intended as a last resort, not as a getaway tactic. I had to be sure this thing does the job well enough to erase this villa, but it's never easy to be certain when you're working with plastic explosives. Besides, this is only my second live detonation and my first while on a mission. My only other experience was during my training with a very exacting ex-demolitions expert with the Indian army and he didn't exactly give me an A that time. I hope I know what I'm doing and don't end up blowing myself up along with Hakam, but if I do, then I guess it's a better way to go than getting winged and drugged and then whisked off on a private jet to a black room where I'm at the mercy of Roger Cordry and a full set of carpentry tools.

'OK,' I say aloud, keeping my voice soft and turning my head to one side to make it harder for him to precisely pin-point my position. 'I'm coming out. Don't shoot.'

'Slowly. Hands in air. Gun in one hand.'

I come out as he says, hands awkwardly above my head, head lolling a bit to one side, dribbling blood.

Not my hands, not my head, not my blood, but in the dark, that won't matter. All he can see from his position is the window with ambient light coming in, the only source of light in the room, and a silhouette standing in front of it. Man, woman, white guy, brown woman, alive, dead, no details visible.

'Hands straight up,' he objects. 'Drop the gun.'

My gun is wedged in my shoulder holster. What I have in my hand is nothing more than Reitmaier's hand and his cell-phone. In this light, at this angle, it will have to do. I let it drop to the floor.

In the light streaming in from behind me, I glimpse a large shadow emerge from the hallway cautiously, training a weapon at me – or rather at the late Detective Reitmaier, who's obligingly propped up before me. Damn, but Swiss detectives are heavy. Must be all that wiener-schnitzel.

'OK,' he says, 'now come for – hold on.' His tone changes as he senses something amiss. 'What are you hold –?'

That's my cue to release Reitmaier's corpse, turn and lunge for the window, even as I hit the button on the detonating trigger in my hand.

One last mad dash for glory, and freedom, and my girls.

The gunfire catches me by surprise.

It hits me in the back like a sledgehammer to the spine. Knocks the breath out of me.

My forward momentum and the gunshot both combine to shove me toward the window.

But even as I lunge at the square hole, I know I'm hit bad.

Then the explosion flares behind me, and the world turns white. Figures. It's a white man's world, after all. We brown folk are just trying to survive in it.

My last thought as I hit the window at a bad angle and crash into it, is my daughters. My sweethearts!

And then the whiteness surrounding me merges with the darkness inside me and I'm out of the game.

# Three Months Later

# 47

## ROGER

Roger is about to tell the stewardess yes, go ahead and close up, she's a no-show, when the brisk tapping of sneakers sounds on the stairway and Kiara's fresh, pretty face appears in the doorway.

'Hey, wait for me!' she says brightly as she comes down the aisle. She's dressed in a casual, offhand but chic outfit. Faded indigos, a simple white blouse, a floppy hat and high tops. They look good on her. Everything looks good on her. She looks great in everything. 'Yay! I made it!'

Roger can't help grinning back as she flops down in the seat across from him. 'You did!'

He nods at the stewardess who locks the door shut and goes into the cockpit to tell the pilot to take off.

She's new. Nice legs, nice everything. Exactly his type . . . but . . . he has something much better right by his side.

He turns his attention to Kiara.

She's much better to look at. Fresher, sweeter, yet on the inside, he knows she's made of real steel. She's not like the young women HR stuffs his staff with to keep him happy. She's something else entirely.

'How are you feeling?' he asks.

'Pretty good, actually,' she answers, removing a tablet and earpods from her handbag. 'Last night sucked but I managed to grab a little sleep.'

There's a hint of something in her face, he's not quite sure what it is. Like she's been crying maybe? Or just down in the dumps? A dark cloud passing across the sun in her eyes. He's tempted to ask her if everything's all right, then thinks better of it. They've come close, closer than he's allowed himself to get to any woman since Gaby, but that's all the more reason to be careful. Respect each other's space. If she has something she wants to talk about, she'll tell him. Besides, he just proposed to her yesterday at dinner.

He slept soundly. That's because he's no spring chicken and is going into this with clear eyes and a battle-hardened heart, and also thanks to the elimination of that Indian bitch who killed Ricky. That was three months ago, but it feels like a huge weight was lifted off his back. He was disappointed at first that Hakam hadn't secured her alive, denying him his chance for some bloody payback, but as outcomes went, it was better than acceptable. His son had been avenged and her being blown to so many pieces that there wasn't even a whole corpse left to identify is the next best thing to torture and maiming.

Ki looks around. 'I could use some breakfast.'

Roger smiles. 'I'm sure we can manage something.'

They chat about the weather, the flight, the plane, Chicago, India, ice hockey versus field hockey. Then they spend a few minutes talking about the island, how remote, how beautifully pristine and unsullied it is.

'This is all like a dream come true, Rog,' she says sweetly.

He smiles. 'If we're going to fall back on cliché, you're the real dream come true, Ki.'

'Then I'm going to use one more cliché and say I feel like the frog who got turned into a princess.'

He laughs. 'Some frog! Compared to you, sweetheart, I'm

the old toad! I can already see the headlines when we get back and news gets out: May–December match! I'm the lucky one here and the whole world's going to be saying it.'

She gives him a skeptical, squinty look. 'I'm trying to see you as the lucky one but nope, no how, no way. I'm the one getting the billion-dollar bargain. Besides, if we're segueing into media ledes, trust me, all they'll be talking about is the new billionairess in town, and how I slept my way into your bank account.'

He laughs. 'Let them say whatever the fuck they like. I know what I have here. The rest of the world can all go to hell.'

She softens up at that, looks away for a minute, blinking away what he presumes are tears of joy. There's the tiniest flicker of that darkness he sensed before, but when she looks at him again, she's all sunshine and roses.

'Let's do this!' she says, pumping her fist in the air.

'Yee-haw,' he goes, matching her. 'We're going to have a good time, aren't we?'

'A great time. Best honeymoon ever.'

They eat breakfast, he deals with a call or two, she takes care of a few things on her phone – 'lab' – and the flight is much more pleasant than usual. Even the stewardess turns her head at the sound of his laughter, and when he happens to glance across the aisle, he notices Hakam noticing as well. The security chief and bodyguard doesn't actually stare but it's in the way he holds his head and torso. Hakam will be riding with them up to Hilo, then staying back on the Big Island. Roger and Kiara will continue onward from there in the same jet, then switch to a helicopter for the last leg. Hawaii is perfect for the wedding: it's more than halfway en route to the island, and it has no waiting period or residency requirement. It's important for business purposes to do this quick and without giving the media outlets and stock market a chance to get a whiff. Which means a complete disconnect from work for the next few days.

Roger doesn't recall the last time he was this relaxed, this much at ease. And at five in the morning, without even the benefit of a good peated single malt? Never.

He's so lost in his reverie that he doesn't notice Hakam trying to catch his eye.

Kiara leans forward. 'Um, I think Mr Abdi wants a word.'

Roger turns his head, frowning.

Hakam looks apologetic. 'I need a minute.'

Roger gives him a look. Kiara doesn't seem to notice. She's busy tapping on her own device, earpods plugged in.

Hakam has been on Roger's shitlist since Goa. Roger may have accepted the Goa outcome as a win, but he hadn't let Hakam see that. Hakam's orders had been to bring the bitch back alive, and in Roger's book, he had failed. He had given the security chief a hard time since then, which was what he deserved. Eventually, Roger will seem to let it go, but reserve the right to bring it up and use as a whip on the man whenever he feels like it.

Right now, he glances at Hakam with mild disgust.

'Go ahead,' Roger says.

Hakam glances in Kiara's direction, just a fraction of a second. His meaning is crystal. This is for Roger's ears and eyes only. Roger makes a dismissive gesture.

Hakam lowers his head slowly. 'We have the DNA tests.'

Hakam's voice is low. He's visibly uncomfortable discussing this in front of Kiara, even though she clearly isn't listening. Roger can hear strains of the music leaking from her earpods. Something folksy and old. Bob Dylan maybe? Woodie Guthrie? Neil Young? Some old hippie shit.

Hakam hands Roger a tablet.

Roger stares at the screen.

It's a picture of an attractive young woman, one of those puffed up, over-made-up, immaculately groomed social media mannequins that pass for celebrities and sex symbols. 'Who is she?'

'Mira Delmore.'

'Who the hell is Mira Delmore?'

'She's the YouTube celebrity who was murdered in San Francisco the week before Monty was killed.'

Roger vaguely remembers Hakam mentioning her in their previous debriefings on the investigations into Monty's murder. 'What about her?'

'Her juvie record was leaked online today. One of those doxxing things on social media. Someone was tired of her fans mourning over her death and wanted to change the narrative. The records were sealed but somehow the person got hold of them and shared them online.'

'What's your point, Hakam?'

'The records show she was a major abuser as a kid. More than your regular schoolyard bully. She did some nasty stuff to other kids, all girls.'

'So?'

'So she made a lot of enemies. There were a whole lot of girls in the same juvenile detention center. Delmore and her pals abused a lot of them, put some in the infirmary, caused permanent damage. It was rough. A lot of young women had good reason to want her dead.'

'And one of them finally caught up with her and paid her back for all her abuse, good for her,' Roger says, rubbing his forehead. He needs a drink.

'Except, maybe there's one with a connection with you. If

we look into each of them, try to hack their records too, then locate their present whereabouts and see what they've been up to, maybe we can find a connection. Someone who was in Zurich and then San Francisco –'

'Why Zurich?' Roger asks. 'We already know Hannah did that one. She admitted it. Reitmaier even spelled out her motive.'

'Maybe Ricky and Monty's killings were connected.'

'Are you saying Hannah killed them both?'

'We think maybe she had an accomplice. Someone else who was working with her.'

'Where is this coming from? It's the first time I'm hearing this theory. Do you have any evidence or are you just spinning windmills?'

Hakam taps the screen of the tablet and hands it back to Roger. The screen now shows a DNA test result and comparison with another sample.

'What am I looking at here?' he asks.

Hakam explains.

Roger stares at him. 'This is verified?'

Hakam nods. 'Double- and triple-checked. I knew you would want to be sure.'

Damn right I would. Roger feels something pass through him. A wave of . . . what? Not nausea. Regret? Self-loathing? He gets a grip on himself. 'OK,' he says, his tone signaling *Enough*. 'Is that it?'

Hakam makes his invisible shrugging motion. 'It's the closest thing we've had to actual hard evidence. It's impossible to be one hundred percent sure.'

Roger thinks about it a minute. He feels his blood pressure spiking. He needs a drink. He needs a whole trolley full of drinks.

Hakam is silent. He folds his hands over his thighs, like a man in church, or a schoolboy in the principal's office.

Roger shoves the tablet into his hand and Hakam grabs it before it falls. He returns to his seat without saying another word.

Roger buzzes once, twice, then keeps the buzzer pressed. The stewardess comes down the aisle at a jogging pace.

'Double whiskey. One rock.'

Kiara sees him ordering and takes a pod out of one ear. 'Are you getting a drink? I wouldn't mind one too.'

'Would you like a soda? Or a wine maybe?'

She makes a face. 'Fuck that. I'll take a whiskey straight up. Single malt, if you have it.'

The stewardess glances at Roger who nods once, decisively. 'Peated all right, ma'am?' she asks.

'I'll kiss you if you make it a double. Straight up!'

The stewardess smiles and jogs back up the aisle.

Roger raises an eyebrow at Kiara. 'Not too early anymore?'

She winks. 'It's after five somewhere, isn't it?'

He grins. Their drinks arrive. He raises his glass to her.

She gets up and comes forward, clinking her glass against his, hard. She slumps into the seat next to him, not asking if he minds. He doesn't.

He intends to get much, much closer to her very soon. Maybe too close for her comfort. Whether she likes it or not.

*The Island, Now*

# 48

## *KIARA*

A woman in a red bikini on a sugar-white beach before a baby-blue ocean.

That's me.

The hunky man in shorts and unbuttoned Hawaiian walking down from the villa to the private beach, weathered, tanned, a little beaten around the edges but all the sexier for it.

That's Roger.

We were married yesterday.

The chopper with his name on the side dropped us off only hours ago. The staff went back with it. Now, we're the only two people on this island and we're pretty much stuck with each other. There's no other way off. The undersea reefs make approach by sea too risky. Even if you survived the rocks and could swim the forty-five miles to the mainland, the sharks and undertow would get you. It's not on any flight paths and no joyriding speedboaters or chopper pilots have any reason to pass this way. It is quite literally the kind of desert island they mean when they ask you the What If question. As in, if you were stranded on a desert island, what books, or movies, or people, would you want to bring along?

All we brought is each other.

We're on our honeymoon after all. We don't need anything or anyone else.

The next three days belong to us and nobody else is going

to steal even a tiny slice of it away. There's no internet, no cell service, no TV, cable, Netflix or landlines. Just a satphone to call the chopper when we're ready to leave. We won't be 'gramming our honeymoon pics for the celeb-obsessed world to drool over, or posting cryptic updates that the gossip websites try to blow up into a scandal.

For the next seventy-two hours, the outside world doesn't exist.

It's just him and me.

And only one of us is going to leave here alive.

Now, I have even more reason to want him dead.

Despite my attempts to warn her of the ambush in Goa, I lost Hannah. Officially, she was never there at the resort, and the Goa Police and Indian authorities listed the deaths and explosion as being the result of some unknown dispute between the Israelis and Reitmaier. No body corresponding to hers was ever found at the scene. But I know that cover-up was Roger's – and Hakam's – doing. They disappeared her and erased all traces of any link to Reitmaier's investigation, Ricky's (or Monty's) murders, the whole shebang. That doesn't matter. I can guess what happened, based on Hakam's reports to Roger. He killed her, if not with his guns, then by the explosion. And that was Roger's doing.

One more member of my family killed by him.

One more reason for me to kill Roger fucking Cordry, my beloved husband.

As if on cue, he leans over the deckchair and kisses me upside down. I let the book I'm reading drop and kiss him back, tasting vodka and cranberry juice and inhaling his familiar aqua-based cologne. His hand reaches for my breast. I intercept it and use it to pull myself to my feet. I lean in close, breathing on his cheek, and feel the stiffening in his Speedos.

'Last one in's a rubber duck,' I whisper, then break free and run, laughing, down to the water. He laughs and runs after me, overcoming my lead with a power sprint, his muscled thighs pistoning.

The surf explodes as we hit it at almost the same instant. I turn to him, arms raised in a victory gesture. 'I win!'

'You cheat!' he responds, laughing.

The incoming tide is waist-high. The water is warm, just a tad above body temperature. It feels great, the sand deliciously cool between my toes.

He grabs hold of my waist and reels me in, finishing the kiss he started on the beach. This time I let him have his way, and when we break off, we're both breathing hot and heavy.

He's looking at me. That same look.

Except, this time I'm not sure what it means, not exactly.

It's not lust as I would have expected. Instead, there's something in his eyes, something I haven't seen since . . . Monty's death.

A klaxon goes off in my head.

He's sad, sadder than he has any reason to be now or at any other time. Why is he so sad? He shouldn't be —

I feel a sting on my right buttock.

I turn, scanning the water for signs of jellyfish. Not that it would be visible: their tendrils can extend a hell of a long way, but that's usually downward into the water, not up here on the surface in the shallows. A bluebottle, maybe? I see nothing in the water, just clear blue aqua layered with frothy suds, like a jacuzzi. I feel my buttock and pull something protruding out of the gluteal muscle. I look at it. It's a dart.

Out the corner of my eye, I glimpse the figure among the trees, at the top of the beach, near the path. I recognize that ramrod straight posture at once. Hakam. He's holding a rifle in his hand, still aimed at me, ready to shoot again.

My body is going numb, consciousness fading.

I turn back to look at Roger, puzzled. Angry. Confused.

'Game's up, honey,' he says as I fall back into the water and the ocean closes her arms around me.

When I regain consciousness, I find myself lying on the chaise lounge in the bungalow. Someone has put a light cotton sheet over me. I remain still, taking my bearings. The bungalow is silent, the ocean and gulls and wind in the palm trees the only sound. From the angle of the sunlight on my arm, it feels like only a couple of hours have passed. Through the window, the ocean soughs softly, regretting forgotten crimes and lost opportunities. She reaches out to the shore, asking forgiveness, never receiving it, repeating it forever.

'She's awake,' Hakam says. He's standing a few feet away from me, out of reach in case I make a move, but close enough to put another bullet in me if I do.

Not a bullet. A dart.

The rifle in his hand has a dart in the barrel. All he has to do is pull the trigger and I'll be out for another couple of hours.

Roger is standing across the room, by the window, a glass in his hand. He's dressed in a light polo shirt and Bermudas.

He turns and looks at me. He has a look on his face I've seen before. In the past year I've gotten to see every side of him, but I've also known that he keeps his darkest, most secret, truest side hidden carefully. On the occasions when it happens to surface while we're together, he either excuses himself or sends me away on some pretext so he can go and take his rage out on the person who's earned it.

This time, it's all directed at me.

I'm getting the full Roger Cordry look of hate.

'Did you really think you'd get away with it?'

I try to sit. My throat is dry, my tongue feels like it's glued permanently to the roof of my mouth. There's a small plastic bottle of water on the coffee table, too small to hurt if thrown. I twist open the cap and gulp it all down. I could drink a dozen like these right now. Instead I look up at Roger.

'What are you talking about? Why did Abdi shoot me?'

He stares at me, sips. To Hakam, he says: 'The bitch still thinks she can talk herself out of it. Tell her, Hakam.'

Hakam: 'I brought it to Roger yesterday, just after you signed the marriage license.'

*After.*

As if reading my thoughts, Roger interrupts harshly: 'It doesn't matter. I'll have the marriage annulled in a New York minute once I bring this before a judge.'

'Bring what?' I ask, trying to clear my throat. It feels parched. 'What are you talking about, Roger? What's going on?'

'Slap her,' Roger says.

Hakam doesn't move. His head turns a fraction toward Roger. 'Maybe we should talk about this first.'

'There's nothing to talk about,' Roger says, 'The bitch murdered my sons. First, Ricky in Zurich, then Monty in San Francisco. I'm going to take her apart piece by fucking piece.'

'As of now, you're legally married to her. If we lay a finger on her —'

'I'm going to lay a fucking hatchet on her!' Roger shouts. He throws the heavy cut glass across the room at me. It strikes the wall just a yard from my head and shatters. I feel

363

the back of my neck, my arm, my cheek prickle as tiny splinters of glass fly everywhere. I reach up and touch my cheek with a finger; it comes away with a pearl of blood.

'That hurt me too, Roger,' Hakam says in the same tone of voice. 'Let's take a step back for a moment. Like I said, she's your lawfully wedded wife. You'll be the first one they suspect and investigate.'

'I don't give a fuck,' Roger says. 'I'll have her hogtied in a cage and hung from Trump Tower if I want. She killed my sons. My beautiful boys. Ricky ... and Monty ... Why Monty? He was the sweet one. The good son. He was a better man than I ever was, than I could ever become. Why did you have to kill *him*, you bitch?'

Roger starts toward me. He's holding a bottle of peated single malt in his right hand, gripping it by the neck like a club. He has murder on his face and in his heart.

Hakam stands and turns to face Roger, blocking his path to me. 'Roger, you need to cool off and let me handle this.'

Roger glares at Hakam. For a moment, I think he's going to use the bottle on him. But either Hakam's size and skill set, or the simple logic of what he's saying, make him stop. He flings the bottle aside, back-handed. It hits the edge of the kitchen counter and breaks, spilling whiskey and broken shards all over the floor.

Roger holds up his empty hands to show Hakam.

Hakam gives him one last look then turns back to me. He's still holding the gun and the barrel comes up again to point at me. He frowns when he sees me standing up.

'He's gone crazy,' I say, 'I'm not staying here with him. Call the chopper.'

Hakam motions with the gun. 'Sit down. We know you killed Ricky and Monty.'

'Then you're crazy too. I was in the car with Monty when he died. You saw that. I couldn't have killed him.'

'You had an accomplice. We don't know who it was but it doesn't matter. But you were the brains behind the whole thing, weren't you?'

'Why would I kill Monty and Roger's other son? I've never even met Ricky!'

I'm telling the truth. Hannah was the one who went to Zurich, after all. She killed Ricky. And Monty too. The only good thing about all of this is that they don't seem to be connecting her to the murders anymore. The bad news is they're convinced I did them. Even though I literally didn't.

'Stop lying, you fucking whore,' Roger says. 'We have your DNA!'

Hakam nods. 'Ricky's place. There was DNA from a bunch of people for whom we couldn't find matches. That was the first piece that clicked. I found a match yesterday.'

'A match with what?' I asked.

'With your DNA,' he says. 'We got your sample off your toothbrush. Our expert confirmed that it came from a sibling to one of the samples in Ricky's apartment.'

'Your sister. Hannah!' Roger says, almost spitting the name. 'When Hakam killed her in Goa three months ago, I thought it was over, we had gotten Ricky's killer. But we didn't know that she had a sister. You!'

'I don't know what you're talking about, Roger,' I say, trying to buy time. This is bad, I don't see any way to get out of it without ending up shot at best. But the longer they talk, the more time I have to figure out something.

Hakam goes on. 'The DNA also matches that found at two other crime scenes – Monty, and Mira Delmore. A You-Tube celebrity who was murdered in San Francisco a few days before Monty. That places Hannah at those two crime scenes as well.'

'The bitch killed both my sons!' Roger yells. 'And then you decided to finish the job. I trusted you. I actually trusted you enough to marry you! And all along, you were playing me.'

'OK,' I say, knowing there's no point going on denying everything. 'It's true. Hannah did kill your sons. But that's the whole point, Roger. Hannah killed them! I didn't. I was with Monty in the car the night he was killed. She could have killed me as well. She didn't care. All she cared about was getting revenge.'

'For your father and brother?' Roger asks, staring at me.

'Yeah. She thought you should feel the same pain my mother felt, so she decided to kill your sons too. Then she would have come after you. But you,' I look at Hakam, 'got to her first and killed her. Her vendetta died with her. I had nothing to do with it.'

Roger laughs. 'You expect us to believe that?' He gestures to the room at large. 'She expects us to believe that! What a crock of shit!'

'You insinuated yourself into Mr Cordry's life to get close to him and then kill him,' Hakam says, the only one who seems completely calm.

'Then why haven't I killed him yet?' I ask, turning aggressive. 'Why didn't I kill Monty when I had the chance? I was with him for months before he died, alone together. I had a half-dozen opportunities. Why didn't I do it? Or do Roger while you were away in Goa killing my sister? I had every reason to, didn't I? Yet I didn't so much as lift a finger against him.'

'You wanted to marry me, that's why!' Roger yells. 'You

wanted to get my money first. So you could inherit it all after you murdered me.'

Now it's my turn to laugh. 'Listen to yourself. You think I could get a hold of your fortune after murdering you? With Hakam and your crack security all over me within a minute of your death? If it was that easy, a thousand women would probably have tried it already.'

'What other reason could you have for being involved with Roger?' Hakam asks.

I shrug. 'It didn't start off that way. It started off with me trying to get close to Monty. Hannah wanted me to kill him and she didn't want to do it because she was afraid she might meet someone who would connect her with Ricky, so she sent me instead. But I couldn't do it. Monty was a good man, a wonderful guy.'

'That he was,' Roger says, quietening down for the first time. He drinks again, looking off into the distance. 'He was the best goddamn son that ever lived. Maybe even too good for me.'

I wait a beat, allowing him his memories, then continue: 'We became really close in those last few weeks. I realized I couldn't punish him for your crimes. He didn't deserve that. When I told Hannah, she got mad. She went off the rails and killed him. I couldn't take it. I broke off with my sister. I never forgave her for killing him.'

'You still haven't answered my question,' Hakam asks. 'Why did you come to Roger next?'

'He came to me, remember?' I say. 'He wanted to continue Monty's work, honor his legacy. I felt guilty over Monty, because my sister had done it, and so I felt guilty in a sense. I wanted to continue Monty's legacy too. Besides, the project was born out of an idea my father had originally, a long time ago. This was my way of honoring him, and paying back what Roger had taken from my family years ago.'

Hakam stares at me. I don't know if he's totally buying this but it's certainly making him think. Roger too. He's staring at me, still enraged and very murderous, but listening to every word. He needs closure too, wants to understand why we did what we did, why his two beautiful sons had to pay the ultimate price for his crimes. He is as complicit in this as we were.

Then something changes in him. He shakes his head, refusing to believe what I'm saying, rejecting it in favor of his own theory.

'You're Louisa's daughter,' Roger says. 'Hannah's younger sister. You knew about the history I had with your family. So you decided to get some payback by taking out my family. Maybe you and your sister planned this together from the start, I don't care about the details anymore. Fuck you and fuck your entire family. I should have gone back to the house that day and taken care of your whore mom and you and your sister. I thought I was being compassionate.'

That galls me too much to keep silent anymore. 'Compassionate? You? Who are you trying to con, Roger? You're a psychopath. You don't care about anyone except yourself. You'll do anything to anyone and not care a damn. You destroyed our lives. My mother never recovered after that day. She knew what you had done. She told the sheriff, the FBI, everyone who would listen. But you bought them all off, used your influence with people in high places to stall the investigation, make evidence disappear, and made the case go away. It destroyed her. Not just losing our dad and our brother, but the injustice of it. She ended up killing herself. She jumped off the Verrazano-Narrows Bridge in February.

It was freezing. They trawled the water but never found her body. She took us to the bridge with her that night, she wanted all three of us to be together, right to the end. But Hannah and I didn't want to die. We tried to stop her. We begged her.'

The tears on my cheeks are real now. I haven't talked about this in years, not even with Hannah. *Especially* not with Hannah. 'We tried to stop her. We held on to her. She fought us, she shoved us back. She shouted stuff at us, just before she fell.'

Roger shrugs, a snarl on his face. 'I hope she fucking suffered worse than my boys suffered. She married a weak man. I offered your father the world. He was too moral. Too high and mighty. He wanted to make his fortune honestly. The fool! Nobody becomes a billionaire by breaking their backs, working hard. You do it off the backs of a million other people. I did him and all of you a favor when I killed him.'

'A favor?' I ask, incredulous. Does this man have no shame at all?

'I spared his family a lifetime of struggle and toil. Better dead than working the coal mines. Fucking prole! If all those other people out there knew it, they'd all be jumping off bridges. Because that's the only direction their lives are headed anyway: straight down.'

Hakam holds up a hand, asking Roger to take a break. Roger glares at me one more time then turns away, walking a step or two toward the counter. He's looking for the bottle of whiskey, then remembers and sees the shards scattered all over the floor. He goes into the kitchen, moccasins crunching over the broken glass, and opens cupboards, looking for another bottle. As his back is turned, I glimpse something behind him, coming down the hallway as slowly and stealthily as a cat.

Hannah.

My heart stops.

Hannah is alive? How? My head spins with scenarios and hypotheticals, trying to make sense of it. But almost instantly, I stop myself.

I stop trying to figure out all the details and celebrate the simple fact that she's alive.

A flood of relief rushes through me at the sight of her, looking thin, pale, but strong, moving with enough surety and control to prove that she's healthy enough, fit, and most of all, very much alive. And if she's alive, then I know the girls are alive too, and safe and well.

That's a load off my chest.

She sees me watching and says three things quickly in sign language:

*Don't look at me.*

*Keep them talking.*

*Be ready.*

# 49

## *HANNAH*

Kiara reads me loud and clear.

She cuts her eyes back to Hakam. He's explaining how they identified her from a blood sample on record with the hospital after Mira Delmore and her girl gang attacked her. He's wrong, of course. That's my blood sample, not Kiara's. I killed Mira Delmore, Ricky and Monty. But of course, they think Kiara did it. That's good. Right now, I need them to focus on Ki, while I get into position.

That's harder than it sounds. Hakam is over there in front of the couch, pointing the dart gun at Ki. Roger is off to one side, by the kitchen counter. There's a wall and a pillar dividing them, and Roger's only partly visible from this angle. If I shoot Hakam, there's a good chance I'll clip Ki too, and if I take out Roger first, Hakam won't give me a second chance. The dart gun alone won't kill me, but it's not the only gun he has on him, and giving Hakam even a second's warning is a second that'll cost me and my sister our lives.

When in doubt, wait.

Roger is rummaging around in the kitchen cupboards, tossing out bowls, plates, sweeping a line of wine glasses off the rack. He's searching for another bottle of whiskey and getting pissed off because he can't find it. Good. The more pissed off he is, the more out of control he'll behave. The best-case scenario is if Hakam turns to talk to him again and they have another face-off. Ki just has to get out of the way at that moment and I can cut both the men down in the same burst. I've already switched the SIG Sauer to Position 3, so it will fire three-round bursts. One or two Radically Invasive Projectile 9mm rounds should bring down even a big guy like Hakam Abdi; they're called RIPs for a reason.

'The fuck is it?' Roger shouts from the kitchen, slamming cupboard doors shut. He's angry and frustrated. Good.

Hakam pauses in his recitation and tilts his head. 'Look in the bar. There are twenty different kinds of –'

'Don't tell me what there is or isn't in my own fucking place,' Roger yells. 'I just want the peated. That's it. I don't care if there's twenty thousand other bottles. I want the fucking peated. Do you get that, fuckface?'

A brief moment of silence. Hakam doesn't respond to that. I can see he's spent some time in the Roger fucking Cordry Institute of Social Etiquette. Probably how he's stayed on the job this long. But there's a new tension in his tight wired body that conveys how much he doesn't like being abused and yelled at. Oh no. Is big bad bodyguard going to go all weepie-weepie now because boss baby threw a tantrum and called him a name? Poor bodyguard. Here. Have another year-end bonus. Make the humiliation go away.

Ki watches me out the corner of her eye, the way I taught her. Her left hand slides along the back of her right forearm, upwards, slowly.

I tilt my head down, acknowledging without taking my grip off the gun, or the sights off Hakam's back.

She's read the set-up. She sees what she has to do to get Roger back into position, so I can take them both out. She's going to do it and is telling me to be ready.

Sis, I was born ready. So were you. Let's do this.

Roger goes over to the bar, elbows and backhands several bottles, knocking them off the shelves. They break and spill alcohol across the already glass-spattered living room floor. The stench of raw liquor fills the air-conditioned room. Finally, he finds something that meets his highly selective taste, twists open the cap and tosses it over his shoulder. He swigs liberally from the bottle. Good. An angry drunk man is even easier to take down.

'I'm going to make you pay now, bitch. For what you and your sister did to my sons. You wanted revenge? I'll show you what revenge really looks like. You two sisters wanted revenge for your family? I want revenge for mine. You're the last of Joe's brood. Once I'm done making you suffer, I'll kill you and that'll be the last of it.'

Kiara says calmly: 'Actually, it won't. I'm not the last one. There's still two more of us.'

Both men look at her.

'The fuck you talking about?' Roger demands.

'Hannah and Ricky,' Kiara says, 'were lovers. She was pregnant with his children when she killed him. Both girls, twins. Ricky's daughters. Your granddaughters. My nieces.'

Now, both men are still. Roger still has the bourbon bottle in hand, half-raised to his chest level, about to drink again, but he's frozen. Hakam is still too, stiller than he was already. They're both stunned. Nicely done, Ki. You distracted them with the one piece of information that changes the whole game. Well timed, sis!

I take the opportunity to move a fraction of an inch forward. I'm almost in position now. Do your thing, Ki, do it soon. You're going great, sis. Let's bring it in now. The SIG Sauer is rock steady in my hands. The past few months have been good to me – and the girls. I was blown clear of the explosion by some miracle, found by Philomena's cousin who helped me get away. The Kevlar vest I had on under my tee shirt saved me from Hakam's bullet. I even hung around long enough to see Hakam watching the fire brigade put out the fires caused by the explosion. The lucky bastard got behind the refrigerator in the villa's kitchenette just in time; the explosion fried some of his hair and blew out his eardrums, but he survived. I wanted to put a bullet in him but I could barely stand on my own. Now, I get a chance to close him out too. As for the cancer, well, the chemo worked and subsequent tests showed it wasn't as advanced as they had feared. It's in remission. I caught a very lucky break, Dr D'Souza says. About time, too. A couple of weeks' rest, exercise, training, a lot of up-current swimming in the river, and I was ready to fly to the continent, take a boat out to sea, and then swim the last few miles to the island. Now, it's showtime.

Roger turns and looks at Hakam. 'Shoot her. Not with that animal control shit. Use a real gun. Shoot her fucking murdering ass and put her down. Do it, otherwise I'll get a butcher knife from the kitchen block and open her up like a fucking –'

'Take it easy, Roger,' Hakam says, 'think about what she just said.'

'There's nothing to think about,' Roger yells, spraying spittle at Hakam. 'She's lying!'

'You know I'm not,' Ki says. 'The girls are cute as buttons, Roger. You can see the resemblance to Ricky.'

'As if I give a fuck!' Roger snarls, swigging bourbon. Some spills on his jaw and down his neck and chest.

'Oh, but you do,' Ki says, rubbing it in now. 'You can scream and yell all you want but you know you care. They're blood. Family. We're all family now, Roger. You, the girls, Hannah and me.'

Roger rushes at Kiara like a bull charging at a waving flag. 'You lie!'

Hakam shouts and turns to restrain Roger before he reaches Kiara.

I jerk my head in a sharp motion even as I move forward smoothly. The broken glass crunches under my shoes but I can't help that. I'm aiming the SIG Sauer at the exact spot where Hakam and Roger's bodylines overlap.

Kiara throws herself to one side, flying through the air.

I fire the gun.

## 50

## KIARA

I throw myself to the side as Hakam fires. I'm quick, but his reflexes are quicker. The dart hits me in the shin, striking nerve and bone. It stings like a bee. I hit the ground awkwardly because I'm twisting in mid-air, trying to avoid the dart. I strike my hip and elbow on the floor, and the side of my head on the wall, and I see stars for a moment, but I'm up and on my feet and running out the door. I saw the gun holstered under Hakam's shoulder, the one that fires real rounds, and I don't want to be in his line of sight if he manages to get it out.

Hannah's first burst of three struck just as I started to move. I saw blood splatter through the air, heard Roger cry out, saw his bottle of bourbon blow up, saw Hakam's torso jerk forward as he fired the dart gun, but I don't know how badly they were hit, and if Hakam is still able and quick enough to get his gun out, turn and fire at Hannah before she can shoot him again. I know she used the three-round burst to avoid having to reload because the SIG Sauer takes only fifteen rounds, and on rapid-fire mode they go almost as quickly as a three-round burst. She's taught me that reloading when your opponent has a full clip is a surefire way to lose a gunfight. She's out in the open, exposed, only about ten feet behind them, and Hakam isn't going to miss at that range. All he needs is to get one head shot off and she's done.

I hear Hakam's gun fire and Hannah's second burst of

three – or is it her third? – and I hear a man's voice crying out in pain. I can't tell if it's Roger or Hakam but I'm already out and running through the sand. I'm still barefoot and the sand is as scorching as the sun even though it's almost sunset.

I know better than to turn back and try to help Hannah. Divide and conquer, that's what she wanted and that's what I'm doing. It worked. It has to have worked.

As I reach the surf line, I hear shouts behind me from the villa.

'Run, Ki!' Hannah shouts.

I feel something go past me, buzzing by my ear.

Then another one.

I see them strike the water ahead and throw up splashes, like rocks skipped on a still lake.

Hakam.

The bastard is still alive, and he's shooting at me.

I hear Hannah's gun speak again and Roger cries out. This time, there's no mistaking the sound of his voice. I've heard him make that identical sound when he comes, somewhere between a desperate sob and a gasping scream.

A pause.

Then one more gunshot.

Head shot.

This time there's no more crying out.

As I plunge into the water, I think: it's over, then.

Roger Cordry is dead at last.

We did it.

We paid him back.

We got our vengeance.

We avenged our mother, our father, our brother, our-selves, each other.

Justice has been served.

My hip hurts, my head hurts and my elbow throbs, but the prickly pain in my shin has gone numb, and my foot is starting to drag. That's when I look down and see the dart dangling from my skin, the tip barely a millimeter in but hanging on for dear life. Sedative dart. Bastard did get me then. But it's already too late, I can feel the drug taking effect.

The water is surprisingly cold.

Roger told me it gets that way this time of year. Warm, pleasant in the afternoon, then suddenly, around fiveish, it goes cold. Something to do with converging currents. He warned me that the flood of cold water means the riptide is close by. If I'm not careful, it'll grab hold of me like a vise and carry me out to the reef. Once out there in the midst of all those sharp-toothed rocks, I'll be done for. Hannah must have got here by bringing a boat close by and swimming through the reefs underwater, using diving gear. It's the only way that makes sense. It's still dangerous, because of the sharks, but if anyone could do it, it's she. And she did. Hakam, on the other hand, got here the easy way: he flew in on Roger's chopper and got dropped in a sling on the far side of the island. Only a couple of miles away but far enough that I didn't catch the sound of the rotors over the surf.

He won't be leaving the same way.

I don't know why he chose to target me at the end. Instead of Hannah. Probably because he was already facing me and heard and saw Roger getting hit and knew that he had a better chance of killing me, unarmed and defenseless against his gun, than Hannah who was behind him and already firing. Or maybe because Roger's last order was to shoot me. Loyal to the end, Hakam Abdi.

I'm almost fifty yards out, only a few feet to the first rocks jutting out of the ocean, when the bullet finds me.

In the back, low and hard. Like a baseball bat swung at my ribs by a very big guy. Hard enough to shatter more than one rib, eat into vital organs. It bites into the center of me; my belly burns like I've swallowed a live coal. The sea salt stings, streaming in to replace the blood that's pouring out.

I gasp and flounder for a minute. My right hand is useless, dangling down into the water, pulling me to the bottom. One-handed, I try to pull for the rock. Another shot hits inches from my outstretched fingers, blasting chips off rock into the darkening air. I feel the rock splinters rake my face, drawing blood. I can't hear anything now, except the wind in my ears, the sound of someone gasping for breath, and the quiet growl of the ocean.

I'm almost at the rock when I start to black out.

My fingertips brush the side, dragging a fingernail loose, drawing blood. My hand slides off, unable to find purchase.

I slip under, the water cool and welcoming, darker than night.

Come home . . .

Come home, Kiara . . .

Suddenly, an invisible pressure pushes against my back, propelling me upward. I start to struggle against it. Let me die, I want to die. But the force, perhaps an air pocket, a current, I don't know what, pushes me toward the surface. I see daylight rushing at me. And then, with a small explosion of expelled water, I am in open air again, gasping, choking, coughing, but breathing.

'Ki!'

The voice is distant, barely audible above the roaring of the surf, the crashing of the waves. But my senses are attuned to her voice. I would hear that voice even in the netherworld.

My blood loss and wounds, as well as the second drug dart, have completely confused my sense of direction. I hardly know which way is up, let alone where the shore is now. The sky swims around me like the kaleidoscopic underside of a carousel top. But I hear Hannah's voice, calling out to me. She sounds strong, unhurt. She would have been wearing a bulletproof vest, unlike Abdi, and while his bullets must have stunned her and slowed her down for a few minutes, long enough for him to come after me, she's still alive and whole.

And that means he's dead now. I imagine him lying face-down in the sand, head blasted open, just like Roger back in the villa, except Roger is lying on his back, staring up at the ceiling, looking straight at the face of the woman who paid him back for all his terrible acts, his punisher, his executioner, the mother of his grandchildren, my sister.

'Hold on, Ki. I'm coming!' she calls out, and I hear splashes as she swims. She's a strong swimmer, but ironically, I'm the faster one in the water. I'm way further out than seems possible. I can't see the shore but I sense it's far away now. The riptide has got me, pulling me out in ice-cold claws to savor its prey. If the sea doesn't get me, the sharks will; the blood will bring them in any second now. And if all three of those things aren't quick enough, the reef will smash my body to shreds like one of Roger's smashed bottles.

I know I'm dying now.

My wound is lethal. Even if Hannah could get to me, there's no way to get me medical help in time. This is one sticky spot I'm not slipping out of, even with my big sister's help.

I feel myself sinking again. The riptide, or air pocket, or

whatever force pushed me back up to the surface, perhaps to hear my sister's voice and know that she's alive, or perhaps merely to taunt me with one last glimpse of the sky I will never see again, now turns on me with a vengeance. I feel myself not only sinking but being pulled down, tugged at by dozens of tiny invisible hands, grasping, pulling, yanking. My body, a rag doll leaking stuffing, corkscrews, tumbles, rolls. I am at the mercy of an unforgiving sea. The blood loss has sapped the last of my strength, and now even those banked reserves have been depleted. The weapon of vengeance is out of ammo.

'Ki, hold on, love, I'm coming.'

She's swimming toward me. I want to shout out and tell her to turn back, the riptide's too strong, it will pull her out to sea. I don't want her to drown too; one of us needs to live, to go back, to care for the girls. We have our vengeance now, our plans, our mission, have all been accomplished; we avenged our mother, killed the monster and the monster's sons, and order has been restored to a bemused universe.

Hannah is free – free of the endless lust for vengeance, free – it seems – of cancer, free of fear; she has more money than she needs to raise the girls comfortably, even luxuriously if desired; she can go ahead with the business of life. I will take our dark secrets to the grave of the ocean with me, like Jack letting go of the edge of that broken door and sinking to the cold heart of darkness.

We have achieved our mission. We have avenged our family, destroyed Roger Cordry's family, killed him, and taken all his wealth. The girls will inherit it once Hannah steps forward and proves that she's the mother of Ricky's daughters. She'll pin Roger's death on Hakam, the bodyguard gone rogue after rebelling against a lifetime of abuse, come to the island to murder Roger and his new bride on their honeymoon. The media will lap it up. The authorities will have a hundred questions but no one to answer them.

Karma has come full circle.

We avenged ourselves by killing Roger and his sons, and at the very end, he got his revenge on us by having me killed.

Maybe it's a just outcome.

I never forgave myself for letting Monty die.

He didn't deserve to die for his father's sins. He was a good man. And I loved him. I still feel the guilt for his death.

*Come home, Kiara, come home to us.*

The tide tugs at me, pulling at the blood streaming through the open hole in my back, calling me back to the womb of mother ocean.

*Come home . . .*

*Come home, Kiara . . .*

'Ki, hold on, I'm almost there!'

I can see her now, a blur growing larger in my peripheral vision.

*Let me go, Hannah,* I want to say, *turn back, go home. Save yourself. Go home to the girls.*

But I have nothing more left.

My mission is done.

*Come home, Kiara, come home to us.*

The wind rises, the waves churn, and just as Hannah reaches me and lunges out, I sink down deep, just out of her reach, and let myself slip away into the soft, furious embrace of our mother, the sea.

Time for me to go home too.

# Acknowledgments

A cracking good thriller needs a cracking good editor. I was blessed with two! Joel Richardson is a master chef who knows just what to ask me to take out, leave in and add more of. *A Kiss After Dying* is a far better novel for his invaluable editorial input. Grace Long was equally invaluable and amazing to the end. Thank you!

The entire team at Michael Joseph has been brilliant at their jobs. I really got lucky making my thriller debut with such a fab bunch! Lauren Wakefield's cover and interior designs are to die for. A huge thanks to Emma Henderson, managing editor; Katie Williams and Lucy Hall, marketing; Ella Watkins and Media Hive, publicity; Deirdre O'Connell, Katie Corcoran, Kate Elliott and Natasha Lanigan, UK sales; Sarah Davison-Aitkins, Anna Curvis and Akua Akowuah, international sales; Helen Eka, production; Sarah Bance, copy-editor; Deborah Hooper and Eugenie Woodhouse, proofreaders.

John Jarrold, a fine agent, true gentleman, genuine friend, and untiring champion of authors: thank you, John!

All my love to my wonderful family, especially my wife, Biki, who read the first several iterations of this novel and gave valuable feedback; my daughter, Yashka, who is always encouraging and supportive; my son, Ayush; and Leia, who wasn't born when I began work on this book, and will turn four the year it's published: someday, you'll read this novel and I hope you'll enjoy it as much as I did writing it!

And you, dear reader and fellow thriller lover, holding this book in your hands. Thanks for taking a chance on an unknown author, and I hope to see you again, nose deep in the pages of my next! Happy Reading!

# He just wanted a decent book to read ...

Not too much to ask, is it? It was in 1935 when Allen Lane, Managing Director of Bodley Head Publishers, stood on a platform at Exeter railway station looking for something good to read on his journey back to London. His choice was limited to popular magazines and poor-quality paperbacks – the same choice faced every day by the vast majority of readers, few of whom could afford hardbacks. Lane's disappointment and subsequent anger at the range of books generally available led him to found a company – and change the world.

*'We believed in the existence in this country of a vast reading public for intelligent books at a low price, and staked everything on it'*
**Sir Allen Lane, 1902–1970, founder of Penguin Books**

The quality paperback had arrived – and not just in bookshops. Lane was adamant that his Penguins should appear in chain stores and tobacconists, and should cost no more than a packet of cigarettes.

Reading habits (and cigarette prices) have changed since 1935, but Penguin still believes in publishing the best books for everybody to enjoy. We still believe that good design costs no more than bad design, and we still believe that quality books published passionately and responsibly make the world a better place.

So wherever you see the little bird – whether it's on a piece of prize-winning literary fiction or a celebrity autobiography, political tour de force or historical masterpiece, a serial-killer thriller, reference book, world classic or a piece of pure escapism – you can bet that it represents the very best that the genre has to offer.

**Whatever you like to read – trust Penguin.**